THE ESSENCE OF LOVING

Jonas braced himself for the final, fatal blow . . . the boar once again made its turn and hurtled itself toward him, but the impact never came. Kate raised her musket to firing position. The earsplitting concussion knocked Jonas flat on his back. He lay there stunned, acrid-smelling gunsmoke writhing sinuously around him, and attempted to gather his scattered wits.

Tossing her musket aside, Kate flung herself on top of him. "Jonas! Oh God, Jonas!" She sobbed hysterically. "I thought I wouldn't get here in time! If that boar had killed you, I don't think I could go on living."

Her words were sweet as honey to Jonas; he held her tightly against him and reveled in the sweet weight of her trembling body. "It's all right Kate . . . It's all right. He didn't hurt me, thanks to you. I can't believe you got him, but you did . . . For the second time, you've saved my life."

She leaned back to gaze at him with tear-bright eyes. "I have, haven't I? Don't you think you owe me something for that, Jonas?"

"What is it you want, Kate? You know I don't have a shilling to my name. I possess absolutely nothing of value to give to you."

"Yes, you do," she insisted, her voice softening so he had to strain to hear it. "Forgiveness. Surely, if you love me, you ought to be able to find it in your heart to forgive me."

"Maybe forgiveness is the very essence of loving," he mused aloud, wiping the tears from her cheeks with both thumbs. "Is that what you mean?"

"Yes," she whispered.

"What an interesting notion," Jonas murmured, distracted from the philosophical debate by the nearness of her lips to his. He drew her face closer and tasted the salt of her tears when he pressed his mouth to hers . . .

KATHARINE KINCAID

Midnight Treasure

ZEBRA BOOKS
KENSINGTON PUBLISHING CORP.

For Aunt Dee, Uncle Bill,
and all the Goods, especially Anna.
With thanks for your encouragement.

ZEBRA BOOKS

are published by

Kensington Publishing Corp.
475 Park Avenue South
New York, NY 10016

First printing: August, 1992

Printed in the United States of America

Prologue

"Stop that! Leave my Grandpa alone!"

Kathleen Elizabeth Montgomery launched herself at the nearest leg encased in dirty, leather breeches and pummeled her fists against the man's hard thigh. In all the excitement, he seemed not to notice, but Kate registered a number of things about him. He was wearing "country boots"—leggings made from lengths of an old blanket tied at the ankle and below the knee—and his shoes had no buckles, only a poor man's tie strings. He also smelled, not the clean, pleasant odor of wig powder and pomade, but the nasty stench of the barnyard, the tavern, and his own unwashed body.

Choking back a sick feeling, Kate pummeled him harder and demanded that he let go of her grandfather. "Leave him be! My grandpa is an important man, I tell you! If you hurt him, you'll be in trouble!"

The rising roar of the crowd all but drowned out her pleas. Distinguishable among the shouts and cries were frightening threats.

"String up the no-good Tory!"

"Naw, hangin's too good for him. Strip 'im naked

5

and ride 'im out of town on a sharp rail!"

"Where's the tar an' feathers? We'll show this Loyalist dog what happens to British bastards!"

Kate's flailing fists slammed into a soft bulge between her adversary's legs. Howling, he grabbed her arm. "'ere, now, l'il gal! Run 'ome to your ma, b'fore we tar and feather you, too!"

"Grandpa! Grandpa!" Kate screamed, struggling to reach the tall figure in the robin's-egg blue frock coat and snowy-white, ruffled, linen shirt.

Grandpa's beautiful powdered wig had fallen askew, blocking his eyes, but as he fought to free himself, his lips formed her name. "Kate! Kate, child, where are you?"

Cheeks and nose berry-red from anger, Grandpa flung aside the wig and glared at the men and women clawing him from every side. "Damned, scurrilous Whigs! Black-hearted, traitorous villains! You dare call yourselves Patriots and Sons of Liberty. Well, I call you knaves of the lowest order . . . Unhand me this instant!" He drew himself up, showing no fear. His eyes flashed golden, and his voice boomed like thunder. "And if you dare lay a hand on my granddaughter, I'll flay the skin off the entire lot of you! I'll see you get a taste of the king's justice you won't soon forget!"

A short, fat woman in a soiled mobcap shoved closer and shouted into Grandpa's red face. "A pox on the king's justice! The king can go soak his head in a pisspot, he can! We'll stand for no more taxation without representation! Ole George an' his parliament has bled us dry for the last time!"

Her words inflamed the crowd even further. Filthy hands tore at the silver lace that lay like a gauzy cloud on Kate's grandfather's blue frock coat. Bits and pieces of fabric—snowy-white and robin's-egg blue— sailed over Kate's head. Her grandfather stumbled and went down under the grasping hands and surg-

6

ing bodies. A silver-buckled shoe spun into the air and dropped out of sight.

"Grandpa!" Kate scratched and bit and kicked to get to him, but there were too many people in the way.

Two big hands suddenly swooped down and caught her around the waist. Still screaming, she was picked up, carried away from the throng to a shop doorway, and dumped unceremoniously onto the dusty doorstep. The fall knocked the breath out of her, and she looked up to find a burly man with stubby brown teeth staring down at her. "Yer the devil's spawn, all right," the man spat, spraying her with spittle. "As feisty as yer grampa. Look like 'im, too, with them tawny red curls and queer yellah eyes. Think yer better'n everybody else, don'tcha? All dressed up like you wuz on yer way t' a queen's coronation. Well, stay here, l'il she-devil, or you'll be the next one t' get it."

Shaking with pent-up fury and terror, Kate backed up against the closed wooden door of the apothecary where Grandpa had often bought sweets for her. It did not seem possible that this was happening. Only moments before, they had been headed for a little shop that carried the prettiest bonnets and hair ribbons in all of Savannah. On the occasion of her sixth birthday, Kate was going to be allowed to pick out her choice from all the bonnets in the store. Six new hair ribbons, one for each of her years, were also on the shopping list. For weeks, she had been looking forward to this day; now, this terrible thing was happening to spoil it.

Kate didn't know what to do—rather, she did know but had already decided not to do it. At first sight of the unruly mob spilling out of Tondee's Tavern and coming toward them down the wide, cobblestoned street, Grandpa had thrust Kate behind him and bade her run for home. He had expected trouble, and it

7

had broken out as soon as someone recognized him. Everyone knew Augustus Montgomery, lord and master of Oak Hill, the biggest rice plantation on the Atlantic coastline. Grandpa's closest friend was Sir James Wright, the English governor of Georgia, and a frequent visitor at Oak Hill.

In the past, people had always listened to Grandpa and respected his opinion, but lately, it seemed to Kate, Grandpa was always having to defend Sir James, King George, and something called Parliament that passed laws and levied taxes on the people who lived in Georgia. It wasn't fair, people said, that the king and parliament could tell them what to do, since neither had ever been to Georgia or even to the Colonies. Even Kate's own papa and mama sometimes argued with Grandpa. Mama was afraid there would be war, with people shooting other people . . . or doing bad things like what was happening now.

Mama would be angry and upset that Kate hadn't gone right home, but Kate didn't intend to run away and leave Grandpa to face the crowd alone. She was no coward. Grandpa often boasted that Kate was the only one in the entire family to inherit the legendary Montgomery spunk. Picking herself up and dusting off her birthday gown of pink silk polonaise trimmed with white satin bows and flowers, Kate waited until the man who had dumped her on the doorstep was looking the other way. Then she darted around him and ran after the procession marching down the street with Grandpa at its center.

Though tall for her age, Kate could only catch glimpses of her grandfather's natural, reddish-colored hair, white face and body. The crowd had torn off most of his clothes, and there were bloody scratches on his face, arms, and chest. She could hardly see the rest of him, but he seemed to be limping. Then someone pulled up a dung cart, half full of manure, whose odor blasted her nostrils as she strained to stand on tiptoe.

The bad people forced Grandpa to climb into the cart where everyone could see him and point fingers. Other people were starting a big bonfire in the center of the street. From somewhere appeared a large kettle and wooden barrels marked with the letters T-A-R. Men and women scooped out chunks of a thick, black, gooey substance and tossed them into the kettle. Using ropes tossed over a lamppost, they hoisted the kettle over the fire. Rag-tailed children helped their mothers drag out big, fat sacks filled with goose feathers. Everywhere Kate looked, there were people—running out of nearby shops and houses, arriving on horseback, leaning out of windows, and standing on wagons and drays.

Peddlers had begun working the area: a woman selling fruit pies, a lantern man banging on his tin wares to draw attention . . . a water carrier brandishing a pewter mug to dip out the water he carried in two stout buckets dangling from a wooden pole laid across his shoulders. Kate couldn't move a step in either direction, so great was the crush of people. Compared to what she heard at home, the language was crude and vulgar, the laughter loud and ill-bred.

Kate watched in tongue-tied horror, tinged with fascination, as a platform made of crates and barrels grew higher and higher beside the cart. When the platform was higher than the cart itself, eager hands helped pass up the heavy kettle that had been cooking over the fire.

The crowd grew suddenly quiet. Grandpa stood rigid and silent in the dung cart. He had stopped fighting when his hands were tied behind his back. A length of rope lay coiled around his neck, and his naked body gleamed whitely in the pale morning sunshine. He seemed to be ignoring the shouts and jeers of the onlookers, or else he couldn't hear them. His eyes were closed, his lips drawn into a thin line,

9

as if he were thinking about something else—something far, far away.

Several big men held Grandpa's arms, while others tipped the kettle over his head. Steam rose into the air, and a hissing sound issued from the big pot as the black sludge within it began to move. A thick stream of the bubbling substance poured onto Grandpa's head. As the tar covered him, Grandpa's whole body jerked, and a scream tore from his throat.

"Long live the king!" he bellowed.

The crowd roared its disapproval and shook their fists at Grandpa. Kate covered her eyes with the palms of her hands. Grandpa didn't deserve *this*, no matter what he had done. He was right to call these people "blathering idiots" and "base-born rabble." That's what they were . . . and Kate suddenly hated these people—these *Americans*, as they called themselves. She hated them with all her heart. With the mob's shouts ringing in her ears, Kathleen Elizabeth Montgomery became King George III's most fiercely loyal subject. As long as she lived, she would never forget this day . . . and if she ever had the chance, she would punish the wicked Americans and make them pay for what had happened here today. If it was the last thing she ever did, she would make them pay . . . and pay . . . and pay.

Chapter One

Conch Cay, Abaco Islands, The Bahamas
1792

Over the sound of her blood pounding in her ears, Kate could hear Edward's heavy breathing as they wrestled each other on the sand near the fringe of surf. He wasn't as tall as she, but he was far stronger; only her determination equaled the odds. She struggled to bring her knee into position to kick him, while he fought to keep her down and outspread beneath him. Finally, she succeeded in kneeing him in the stomach.

"Oof! That hurts! . . . Leave off, Kate!" he cried.

Seizing the advantage, she sank her teeth into the flesh and bone of his bare shoulder and bit until she tasted blood. He swore and let go of her wrists. Quick as a cat, she relaxed her jaws and rolled out from under him, then leaped to her feet, panting and outraged.

"You jump on me again, Edward Garvin, and I'll bite off your bloody nose!"

Turning her head, she spat out the salty taste in her mouth, while he got to his feet, gripping his savaged shoulder and gasping for breath. They were both breathing hard—Edward from thwarted lust and she

11

from fury and the exertions of the past few minutes. The strong breeze off the darkening ocean dried the perspiration on her forehead and flattened her father's shirt against her full breasts. Edward's gaze clung to them, but she refused to succumb to the impulse to fold her arms across her bosom. Edward would just have to learn to control himself. She wasn't going to start wearing a bodice, blouse, and skirt to go wrecking . . . Besides, he had seen her often enough in male clothing to have gotten used to it; everyone else on the island had stopped complaining, even Mama, who deplored such unfeminine attire.

"I wouldn't be jumpin' on ya if you'd quit stallin' and marry me, Kate," Edward grumbled. "This has been goin' on too long, and you know it. Why won't ya give in and say you'll have me?"

Kate tossed back her single, long braid and regarded Edward with a deep scowl. Aside from the anger this latest incident provoked, she didn't particularly like what she saw. Edward Garvin had dirty-blond hair, pale gray eyes, and a squarish, muscular body that might appeal to some women but didn't to her. Despite his blondness, he was dark, taciturn, and brooding. He almost never smiled, and when he did, it was a mean, grudging quirk of the lips . . . Illiterate, boorish, and cruel, he would beat the slaves he was supposed to oversee, if he had his way, and Kate had no doubt that if she did marry him, he would end up beating them anyway, and probably her, too. Marriage into the Montgomery family would make Edward virtually the king of Conch Cay, what with Papa being no good at all these days . . . No, she wouldn't marry Edward if he were the last man on earth.

"We don't suit, Edward," she told him coldly. "If you're so desperate for a wife, I advise you to look for one in Nassau or, better yet, on one of the other cays or Out Islands. There's bound to be another planter somewhere who'll make you an offer similar to Papa's—especially if his family lives alone like we do and will be gaining an overseer as well as a son-in-law. In the middle of the ocean, good overseers are every bit as hard to find as husbands."

"Drat it all, Kate! It's not just the forty acres of my own that your pa promised me—or takin' over the whole two hundred and twenty when he dies and leaves it all to you; it's *you* I want . . . I ain't much with words, but I . . . I promise I'll be good to ya. I'll treat ya right and take care of ya . . . an' t'gether we can make Conch Cay the finest plantation in all of the Bahamas."

"Oh, Edward." Kate made a disparaging motion with one hand. "Why are we discussing this, again? Can't you see that you'd be getting a bad bargain? First, I don't love you and don't think I ever can. Second, we're only hanging on here by our fingernails. God alone knows how long we'll last. The soil's too thin to support a decent cotton crop, and when we finally do manage to grow one, the chenille bugs come along and destroy it. Don't you understand our situation? We're barely making it! Half the planters on the other cays and over on Big and Little Abaco have given up and gone elsewhere to make their fortunes. Soon, we'll be the only ones left."

She spoke as if to a half-wit, saying things Edward very well should have known by now. As usual, Edward hardly seemed to be listening. He scratched his stubbled jaw, his craggy face brooding and petulant. A half-moon of grime adorned each of his stubby fingernails, Kate noticed, and she shuddered at the thought of those dirty hands touching her.

"We don't need no cotton crop," Edward insisted after a moment. "We got wreckin'. And between wrecks, we got salt rakin'. When it comes t'fillin' our bellies, the sea is full of fish, crawfish, and conch, and

13

if you've a taste for pork, there's lots of wild hogs over on Big Abaco. We can have a good life, Kate, better'n you'd have if you an' your family up and went back t' Georgia."

"The one thing we *won't* do is go back to Georgia!" Kate flared. "But that doesn't mean I'll marry *you*."

Swinging away from him, she started walking down the sandy beach. Overhead, scudding black clouds promised bad weather and a dark night, excellent conditions for wrecking—the one thing they could always count on. Ships bound for almost anywhere had to cross the Gulf Stream and thread their way through the Bahamas, negotiating treacherous reefs and shoals unmarked on any map. Many didn't make it; quite a few broke up off the Abacos, and when they did, Kate, Edward, and others like them, salvaged what they could of the survivors and cargoes, then ferried them to Nassau. There, whatever the sea washed up, excluding only the captains and crews, could be sold on the open market at inflated prices. The Bahamas had long been home to wreckers, pirates, and privateers; when all else failed, these three activities fed and clothed the impoverished inhabitants.

"I don't know why you even mention going back to Georgia," she grumbled. "You ought to know how I feel by now. I hate wrecking, but I wouldn't go back to America if someone offered me a thousand acres of prime Georgia bottom land and two hundred slaves to go with it. No matter what Mama says, Papa was right to get us out while he could. The rebels as good as killed Grandpa; in time, they would have destroyed all of us. The way they treated Loyalists will go down in history as a worse sin than wrecking could ever be."

"So ya might as well make the best of things an' marry me, Kate." Edward smirked triumphantly, as

14

if he'd made his point. Shirt in hand—it had been lost during their scuffle—he matched her long strides down the beach. "If ya won't go back t' America, an' yer pa can't get no land grant noplace else, then you're stuck here for the rest of yer life . . . an' I don't see no suitors stormin' the island t' beg for your hand. All there is is me, an' I'm gettin' damn tired o' waitin'."

"Well, I'm not marrying you and that's that, Edward . . . Some other man will come along."

She forbore to mention the name of one who already *had*, a man they had rescued four months ago as his ship was going down. Edward had been irrationally jealous almost from the moment they dragged Jonathan Irons from the surf, more dead than alive. Even in his half-drowned state, and despite being a hated American, Jonathan had stirred something to life in Kate, something she had been unaware existed within her. He was the handsomest man she had ever seen, with eyes as blue as the turquoise seas surrounding the Abacos, a smile at once merry and devilish, a lean, lithe body, tan from the waist up . . . a hated American, yes, but a man who seemed able to banish all the ugly feelings simmering inside her with one rakish, teasing grin.

Jonathan had been as smitten as she. It had been fairly easy to convince the handsome, dark-haired sea captain to abandon his suspicions that a light had been deliberately misplaced to make him think the island was in one location, when actually, it was in another . . . causing him to run aground on a reef.

Later, Kate learned that Edward *had* been guilty of the deed, but by the time she discovered this, Jonathan was already dead. He'd gone out fishing by himself in a one-man dory and never returned. Two days later, following a series of violent rain squalls, they'd found his battered body washed up on the beach and pieces of the dory smashed against the rocks.

At the time, Jonathan had not yet convinced Kate to return with him to Salem, Massachusetts, from whence he had come, but she had been tempted. A few more stolen kisses and Kate might have surrendered everything—not only her virtue, but her duty to family, her loyalties, her political beliefs, and even her love for the chain of picturesque islands and cays set like emeralds in the sparkling turquoise sea.

Edward wasn't the only one who hadn't mourned Jonathan's death; the relief of her parents had been glaringly apparent. Kate had thought she'd hid her feelings well, but Mama, especially, had recognized Jonathan as a threat, someone who might take Kate away from the island and leave the elder Montgomerys and their dependents stranded and nearly helpless to fend for themselves in what Mama regarded as a harsh and bitter exile. Of course, she would never have done that, Kate told herself. Somehow, some way, she would have found the means to provide for them before she left—*if* she left.

Now, Papa and Mama wanted her to marry Edward, who did, after all, seem to be her only suitor. Blind to his ambition, Papa mistakenly believed that Edward could be controlled, but Kate knew better than her father just how pushy and aggressive Edward could be. She also knew how weak her father had become; most of the time he wasn't even sober. Had she never discovered the lure of passion with a handsome, cultured, well-educated man like Jonathan Irons, Kate might have been willing to settle for Edward. But now, the idea was unthinkable. Another man would come along. She just hoped that the next one wouldn't be an American, thereby arousing such profound inner turmoil and conflict.

As was her wont, whenever she fell to brooding over Jonathan and what might have been, Kate mentally ticked off the long list of grievances she still harbored against Americans. Time had dulled the burning need for revenge, but Kate hadn't forgiven—nor forgotten. First, there was the death of her grandfather. After his tar and feathering, Augustus Montgomery had never been the same; he died, broken and humiliated, several months after the ugly incident. Then there was the demise of her younger brother, Robin, from fever on Tynbee Island off the coast of Florida. Loyalist refugees had suffered grave hardships there while waiting for ships to take them to Nova Scotia, Bermuda, or the Bahamas, to begin new lives. Neither Mama nor Papa had fully recovered from Robin's death—or indeed, from losing Papa's inheritance, the elegant Georgian plantation, Oak Hill, its blooded stock, the many slaves who had worked it, and the accompanying positions of influence and affluence in Georgian society.

Mama, in particular, mourned the loss of that genteel life. Mama's relatives had sided with the Patriots and still enjoyed pampered lives back in Georgia, but because their pretty, young daughter, Sybil, had married into a staunchly Loyalist family, they had disowned her, forcing Mama to emigrate, along with her husband. Sadly, over the years, Mama's resentment and anger had settled on William, Kate's father, which was why Papa now found his only solace and comfort in cheap rum. That left Kate to manage as best she could to take care of Mama, Papa, and the slaves they had brought with them—sixteen people in all, including Edward, who was as much hindrance as help, at times.

Thinking of all this, Kate ignored Edward as they trudged down the beach toward the spit of rock that jutted out into the sea and provided an excellent vantage point from which to watch for passing ships. On a black and stormy night such as this, there was

17

an excellent chance that a wreck might occur, and if it did, Kate wanted to be first on the scene, before the inhabitants of Abaco and the other cays spotted it and raced to recover the prizes.

She lifted her face to the wind and inhaled deeply, scenting rain on the tangy, salt-laden breeze. In the gathering darkness, the sea was a leaden gray color, the surf startling white as it clawed the shore. The waves were already six or seven feet high, crashing on the sand with a vengeance and boiling around the big rocks which dotted the beach.

Edward suddenly spoke up, his tone belligerent. "I wish you wuzn't so unreasonable about lettin' me go out in a dory with a lantern. Then we'd be sure of a wreck, tonight."

"No," Kate said. "I won't be party to *causing* a wreck. Too many people die passing through the Bahamas, as it is. Besides, it's too dangerous. You yourself could get killed in rough seas, going out alone."

"I wouldn't be alone if you came with me—or else I could take Cal. I ain't no wet-behind-the-ears sea-captain who can't handle a small boat in a storm. No matter the weather, I know these waters like I know my own bed."

This was a slur on Jonathan, and Kate felt compelled to defend the young man whose loss still pained her and whose apparent lack of seamanship still surprised and disappointed her. "You never should have given Captain Irons that dory and encouraged him to go bonefishing by himself; you knew a storm was brewing . . . He didn't. These waters were new to him. And it was your fault in the first place that his ship grounded and went down. Profiting from a wreck is one thing, but causing the wreck itself is nothing short of murder . . . I haven't stooped that low, Edward, at least, not yet."

"I didn't kill him; he killed hisself. An' I don't see

18

what difference it makes how his ship sunk. Nobody'll ever know I done it; he wuz the only survivor. If we all keep quiet like we agreed, there ain't gonna be no problems on account of it."

"I'm sorry I promised to keep the whole thing a secret," Kate snapped. "Jonathan told me he had family back in Massachusetts, an older brother—Jonas, I believe he said his name was, who's probably worried himself sick wondering what happened. I still think I should have written him a letter and let him know how Jonathan died. I imagine Jonas Irons thinks Jonathan went down with his ship."

"'Course, he thinks that . . . an' we don't want him thinkin' anything diff'rent. How would it help your ma and pa if Irons's brother knew he survived the shipwreck but got drowned fishin'? The brother might get t' wondrin' about *our* part in the sad business, 'an he could turn up here someday with guns mounted on his bowsprit an' blow Conch Cay all t' pieces, just t' git even. No, yer pa's right. The less said about the whole thing, the better. Nobody needs t' know we had anything t' do with that wreck."

Kate clamped her jaw shut and walked faster. A man—a very special man, for all that he was an American—had died in a tragic accident, and all her family could think of was protecting their own selfish interests. Never mind that she shared those interests; their attitudes sickened and disgusted her. She arrived at the rocky spit of land and began clambering over the boulders, climbing upward to the shelf of rock that jutted into the sea. Edward followed. When she reached the top, she searched in a rocky crevice for the canvas-wrapped bundle that held a few items meant to make them more comfortable as they undertook "wreck-watching."

There were a couple of blankets, a long, narrow case containing a spyglass, a folded piece of canvas to rig up a windbreak, a tin lantern, and two surtouts made of oilcloth to protect them from rain and seaspray. There was also a haversack containing rock-hard ship's biscuit and a jug of rum. All had been salvaged from previous wrecks. If they witnessed a wreck tonight, they would hurry and join Cal, Benjamin, and Fish, the family's three hardiest male slaves, waiting farther down the beach with two dories, ready to push them into the surf and row out to the rescue.

Kate located the bundle, hastily opened it, and tossed a surtout at Edward. "Here, put this on . . . the rain's coming."

As she said it, a few drops splattered her face. She shrugged into her own surtout, then unfolded and shook out the square of canvas in the pack. Edward helped her tie it down, tent-fashion, to iron spikes pounded into the rocks on a previous vigil. They both climbed beneath it, taking shelter just as a sheet of rain drove across the water.

No sooner had they gotten settled, when Kate removed the spyglass from its velvet-lined case, raised it to one eye, and began a slow, steady sweep of the black horizon, searching for a pinprick of light or a flash of white sail. Edward gnawed at a ship's biscuit and swigged from the jug while she undertook the first watch. Then he belched, stretched out on a blanket, and began to snore.

The wind plucked at the canvas. Rain pelted it. The only sound was the boom of the sea slapping the rocks below. Kate rejoiced that Edward had gone to sleep. Otherwise, he might try to take advantage of the darkness and isolation to have his way with her. She was growing Godalmighty tired of always having to fend him off; fortunately, after a rebuff such as tonight, he usually retreated to lick his wounds and didn't bother her for a time.

She didn't know how much longer she could put

him off, especially with Mama and Papa encouraging him. Lately, he had grown much bolder, trying to take by force what she wouldn't freely give him. If he did force her, she supposed she would *have* to marry him. Maybe that's what he was counting on . . . or maybe, he just figured that eventually he would wear her down. Papa wouldn't approve of rape, however, and Kate decided that she really ought to tell her father about Edward's behavior—if she could catch him when he was sober. Lately, Papa was rarely sober. Unfortunately, on the rare occasions when he was, Mama's strange moods soon drove him back to the bottle.

Suddenly, Kate felt trapped, disheartened, and manipulated. She loved the islands, especially Conch Cay, and hoped to be able to hold things together and stay on, though others were giving up. But in order to do that, she needed to find some other means of making a living, and she had to convince Edward to keep his distance. She wished she could produce another female for Edward to marry, someone plain, simple, and biddable, who'd be thrilled to have a hard-working overseer for a husband; that would leave her free to concentrate on the greater problem of survival.

Not that Edward was all bad, of course. If one overlooked his coarseness and lack of education, he had much to recommend him. He worked as hard as any of the slaves—often harder. The entire family, herself included, had come to rely on his strength and skill when it came to difficult jobs that needed doing or farming problems that must be solved. Nor was his ambition so outrageous. It just needed to be channeled into more constructive activity, something which would enable all of them to survive and maybe even prosper. What that activity could be, Kate had no idea.

The island's thin soil yielded barely enough fruits

and vegetables to relieve the boredom of constant fish and seafood. Cotton had proved disastrous, and wrecking was much too uncertain, not to mention morally questionable. Turtling? They could certainly increase their catch of the huge turtles that came ashore to lay eggs, but everyone went turtling. There were fewer turtles now than there had been even a few years ago. Of course, there was always salt-raking, but it didn't pay well, because everybody did that, too, causing a frequent glut on the market.

Maybe she would have to give in and permit Edward to make use of decoy lights, after all. Many of the passing vessels were American, and if anybody deserved to be shipwrecked, they did. She mustn't let her feelings for Jonathan undermine her toughness and will to survive. Perhaps her femininity was making her weak when she needed to be strong. She had sixteen mouths to feed beside her own. The slaves had long been wearing rags and going barefoot, and Mama and Papa weren't clothed much better. Something had to be done—and soon, to change their circumstances, which were growing more desperate with each passing day.

Squinting into the spyglass, Kate scanned the rain-lashed ocean. About two hundred yards offshore, the waves were tossing up great flumes of spray as they broke over the submerged reef. This particular reef, appropriately called Dead Man's Reef, had provided most of the wrecks from which the Montgomerys had profited thus far. Stretching almost the entire length of the cay on this, the windward side of the island, the vast section of honeycombed coral was home to grunts, groupers, parrotfish, and many others. There were only two breaks in it, and if you didn't know where those breaks were, you inevitably smashed to pieces trying to get to shore.

Once inside the reef, the waters grew calmer, cradling a magnificent stretch of white sand beach.

One could also approach the cay from the leeward side; a sheltered, natural harbor existed there, but the shoreline was rocky, the beach small, and the water barely deep enough to accommodate large, ocean-going vessels. Ships always passed on the windward side, skirting the reef while at the same time seeking the shortest possible route to Nassau at New Providence, or else traveling straight through the Bahamas en route to more southern ports.

Because of the scimitar shape of the cay, a light at one end would have effectively warned passing ships to keep well out to sea, while a light at the opposite end offered encouragement to come in dangerously close . . . and if one took out a dory and anchored with a stationary light, ship captains could hardly help mistaking the location of the cay altogether and plowing right into the reef, as Jonathan had done.

Until Edward had taken matters into his own hands, the Montgomerys had sought neither to guide nor to deceive the many passing vessels. However, as conditions on Conch Cay worsened, the temptation to tip the scales in their favor grew greater, causing Kate to endlessly debate the issue, as she was doing now. When a ship suddenly did appear, she almost missed it, so involved was she in her own thoughts. A slow-moving light on the northeastern horizon caught Kate's eye. Shifting her position on the bunched blanket, she fixed the spyglass on the tiny, bobbing object.

It was definitely a ship—headed in the general direction of Conch Cay. Knowing she had a few minutes before she needed to wake Edward, Kate used the time to calculate how long it would take the vessel to reach them and how close it would come to the reef. This near the Abacos, a wary captain would have lookouts posted and be taking frequent soundings, but on a night like this, such diligent precautions could not save him if he miscalculated even slightly . . . and he was lost altogether if lights appeared in the wrong places.

Restless and impatient, she scanned the sea again, where a second light riveted her attention. Startled, she trained the spyglass on it and wondered how she could have missed it earlier. Visible even without the spyglass, it stood almost straight out from the cay. As she adjusted the focus on the instrument, she saw that this was no ship, but a small dory—much like the ones Cal, Benjamin, and Fish were guarding farther down the beach.

Who would be out fishing on a night like this—and in Conch Cay waters?

"Edward! Edward, wake up!" Roughly, she shook his shoulder.

"Huh? . . . What is it?" He sat up, knuckling his eyes.

"Someone's out there—laying a trap for *our* ship!"

"What ship?" he demanded, snatching the spyglass out of her fingers.

"There! To the north . . . Do you see it?"

"Yeah . . ." His tone brimmed with satisfaction. "And she's headed right where we want her."

"But that dory out there! Who could it be? These are *our* hunting grounds. Nobody else has the right to go out there and lure a ship onto *our* reef!"

The unfairness of it made her voice shake. She couldn't stop the inhabitants of the other cays—Green Turtle, Great and Little Guana, and Man O' War—from salvaging a vessel sinking off Conch Cay, but she could—and would—try and stop anybody who dared enter their territory to cause a wreck under her very nose.

"I'll go to Nassau and demand an investigation!" she fumed. "I'll petition Lord Dunmore himself. This is outrageous! How *dare* they, whoever they are! Well, they better not think to take all the booty for

24

themselves . . . Come on, let's get back to Cal and the others."

She started to scramble out into the rain, but Edward clamped a hand on her surtout. "Take yer time, Kate . . . We got plenty of time. Hell, the ship ain't even wrecked, yet."

"But she will be, soon! That light is placed just right to make the captain miscalculate where the island is. He'll try and pass west of it, instead of east. That'll put him right onto the reef!"

"Slow down . . . there ain't no need t' hurry."

Something in Edward's tone made Kate study him more closely. It was too dark to see his face, but the flash of his teeth told her he was grinning.

"What is it?" she demanded, her suspicions growing by leaps and bounds. "You *know* about this, don't you?"

When he didn't answer, she screamed at him. "Who is it out there in that dory, Edward? Goddamn you, who is it?"

"Friends of ours, Kate . . . All right, maybe not friends, but people we know."

The truth crashed over her like a wave. "It's Cal, Benjamin, and Fish, isn't it?" she accused. "You sent them out on a night like this with no thought at all for *their* safety, much less the safety of any passing ships."

"They didn't mind . . . they *wanted* t' go out. I promised 'em a share of the salvage."

"Cal wouldn't approve of a deal like that—nor Benjamin, either . . . What did you do? Threaten to sell their wives and children?"

"Don't worry about it, Kate. What I threatened is between me and them. I'm overseer here, an' I got yer pa's consent t' handle things *my* way."

"Well, you don't have *my* consent, damn you! You aren't the boss on Conch Cay and never will be!" She struck him hard across the face, so enraged that she

25

had to do something—anything—to release her anger.

In answer, he grabbed her about the waist, dragged her to him, and ground his mouth down hard upon hers. It wasn't so much a kiss as a violent attempt to assert his authority. Kate kept her mouth closed and pounded on his shoulders, until he finally let go. When he did, for the second time that evening, she spat out the taste of him, then wiped her bruised and violated lips.

"You've gone too far this time, Edward," she grated. "For this, I'll see you thrown off Conch Cay."

"Ya won't git rid of me as easy as all that, Kate . . . I'm the one who supplies your pa with rum, have you forgot? An' I'll bet there's plenty of rum—an' whiskey, brandy, an' maybe even champagne—on that ship. We need that ship bad. So ya might as well forgit yer scruples an' help me save everything we can—except the crew, o' course. We don't want the crew carryin' tales t' Nassau, do we?"

"We'll save the crew, too, if at all possible," Kate insisted furiously. "They're human beings, for God's sake."

"They won't be that far from shore," Edward callously reminded her. "They can swim fer it."

"You're a heartless, depraved monster, Edward Garvin, no better than the fiends who tarred and feathered my grandfather!"

"Jus' think of the poor bastards as Americans," he retorted. "An' ya won't feel so bad about it. Now, come on. Let's git the other dory, before every last wrecker in the Abacos realizes what we're up to and gits there first."

Chapter Two

"What in bloody hell is that damned light doing out there?" Captain Jonas Irons demanded of his navigation officer, Garrod Brown. "I thought I signed you on because you claim to know the Bahamas better than most, and you swore to keep me from piling up on a reef like my poor, godforsaken brother!"

Garrod Brown, ashen-faced in the dancing lantern's glow, blinked the rain from his eyes and cast a frightened glance toward the light in question. "I do know these waters, Cap'n. Our position is exactly as I told you. We're approaching the Abacos off our starboard bow. The latitude and longitude is . . ."

"I don't give a rat's tail for our latitude and longitude! What I want to know is why that light is sitting out in front us, not moving an inch in either direction!"

"I . . . I don't know, sir! By my calculations, it shouldn't be there. It might be one of the cays, sir, but I really don't see how that's possible. Then again, maybe it is. You see, sir, Great and Little Abaco lie on the Little Bahama Bank in a cluster of more than eighty cays and two hundred rocks, forming a crescent southward from the Mantanilla Reef to the tip of Great Abaco, which is, I believe, called Hole in the Wall . . ."

"Quit babbling, you fool!" Jonas roared into the wind and rain buffeting the quarterdeck. "If that light does indicate the location of one of those eighty cays, we will all very shortly be getting a close-up look at the Little Bahama Bank and all the sharks, eels, sting rays, and barracudas who inhabit it."

"Yes, sir. I'm sorry, sir."

"You're *sorry?* There's no room for 'sorry' on this ship, Brown! Get below, and don't come out of your cabin until I personally come after you, which I damned well intend to do in the afterlife, if I don't make it in this one!"

"Yes, sir." Looking quite cowed and terrified, the man staggered across the heaving deck and disappeared down a hatch opening.

Jonas paid him no more heed than he gave the rocking motion of the ship as he limped past the foremast and leaned over the bowrail, straining to see through the rain and darkness. The distant light was clearly visible to the naked eye, now, and it hadn't moved right or left, forward or backward. The up-and-down motion could be attributed to his own ship's motion, not to the light's. It was time to decide which way to run past it—to the east or to the west. He couldn't stay on his present course, or he'd run right into it. Was the light meant to deceive him and lure him onto a reef? He had heard of such things happening in the Bahamas, where the wreckers were renowned for their greed and avarice . . . But it could just as possibly be the light from some innocent planter's cottage on one of the outlying cays.

At this point, he couldn't even be sure he had reached the Abacos. The weather had been abominable ever since he left Salem. Rain, high winds, and rough seas had followed him down the coastline, and a squall off the Carolinas had blown him halfway to Bermuda—by *his* calculations, not Brown's. The worthless navigator had insisted they weren't more than twenty miles out from Savannah.

Jonas swore under his breath and wished to God he had never allowed his younger brother, Jonathan, to captain his own ship, instead of continuing to serve as Jonas's navigator. Jonathan would have known exactly where they were; more importantly, Jonas would have known where Jonathan was. His younger brother would not have disappeared from the face of the earth, leaving Jonas wracked with guilt but determined to discover the young man's fate and that of his newly renovated ship, the *Patriot*, not one small trace of which had thus far been found.

But there was no point now in grieving over Jonathan or mulling the mystery of a gold watch fob turned up in Nassau—a salty, sea-captain's watch, inscribed and dated, which Jonas had given Jonathan on the occasion of his twenty-first birthday and which Jonathan was never without. There would be time later to discover how the watch had wound up in a Bay Street shop, where it was spotted by a close friend of the Irons brothers, Captain Talbot Daniels. Headed for Neuvitas, Cuba, with a cargo of apples, potatoes, onions, leather harnesses, and blacksmith tools, Jonathan, his entire crew, and cargo had apparently perished in a storm somewhere off the Abacos, probably on a night very like tonight, and in the same general vicinity.

If Jonas didn't make the right decision, another Irons—the last of them—would simply vanish into the mists of memory. Neither Jonas nor Jonathan, the only offspring of Bartholomew and Martha Irons, now dead some ten years past, had ever found the time or the right women to marry. Most women severely minded their husbands going to sea so much, not to mention being totally preoccupied with business matters during the brief periods when they were in port. For his part, Jonas had never missed marriage and family life; like his father before him, he was happily wedded to the sea. He wanted no wife to distract him, as his mother had tried so long and so futilely to distract his father.

Only Jonathan had occasionally complained of their monklike existence, and these complaints now haunted Jonas as he faced his own possible demise. "So who's gonna inherit this growing family empire, Big Brother, if we never get married and sire some children?"

It was too late for Jonathan—handsome, laughing Jonathan, whom all the girls adored—and now, it might be too late for *him*. Not that Jonas cared a whit about siring children, creatures as strange and alien to him as two-headed cats . . . but he would damn well regret never knowing what had happened to his brother, whom he deeply loved in his own gruff way. The appearance of Jonathan's watch suggested foul play, and Jonas could never lay his brother's spirit to rest, so long as the mystery of his death remained unsolved.

"God help us all," he murmured, swinging away from the railing.

He started shouting orders, and dark figures in rain-slickened oilcloth ran to obey. The *Liberty*'s timbers creaked, and her sails luffed, as she came about, preparing to set a course due west, instead of south. Taking a chance that what he had sighted might be the island of Grand Bahamas, instead of the Abacos, Jonas decided that this was the most prudent course of action, given his uncertainty. If the Grand Bahamas did indeed lie ahead, veering west would save him, and if it was the Abacos, he still stood a chance of passing between a cay and the main body of the Abaco chain. Just in case, he ordered soundings to be taken continuously.

Then he limped in the direction of his cabin to retrieve his logbook, his brother's watch, and a few

30

additional valuables he did not want to lose if, despite all his prayers, curses, and precautions, the ship grounded on a reef and went down.

Kate did not have to wait long to witness the terrible consequences of the misplaced light on the dory manned by Cal, Benjamin, and Fish. The ship they had been watching—a double-masted, square-rigged brig under full sail—did exactly as she feared. It altered course and headed straight for the reef. Had there been lightning or stars and moon, the ship's lookout might have spotted the white water frothing over the reef, but the blackness of the night and the pelting rain hid the surf until the ship was almost on top of it.

Watching from the rocking dory in the relatively calmer waters inside the reef, Kate knew the exact moment when the ship's captain became aware of impending disaster. The crew aboard the brig made a valiant effort to trim sail, but by then, nothing could save them. A loud cracking and splintering sound signaled the impact of reef and hull, followed by a noise that resembled the groan of a living creature being torn apart.

Kate gritted her teeth and momentarily closed her eyes, loathe to watch the final moments of the mortally wounded vessel. "God have mercy," she murmured under her breath, well able to imagine the terror and panic reigning aboard the stricken ship.

"It's gonna be a clean wreck!" Edward exulted from the stern, where he was handling the tiller.

By a clean wreck, he meant that the vessel would go down fast and not linger, hung up or partially hung up while the surf pounded her to pieces. She had a big enough hole in her hull that her cargo would be released immediately. Unfortunately, the captain and crew stood a slim chance of surviving. There

31

hadn't been time for the lowering of a longboat, and any crew or passengers would soon be tossed into the brine. While Edward watched for floating hogsheads, crates, barrels, and other salvageable items, Kate kept an eye peeled for struggling bodies. Any survivors had to reach the calmer waters before she and Edward could risk picking them up—lest they, too, be dashed against the reef—and doing that would not be easy.

Kate knew that the undertow near the reef was fierce, plus the sinking ship created its own powerful undertow. Dazed or injured survivors hadn't the strength to fight the sea's relentless grip. Only the most powerful, determined swimmers stood a chance of cheating death. How many would die tonight? she gloomily wondered. A ship the size of this one likely had a crew of ten to twelve, and if she carried passengers, the death toll could rise even higher.

This was the part of wrecking that Kate hated most—the panic, the futile struggles, the shouts and cries of dying men moments before the sea sucked them under, when all she could do was watch helplessly and pray for their souls. Edward relished the excitement and challenge of these awful moments, but Kate dreaded and despised them. She would much prefer going out the next day and calmly collecting what had washed ashore. But she couldn't afford to sit back and wait. Other wreckers might arrive at any moment, eager to brave the storm's wrath and snatch the treasure before it was ruined. Cal, Benjamin, and Fish should be arriving as soon as they safely negotiated the reef. It was time to stop thinking of the victims and start searching for the salvage.

Behind her, Edward suddenly shouted: "Look! Over there! A whole fleet of hogsheads!"

Kate squinted into the driving rain, which by now had found its way in cold dribbles down the back of her neck. Despite the fabled warmth of the Bahamian climate, Kate was so chilled that her teeth were chattering. Then she saw them—a bevy of barrels bobbing like fat brown ducks on the spumy sea. She focused her attention on them, hoping to distract herself from the reality of drowning men, whose anguished cries were already carrying across the water. She leaned forward against the long, wooden oars and started rowing. It required all her strength to fight the waves, and Edward came up beside her, sat down on the bench, and took one of the oars. Together, they mastered the waves and propelled the pitching dory toward the barrels.

Kate had always found it odd that filled barrels could float for a time after being cast upon the water, but float they did, until they became waterlogged and finally sank. This was the main reason for speed. Many things quickly spoiled when exposed to salt water. Fortunately, not everything did; in a few days, it would be possible to go out in the dory, peer into the crystal clear waters, and locate more sunken booty—crates, barrels, lengths of pipe, and so on, much of which could be recovered. Fish especially, was an excellent diver. Still, the longer they waited, the greater was the chance of spoilage. What brought the highest profit in Nassau was usually what they salvaged the soonest after a wreck. This fact gave Edward all the reason he needed to focus on salvage, rather than survivors.

God have pity on those poor drowning wretches, Kate prayed silently, and bent once again into the oar.

It was useless. He was going to die. Jonas knew it in his weary bones and burning lungs. The sea embraced him like an impassioned lover, and he experienced a moment of near surrender; if he had to die, this wasn't a bad way to go—locked in the arms of the demanding mistress he had always cherished. It would be so easy to just give up; with the *Patriot*, the *Liberty*, and his brother gone, too, he didn't have much left to live for. Irons Shipping Company only consisted of four ships—and the third and fourth were in Salem dry dock, undergoing cleaning and refitting, which he could not now afford, having lost this cargo on top of the *Patriot*'s.

But despite his financial problems and his utter exhaustion, Jonas could not seem to stop fighting to survive. His body was determined to save itself. With long, powerful strokes, his arms resisted the downward tug of the sea. His legs kicked frantically—propelling him toward the surface and life-giving air.

His head broke water, and he managed to steal a huge gulp of air before he was again sucked under. He banged and scraped along something hard and sharp that rent his flesh in a dozen places, and guessed he was being battered against the *Liberty*'s barnacle-encrusted hull. If so, he stood little chance of escape, for he knew the hull was fast sinking, dragging him down with it.

The speed with which the ship had succumbed to the reef still amazed him. Once impaled upon it, gouged and torn open, she had immediately begun to break apart. There had been no time for launching the longboats, issuing last-minute orders to the crew, or checking on the navigator he had sent below . . . Jonas wondered if Garrod Brown had even made it on deck. Those like himself already there had been quickly tossed or swept overboard. He himself had clung to the mainmast as it toppled into the ocean.

As despair closed in on him like a hungry shark, he searched his mind for a reason to stay alive. He and Jonathan had been poised upon the brink of brilliant economic success. Another fruitful trading voyage by either of them would have lifted their fledgling shipping business out of the red and firmly established it as Salem's finest, upcoming, young firm. Not for the Irons brothers the uncertainties and constraints of sailing ships owned by other men. Jonas had too often witnessed his father's frustrations at not being able to choose his own ports and cargoes.

So Jonas and Jonathan had set out to become their own masters, and they had come so close . . . so tantalizingly close to fulfilling their dreams! Now, those dreams lay shattered and broken at the bottom of the sea, and Jonas suddenly felt a spurt of such raw rage and boundless fury that it gave him an almost inhuman strength. Once again, he fought his way to the surface, gulped air, and trod water long enough to shake the spray from his eyes and ascertain which way the waves were running, his only clue to the direction of land, salvation . . . and revenge.

He would keep living if for no other reason than to find out who had placed that light to lure him onto the reef . . . and who had sold his brother's watch to a gem shop in Nassau. He would stay alive to mete out justice and gain revenge on the conscienceless bastards responsible for wrecking ships and taking pocket watches from dead men. He burned with a fever to wrap his fingers around the necks of as many murderers as he could discover. No, he would not die this night. God help him, *he would not die!*

Kate dragged the last of the hogsheads up on the beach, past the reach of the waves, then sat down a moment on one of them to catch her breath. She hated to admit to any weakness or need for rest, but she suddenly felt as if she could not budge another step. The four men—Edward, Cal, Benjamin, and

Fish—were already clambering back into the dories and shoving them out into the surf en route to retrieve more booty; maybe they wouldn't notice her absence in the rain and darkness, and she would have a short respite before she had to carry or drag more heavy loads to safety.

She pressed a hand to her side where a painful stitch made the simple act of breathing difficult. Bad as the stitch was, it was nowhere near as bad as the cramping in her lower abdomen. Why tonight, of all nights, did the curse have to pay her a visit? And why did it have to bring cramps, a headache, and a backache all at the same time?

Being female was so unfair. Most of the time she could and did ignore her gender; she could row, sail, plant, harvest, fish, swear, fight, wreck, and ride a horse as long and hard as any man. But once a month, her femininity caught up with her, reminding her that no matter how much she might wish otherwise, she still lived in a woman's body . . . and that body ruled the rest of her. That's what it was doing now—ruling her, sapping her strength and willpower, making her feel weak and nauseous, to the point of being unsteady on her feet.

She didn't think she could roll or carry another barrel up the beach right now if her life depended upon it. The cramping in her lower belly made her bend over suddenly and utter a low groan—half in pain, half in protest. She cursed the double inconvenience of having to conceal her condition before the men got back with more barrels and crates to haul. Even in the darkness, a dark stain on her tan breeches would be noticed, especially if Edward lit a lantern to better assess their catch.

Muttering over the indignity of it, Kate crept behind a barrel, tore off a piece of her long shirt, wadded it up, and stuffed it down her trousers. That, at least, should prevent discovery. Unfortunately, she could do nothing about the discomfort. It would be a long time before she could take to her bed and allow Bell to prepare one of her special remedies—a mixture of tea and one of her mysterious herbs and powders—which inevitably eased the cramping. Thank God for Bell's teas; without them, the Montgomerys might not have survived this long.

Peering into the darkness, Kate saw the two dories rising and falling as they broached the waves headed out to sea. Thank heaven, she'd been left behind this trip! She decided to sit awhile, then do something to distract herself from the cramps—count the barrels perhaps, or search farther down the beach for whatever might have washed ashore on its own. Thus far, there had been no sign of survivors, and Kate doubted there would be any. The ship had gone down too fast, and the sea was especially rough tonight. She tried not to think about the fact that Edward had caused the wreck, thereby murdering men as surely as if he'd done it with his own two hands.

Later, she would deal with the problem of Edward, perhaps by forbidding Cal, Benjamin, and Fish ever to obey such a heinous command from him again. She must get Papa sobered up and speak to him about it. Edward obviously had no intention of listening to *her;* he might start sending out Fish on a regular basis, even on calm nights, not just stormy ones. Fish would go, just for the hell of it; he liked rum as well as Papa, and a little bribery went a long way with Fish.

Sighing over the situation, Kate rose to her feet and tipped back her face to see if it had quit raining. It had, but the air was thick with moisture. She rummaged around for the lantern, fumbled in the dark to light it, then set off resolutely down the beach. The lantern cast a small circle of light which barely penetrated the mist writhing out of the nearby forest of pine and mahogany. The many trees—some appearing to grow straight out of rock—were an island irony. They gave the Abacos the appearance of great fertility, but once the trees were cut or burned, the soil soon washed or blew away, leaving only barren sand and rock.

Kate walked a good distance, spotting nothing of interest, but her cramps eased slightly, and she turned to go back with less dread and weariness. Halfway to the heap of salvage, she spotted what at first glance appeared to be a log rolling over and over in the waves. A glimpse of something white propelled her toward the surf to investigate. Setting down the lantern out of the ocean's reach, she ran to the water's edge, where the log revealed itself to be the body of a man clad in black boots, trousers, and a white shirt almost torn to shreds. It was the shirt that had caught her eye.

Splashing into the shallows, she hooked her hands beneath the man's armpits and started hauling him to shore. He was very tall—taller than Edward—and very heavy, like a dead weight. In all likelihood, he *was* dead, poor, battered, drowned sod. Kate alternated tugging and rolling him until he was safely past the claw of the surf. Then she quickly retrieved the lantern and shone it full into his face, searching for signs of life.

The man's features were achingly familiar—so much so that her heart slammed painfully in her chest, and her breath departed her lungs in a loud gasp. So great was her shock that for a moment, she suspected fate of playing a cruel, heartless joke on her . . . *The man was Jonathan.*

But no, it couldn't be. Jonathan was buried deep in the pine forest behind her. Maybe her eyes were playing tricks. Twice, she had pulled Jonathan from the sea's clutches, but perhaps her love for him was so strong that the mere similarity of circumstances had

38

caused her to superimpose Jonathan's features on the face and body of this stranger's.

Only he *did* look like Jonathan—the same dark, curling hair, the same golden-bronze skin, the same hawkish nose and finely chiseled lips that managed to be masculine, sensuous, and temptingly kissable, all at the same time. Dear God, he even had the same deep cleft in the bold, square chin!

With trembling fingers, Kate brushed back the wet hair on the man's forehead. Ah, there was something different. A white scar slashed across his brow, neatly bisecting one thick, black eyebrow. This man was also more muscular, Kate decided, glancing quickly down his body. His shoulders were broader, his chest wider, his thighs more reminiscent of tree trunks in the forest. Still, he bore an amazing resemblance to her lost love. If he opened his eyes, would they, too, be the exact color of the turquoise sea flashing in the sunlight?

She would probably never know, because this man was most definitely dead. At least, he didn't seem to be breathing. Coming to her senses, Kate dropped to her knees, set down the lantern, rolled him over on his side, and started pounding on his back. She knew of no sure method for reviving drowning victims, but Bell advised forcing them to vomit and expel the seawater they had swallowed. So that's what Kate did—tried to get the man to vomit. Repeated thumping between his shoulder blades didn't seem to work, so she rolled him onto his back again, and sat down with a bounce on his midsection.

Immediately, water gushed from his mouth. She quickly turned his face to the side, then bounced on his abdomen a second time. More water gushed forth. The man coughed, heaved, then drew a long, shuddering breath.

"That's it, *breathe!*" she instructed excitedly.

For a moment, he didn't move, then his eyelids

39

twitched, a groan emerged from his chest, and he opened his eyes. Kate found herself staring—incredibly—into Jonathan's sea-blue eyes . . . those uniquely colored eyes that had no comparison in nature except for the blue-green of the Abaco sea on a fine, fair day.

Chapter Three

At first, Jonas thought he had died and was awakening in the hereafter. He felt a mild spurt of interest; now, he would discover if there really was a heaven and a hell, and if people actually went to one or the other when they died. Where had he wound up? He didn't feel as if he rightly belonged in either place—heaven being too good for him, and hell a bit worse than he deserved.

As feeling returned to his stiff, chilled limbs, he realized that he hadn't died, after all. The back of his neck felt gritty with sand, his stomach hurt, he was shivering from wet and cold, and someone was shining a light in his eyes. He stared hard at the intruder, half expecting to see angel wings fanning the air overhead. What he saw was no angel, unless angels these days came with hair tucked under an oilcloth hood, a smattering of freckles across the bridge of a straight, regal nose, and eyes more like a cat's than a human's.

Gradually, it dawned on him that the pale, aristocratic face looking down at him belonged to a female, and whoever she was, her surprise more than equaled his; indeed, she looked downright thunderstruck.

"I'm not dead," he tried to say, but his voice came

out in a croak.

"Who are you?" she gasped in a low, husky voice. "What's your name?"

"What's yours?" he countered warily, first clearing his throat.

"Kate," she said. "Kate Montgomery. You don't know me . . . do you?"

She sounded half wistful, as if she wished they *had* met somewhere before, perhaps in a previous life. He reached up a hand to brush back her hood so he could get a better look at her. The lantern light revealed hair a dark red color, the shade of chestnuts. Then he realized that her hair was damp, and when dry, might be a different color altogether. She wore it in a single, fat braid that fell down her back, so he couldn't see how long it was. She was, he noticed, dressed in a man's clothing; he caught a glimpse of a man's shirt and breeches beneath the rain gear, and a well-worn pair of boots, much like his own, on her feet.

He glanced back to her eyes. They were odd and compelling—gleaming yellow in the light, like a calico cat's. Absurdly long lashes framed them. She had full, soft lips, slightly bluish in color, but pinkening as he studied them. The thought came to him that she wasn't what a man would call "pretty," her jaw being too angular, her cheekbones too prominent, her gaze too direct and disturbing. But she was certainly striking, bold, even exotic. Or maybe he just hadn't taken the time to look at a woman's face for so long, that he would have found almost any female attractive, especially as close as he had come to death this night.

"Did you see anybody else on this beach? Anybody off my ship?" he rasped, ticking off his crew in his mind—Musket Jones, his reliable first mate, Donald Fell, his helmsman, Garrod Brown, his navigator . . . God, how he dreaded having to tell their families that they were never coming home. With the exception of

42

Brown and a couple others, his crew had been with him for years; they were good, competent men whose loss he could not yet assimilate.

"No . . . I've seen no one," she answered. "I . . . um . . . was taking a walk when I saw your ship foundering. Two dories have already gone out searching for survivors. It was just luck that I found you here on the beach."

He saw in her eyes that she was lying; probably, her father, brothers, husband, and everyone else in her family were out collecting salvage, not survivors. And if *they* were the ones responsible for that misplaced light, they would soon wish he had died, instead of washing up on shore.

"Wreckers . . . You're wreckers," he gritted through chattering teeth. He tried to sit up, but his entire body protested the action.

She helped him. "You can't blame us for saving whatever we can before the sea gets it."

His head was spinning, his limbs boneless. Now was not the time to mention the light. "Oh, I don't blame you for taking advantage of my misfortune. This is a cruel, godforsaken world; you have to look after yourself first, if you want to survive in it."

Even to his own ears, the comment sounded harsh and bitter, but that was how he felt at this particular moment. The woman—or girl, rather, she looked quite young—did not dispute it. Instead, she kept a firm grip on his arm.

"Are you injured?" she inquired. "Can you stand and walk? I'd like to get you away from this surf."

He rose unsteadily to his feet. Once there, he had to lean on her until the dizziness passed. "I can walk. Nothing's broken, but I took a hell of a pounding against the ship's hull before she went down."

"You're lucky to be alive," she sympathized.

"And lucky you came along to drag me out of the surf when you did."

"Oh, well . . ." She made a disparaging motion with her hand. "As I mentioned before, I was just walking along the beach when I saw your ship in distress."

"Right . . . Perfect night for a walk on the beach. Dodging lightning bolts is so invigorating. And there's nothing like a steady downpour for washing laundry while it's still on your back."

His sarcasm wasn't lost on her. "All right, I *was* watching for a wreck," she admitted. "It's the kind of night when wrecks usually occur. You should be glad I was here, or you'd be dead by now."

"I *said* I was lucky you came along."

"But you haven't thanked me yet."

He clamped his jaws tightly together. The one thing he wouldn't do was thank her—especially now, when it was almost certain she had been involved in placing that light.

"Come along," she ordered, tugging on his arm. "If you can walk, then let's walk."

She picked up the lantern with her free hand and set out. He followed, limping worse than ever, his bad leg hurting like hell. She stopped.

"You *are* injured. Something's wrong with your leg."

"What's wrong with my leg didn't happen tonight. It happened years ago. Think nothing of it. I never do—at least, I try not to."

They started out again, but hadn't gotten very far before she again stopped. "How did you hurt it? You're limping badly."

Exasperation and pain made him snap at her. "It's nothing, I told you!" Then, seeing her expression, he sighed and explained. "I fell out of the shrouds—the sails—when I was eleven. Broke my leg. When it healed, I had a limp. It's not usually this bad; tomorrow, if it's sunny, the limp will all but disappear. Foul weather always aggravates it."

44

She regarded him with unnerving intensity. "And the scar on your forehead? How did you get that?"

He thought her unusually nosy, but she had, after all, saved his life, so he indulged her curiosity. "A cable snapped loose in a storm and laid my forehead open to the bone."

Her remarkable eyes lingered on his scar, warming him as if she had touched him, but all she said was "Oh."

They made slow progress up the beach, and when they got where she was headed, Jonas took a good long look at the hogsheads already piled there— booty that head come from the hold of his ship. Seized with sudden, bitter amusement, he threw back his head and laughed.

"What's so funny?" she demanded, yellow eyes flashing.

Regaining control, he sat down on one of the barrels. "You picked the wrong thing to salvage, that's all. What's in these barrels has probably already been ruined."

"What *is* in them?"

"Rice mostly, but there's also corn and wheat flour."

"You packed rice, corn, and flour in barrels instead of sacks?"

"Deters the rats. Wood is harder to chew through. Stores longer, too. Especially the corn, which has a tendency to spoil in the stuffiness of a hold."

"Where were you bound?" she asked, her eyes narrowing suspiciously.

He decided not to lie about it, though he suspected she wouldn't like the answer. "Nassau . . ."

He was right; she didn't like the answer. "But you're an American! American trade isn't welcome in Nassau, as I'm sure you know."

"And you're a Loyalist, or you wouldn't oppose trading typical Bahamian products like salt, wood,

45

and turtles for badly needed commodities such as corn, rice, and flour."

Her face suffused with heat and color, endowing her with a sudden, vibrant beauty that caused him to revise his opinion that she wasn't pretty. Anger made her downright stunning. "Who authorized you to trade in the Bahamas?" she demanded imperiously.

"Lord Dunmore." He crossed one leg over the other, made himself more comfortable atop the barrel, and absentmindedly rubbed the throbbing knee of his bad leg. "If you don't like it, you'll have to take it up with Dunmore himself. I'm not the only one he's authorized. I know of several Salem firms to whom he's given the nod. And why shouldn't he? In case you haven't heard, the war's been over for quite some time."

"It will *never* be over! Not for those of us who lost everything we had and were driven from the country like the worst of traitors."

"You deny that you sided with a despot?"

"Of course, I deny it! *You* are the ones who were traitors. We were only being loyal to our king and mother country."

He would have laughed a second time if she hadn't looked so serious and outraged. "And just how old were you when you pledged undying faith to a greedy old man living on the other side of the ocean?"

"What does age have to do with it? I was old enough to have witnessed my grandfather being tarred and feathered for his beliefs."

"And I was old enough to see my uncle die of a bayonet thrust he took in a battle with the redcoats. But I'll wager that neither of us really understood the issues at the time. At age twelve, I only knew that I wanted to kill the lobster backs and cover myself with glory."

"It isn't right that you come here to gloat over our misfortune and profit from our poverty," she said

46

primly, her full, luscious lips curving downward and her brows dipping in a scowl. "So I can't say I'm terribly upset that your ship struck that reef. At least now you won't be making money off poor wretches who were tossed out of your country on their behinds."

Anger rose in him like a floodtide. "Eleven men went down with my ship," he grated. "You've had half a lifetime to get over your grief and anguish over what happened to your family. I've only had ten minutes to recover from my losses. Forgive me if I don't care to debate political issues at the moment."

"I'm sorry," she offered after a moment's silence. "It's just that most Abaconians, myself included, would prefer to have nothing to do with your countrymen."

"So this *is* the Abacos, I take it." And Garrod Brown was right, after all, he thought, with a stab of regret that he'd been so harsh on the man.

"Yes," she confirmed, adding reluctantly: "Welcome to Conch Cay . . . We don't have a great deal, but what we do have is yours to share for however long you stay with us."

"Does that mean you intend to return my property to me?" He nodded toward the barrels.

"No," she challenged, looking him in the eye as directly as any man. "By the law of the sea, whatever we salvage belongs to us. When we take it to Nassau, we need only give the royal governor his share and the rest is ours."

And Dunmore profits either way, whether he trades with Americans or they shipwreck somewhere in the Bahamas, Jonas thought bitterly. "Have you another dory available then?" he asked. "I'll pay for the use of it. Perhaps I can save something on my own that you might miss."

She tilted her head as she soberly assessed him. "Aren't you a bit weak to make the attempt? You nearly drowned tonight. I suggest you be satisfied that you still have your life, and forget about everything you've lost."

"Forget those eleven men, you mean."

She looked slightly abashed, but then shrugged philosophically. "What else can you do? The sea has claimed many men. Anyone who goes out on it knows the risks involved. I assume you're the captain of that ship; if so, then you of all people should be aware of those risks."

"I *was* the captain . . . My name is Jonas," he said, watching her carefully. "Captain Jonas Irons."

Her eyes widened as he said his name, and her face paled. He would bet his last shilling she had heard the name before—with a slight variation. "You seem familiar with the name Irons. Perhaps you've met my brother—Jonathan. My parents had an affinity for names starting with the letter J."

"N-No," she denied. "I've never met anyone by the name of Irons before."

"Then you know nothing about his ship, the *Patriot*, that sank in a storm off the Abacos about four months ago."

"No, nothing!" She responded too quickly and vehemently. "We get lots of storms in these waters—lots of shipwrecks."

She looked positively guilty, now. Her face had gone whiter than a shroud—the little liar! He had to restrain himself from wrapping his fingers around her slender neck and choking the truth out of her. Undoubtedly, she knew all about the *Patriot*, his brother, and perhaps even his brother's timepiece, safe in his buttoned shirt pocket. He couldn't wait to see her face when he showed her *that*. But before he took any further action, he needed to be sure about the light. It might have been the very same light that misled his brother. If so, how many, besides this girl, were involved in the heartless business of murder and

48

wrecking? He was amazed she had bothered to drag him from the surf. Probably she had only been looking for another fine watch to pilfer and hadn't counted on his still being alive.

He glanced out to see where a dark shape loomed in the water. "Is that your husband—or father—returning?"

"Neither . . . I'm not married, and my father is too old for this kind of excitement. That's our overseer, Edward Garvin, and three of our slaves."

"How convenient," he drawled. "Your family couldn't have been too impoverished when it took refuge in the Bahamas; you were able to bring slaves with you."

"We lost more than two-thirds of our people!" she erupted. "We were fortunate to retain any, after the fevers that carried off not only the slaves but my brother on Tynbee Island."

"Tynbee Island? Isn't that near Saint Augustine, Florida?"

"Yes," she spat. "It's where we fled in terror for our very lives. After that, we came here, and this is where we've been living—or should I say, barely surviving—ever since."

He cast a scornful glance over her roughly clad, barely visible figure. She was tall for a woman, and from what he could see of her body, lusciously endowed. She did not appear to be starving. True, her clothes left something to be desired—as did her manners—but she was every inch a sensual, blooming female. He felt his groin swell in response to her and cursed this very masculine reaction to a woman likely no better than a murderess.

"Don't expect me to say I'm sorry," he growled. "It's difficult to summon sympathy for people caught in the act of stealing me blind."

"Wrecking isn't stealing! Everyone knows that. You would do it yourself if you had no other means to keep body and soul together, and the opportunity came along."

"Did the opportunity just come along? Or did you perhaps help to create it?"

"I did no such thing! If you're accusing me of something, why don't you spit it out, instead of making sly insinuations?"

Oh, she was a picture of self-righteousness, now. He could almost believe she *hadn't* had anything to do with that light—only he wasn't that stupid and naive. Someone had lured him—and probably also his brother—onto that reef, and he was damned well going to find out *who* and punish the person for it. Whoever had done it would pay with his—or her— life. A life for a life. On that, he was decided.

"Here come your friends." He jerked his head in the direction of the beach. "Don't forget to introduce me. I want to see their expressions when you tell them my name. I have a feeling they'll look as shocked and guilty as you did."

Her eyes widened even more, if that were possible. "I have nothing whatever to feel shocked and guilty about! I've never heard of you or your brother . . . If I'd known you were going to be so churlish and ungrateful, I assure you I never would have bothered to rescue you!"

"Why *did* you rescue me? Were you suddenly overcome by a fit of conscience? In your line of work, that must be a rare occurrence."

"More likely I was overcome by a fit of lunacy! I'm only in this line of work because you and your kind drove me to it! I see now that I made a great mistake in saving you; I should have let you drown. I wish I had. Then I wouldn't be having this ridiculous conversation."

Spinning on her heel, she stalked away from him and marched down the beach toward the shadowy figures fighting the surf to pull the heavy-laden dories ashore—dories loaded down with even more of his precious cargo. Jonas sat where he was, still too weak, stiff, and sore to move any more than necessary. Had he been rash and unwise to have played his hand so soon? If the girl *had* done everything of which he accused her, then he didn't stand much chance of gaining revenge in his present weakened state. What was there to prevent this Edward Garvin and the three black men he could see climbing out of the boats, from overpowering and killing him?

He had been a fool to reveal so much, and wouldn't have, had the girl not goaded him into it. Warily, he looked around for something he could use to defend himself. A short distance away, a piece of driftwood lay half buried in the sand. Rising he limped over to it and picked it up. It was heavy enough to do real damage, but he wasn't sure he was strong enough to wield it effectively.

Lacking pistol, knife, or sword, he would have to try. The only other thing he could do would be to grab the girl and threaten bodily harm to her if anyone lifted a menacing hand toward him. There *was* a certain fragility to her bone structure. He was sure he could snap a wrist, arm, or even her neck with hardly any effort . . . and he'd do it if he had no other choice.

Holding the driftwood out in front of him, he awaited the arrival of the four men in the dories. Carrying crates he recognized as containing saws, augers, and other tools, the men tromped up the beach toward him. The only white man, obviously the overseer she had mentioned, struck him as a strong, surly sort of fellow, who did not look at all pleased to see him. Apparently, the girl had already identified him, for the first words out of Edward Garvin's mouth were his name.

"Jonas Irons? Kate here says yer the cap'n of that

51

ship out there. Too bad ya didn't see the reef. Black night like this anything can happen."

"Guess I was too busy poring over maps in my cabin . . ." Jonas prevaricated, keeping a firm grip on the driftwood. "When I went below, everything was fine. The next thing I knew the ship was breaking apart at the seams."

"That a fact?" Edward Garvin smirked unpleasantly. "Then ya didn't really see nothin' b'fore ya hit that reef."

"Nothing I'd admit to when I'm outnumbered five to one." Jonas hefted the wood, letting the other man know he wasn't afraid to use it, but also that he wouldn't fight unless forced into it.

Garvin turned triumphantly to Kate Montgomery. "Hell, he sounds like a reasonable man t' me, Kate. But if he gives ya any more lip, you jus' holler. Me an' the boys'll be happy t' bash in his head fer his trouble."

"No! No violence, Edward. I already told you that," Kate Montgomery snapped.

"I ain't fixin' to be violent," Garvin denied. "But you said he was mad about his ship goin' down, an' real anxious t' place blame. I'm jus' warnin' him that we don't cotton t' bein' called murderers. What we are is wreckers, an honest occupation in these here parts! We jus' go out and haul in whatever the sea sends us."

Another liar! Jonas thought furiously. Searching for support, he scanned the faces of the three, silent, black men who offered no comment one way or the other and for the most part, kept their eyes averted . . . except for one. Jonas focused his attention on the largest and strongest of the three slaves—a giant of a man with a broad, round face, gentle features, and disapproving eyes. Everytime the giant's gaze touched Kate Montgomery, something flickered in his expression. Some soft, protective emotion warred

52

with his obvious displeasure at being where he was, doing what he was doing.

That's the man who'll eventually tell me what I want to know, Jonas thought.

He must be patient. He must watch and wait. Sooner or later, he'd discover the truth of this night—and the facts about his brother's disappearance. There would be clues and irrefutable evidence. If he bided his time, he could eventually get all the proof he needed. In the meantime, he must strive to overcome the damage he had already done by revealing too much to Kate Montgomery.

"There's plenty more where that came from," Jonas said, nodding toward the crates and barrels. "Hadn't you better get back to work? I offered to help, but Miss Montgomery here turned me down."

Kate's eyes blazed, turning to gold fire in the lamplight. "You never offered to help! What you wanted was to salvage things on your own!"

"That was before you so graciously enlightened me concerning the laws of wrecking. Now, I'll be glad to help for a mere percentage of the take. I don't know how else I'll get home again. The money I brought with me is somewhere in Davy Jones's locker."

"How big a percentage?" Garvin demanded, eyeing him with greedy interest. "You'd be a big help tellin' us what t' go after first."

"Fifty percent . . ." Jonas tried, knowing the amount would never be accepted.

"Ten percent and not a shilling more," Kate Montgomery protested, her husky voice vibrating with anger.

"Forty," Jonas determinedly bargained.

"Twenty."

"Thirty . . . Take it or leave it, Miss Montgomery. If you refuse, I won't lift a finger."

"Twenty-five or you can go to hell and back."

"Twenty-five, it is," Jonas abruptly agreed.

Without boats and manpower, he couldn't rescue a single barrel. Still, he resented having to bargain like a fishwife for a share of what should have been wholly his. He consoled himself with the thought that he would have settled for less, just to be able to get anything.

"Are you sure you're strong enough to go back out in a boat?" the feisty, golden-eyed female challenged. Her amazing eyes skewered him as if he were less than the man he knew himself to be.

"Do you intend to go?" he drawled, deliberately provoking her.

"Yes," she answered.

"If a mere woman can do it, I can," he assured her. "The fact that I'm battered and half drowned only makes us equal—though I believe I still have the edge on you."

"In a pig's eye!" she spat.

Edward seemed delighted by their mutual animosity. "Glad t' see you know how t' put a woman in her place, Irons. Not that Kate Montgomery is jus' *any* woman, mind ya, but she keeps forgettin' that she ain't a man, neither."

"Then we'll just have to remind her, won't we, Mister Garvin?"

Kate locked glances with him, letting him know that she would never forgive him for maligning her gender. He met her gaze unblinkingly; females *were* weaker than men, and the sooner they realized it, the better. He never had been one to flatter and cajole women. Jonathan had been the honey-tongued seducer of silly young chits; he told them how smart and clever they were, and they invariably believed it and tossed their skirts for him—more fools, they.

"Shall we get started?" He slid easily into the role of command, a role as familiar as a well-worn coat or pair of high boots.

Garvin didn't argue. He and the three slaves headed back toward the boats. Only Kate stood there, looking quite mutinous, as if she wanted to throttle him. She wouldn't take a step until she was damn good and ready. In that moment, Jonas realized that *she* was the true figure of authority; Edward Garvin wanted the power but hadn't figured out how to wrest it from her . . . which meant that whatever had happened tonight or in the past, Kate Montgomery had definitely been involved. More likely still, she had been in charge.

Chapter Four

Sybil Montgomery awoke from a terrifying dream and clutched the bed linens with sweaty, trembling fingers. "Bell? Bell, where are you?"

But it wasn't Bell who answered her summons. Her husband, William, snapped upright beside her. "What is it, Sybil, darling? It's me, William. Tell me what's wrong."

Sybil heard him rummaging around on the table next to the bed, and a moment later, light banished the oppressive blackness of their bedchamber. William's gaunt, concerned face—no longer handsome as it had been in his youth—filled her field of vision. Her nostrils flared at the odor of the spirits he breathed in her face.

"Bell, I want Bell," she said, closing her eyes in revulsion. William's sallow, rum-ravaged features, graying brown hair, and bloodshot eyes—those dark, velvet eyes that had been her undoing!—disgusted her beyond measure.

"Now, Sybil, honey . . ." he said patiently. "Bell's gone home with Gilbert, and last I looked, we were having a bit of a blow outside. You wouldn't send me out to fetch her on a night such as this, would you?"

"Where's Kate then?" Sybil demanded. "If I can't have Bell, I want my daughter."

"Dearest love, Kate's not here either. Don't you remember? She and Edward went down to the beach to watch for a wreck. But I'm here. Just tell me what you want. I can do anything that needs doing."

"No, William, you cannot. You are a useless old sot, incapable of doing anything . . . I want Bell! I want to go home! I want my baby, Robin, back again! I want everything to be as it was when I was young and beautiful—the belle of Savannah, and I could have any man I wanted! Oh God, why did I have to choose you?"

She started to sob, the terrible dream still so vivid in her mind that she could remember every detail. She had been wearing a white silk gown, trimmed with violets and forget-me-nots, and floating across a polished wood floor to the strains of a string orchestra. Nearby was a table laden with all her favorite childhood foods: a clove-studded ham, black-eyed peas, a plump, roasted turkey, tarts and pastries of all kinds, a frothy syllabub . . . The air was scented with flowers, and candles gleamed everywhere. Men were vying for the privilege of the next dance with her, and Sybil knew that her life would be an endless succession of lovely gowns, mouth-watering foods, slaves wearing white gloves fulfilling her every whim. She would always be the center of attention, adored by family, friends, husband, and children . . .

"Did you have another one of your nightmares, my dove?" William inquired solicitously. "Have you a headache? Shall I fetch some of Bell's powders to make you sleep?"

"No! No, you fool!" Sybil jerked away from him and hid under the bed covers. "Go away! Leave me alone! The snakes will devour me, and you will sit there and watch, helpless and useless as ever. Well, this time, I won't permit you to watch my suffering."

William's voice came to her, muffled but calm.

58

"Dearest love, there are no snakes here in our bed. You must have been dreaming of Tynbee Island and the swamplands in Florida."

She threw off the bed covers and screamed in his face. "The snakes were eating me alive only a moment ago, you fool! They ate the violets right off my gown. They ate the cloves out of the ham. They drank up every last drop of that lovely syllabub."

"I think I had better go and fetch Bell, after all." William sighed. "She's the only one who can deal with you when you get like this."

"Stay here!" she snapped, grabbing the sleeve of his nightshirt. "I know where you're going—not to get Bell, but to fetch your precious rum. That's all you care about. The snakes can eat me alive, and you won't care a fig, so long as you can drink until you can't stand up anymore."

"I'm not drunk, tonight, Sybil. But you're making me wish I were. Can't I go fetch Mattie, at least? Her hut is closer than Bell's. Mattie will come keep you company and make you feel better."

"Mattie despises me!" Sybil sobbed. "She cares only for Kate! If you bring Mattie, she'll tell Kate I was bad tonight, and then Kate will look at me with pity and loathing in her eyes. You know I can't stand to be pitied! If she comes to hate me, Kate may desert us, William! Then what will become of us? Kate will leave here and go someplace else, and the snakes will come and devour us, and we shall all die . . . Bell, Gilbert, Mattie, Cal . . ."

Sybil could feel herself slipping into hysteria, and beyond the hysteria was an even darker place, a yawning black pit. If she ever fell into it, she would never get out again. That was what frightened her so much. The pit held snakes, spiders, and all sorts of other creeping, crawling, slithering creatures, such as there had been on Tynbee Island. Only Bell could pull her back from the precipice . . . could stop her

59

from plunging down . . . down . . . down . . .

"Bell! I want Bell!" she screamed, clinging to William's shirtfront.

"All right, Sybil, I'll get Bell. But I don't know if it's a good idea to depend so much upon Bell and her strange herbs and powders. Not only does she refuse to tell anyone what's in them, she won't say what she's chanting when she sings all those songs over you . . . I don't like it. The other slaves are afraid of her, you know. They say she practices black magic. White people shouldn't mess in the ways of black folk, Sybil. It isn't healthy."

William kept talking as he dressed, and Sybil collapsed breathlessly upon the pillows, hardly listening to anything her husband said. She felt drained of energy, as if the blood had seeped right out of her. It was tiring to be so afraid . . . but thank God, she no longer had to worry that Kate would desert them for a reason other than becoming aggravated and impatient. The Demon Lover—the devil in the guise of a handsome young man—was gone forever, his drowned body washed up on the beach. God willing, Kate would marry Edward and stay here forever, looking after all of them.

She must ask Bell if there wasn't a potion or love charm that would cause Kate to fall in love with Edward. Yes, that's what was needed, a little help from the spirit world. Once Kate married Edward, Sybil would be safe; never again would she be uprooted, torn away from all she knew and loved, and forced to journey to an inhospitable land to live in poverty and uncertainty. The hell she knew was better than the one she could only imagine; here, at least, Kate kept them all fed and clothed. Whatever small luxuries brightened their dreary lives derived from Kate's efforts, not William's. Oh, yes, Bell *must* know of a potion or spell that could make Kate look at Edward the way she had watched her Demon Lover

60

when she thought no one aware of what she was doing.

In her own way, Kate was a beauty—not as beautiful as her mother, of course, but she did possess a potent allure that attracted men like flies to honey. Lying limp and languid on the bed, Sybil plotted how to get Kate and Edward together quickly before some other survivor of a shipwreck washed up on the beach, saw Kate, and convinced her to abandon her mad mother and drunken father to pursue a life with him.

It was dawn before the last of what could be salvaged from the *Liberty* was rowed ashore and dragged above the reach of the waves. Kate had Cal and Benjamin cover the cache with a huge fishing net; then she set Fish to guard it until later in the day, when she and Edward would go through everything and decide what to do with it. In this, as in the actual salvaging, Jonas Irons's advice could save them much time and effort. The surly sea captain had known exactly which items ought to be saved first— with the result that their profits from this wreck would now be much higher than they might otherwise have been, justifying the ridiculous percentage she had agreed to pay him.

Casks of fine wine and brandy had taken precedence over the remaining hogsheads of flour, and barrels of salt pork and beef had won over the corn. They had also managed to save kegs of nails and oakum, as well as two of the ship's masts, which Jonas claimed would be valuable to shipbuilders, along with some of the brass fittings attached to floating pieces of wood.

The last thing they had saved was a coal-black cat, drenched and shivering, but managing by sheer effort of will to cling to a battered, bobbing plank.

61

Jonas had matter-of-factly tucked the creature inside his shirt, so the warmth of his body might help revive it. The gesture had deeply touched Kate, reminding her that other than Jonas, the half-drowned feline was the only other living creature they had rescued from the storm-tossed sea. No one else had been spotted hanging onto debris; the entire crew of the *Liberty* had obviously perished.

Another reason why the gesture brought tears to her eyes was that it reminded her of Jonathan. Jonas's brother might have done a similar thing, for he had been a man of tender sentiments, unafraid of expressing them. His first remark to Kate after she and Edward pulled him from the sea had been: "Have you descended from a star, fair one, who gazes down at me with eyes like molten honey?"

How different was Jonas Irons! Though he reminded Kate of Jonathan in appearance—and in his solicitude for the cat—Jonas possessed a different personality altogether. He was gruff, harsh, and suspicious, whereas Jonathan had been grateful, kind, and charming. Jonathan's smile could have lit candles; Jonas hadn't yet smiled, so Kate couldn't gauge the effectiveness of that attribute. She doubted he ever did smile.

No two brothers could have been more dissimilar, Kate decided, surreptitiously watching Jonas Irons throughout the night. She remembered Jonathan as being outrageously handsome, but despite having the same color eyes, the same dark hair, and the same pleasing, symmetrical features, Jonas's face struck Kate as being a far more rugged, granite-hewn version of his brother's. The scar, of course, gave Jonas a sinister air, but the scar and the limp weren't the only things that kept Jonas from being as attractive as Jonathan.

Kate saw no warmth in those sea-blue eyes—no softening of that finely chiseled mouth. Danger crackled in the vicinity of Jonas Irons, charging the air with hidden menace. He must never find out that his brother had reached this island, Kate thought. No telling what he might do. She would have to warn all of the inhabitants on Conch Cay to keep their mouths shut, especially the slaves, some of whom were prone to blurting things better left unsaid.

The first problem would come when she introduced him to the household, and the hour was fast approaching when those introductions would have to be made. They were all exhausted now; it was time to quit. She must go home, prepare a bag of food, and send Old Tom down to the beach to stand guard with Fish, who would probably curl up and go to sleep once he had eaten. If anyone approached by boat or beach, Old Tom would awaken Fish, and the two make certain no one took any of the night's booty.

Stretching to relieve a crick in her neck, Kate motioned Edward over to her. Jonas Irons was busy limping up and down the beach, still restlessly scanning the surf for any signs of salvage, or more likely, survivors. By now, he must know it was hopeless, but he refused to quit—stubborn, ornery fool. He had no better sense than she did.

"Edward," she said urgently, keeping her voice low. "I'll keep Captain Irons down on the beach long enough for you to go up to the house and tell Mama and Papa and the slaves to be careful to act as if they've never seen or heard of anyone named Irons."

"Yeah, good idea . . ." Edward muttered. "'Cept, I think *I* should stay here with him, and *you* should go and warn everybody."

Kate squinted to better see his face in the pale light of the overcast morning. "Don't argue with me, Edward . . . I said *you* were to go ahead. Take Cal and Benjamin with you. They can spread the word quickly among the slaves, especially Cassie, Daisy, and the children. Cal will understand the necessity of keeping quiet, but remind Benjamin how important it is; he must make certain Daisy doesn't say something foolish and revealing."

Edward planted his feet in the sand and regarded her belligerently. "I ain't about t' leave the two of you alone t'gether," he insisted. "I know what happened the last time a man named Irons washed up on shore, an' I'm gonna make certain it don't happen again."

"For heaven's sake!" Kate exploded. "What happened then was none of your business! And anyway, I won't be alone with him because Fish will still be here!"

"Fish ain't no pertection against a man gittin' under a gal's skin like that other Cap'n Irons got under yours. I ain't leavin' you alone with 'im. Not when the other one had you purrin' around his legs like a cat lappin' up cream in one hour flat after we drug him from the sea."

"You do as I say, Edward! I don't have to explain myself to you or anyone, and I certainly needn't account for my behavior to a mere employee."

He grabbed her arm and pulled her closer. "I ain't always gonna be a 'mere employee,'" he hissed in her ear. "One of these days, I'm gonna be your husband, ya hear? And then we'll jus' see how much explainin' you got t' do t' me."

"I told you that would never happen! You're overstepping yourself again, and I've had about all of it I'm going to take!"

Just then another male voice spoke behind Kate. "Having a difference of opinion with the hired help, Miss Montgomery?"

She whirled to see Jonas Irons standing tall and muscular against the horizon, his very masculine, broad-shouldered, slim-hipped body silhouetted against the brightening sky. For a moment, her throat convulsed, and she found it difficult to breathe, much less speak.

"Nothing I can't handle by myself," she haughtily informed him, wondering how much he had overheard. "Edward, go at once and do as I said. Captain Irons and I will be along shortly, as soon as I've counted the crates and barrels so if one of them mysteriously disappears, I'll know it."

Jonas's black brows lifted sardonically. "You don't trust your own people, Miss Montgomery? Or is it perhaps that you don't trust me?"

"Trust should never preclude taking normal, prudent precautions, Captain Irons. In the wrecking business, one can't be too careful."

Jonas gazed past her at Edward. "Don't worry about leaving her alone with me, Garvin, if that's what the two of you were arguing about. I couldn't ravish a woman this morning if I wanted to—and I assure you I don't want to."

His comment brought a hot rush of color to Kate's face. Didn't he find her in the least attractive? True, she wasn't dressed for the delicate business of seduction, but Jonas's brother had been able to see past the limitations of her attire. He had thought her beautiful right from the start.

"Awright, Irons . . . I guess I kin trust you. Truth is, it's Kate herself I wuz worried about. When it comes t' men an' knowin' what's right for her, she ain't got a lick of sense."

"Edward!" Kate spun around on her heel, ready to boot the presumptuous lout into the sea, but Jonas Irons's deep-throated laughter stopped her cold. Forgetting Edward entirely, she rounded on the chuckling sea captain. "How dare you laugh at me— you big, braying ass! Surely, you don't imagine I could ever be drawn to the likes of you! If you were a fish, I'd have thrown you back again, having judged you too ugly to keep!"

Jonas Irons stopped laughing, but a smirk played about his fine lips, and amusement twinkled in his blue-green eyes. In that moment, Kate realized that Jonas was every bit as handsome as his brother—maybe more so. Jonathan's smile had come so easily, but Jonas's, being a rare event, was somehow twice as devastating. Her heart did a queer little flip-flop, and she found herself half smiling—at what she wasn't sure.

"I'm sorry if I repulsed you with my ugliness," Jonas Irons said, abruptly sobering. "My brother had all the good looks in the family—and the charm. Forgive me if I keep saying and doing the wrong thing, but I have so few opportunities for conversing with the gentler sex that I'm sadly out of practice."

"I'm not gentle," Kate responded. "I'm as tough as any man. Remember that, and we'll get along fine."

"I'll help you tally the barrels and crates," Jonas offered as Edward headed away from the beach. "*Mister* Montgomery . . ."

Kate slanted him a sideways glance but decided not to respond to the gibe. To do so would only give him a victory, and she did not intend to give him anything, least of all, easy victories.

"All right . . . You can check my count. You start on one side, and I'll take the other."

He nodded, and they spent the next few minutes counting. When that was done, and the count didn't tally, they repeated the process. Finally, they both arrived at the same number. By then, Fish was already asleep, lying curled on his side in the sand, his thin, lanky body lost in deep slumber.

"Some guard you have here," Jonas commented, nudging the young black man with his booted foot.

"He's exhausted, that's all." Kate heard the note of defensiveness in her own voice and frowned. "Of course, sleep is what Fish does best even when he's not exhausted. Sleep, fish, and eat—that's his idea of the perfect life."

"And you? Aren't *you* exhausted?" Jonas Irons

queried, coming toward her around the barrels. "You have circles under those calico cat-eyes, but I don't see you slowing down any."

"I haven't time to slow down! There's too much to do . . ." Unnerved by his nearness, Kate sought to change the subject to something other than herself. "Speaking of cats, how is that creature you have tucked into your shirt?"

He paused and reached into his slightly bulging shirtfront. "Sleeping and purring, at the same time. Now that it's dry and warm again, I suppose I can get rid of it."

Holding the animal by the loose skin at the back of its neck, he withdrew it. The cat yawned and stretched in midair. When he tossed it to the ground, it landed on all four paws and immediately wound itself around his leg and meowed to be picked up again.

"It would appear you have a friend for life," she noted. "Does your friend have a name?"

Jonas seemed to think a moment. "Whiskers," he finally said. "I think his name is Whiskers. He belonged to our cook—a good man whom we called 'Oatcake,' because he used to make a curious, rather tasteless concoction he called an oatcake to serve with our morning coffee. I expect I'll never eat them again, now that Oatcake's gone. The least I can do, I guess, is look after his precious cat."

He bent and picked up the animal, allowing it to curl against his chest. As Jonas Irons's large, calloused hands idly stroked the sleek, black fur, Kate couldn't help wondering if he would be as gentle when he touched a woman. His blue-green eyes looked out over the ocean, which was still pounding on the shore but with less violence than during the night.

"It still doesn't seem possible that Whiskers and I are the only survivors," he said, more to himself than

67

to her.

Despite herself, Kate's heart went out to him as he struggled with his loss. She stepped closer to him and impulsively put a comforting hand on his forearm. "I'm so sorry," she said. "I can understand how you must feel."

"Can you, Miss Montgomery?" The brilliant eyes came back to her face, and they were as chilling as a cold wind blowing straight from the north.

She hurriedly removed her hand. "Just because I'm a wrecker doesn't mean I have no feelings . . . I always mourn the lives that are lost when a ship goes down."

"But you get over it quickly. Your kind always does."

His callous assessment of her character wounded Kate more than she would have thought possible. "I think it's time you meet the people I'm doing this for—then maybe you'll better understand *why* I do it."

"By all means . . . I'm anxious to meet the other inhabitants of this little island. Does your family own the whole thing, or only a portion of it?"

"We own over two hundred acres—which is almost the whole island but not quite. What we don't own isn't worth owning. It's barren rock or pure sand. My father received the only land grant on this particular cay. There are more settlers—and wreckers—on Big and Little Abaco, as well as scattered throughout the other cays."

"Do you do anything besides wrecking?" He fell into step beside her as she headed inland, away from the beach.

"Oh, yes . . . We rake salt, go turtling and fishing, and we plant, of course. Cotton was our main crop until the chenile bugs destroyed it. Now, we're experimenting with indigo, but I'm not holding my breath waiting for amazing success. The soil is poor and doesn't yield much of anything."

"It yields some nice timber," he noted, eyeing the trees through which they were passing en route to the house.

"Yes, but as soon as you cut them down, the soil washes away, and you're left with nothing. When we first got here, we cut and burned lots of timber, in order to clear the land for planting. That was a big mistake, because the first big storm swept away the soil like a huge, big broom."

"Interesting . . ." Jonas Irons murmured.

She sneaked a glance at him and saw that he was studying the trees intently, as if he had plans for them. Well, he wouldn't be staying long enough to formulate plans, she thought indignantly. As soon as possible, he must leave and go to Nassau, along with the salvage. Every moment he remained on Conch Cay increased the chances of his finding out what had happened to his brother and of discovering Edward's use of lights to lure ships—including his and his brother's—onto the reef. It also increased the chance that she might start finding him as attractive as Jonathan . . . God help her!

As soon as the sea calmed down, he must leave, Kate decided. And whenever that was, three or four days at most, it wouldn't be a moment too soon.

Chapter Five

Sybil Montgomery's slave, Bell, did not consider herself a slave, except in the eyes of white folks. In her own eyes, she saw herself as a person of great power and influence, which she was, among all those of black or brown skin residing in the Abacos. Even beyond, in the rest of the Bahamas, her reputation was slowly but surely spreading. People called her Obeah Woman, and both slaves and free blacks sought her help to cure illnesses, punish enemies, become lucky in love, or gain power over others. They also sought it to overcome hexes and bad influences caused by people using Obeah against them.

Bell was a busy woman, but no one kept her as busy as Sybil Montgomery, through whom Bell exercised her considerable power to influence everything that happened on Conch Cay. When "de massah" came to fetch her in the middle of the night, Bell did not complain, but simply gathered up her box of herbs and "remedies" and trudged after him toward the house.

There, she dosed the mistress with jumbey-laced tea—jumbey being a local herb with sedative effects—and then sat down in the mistress's rocker in the parlor to await the morning. If not for "de massah," it might have been a peaceful, quiet time, when Bell could have ruminated on several problems and conjured solutions for them. As it was, "de massah" was in a talkative mood and refused to go back upstairs to bed.

"Bell, I don't think your mistress is getting any better," Massah William said, sitting down across from her with a glass of rum in his hand. He was still in his nightshirt, and his graying hair stuck up all over, while his hairy legs stuck out below—a sorry excuse for a man, if ever there was one, Bell thought contemptuously.

"Isn't there some herb or remedy you could give her to prevent these nightmares before she has them?" he plaintively inquired.

"Cain't think of none, Massah William. De mistress bin sick in de head evah since de young massah died. Cain't nothin' mah magic do 'bout dat. I'se doin' de best ah can, jus' t' keep her from gittin' worse."

"Yes . . . yes, I know that, Bell. I'm not questioning your competence or devotion to her, far from it. I just wish there was something more we could do. It breaks my heart to see her like this. In her youth, she was such a gentle, sweet, tenderhearted girl; now, even when she's rational, she's so snappish and sharp-tongued. Maybe I ought to take her to Nassau and seek medical advice again. Might be there's a new doctor there could shed more light on our sad dilemma."

Bell quit rocking and sat still as a thief hiding in the larder. Over the years, there had been many threats to her supremacy—many efforts to improve Sybil's condition through interference by white practitioners. Bell had dealt calmly and swiftly with each one, allowing a temporary improvement to occur, and then as soon as the family's jubilation died down, manipulating things so that the mistress

72

became more dependent upon her than ever. Nevertheless, the thought of a new effort being mounted made Bell's stomach roil and her heart rattle in her rib cage.

"You done tried evahthing you could, Massah William," she assured him. "Ain't no white man's medicine gonna heal whuts ailin' de mistress. Best you leave her in Bell's lovin' hands. Ah tek care o' her like she mah own sweet chile . . ."

William sat cradling the untasted glass of rum, and looking terrible—all pale and trembling. Self-denial always made him miserable, Bell knew. Once he had downed the rum, his color would improve.

"Drink up, Massah William. Sometimes, drinkin' be justified foh medicinal purposes, an' 'pears t' me dis be one o' dem times."

"I'm glad *someone* understands why I drink," William mumbled, raising the glass and taking a hefty swallow.

Bell resumed rocking. If Massah William drank enough, chances were he wouldn't remember this conversation, come morning. Things would stay as they were, with Bell in control, and those who didn't like it, couldn't do a thing about it. The only person on Conch Cay with enough guts to challenge Bell's position was the young mistress, but Miz Kate was much too busy keeping food in the larder to know or care what Bell was up to. Mattie knew, of course, and did her best to thwart Bell whenever she could, but without help from one of the whites, Mattie was essentially powerless against Bell's magic.

Yes, Bell thought as she rocked: A person could be a slave and still be more powerful than anyone thought possible, if she knew how to use her power to good advantage. As she often told Gilbert when they lay in their bed together at night, a slave could make a slave out of her owners, if she just knew what she was about. Poor old, stupid Gilbert didn't understand

73

what she meant by that, but he would always nod his grizzled head and agree with her. "Whatevah you say, Bell, honey. You de one wif de brains in dis outfit."

Bell dozed for a while, and Massah William drank, and at some point in time, de massah went back upstairs. The creak of the front door opening alerted Bell to the presence of someone new in the house. She leapt from the rocker, stilled it with her hand, and hurried into the hallway to see who had arrived. To her relief, it wasn't Miz Kate, but Edward—sly, cruel, ambitious Edward—who, despite all his faults or perhaps because of them, was every bit as easy to manipulate as Miz Sybil. Except when he got mad and mean.

"Bell?" he questioned when he saw her. "What are you doin' here?"

"De mistress had one of her spells, ag'in," Bell informed him with the quiet dignity that intimidated whites and blacks alike. "De massah done come an' got me, 'cause ah'se de onliest one who kin help her."

"Well, you'd better awaken the master and mistress an' tell 'em we got unexpected company . . . Jonathan Irons's brother washed up on shore t'night."

Bell put a hand to her plump bosom to keep her heart from leaping clean out of her chest. "Miz Kate's Demon Lover gots a brother? How's come ah didn't know about 'im before dis?"

Edward snorted. "Could you have stopped him from comin' if you did know?"

"Ah might coulda done somepin'. Does he know whut happent t' Jonathan Irons?"

"Not yet, he don't . . . an' you better make sure nobody tells him. Kate sent me to warn everyone t' be careful what they say in front of 'im. Can you keep Miz Sybil from blabbin'?"

"'Course, ah can . . ."

"Then you better do it, real quicklike. They'll be

74

comin' up t' the house soon. Ain't no place else for him t' stay on the island."

"But how long he gonna be here?" Bell narrowed her eyes as a new thought struck her. "An' whut's he look like? Jonathan Irons wuz a right handsome man. Poor Miz Sybil gonna have herself a conniption if dis Jonas feller is even half as good lookin' as de one who died. Y'all know how she felt about *him;* she shore didn't shed no tears when he got drowned fishin'."

"Neither did I," Edward reminded her. "If I have anything t' say about it, he won't be here a minute longer'n he has to. Soon as the sea calms down, me an' Cal will take him t' Nassau."

"Ah'll do everthin' ah can t' help," Bell promised. "I'll cast a spell on de sea t' make 'er calm down real quick."

"You do that," Edward urged, his tone slightly contemptuous.

Like most whites, Edward professed not to believe in Bell's magic, but Bell knew that he really did. For all his bossiness, Edward never tried to boss her around the way he made other slaves toe the mark, and he went easy on Gilbert as well. The less book learnin' a white man had, Bell had discovered, the more prone he was to the same superstitions that ruled black folks. And Edward had precious little book learnin'.

"While ah'm wakin' up de massah an' Miz Sybil an' castin' spells, whut you gonna do?" Bell bluntly demanded.

"Git on down t' the slave huts and spread the word that I'll tan the hide offen anybody that lets slip a single word about Jonathan Irons to his brother."

"You better think of a worse threat den dat, 'cause Miz Kate won't let you whip nobody, an' de whole world knows it."

Edward shot Bell a dirty look. "I don't need a worse

75

threat; they know I'll get 'im one way or another, when Miss Kate ain't around t' see it."

Bell pursed her lips but didn't dispute the boast. What Edward said was mostly true. He had been known to wait until a man least expected it, and then cuff him around and black his eye or bruise his ribs, and claim something else had happened to him. Sometimes, Edward took out his ire on the wife or children of a wrongdoer. He would force them to some task beyond their strength, and then punish them when they failed to perform to his satisfaction. Such punishment might consist of more work, scanty rations, and even withholding fresh water for drinking, cooking, and bathing. Water was a precious commodity on the island, and not a drop was wasted. Yes, there were many ways to punish and demean the slaves that Miz Kate never knew about.

Bell occasionally managed to thwart Edward's schemes, but she didn't go to the trouble too often, and when she did, she exacted her own payment in return. Everything in life had a price, she had learned long ago, and if a person wanted to survive, they must pay handsomely for the privilege. The price she paid for her own unique position was spending more than half her lifetime in the company of a difficult, querulous, half-demented white woman.

As Edward exited the house on his way to the slave quarters, Bell headed for the bedchamber. She didn't relish waking either de massah or Miz Sybil, but she had no choice. The two must be told about the Demon Lover's brother. What his arrival would mean to all of them, Bell could only speculate. As she did so, she shuddered with mingled fear and anxiety. This threat must be dealt with, and the sooner the better. This time, there must be no mistakes.

Jonas was surprised when he saw the house where

76

Kate Montgomery lived with her aging parents. It was two stories high, built of wood over a masonry cellar, and had a veranda along the front of it, but no balcony above. Small, old, and weathered, it possessed none of the elegance he associated with plantation houses in America. The design was plain and utilitarian, and the wood had been patched in many places, as though boards were frequently torn loose during storms and high winds.

Somehow, he had expected something more substantial, a stone or mortar structure of spacious, graceful proportions, but apparently, Kate Montgomery hadn't been lying when she complained of her family's poverty. Beyond, down a foliage-lined trail, he glimpsed huts consisting of thatch and wattle. Out back, there was also the traditional cook shed found in warm climates, where the cooking was always done separate from the house so as to lessen the danger of fire consuming the main shelter. Jonas could see smoke rising from the top of the cook shed even at this early hour.

Chickens scratched in the sand, and lizards scurried out of his path. If the house lacked charm, there was plenty to be found in the yard, where flowering trees and bushes abounded. Next to the steps leading up to the veranda was a small shrub with delicate pale blue flowers and bright green leaves. It caught Jonas's eye as he followed Kate Montgomery's ramrod-straight back.

"Wait a minute," he called out to her. "What do you call this?"

He indicated the shrub with a nod, his hands still full of Whiskers, who meowed loudly everytime he sought to put him down. Kate's eyes softened as she glanced down at the blooming plant; they had softened once before when the subject of the cat arose, so perhaps she wasn't as tough as she would have him believe. Anyone with a soft spot for animals and

77

flowers couldn't be all bad, he mused—even if she was a wrecker.

"Plumbago," she informed him. "Why are you so interested in what grows here? First, the trees, now, the flowers . . ."

"I'm always curious to get to know a place," he answered. "And even more curious to get to know the people in it."

At that, she stiffened slightly, and her eyes darkened. He decided that her eyes were actually the color of a golden wine he had once enjoyed—the best he had ever drunk, in fact. It had gone down smooth as satin, yet warmed him like a fire kindled deep in the pit of his belly. He wondered if she would affect him in the same way. He could imagine himself growing drunk on her kisses; if she kissed as well as she provoked a man, she could light a real bonfire in his belly.

"Please don't accuse my parents of any wrong-doing," she said suddenly and quietly. "They are . . . fragile. Not like me at all. Life has dealt so harshly with them that neither can face reality anymore."

"So you have become the parent?" he probed.

"In a way . . . I make all the important decisions and do most of the work, though I do have help, of course."

"Of course . . . Edward is falling all over himself to assist you, except he wants to do things *his* way, not yours."

Her chin lifted, and her eyes flashed fire. "That's *my* problem, not yours. All I ask is that you don't frighten or abuse my parents by making ugly accusations. They have enough problems to worry about without you marching in and hurling insults."

"I wish *I* had someone to defend and protect *me* the way you do your parents. Don't worry, little tigress.

78

I'll do my best not to alarm your cubs. Obviously, *they* aren't responsible for my losses tonight.''

She whirled on her heel and mounted the rickety, veranda steps, which creaked loudly in protest. Quickly depositing the cat on the first step, Jonas ignored its complaints, avoided a loose board, and kept pace behind Kate Montgomery. She swept into the house, and the first person he saw as he entered after her was a short, plump Negress dressed in a shabby red gown and white mobcap, who dropped a brief curtsy in Kate Montgomery's direction.

"Bell, where are my parents?" the girl inquired over the cat's loud meows as it scratched at the doorpost. "I've brought home a guest."

"Sounds like you brung home *two* guests, Miz Kate. De massah be waitin' in de parlor, an' de mistress is still gittin' dressed. She be down shortly."

The black woman's eyes cut to Jonas. Her manner seemed deferential enough, but he had the unnerving feeling that she would take a meat cleaver to his heart if she had the chance. The piercing black eyes were definitely hostile. He returned her glare steadily, and she dropped her gaze after a moment, but the show of servility didn't fool him one bit. For some reason, the woman despised him. He cast a quick glance over the rest of her. Several necklaces of shells adorned her ample bosom, and gold hoop earrings peeped out from beneath her mobcap. Her feet were bare, but shell necklaces encircled each ankle. She looked more the queen than the slave, and he wondered about her position in this odd household.

As if in answer to his unspoken question, Kate said, "Perhaps, you'd better go back upstairs and help Mama finish dressing, Bell. She'll have to meet Captain Irons sometime; it might as well be this morning."

"Yes, Miz Kate, ah do dat. Ah only hope she ain't gonna be too upset wif comp'ny in de house. You

79

know how she gits sometimes."

"I'll do my best not to upset her too much," Jonas said dryly, beginning to resent the woman before he'd even met her. "Believe me, if there were anyplace else to go on this island, I'd go there."

Kate frowned at the comment. "Mama's ill much of the time—and confused. She isn't always sure where she is or who *we* are. You must excuse her if she says things that sound peculiar."

Jonas nodded, sorry he had mentioned anything. Kate crossed the hallway in front of him and opened a door, while the woman named Bell went up the staircase to the second floor. "The parlor's in here . . . Good morning, Papa. Bell said I'd find you here. I want to introduce you to someone."

She stood aside for Jonas to enter. Jonas did so and took the extended hand of the slender, sallow-faced, gray-haired man who rose from a chair to meet him. Noting his look of befuddlement, Jonas said politely, "Pleased to meet you, Mister Montgomery . . ." and then waited for a response.

"Um, yes . . . William . . . Please call me William," Kate's father muttered.

A whiff of rum assaulted Jonas's nostrils, leaving no doubt that Kate's father had been drinking. Though neatly dressed in a planter's tan-colored jacket over a lighter shade of breeches, William Montgomery's unsteady hands, bleary eyes, and shaky, uncertain manner all attested to his love of the bottle. On a table nearby, Jonas spotted a glass with a few remaining drops of an amber liquid coating the bottom. Kate saw him looking at the glass and defensively stepped closer to her father and touched his arm.

"Papa, this is Captain Jonas Irons, whose ship ran aground on Dead Man's Reef during the night. I've invited him to stay with us until the seas calm down, and Edward can take him to Nassau. It shouldn't be more than a couple days, at most."

She's in a hurry to get rid of me, Jonas thought, only I don't intend to leave until I have proof about that light and know the truth about my brother.

"I understand from Edward that you're the only survivor of that shipwreck, aren't you, Captain Irons?" William Montgomery said. "A tragedy, that. Here, sit down while we talk. My stomach's a bit unsettled this morning, and I've been dosing myself with a touch of rum. Brandy would be better, but we've none on hand, at the moment. Would you care for a glass?"

"No, thank you . . . but help yourself, sir. Perhaps later, your daughter will want to fetch you some of the brandy that's down on the beach. There's a half-dozen casks that came from my ship."

William Montgomery's bloodshot, brown eyes lit up. "You don't say! Why, that would be a welcome change from rum. Probably just the thing to settle my stomach."

"I doubt it," Kate retorted, flashing Jonas an angry look. "In any case, I wouldn't want to open a whole cask just for one little dose of brandy. Think of what that brandy will bring in Nassau, Papa."

"Oh, it will bring plenty, that's sure . . . but we really should keep a cask here, for medicinal purposes, if nothing else."

"Tea is excellent for unsettled stomachs, Papa," Kate disputed. "Can I fetch you some, Captain Irons, while you get acquainted with my father?"

"Yes, I would appreciate some tea," Jonas assented—and some food, too, he added silently. As the thought formed in his mind, his stomach growled loudly. He couldn't prevent the rude sound; he hadn't eaten since the noon meal the day before.

Instead of blushing as most young women would do, Kate Montgomery merely raised her eyebrows. "I'll see if Mattie has breakfast ready while I'm

81

fetching your tea," she said. "You must be hungry as well as exhausted."

"No more so than you must be." Jonas wondered if she had given a thought yet to her own needs; it didn't seem so. Her concern was all for everyone else—her mother and father, his rumbling stomach . . .

"I must send food down to the beach for Fish as well, and also quiet that poor famished cat," she continued, brushing aside the suggestion that *she* might be hungry and tired, just as she had brushed it aside earlier, when he'd mentioned it.

As she left, Jonas took a seat on a plain, wooden chair to the right of William Montgomery, but the old man waved a hand in objection. "Take my wife's rocking chair, Captain Irons, or one of the padded ones over there against the wall. They're much more comfortable."

"No, this will be fine . . ." Jonas assured him. "My clothing is still damp. I wouldn't want to ruin the fine needlework on the backs of those chairs."

The needlework was the only thing of delicacy and quality in the room; all else was plain and rudimentary, except for the rocker, which Jonas could see was a cherished piece of furniture. Its wood gleamed from many polishings, its graceful design and intricate floral carvings set it apart. The lovely old rocker stood out from the rest of the furnishings like a swan stands out from sparrows.

"I'll be glad to lend you some of my clothes—if they fit," William Montgomery offered.

Jonas eyed his host's slender frame and shook his head. The man was almost emaciated, his wrists and elbows more fragile-looking than a woman's. Kate could not have inherited her robust strength and vivid coloring from her father; he seemed but a pale imitation of his daughter, and his eyes were brown, not golden, like hers, nor had his hair ever been that red.

"Mine will dry soon enough," Jonas pointed out. "I can make do."

A silence fell afer that. It seemed to Jonas that William Montgomery ought to have many questions to ask him, but the old man looked strangely ill at ease and reluctant to discuss Jonas's mishap off the coast of his island. Instead, he finished off the few remaining drops of rum in his glass, then sat morosely studying its empty depths, as if forgetting all about Jonas. His inattentiveness may have been due to his drinking, but Jonas considered it more a form of evasiveness.

"Don't you want to know the name of my ship or where I was headed?" he finally demanded, his temper stretched to the breaking point. "Aren't you curious to learn anything about me? Or do shipwrecks occur with such frequency in these waters that they no longer even interest you?"

William Montgomery blinked and sat up straighter. "But of course, I want to hear about your ship. You must forgive me. I didn't sleep well last night. My poor wife was having nightmares and kept me awake all night."

"I, too, was awake all night," Jonas curtly reminded him. "And so was your daughter."

The old man shrugged. "Ah, but you are much younger than I. As for Kate, she is never tired, never depressed, never defeated. She inherited her strength from her grandfather—my father, who was exactly the same way for most of his life. Amazing, isn't it? I never could figure out how a man as lacking as I am in admirable qualities, could have managed to pass so many of them on to my daughter. Where I am weak, Kate is strong. Where I am vacillating, Kate is decisive. She's the very image of her grandfather, too—in a feminine package, of course."

"She's strong and opinionated, yes, and drives

herself hard, but I wouldn't say she never tires," Jonas disagreed. "Several times during the night, I noticed she was extremely pale and drawn. She almost seemed to be in pain. Of course, she would never admit it, but . . ."

Just then the door flew open, and a small, thin, white woman stood on the threshold. She poised there a moment, staring at Jonas, her hazel eyes wide and disbelieving. Her graying, dark hair was piled high on her dainty head, and fat curls dangled girlishly against her rouged cheeks. She wore a gown heavily bedecked with lace, but the lace had yellowed with age, spoiling the effect of elegance.

The edges of her sleeves were frayed, Jonas noted, rising from the chair, and her toes were poking through her slippers. Still, the woman had presence; she was a lady from the top of her head to the hem of her faded gown, and she stood regally as a queen awaiting the adoration of her subjects.

"Mrs. Montgomery?" Jonas said uncertainly. The look in the woman's eyes was strangely disconcerting. She seemed to be looking *through* him, not at him, and she suddenly gave a startled shriek and threw herself in his direction.

"No, no, no! It can't be *you*, again!" she screamed, beating on his arms and shoulders.

He caught her before she stumbled and tripped over her skirts. Her head snapped back, and the face she turned up to him was filled with horror and utter loathing. "Why have you come back?" she shrieked. "Demon! Devil! Whoreson!"

Her fingernails raked across his cheeks. Jonas grabbed her hand before she could claw out his eyes, and she sank her teeth into his thumb and bit down like a fox, cutting to the bone.

Behind her, the black woman cried: "Miz Sybil! Miz Sybil, no! You done made a mistake!"

And then Kate's voice sounded: "Mama! Stop

84

that, at once! Stop it, I tell you!"

The woman finally stopped biting him, but hatred still poured out of her, drenching him as if with acid. "I hate you! Go back where you came from! You shan't have her! I won't permit it—I've lost too much already . . . Oh, God, too much, too much!"

Chapter Six

Jonas was too stunned to do much of anything after the distraught woman's attack. He simply held her away from him, so she could do no further damage. Both his thumb and his cheek were bleeding, but the blood and pain were minor compared to the anguish of his turbulent thoughts. What was she saying? Who did she think he was? Not Jonathan, surely. What could Jonathan ever have done to her to provoke such a violent outburst?

Bell and Kate rushed forward and tried to reason with her, but it was like trying to reason with a mad dog. "Mama, this man isn't who you think he is . . ." Kate cried desperately. "This is Captain *Jonas* Irons."

The emphasis on "Jonas" was unmistakable.

"You said it wasn't *him!*" Sybil Montgomery screamed, ignoring her daughter and rounding on the black woman. "But it certainly *is* him. I'd know him anywhere. This is the man who tried to steal my precious baby and take her away from me!"

"No, Miz Sybil! It ain't," Bell denied, taking the woman's arm. "You done made a mistake . . . Come along now, you're all upset an' talkin' foolish. Ole Bell will fix you somethin' t' calm yer nerves."

"Wait a minute," Jonas growled, as Bell and Kate

started to lead Kate's mother away. "I want to know who I look like and why she hates me so much. She's not leaving here until I get an explanation for her behavior."

William Montgomery plucked at his sleeve. "She's ill, sir, can't you see that? She doesn't know what she's saying."

"She thinks you're the man I was once going to marry," Kate coldly explained, meeting him eye to eye. "You look a great deal like him. The resemblance is actually quite startling. But it's no one you know or could ever have met."

"What's his name?" Jonas demanded. "Damn it, *tell me his name.*"

"John . . ." Kate said levelly. "John Merrick. He had—has—blue eyes just like yours."

She's lying through her teeth, Jonas thought furiously. She can't even decide if this John Merrick exists in the past or present tense. What she really meant to say was Jonathan, but she stopped herself just in time.

"Let the slave woman see to your mother," he grated. "You and I will discuss this further."

"There's nothing to discuss, Captain Irons. My mother isn't well. Anyone living here will tell you that. She's made an unfortunate mistake. I'm sorry she's upset you, but there's nothing to be gained by making an issue out of it."

"Making an issue out of it! I want to know the truth! And I'm damn well staying on this island until I learn it."

"If you insist on upsetting my mother further, you're going to have to leave this house. Bell, take Mama back upstairs and see to it that she receives medicine to calm her nerves. I'll be up later."

"Yes, Miz Kate . . . I tek care o' dis poor sick chile."

"I'm not sick," Kate's mother protested, but all the fire had gone out of her. She stood now like a wooden doll, staring vacantly into space. "Send him away, Kate," she urged in a dull, listless tone. "Don't let him stay here. He's a demon just like the other one."

"Nonsense, Sybil," William scolded. "There was no other one—not really. Kate would never have left us. She loves us too much to desert us in our hour of need."

William went to his wife's side and smoothed back the hair that had come undone and tumbled down around her shoulders. "Come along, dear. I'll go up with you. Bell and I will look after you and keep you safe. Please excuse us, Captain Irons."

Jonas was about to fire off more questions, but one look at Kate's drawn, white face convinced him to hold his peace a few moments longer. She knew everything there was to know; he wouldn't get what he wanted by badgering a crazy, old woman. He waited until William, Sybil, and Bell had left the room, then he shut the parlor door firmly behind him and leaned against it, blocking Kate's escape, if she tried to make one.

"All right, talk . . ." he said. "I'm not stupid. I know you're lying. Tell me everything you know about my brother."

For a split second, he thought she might break down weeping. She seemed on the verge of tears, but then, she straightened, glared at him with that fiery golden light in her eyes, and began to speak—spouting more lies.

"I don't know anything about your brother. I've already told you that, but John Merrick looks enough like you to be your twin. That's why I reacted as I did when I first saw your face. The similarity caught me by surprise."

"What about your reaction when you heard my name? Don't deny that you did react. I know my name was familiar to you."

"You don't know anything of the kind. I was just

89

amazed that your name wasn't Merrick. I thought at first that you might be John's brother, except he never told me he had a brother."

She was an excellent liar; he had to give her credit for that. Another man might be tempted to believe her, but he wouldn't believe anything that couldn't be proved. Her guilt, her secretiveness, her shock at his name and appearance, her mother's response to him, all combined to convince him that she was lying. Jonathan had undoubtedly come to this island; so where was he, now? What had happened to him that no one wanted to admit to his existence?

"Where *is* this John, if indeed such a person actually lives and breathes?"

"Gone for good. I sent him away. He wanted me to marry him and leave the island, and I wasn't prepared to do that. I could never walk out on people who need me."

"People who *use* you, you mean. Your mother is your father's responsibility, not yours."

"No one asked you to criticize the way we live! You don't know anything about our problems," Kate snapped.

Despite her anger, she had grown increasingly pale, to the point of looking ill and on the verge of collapse. No wonder. After last night, she must be as desperately in need of rest and food as he himself. He wanted to pursue the issue, but couldn't help feeling as if he were bullying her. No matter how depraved and deceitful she was, she was still a female—a human being—and he wasn't accustomed to being cruel, especially to women.

"You're right," he conceded with a ragged sigh. "I don't know you, but I intend to know you very well before I leave here. I intend to know everything about you. If you have any dark secrets, Miss Montgomery, they won't remain secrets for long."

"I have no secrets! I am just what you see—a

woman struggling to survive and keep her family from starving."

Jonas snorted, eyeing her slender but voluptuous figure with ill-concealed skepticism. She had removed the rain gear sometime during the night, and her shirt and breeches hid very little of her blatent femininity. She was a woman, all right; no man could deny that. But her very attractive exterior could well be hiding a rotten, poisonous core.

"What I see is a young woman who dresses like a boy, works like a mule, and lies like a rug. She claims she isn't tired, when the truth is she can barely stand up. She probably hasn't eaten a decent meal in days and won't get one until she goes out to the cook shed to cook it for herself."

"That's not true. Mattie will . . . will . . ." She paused and abruptly gripped her lower abdomen. A spasm of pain crossed her pale, twisted features.

"What is it?" he demanded. "Are you all right? You look as if you're about to faint."

No sooner had he said the words when Kate reached for the back of the rocker and white-knuckled, clung to it. "I've never fainted in my entire life," she gasped. "And I certainly won't do it, now—most definitely not in front of you."

He crossed the room in two strides and caught her just as she crumpled to her knees. He lifted her, stepped around to the front of the rocker, and sat down on it with her in his lap. Her weakness did not surprise him; his own legs were shaky from fatigue and the buffeting he had taken from the sea. Also, he had grown light-headed from lack of food and drink. "If this isn't fainting, what is it, Miss Montgomery? Your legs don't seem capable of supporting you at the moment. And neither, frankly, do mine."

She struggled weakly to get free of him. "It's nothing . . . just a touch of . . . of stomach trouble."

He wouldn't let her up for fear she would collapse

again and he along with her. "What do you mean—stomach trouble? You haven't got a bun in the oven, have you? Stomach trouble in a female usually means she's pregnant."

A red stain climbed up Kate's aristocratic cheekbones. "Of course, I'm not pregnant! It's just the . . . the wrong time of the moon. I don't feel well right now, that's all."

He kept his arms clamped tightly around her middle. "Sit still a minute. Relax and get hold of yourself. Whatever's wrong with you won't be helped by being stubborn and falling on the floor from dizziness."

Did she mean what he thought she did by "the wrong time of the moon?" His experience with women had been limited to his mother—who had gone to great lengths to hide feminine mysteries from her two sons—and to the occasional whore who eased his male frustrations. He did know he didn't want a collapsed woman on his hands, so he held her against him, forcing her to remain seated until the spell of weakness passed.

She gave a small sigh and leaned awkwardly against him. "I hate it when this happens," she whispered forlornly. "Once a month, I'm no good to anybody. I get so tired, feel like I want to weep all the time, and can't seem to ignore the cramping in the pit of my belly. I don't know why God cursed women like this; it isn't fair. If I knew where to lodge my complaints, I'd complain long and loud . . ."

She was rambling, talking more to herself than to him, and he realized that she was even more exhausted than he had suspected. He recalled how hard she had worked all night, hauling boxes and barrels too heavy for most men, never permitting herself even a moment's rest. He felt a wave of compassion for her—and something else, a heated stirring in the sensitive spot where her soft, round

92

bottom rested on his lap.

Acknowledging her nearness, his senses suddenly roared to life. He became almost painfully aware of the swell of her breasts pressed against his forearm, of the scent of the sea on the soft, silky hair tickling his nose, of the warmth and sweet weight of her. She made a wonderfully stimulating armful, being rounded where she ought to be rounded, her curves easily discernible through the thin, damp fabric of her boy's clothing.

He set the chair to rocking, hoping to distract himself, and without thinking, brushed her tousled hair back from her forehead. At his touch, she sighed deeply and relaxed. He glanced down to see her eyelids drooping, her incredibly long lashes brushing her cheeks. She couldn't keep her eyes open, and he felt a sharp stab of annoyance at her father—and Edward, the overseer, who would let a young woman work so hard that she was ready to keel over from exhaustion.

Why, she was little more than a slave—or a prisoner—on this godforsaken island. Her parents obviously opposed her marrying. Whether or not John Merrick actually existed, there could be no doubt that Kate Montgomery's family dragged on her like an anchor around her slim neck. The girl had enormous responsibilities which she apparently could not escape, even if she desired to do so.

However, *her* problems were not *his* problems, and he ought not to be sitting there, like some half-wit, permitting his sympathies as well as his body to be aroused. He shifted in the rocker, seeking to remind her that he was still there. She muttered something unintelligible, and her bottom ground even more deeply into his lap, provoking a full-blown physical arousal. The urge to wrap his fingers around her full breasts and discover the exact shape and feel of them nearly overcame him. Would she even notice, tired as she was?

She seemed oblivious to what she was doing to *him*. Gritting his teeth, he resisted the temptation to touch her; never had he taken advantage of a woman in any way. Jonathan had been the one who usually managed to get what he wanted from women for free, but Jonas scrupulously paid for all of his sexual encounters, generously rewarding his partners for the privilege of touching them. Neither wanting nor needing emotional entanglements, he preferred to keep his relationships with women as cold-blooded business arrangements. Innocent virgins he avoided like the plague.

This sudden physical attraction to a young woman he disliked and mistrusted surprised and dismayed him. He didn't understand it. Worse yet, he felt powerless to control it. He actually wanted to ravish the girl sleeping so trustingly in his lap!

Her utter relaxation and even breathing told him that she had slipped unawares into a sleep of complete exhaustion. If indeed she wasn't feeling well, as she claimed, then her energy and hard work during the night were all the more remarkable. She was really an extraordinary young woman, he mused, and then he frowned in annoyance at himself and at her. Maybe she had fallen asleep in order to avoid his questions. Perhaps she was feigning illness so as to distract him.

He must remember that she was a wrecker. Anyone who callously claimed the fruit of another's misfortune—God alone knew how many others had been robbed besides himself—did not deserve his admiration, his lust, or even his curiosity. He had already discovered enough about her to justify a good dose of hatred. The only other human being on the face of the earth whom he truly cared about was Jonathan . . . and this not-so-innocent chit had yet to prove that she had never met his missing brother.

Despite his dark thoughts, Jonas couldn't bring himself to dump Kate Montgomery on the floor . . . so he merely sat quietly, watching her as she slept and trying not to think how very sweet and desirable she looked in his arms—this strange young woman he had every reason to despise, but had somehow come to pity, and even, perhaps, to admire.

Drifting in a sea of the first real comfort she had known for days, Kate could hardly distinguish between reality and fantasy. A layer of cotton wool encased her senses, and it was a struggle even to think. She knew she was in a man's arms, being held tenderly and lovingly, the cramping and fatigue gradually ebbing away, but everything seemed dreamlike and insubstantial. If only it were Jonathan holding her! She wanted Jonathan to hold her forever, wanted to feel his lips pressed against hers in one of those languorous, drugging kisses he had been so good at giving. Oh, my lost love! she thought. I miss you so much. I mourn what we almost had— could have had—if you hadn't drowned that day.

Grief twisted her heart, the agony of losing him as fresh and exquisite as it had been on the day she found his battered body wedged between two rocks on the beach. Seeing his brother—gazing again into those blue, blue eyes—had brought it all back: the grief, regret, bitterness, anger . . . and the memory of what it had been like to desire a man from the very depths of her being.

She remembered how Jonathan's kisses had brought a heaviness to her breasts and a damp, swollen feeling between her legs. She had wanted him to touch, caress, and fondle her body, and keep kissing her until the hunger she felt for him was finally appeased. She never had satisfied that hunger, and it was still there, tormenting and frustrating her, like an itch she dare not scratch.

She stirred restlessly, the hardness beneath her buttocks both familiar and alien. She knew what that hardness was, but her knowledge was incomplete. She had never let Jonathan—or any man for that matter, including Edward—get close enough for her to discover all the intricacies of a male's anatomy. Edward revolted her, but Jonathan . . . She mustn't think about Jonathan anymore, she scolded herself. That was over and done with. Finished. She wouldn't be thinking of him now, were it not for his brother, whose every move, every gesture, reminded her in some way of the man she had loved and lost.

She ought to wake up and run. It was dangerous to be so close to this man . . . to let him cradle her in his arms like this. Only she was so tired . . . so mentally and physically weary of always having to be strong and capable, of having to look after people and solve problems. She had depleted her strength and needed rest and comfort like a plant needs sunshine and rain. Without them, she couldn't go on any longer. She would simply wither and die.

Succumbing to the inevitable, she burrowed more deeply into the strong, warm arms that held her. Flaring her nostrils, she relished the salty-sea scent of this man who wasn't Jonathan but who awakened the same feelings that Jonathan had. Forbidden fantasies beckoned. In her half dreamworld, she was loved and cherished . . . desired and adored. She didn't fear poverty, hunger, or losing her island home. She was cossetted and protected; no harm would ever come to her or those who looked to her for help. She had someone to share the heavy burdens she had labored so long and hard to carry alone.

Her dream-lover's breath caressed her forehead, and she turned her face up to his like a blossom seeking the sun. His nose brushed hers. More by instinct than actual intent, she met his lips with her own. For a moment, he hesitated, then his mouth opened slightly and covered her mouth. He tasted sweet and somehow very masculine. She sensed from the way he kissed her that he was every bit as ravenous as she.

Winding her arms around his neck, she opened her mouth to his seeking tongue. He plunged it inside her mouth, withdrew, and plunged it again. She felt the invasion with every fiber of her body and helplessly welcomed it. It had been so long since she had been well and truly kissed . . . since she had wanted to give what a man wanted to take.

His hand moved over her body, searching out the fullness of her bosom. Instead of being repulsed, as she would have been had Edward taken such a brazen liberty, she luxuriated in the possessive caress. His hand cupped her left breast, and she thought he must surely be able to feel the acceleration of her heartbeat and the tightening of her nipple.

The kiss went on and on—lasting far longer than she had ever kissed Jonathan. She couldn't be sure she wasn't imagining the wondrous sensations flooding her body. She felt warm all over, as if she were glowing from the inside out.

It's only a kiss, she told her bemused self, but it seemed as if she were surrendering everything she had to this man. He was taking something she had never given anyone—not even Jonathan. Her limbs felt immobile, entwined by the softest silk imaginable. He could have stripped her naked, and she would not have resisted. She floated in a languorous sea, as warm as bathwater and gentle as a salt pond.

When it ended, she still could not open her eyes. Kiss me again, she silently begged. Let me float here forever . . . Pretend you love and want me—pretend you're Jonathan returned from the dead.

What happened next jarred her teeth in her mouth and jerked her back to reality with brutal force. In

97

one swift movement, she was shoved out of the warm nest of Jonas's lap. Unable to react fast enough, she hit the floor with a loud thump, landing flat on her bottom.

"Witch!" he hissed, jumping to his feet and towering over her. "What in hell do you think you're doing?"

His face had gone blacker than a thundercloud. Terror rose thick in Kate's throat. She could think of no answer to the furious inquiry. He reached down, grabbed her by the shoulder, and hauled her upright. She stood trembling on wobbly legs, gazing into eyes as dark as granite, and almost choked on the humiliation of the moment.

"Don't think your sex will save you if you had anything to do with my brother's death or disappearance." His hand on her shoulder tightened like an iron claw. "You can't kiss your way out of murder. I'm not some mewling, milk-faced boy who believes everything a pretty girl tells him. I'm a man, and I'll take a man's revenge on you."

Her own anger rose to meet his; how dare he kiss her one moment, then maul and threaten her the next!

"I didn't kill your brother, and I had nothing to do with *your* shipwreck either! You ungrateful, misbegotten swine! Get out of this house!" she spat in his face. "You aren't welcome here any longer. For all I care, you can starve—and if you dare come within ten feet of the salvage down on the beach, I'll tell Fish and Old Tom to shoot you."

"Is that what you did to my brother—kill him, when he demanded a share of his own salvage?"

"I swear I've never met your brother!" she shouted. "I wish I had never met you! Go on, get out of here! And take your squawling cat with you!"

They both heard the cat just then, meowing outside the open window. Kate guessed that the reason she hadn't heard it in a while was because she had been too busy kissing this scoundrel of a sea captain, fantasizing that he was her beloved Jonathan. How *could* she have done such a thing? What insidious weakness had come over her?

"Get out! Get out!" she screamed at him.

He swept her a low, mocking bow. "With pleasure, Miss Montgomery . . . With utmost pleasure."

Then he was gone, pivoting on his booted heel and exiting the parlor and house faster than she could call him back—not that she had any desire to call him back, after the way he had treated her.

"Bastard!" she muttered under her breath, so mortified she could scarcely breathe. "The man is a total, complete bastard!"

And I am an utter fool, she added silently. What in God's name had ever possessed her to permit such intimacies? And what would she do if he refused to leave the island, after all?

Chapter Seven

Stiff with anger, both at himself and at Kate Montgomery, Jonas tromped back down to the beach and headed in the direction opposite of where they had left the salvage. He couldn't imagine what had gotten into him—kissing and caressing that little she-devil! Practically permitting her to seduce him. He should have dumped her on the floor the minute she cuddled up to him. Did she think that if she was "nice" to him, he would forget his suspicions— maybe even let her keep all the salvage? If she did, she had another think coming!

The sun was trying to poke through the gray clouds overhead, the beach rapidly drying in the offshore wind. Suddenly so parched he couldn't stand it, Jonas resolutely forced his thoughts away from the infuriating little tease and began looking for anything that might contain a few mouthfuls of rainwater before it all evaporated. He found a cluster of large, pinkish shells—each holding several sips of water—and carefully drained them, ignoring the few grains of sand that went down with each swallow.

The black cat, who'd been following at his heels and meowing plaintively all the while, lapped up some water, too. When his thirst was slaked, Jonas started searching for a sheltered spot where he could lie down and sleep for a couple hours. His hunger would have to wait until he felt strong enough to start looking for coconuts or other indigenous foods. There had to be something to eat on this island; Kate had mentioned turtles. If he had to, he'd kill one with his bare hands. Failing that, he could always eat the damn cat, he supposed.

For the moment, sleep took precedence. He was nearing the very limits of his endurance. Every muscle in his body ached, his head throbbed, and he felt slightly nauseated. Examining his side, he found purpling bruises on his rib cage beneath his shirt. His arm and leg on that same side felt tender and probably sported bruises, too.

It's been a hell of a night, he thought, picking a level spot set back from the water's edge, where a patch of trees promised shade if the sun came out in earnest. The sand was damp and cold when he lay down upon it, but he would not have cared if he had to lie in a puddle, so great was his fatigue. At least, the trees cut the wind. The cat promptly jumped on his chest and curled up there, purring contentedly. Jonas was too tired and dispirited to push it away. Closing his eyes, he gave himself up to the weariness tugging at his bones.

Instead of sinking into oblivion, he was plagued by erotic dreams dancing through his brain—Kate Montgomery shedding her clothes for him, revealing a body that was white, firm, and voluptuous. Every man's fantasy of the ideal female, she taunted him with her pure perfection. Tossing back her long, coppery hair, she wet her lips in anticipation of his kisses, and extended a hand to him. Inflamed, he tried to embrace her, but tease that she had already proven herself to be, she disappeared like a wraith into thin air.

Abruptly, his dreams turned chaotic—filled with images of his crew members fighting gigantic waves as they tried to save themselves. The same waves tossed him about like a piece of driftwood, and he kept struggling to gasp a breath of air before water again sucked him under, rolling him over and over, dashing him against hard objects. A voice kept calling his name. He was sure it was Jonathan, and once, he thought he saw Jonathan's face and Jonathan's hand—or was it Kate's?—reaching out to him across the waves.

He nearly leaped from his skin when someone actually touched his shoulder. Spilling the cat onto the sand, he sat up, wiped his eyes to clear the sleep from them, and found Kate Montgomery kneeling at his side.

"Here . . ." she said, thrusting a knapsack at him. "You don't deserve it, but I brought food, as well as a few other things I thought you might need. My conscience kept bothering me until I had no choice but to do something. You certainly didn't make it easy for me to find you; I've been searching for the past half hour."

Having no idea how long he'd been sleeping, Jonas eyed the sky, still overcast, and tried to guess the time of day. It seemed to him that the wind had picked up and the waves pounding on the beach were as high as ever, if not higher. "Is it still morning?" he asked.

"No, it's late afternoon," she informed him.

He took a good look at her then; she appeared refreshed. Her color had returned and with it, a good measure of her unusual beauty. Her oddly hued eyes still had dark circles under them, but her hair had been brushed until it shone and fell in a fiery, red-gold tangle down her back almost to her waist. Also, she had changed out of the shirt and breeches. Now, she wore a simple, white bodice beneath a faded blue apron covering a long, darker blue skirt.

The clothes were plain and worn, but cleaner and

103

more appropriate to her gender than her previous attire. He decided that she really didn't need anything fancy like silks and satins in order to be striking; he would have stopped to look at her anywhere. Not only did her hair and eyes draw attention, but those high cheekbones and that straight, regal nose suggested royalty in her background. Maybe it was her natural haughtiness that so tempted him to conquer and tame her. He hadn't instigated the kiss they had shared, but he hadn't refused it, either, he guiltily recalled.

Ashamed of the way she affected him, he took the knapsack as humbly as any commoner. "Thank you for thinking of me," he said with studied politeness and gravity. The cat rubbed against his calf, meowing hungrily, providing a welcome distraction. "Did you bring anything for my friend, Whiskers?"

"If he doesn't object to fried grouper fingers, there's plenty for him, too."

"Grouper fingers? I didn't know groupers had fingers." His mouth suddenly watering, Jonas tore open the knapsack. "Whatever they are, I'm sure I'll have no trouble eating them."

"They're not really fingers," she explained. "They're pieces of fish. Mattie often prepares them. She rolls long skinny slices of grouper fillet in flour or cornmeal, then fries them in oil. You'll find them right on top."

Jonas located the grouper fingers immediately, unwrapped them from a cloth, and popped one into his mouth. It melted on his tongue. "Delicious." He sighed, breaking off a portion for the hungry cat.

For several moments, he and Whiskers made a serious business of eating, while Kate silently watched. He wondered what she was thinking and if she was still angry. His own anger had mysteriously drained away. He was too hungry to worry about it or question her motives for bringing this peace offering. As he stuffed himself with the fish, a wedge of slightly moldy cheese, and a thick slice of juicy, orange papaya, he began to feel positively benevolent. It was amazing what food could do for a person.

Maybe he had misjudged Kate Montgomery, he thought hopefully. Maybe she really didn't know a thing about his brother. If in fact she didn't, there was nothing to stop him from being friendly. She needed a friend. Wrecking was no life for a woman; someone should tell her that. And also tell her that she was entitled to have a life of her own. Her parents were taking advantage of her. With an overseer and a houseful of slaves, the Montgomerys didn't need their daughter to look after them; they ought to be able to manage very well on their own.

"Thank you again," he said when he had finished. "I was wondering what I was going to do about my rumbling stomach."

She sat back on her heels and regarded him warily, as if fearing he might do something objectionable, possibly even violent. "Captain Irons, I've been thinking about your situation," she began, holding up her hand to forestall any comment he might make. "No, let me finish . . . I hardly blame you for thinking the worst of us. After all, we *are* wreckers. But we didn't *cause* your wreck, nor did we have anything to do with whatever you think happened to your brother."

The certainty again took hold of him that she was lying. He opened his mouth to mention the mysterious light, then abruptly snapped it closed. There was no point in arguing or revealing anything further. Instead, he'd hear her out and learn what she suggested he do about his situation.

She took a deep breath and continued. "My father and I have discussed it, and we have agreed that your suffering demands some sort of compensation on our part. As I mentioned before, we'd like you to stay with us until the sea calms, and when it does, Edward and I will take both you and the salvage to Nassau. There, instead of handing over the small share upon which we agreed, I'll split the profits from the entire operation with you. You should then be able to afford to return home. I realize that half the profits from the salvage won't restore your ship or your men—or for that matter, your brother—but under the circumstances, it's the best we can do. Whatever you may think, we aren't monsters or murderers, Captain. We're decent people, and we do have consciences . . ."

Jonas stared at her. Whatever he had been expecting, it wasn't this. If she wasn't lying, the offer was more than fair. If she was, it was actually brilliant—the perfect maneuver to throw him off the scent and convince him of her innocence. "Why, I hardly know what to say, Miss Montgomery . . . You've caught me by surprise. I must think about your offer. Whether or not I'll be prepared to leave here when you are, I can't say as yet."

"But you have to leave! This is *our* island, and we won't permit you to stay."

So she was still trying to get rid of him as fast as possible. The thought disappointed as much as angered him, fueling the fire of his suspicion. Remembering his resolve, he struggled inwardly not to show it. "All of the cay isn't yours," he calmly countered. "If you'll just point out the part that isn't, I'll stay out of your way."

"*Most* of it is ours. I've already told you; what doesn't belong to us is barely habitable. How would you live? What would you eat? And why on earth would you turn down half the profits from the salvage?"

"The *truth* is more important to me than any profits, Miss Montgomery. Let me repeat: I'm not

106

leaving here until I have the truth."

Her eyes sparkled, whether from tears or fury, he wasn't sure. Maybe it was both. "Why won't you believe me?" she wailed, reminding him of a little street urchin, caught stealing apples from the tree behind his house in Salem. She, too, had protested her innocence, though her pockets had been bulging with fruit.

"Probably because you haven't convinced me of your sincerity. I don't really know you, Miss Montgomery. I haven't taken your measure as they say, and don't know whether I can trust you or not. What, for example, were you trying to do when you kissed me this morning?"

She glanced down at her hands, nervously plucked at her skirt, then brought her gaze back to him. "I wasn't trying to do anything . . . I didn't mean to kiss you—or let you kiss me. Somehow, it just happened."

"Well, then . . . did you enjoy it?" he probed, wanting very much to know if she had been as affected by it as he had been.

"Yes . . ." she whispered, again dropping her eyes. "I enjoyed it more than I would have thought possible."

For once, an honest answer, he thought, elated. She couldn't be faking the blush on her cheeks. The urge to enfold her in his arms and resume kissing her surged through him, but a sudden awareness of his own sweat and dishevelment held him in check. He badly needed a bath and a shave.

"I hate to change the subject, but is there somewhere I could wash—or better yet, swim? Not in salt water, of course. I was thinking of a pond or stream. Until I'm clean, I can't make decisions about my future, and I certainly can't reveal my own reactions to that kiss."

She slanted him another wary glance. Then,

unexpectedly, she smiled—a beautiful smile that lit her face with breathtaking radiance that warmed him from head to toe. "You really aren't as dour as you seem, are you? You *do* have a sense of humor."

"What I have is a nose, Miss Montgomery, and right now, I'm not overly fond of the way I smell. It puts me at a great disadvantage in discussing personal, intimate subjects like kissing with a young lady."

Her nostrils flared ever so slightly. "I see what you mean," she said in the husky voice that sent shivers down his spine. "However, you mustn't assume that ponds and streams are easy to come by in this part of the world, Captain. Fresh water is a scarce and valuable commodity. Fortunately, the island does boast a small pond that might be deep enough for a swim after last night's rain. Do you feel up to a good walk?"

"After those grouper fingers, I feel up to anything."

She rose swiftly to her feet, which were, he saw, bare. Bare, pink, and feminine. He caught a flash of well-turned ankle as she whirled away from him, and he could hardly tear his eyes away from the intriguing sight. He hadn't noticed her ankles or feet when she wore breeches and boots; he'd been too mesmerized by the womanly flare of her hips and the shape of her bottom.

"Come along then . . ." she urged. "I'll show you where it is. I suspected you might be anxious to clean up, so I put soap and a linen towel in the sack, as well as a clean shirt and one of my father's razors. Not knowing if you'd be willing to return to the house with me, I came prepared."

"You seem to have thought of everything."

Marveling anew at her efficiency—and also at her ever-increasing comeliness, Jonas grabbed the knapsack and scrambled after her, following as she turned

108

inland away from the sea. The forest through which she led him held many species of trees, most notably sea grape, screw pine, and several varieties of palm. As they left the coastal area, one particular type of pine tree predominated, the same as he had noticed on the journey to her house. A sturdy, plentiful timber, it possessed excellent potential for building homes and more importantly, boats.

He also spotted some fine hardwoods: dogwood, horseflesh, and wild tamarind, as well as a tall, attractive tree whose foliage grew in a rounded, circular shape. He wondered if it was the tree called maderia, which produced wood often used for furniture. He had seen some Bahamian-crafted furniture in Nassau and admired its quality, though to him, such good wood seemed wasted on mere tables, chairs, and cabinets. Having grown up surrounded by ships and shipyards, Jonas couldn't help viewing the island as a natural location for shipbuilding. He wondered why the Montgomerys hadn't thought of exploiting the abundant forest for that purpose, or at least, for its lumber to be used for other things. Perhaps they had, but lacked the knowledge and manpower to mount a lumbering operation. No, they had enough manpower; but lumbering was no more a proper occupation for a woman than wrecking.

Kate Montgomery probably didn't know anything about the business, but he did. Maybe she would consider allowing him to remain on the island on the pretext of investigating the possibility of building ships in the area, perhaps on one of the adjacent cays. The more he thought about it, the better the idea seemed. Wood was plentiful, land probably cheap, and the sea close at hand. Most important of all, the only way to get around in this part of the world was by water. Ships had to come from somewhere; why not produce and sell them locally, undercutting the high prices demanded by shipyards in England and America?

He must think about this seriously, Jonas decided, not just view the idea as an excuse for remaining long enough in the Abacos to discover what had happened to his brother.

But first, he must undo the damage he'd already done to Kate Montgomery's good opinion of him. He must win her confidence—make her forget why he was really here. Perhaps if he spent his time wooing her instead of fighting her, she would let down her guard and enable him to get to the truth of things. By bringing him the knapsack, she had struck a truce, and he must be careful not to resume hostilities or declare full war. His position was precarious. If he stayed at her house, he had a much better chance of observing everything. Yet he doubted that he could learn much in the few days he would have before she insisted on taking him to Nassau.

If he were forced to leave the island, he would simply have to return on his own. One thing was certain: the answers to all his questions were here, on this very cay. And he wasn't leaving for good until he had them.

As Kate had expected, the pond she had mentioned to Jonas was deep enough for swimming after last night's rain and the recent bout of stormy weather. Located on a part of the cay judged unsuitable for farming by her father, the pond was hemmed by pines on one side and a marshy area on the other. Here, the livestock roamed, but Kate did not see the small band of half-wild mares and foals, or her own feisty stallion, Neptune, when she arrived at the pond with Jonas Irons in tow.

This far inland, the heat was oppressive, and she wished that she herself could doff her clothing and go for a swim in the warm, slightly brackish but fresh water, which was wonderful for bathing and washing one's hair. But of course she couldn't—not with Captain Irons around to watch. Nor did she intend to stay and witness his bath. He could undoubtedly find his way back to the beach, and from there, to the house in time for the evening meal . . . if he was so disposed. Nothing had been settled yet between them, but if he accepted her offer of staying at the house, then he must also accept the limitations she and her father placed upon his visit. One way or the other, he wouldn't be staying long on Conch Cay. On that, she and her father were firmly decided.

"This is a pretty place," Jonas Irons said, coming up beside her. "Will you join me for a swim?"

She was about to give him a stinging refusal, but as she turned to look at him, she saw that he was grinning—a roguish, teasing grin that implied he wasn't serious. His blue eyes caught and held hers, and she knew he was thinking of the kiss they had shared. Heat crept up her neck, reminding her of the danger she faced in being alone with this man. She should have brought Mattie with her, she belatedly realized, only she hadn't wanted any of the slaves to spend any more time than absolutely necessary in his company.

Mattie hadn't yet seen him, but her curiosity was mightily aroused; she had plagued Kate with questions about the shipwrecked captain who so much resembled his dead brother. No matter that Mattie was normally the most sensible and reliable of females; when it came to the brother of Jonathan Irons, Kate was becoming more and more afraid that Mattie would be the one to let something slip. Mattie had been Jonathan's staunchest defender, to the point of encouraging their relationship in the face of everyone else's disapproval. How had Kate ever forgotten Mattie's piercing observations?

111

"Y'all cain't be married t' yer fam'ly, Miz Kate. It's time you done got yerself a husband, an' that no-account Edward just plain ain't good enough fer you!"

Mattie hadn't minced any words on the subject, and while she was frying grouper fingers for Jonas to eat, she had shared a few more of her radical opinions. "Ah think you oughta tell the man what happened to his brother an' not try and keep it a secret. He's bound t' find out sooner or later . . . and when he does, he'll be plumb mad, an' with good reason."

"Well, you're the only one who thinks that way, Mattie, so I'll just thank you to keep quiet and not let on that I ever met Jonathan Irons."

"Have it yer own way then, missy," Mattie had huffed in her uppity way. "But ah b'lieve you'll live t' regret it!"

I probably will live to regret it, Kate thought, but what else can I possibly do? I can't very well admit that I've been lying right from the beginning; there's no telling *what* Jonas Irons might do it he finds out the truth.

Being careful to let none of her fears and worries show in her face, Kate shook her head no in answer to Jonas's invitation to join him for a swim. "Sorry, but I doubt that pond is big enough for both of us," she informed him. "Besides, I'm a virtuous woman and shouldn't even be alone here with you, much less join you for a swim."

He dropped the knapsack on the ground and began peeling off his shirt. "Why *are* you alone with me, then? I wouldn't have thought that your family—or you yourself—would allow it. Have you always had the freedom to do whatever you wish? I'm actually quite amazed at the life you lead on your little island in the Abacos, cut off from the rest of the world."

112

She couldn't seem to avert her eyes from his emerging chest. He was very muscular, and the curly hair covering the broad planes of his chest looked darker than the hair on his head. In fact, one whole side of his body looked darker than the other, but before she could ascertain why, he half turned, shielding that side of him from view.

"No one tells me what I can or can't do; I've been in charge too long for that," she finally responded to his question. "I knew you needed food, so I brought some. I wasn't planning to stay long in your company. Indeed, it's past time that I be going. Dinner will be served at sunset. If you wish to join us, you're most certainly welcome. I'm sure you can find the house by yourself."

He tossed the shirt to the ground, kicked off his boots, and started unbuttoning his pants. "Are you sure I can't persuade you to stay? We still have a great deal to discuss . . ."

"We can discuss it at dinner," she hurriedly assured him, dragging her glance away from his hands with a great effort of will. "Providing you decide to accept our hospitality and respect our wishes regarding your stay here, I'll see you then."

He paused before tugging down his trousers. "And if I don't?"

"Why then, you can get your own dinner, Captain—and failing that, starve. I'll not rescue you again. This is my last and final time."

"Then I suppose I have no choice but to join you for dinner, however much I'd prefer that *you* join *me*, instead."

"No choice at all, Captain. Enjoy your . . ." She stopped midsentence and spun around, facing away from him. "You could at least wait until I've gone!" she sputtered, flushing with embarrassment. "Aren't you ashamed to be stripping naked in front of me?"

"Not in the least," came his amused reply. She

113

heard a splash and then a deep sigh. "Ah, this is heaven on earth—good for whatever ails you. You really ought to try it. The water is wonderfully warm, but at the same time refreshing."

She had to resist with all her might turning around to watch him. She could well imagine what he looked like with the water sheeting off all those muscles. "I already know what it feels like, Captain . . . I've come swimming here before."

"With or without company?" he inquired. "I'm sure it's even nicer when shared with a close companion."

"The only one I've shared it with is Neptune," she hotly informed him.

"Neptune? Not John Merrick? Who the hell is Neptune?"

"Never mind!" she shouted. "Just never mind . . . I'll see you tonight! Or maybe I won't. It doesn't make any difference to me. My obligation to you is *over*."

She strode away from him as fast as she could—too fast to hear any replies he might have made. She didn't think he tried to make one. The only thing she heard was something that sounded suspiciously like laughter . . . only she wasn't going to turn around to find out. What did he have to laugh about anyway? And why—oh, why—did he have to be so impossibly virile, handsome, and challenging?

Chapter Eight

As she carried platters of food back and forth from the cook shed, Mattie made certain she got herself a good, long look at Jonas Irons, who was eating dinner with Edward, Miz Kate, and her father. In Mattie's opinion, this Captain Irons only looked a little bit like his dead brother and was easily the better man of the two; any fool could plainly see that the older of the Irons brothers was a real man, while the younger had been a flirtatious, unsettled boy, his charm and attractiveness not withstanding.

This one possessed maturity and authority; unlike the other, he didn't appear much given to sweet talk. As much as she had liked Jonathan Irons, Mattie had worried that he was a mite too slick for her innocent Miz Kate. Yes, Mattie decided, she liked Jonas far better than she had his brother. Of course, any man was a better choice than Edward, who didn't figure at all in Mattie's view of Miz Kate's future.

She could tell that Miz Kate liked Jonas, too—and that *he* wasn't indifferent, either. The girl kept eyeing him, and then looking quickly away when their eyes met, while Captain Irons boldly studied Miz Kate and tried to intercept those furtive glances. A powerful attraction already existed between them; Mattie was sure of it. She hadn't seen Miz Kate this aware of a man before or since Jonathan Irons, and that was the one thing that worried and fretted her: Jonas Irons would be powerfully angry when he discovered what had happened to his brother. Miz Kate should have told him the whole story straight out and not tried to conceal everything. Lies only led to more lies, and sooner or later, the liar got caught.

Maybe I should tell him myself, Mattie thought, and spare Miz Kate the bother and heartache.

It wouldn't be too difficult to take Captain Irons aside and explain that the Montgomerys were afraid to admit to the truth for fear of retaliation. Edward had, after all, lured both men's ships onto Dead Man's Reef. She'd be sure to make it clear that Edward was the one at fault, not Miz Kate or her father; the overseer had forced Cal and the others to signal passing ships with a lantern. If they didn't do it, he had threatened to have them locked up in gaol in Nassau for several months—and there'd be no guarantee that when they returned, they would find their families still on the island.

Edward was so sure that he'd soon be Miz Kate's husband and the new master of Conch Cay that he was making all sorts of rash threats and promises. Mattie wished she knew how to prevent such a misbegotten marriage, but with the master, the mistress, Bell, and Edward himself all against her, she didn't know what she could do—except maybe tell Jonas Irons the truth and hope that he'd change the situation. Surely, he'd demand that Edward be punished and maybe do the job himself.

If Edward suddenly disappeared, then all Mattie would have to worry about was how to keep Bell in line. Though a black woman and a slave the same as Mattie, Bell had huge aspirations that extended to running everything. She could not, of course, manipulate Miz Kate to her heart's content, but once Miz Kate married and had to obey her husband, then

Bell could manipulate *him*. That was why Bell wanted Miz Kate to marry Edward. If Kate married another man instead—an outsider like Jonas, say— then Bell would have to start all over plottin' an' plannin' how to get her way.

Thinking of all this made Mattie's head spin, but she never let on to anyone at the table that she had anything on her mind except filling their plates. Jonas Irons complimented her more than once on the excellence of her cooking, and each time he did, she grew more convinced that she really ought to speak to him. If he stayed at the house tonight, she'd have the perfect opportunity; the bed in the tiny guest room was already made up, but later, she could take him soap and towels, normally a job she'd give to little Ruthie, whom she was training in household duties. This time, she'd do it herself and hope to find a few moments to speak to him alone before he went to bed.

While Jonathan's death appeared accidental, Mattie still counted it mighty strange that an experienced sea captain hadn't been able to find safe harbor during a storm. Cal had shown him the breaks in the reef and cautioned him about sudden wind shifts and peculiar cloud formations that usually preceded violent weather. There was no good reason why he hadn't made it back to shore in time. Nor should his body have been quite so battered, if all he had done was drown. True, there were some big rocks on the beach, but could they alone account for his head being so bashed in when Miz Kate found him?

In Mattie's opinion, they couldn't, but there was no sense fretting Miz Kate by voicing her suspicions. Miz Kate had been torn up bad enough as it was. Could she possibly warn Captain Irons to take care, without revealing that she wasn't sure that his brother's death had been accidental?

As Mattie was removing an empty platter from the

table, Kate suddenly touched her arm. "Mattie, Captain Irons has decided to accept our hospitality and stay at the house, instead of down on the beach. Will you see to it that the guest room is readied?"

Mattie smiled at the young woman, thinking she looked especially lovely tonight with her shining hair and glistening eyes. Miz Kate had slept only a few hours this afternoon, but the rest had done her a world of good—either that, or she was already half in love with Captain Irons. To Mattie's eyes, Miz Kate hadn't looked this pretty since before Jonathan's death.

"Ah done already seed to it, Miz Kate. Except fer a few little comforts, de room is ready whenever Cap'n Irons wants t' bed down in it."

"That won't be long now," Captain Irons said. "I can use a good night's rest."

"Still don't see why he has t' stay here in the house," Edward grumbled to no one in particular. "I could find him a bed in the slave quarters or even in my own house."

"He's a guest, Edward," Kate responded. "Not yours, but *ours.* Of course, he should stay here in the house."

"If it's Kate's reputation that concerns you, Edward, you needn't worry," Kate's father admonished. "Her mama and I are here, so there's no cause for gossip or speculation on anyone's part."

Massah William's speech was slightly slurred from drink, and Mattie knew for a fact that Miz Sybil was already in a deep, unnatural sleep, induced by one of Bell's teas. Neither parent would be much of a chaperone tonight, so Edward had good reason to worry—not because of gossip, should the slaves spread the word to slaves on the other cays—but because Jonas Irons was a good-looking man and Miz Kate a beautiful woman. It was only natural that

118

they should be interested in each other . . . as indeed, they appeared to be, and Mattie fervently hoped that they were.

Mattie decided then and there that she would send Cassie and Daisy home early tonight, so that there would be no one in the house or the nearby cook shed except herself—and as soon as she'd had a word with Captain Irons and was sure he was taking the news about his brother all right, she would depart. Captain Irons and Miz Kate would then be as good as alone in the house. Human nature could take its course, and with any luck at all, Miz Kate might get a husband far better suited to her than Edward.

Miz Kate deserved her own life, whether it be here on the island or somewhere far away, Mattie thought for what must be the thousandth time. It wasn't right that she worked harder than anyone else, bore such heavy burdens of worry, and wasted all her youth and beauty looking after two people too wrapped up in bitterness to consider their own daughter's needs. Mattie loved Kate as well as she loved her husband, Cal, her daughter, Ruthie, and her two little sons, Ernest and Baby David.

Having practically raised Kate, she took great pride in Kate's strength, competence, and family loyalty—until she saw that those wonderful qualities were dooming Kate to a life of servitude, as surely as if Kate had Mattie's own skin color. If only one of them could escape slavery, Mattie was determined that it should be Kate—and Jonas Irons might be the very man to rescue her.

Carrying a load of dirty dishes back to the scullery adjacent to the cook shed, Mattie instructed Cassie and Daisy to scrape the plates clean, but "leave the washin' 'til mornin'. It's late, an' you gals mus' be tired."

Cassie and Daisy exchanged glances of surprise. It wasn't often Mattie let them escape before all the work was done.

"Y'all feelin' all right, Mattie?" Daisy asked, her fat, round face glistening in the heat of the small, stuffy building.

"Ah'm feelin' fine . . . Go on home t' Benjamin, an' git 'im some supper, Daisy. After bein' up all last night, ah expect he's right hungry an' sleepy."

"You really mean we can quit, now? Ah can go home, too, Mattie?" Cassie pleaded, batting her big brown eyes in her pretty moon face. "Liza an' Ollie are bound t' be hungry, by now, too."

Liza and Ollie were Cassie's small children, their father unknown. Cassie was unmarried, but everyone suspected Fish of having sired her babies. It was a well-known fact that Fish often visited her hut, though he always denied that the babies were his. Liza looked just like him—same nose and mouth— but Ollie reminded Mattie more of Edward. The chubby toddler was lighter-skinned, too, but no one had the nerve to mention *that* fact, at least not out in the open. In all probability, Cassie and Fish would eventually wed. There was no one else for either to choose from, unless the Montgomerys were willing to purchase a slave from Nassau or one of the other cays in the Abacos. With money as scarce as it was, Mattie thought that possibility unlikely.

"Git goin', both of you. I'll finish up here. Ah don't expect anyone t' stay up late t'night. Soons ah git Cap'n Irons settled, ah'm leavin', too."

"He shore is a handsome one." Cassie sighed. "Weren't fer dat scar over his eye, he'd be very bit as good lookin' as de other one—maybe even more so."

"Hush up about dat other one!" Mattie snapped. "An' you, Daisy, don't you mention him neither. If one o' you gals say a thing about 'im, ah'll make you wish you hadn't!"

"Oh, we won't!" Daisy denied. "Massah Edward

said he'd kill me if'n ah opened mah mouf."

"He probably will," Mattie assured her. "The cap'n may find out sooner or later, but jus' make sure it don't come from either of you."

"It won't!" they both promised, but Mattie wondered how long they could keep the secret. Neither Cassie nor Daisy were known for keeping secrets, except for the matter of Liza's and Ollie's daddies, which was really no secret at all.

Their featherheadedness was one more reason why Mattie should do the tellin' herself. If she didn't, the truth was bound to come out the wrong way; then there'd be no chance of getting Miz Kate and Captain Irons together. She must do it and do it soon. This very night. Her mind made up, she shooed Cassie and Daisy out of the scullery and then fetched the soap and towels she would take to his room as soon as he had retired.

The evening meal had barely ended when Kate's father left the table, stumbled toward the stairway, and unsteadily mounted it in search of his bed. Kate rose and offered to see Edward to the door, so that he, too, could depart and gain a much-needed rest. But Edward stubbornly remained seated, claiming to be in no hurry.

"Well, I'm not going to argue," Jonas Irons drawled. "If you'd be so good as to point me in the right direction, Miss Montgomery, I'd be delighted to embrace the comforts of your spare bedchamber."

"It's up the stairs . . . Just follow my father," Kate said. "Second door to your right."

Jonas Irons stood and bowed to her, his smile slightly mocking, echoing the looks he had been giving her all night. "Thank you for another delicious meal and for inviting me to your house. I'm glad I don't have to sleep on the beach or in a slave hut tonight. I find myself humbly grateful for any shelter I can get. I smelled more rain on the wind when I made my way here. Bad weather may be here to stay for a while. Will you be going to bed—or will you and Edward be wreck-watching again tonight?"

"Ain't none of your business what we do," Edward snorted, obviously still out of sorts that Jonas was staying in the house. "Whatever we do, we won't be needin' yer help."

Kate moved uneasily around the table. Edward had been spoiling for a fight all through dinner, but she wasn't going to let him have it—not now, not ever, for that matter. "I don't plan on wreck-watching this evening, Captain Irons. The truth is I haven't totally recovered from last night. Sleep well, Captain. The weather may surprise you. By tomorrow, it could be beautiful again, the sea as calm as a pond. In a day or two, we'll probably be able to leave for Nassau."

"It *could* be, but my guess is it won't," he said, not explaining why he thought so. "Good night, Miss Montgomery—Edward. I'll see you in the morning, I presume."

Only after Jonas had left the room and gone up the stairs did Edward push back his chair. "He don't seem nothin' like his brother, but I still ain't about t' trust 'im."

"Hush!" Kate hissed. "He might hear you."

"You jus' better not go throwin' yourself at 'im like you did the other one," Edward growled in a low tone. "I seen the way you wuz lookin' at 'im all through dinner. Why, you could hardly eat. An' I seen the way he wuz lookin' at you."

"Go home, Edward . . . You didn't see anything. It's all in your mind," Kate protested, distressed by his observations. She had been hoping no one had noticed her preoccupation and lack of appetite. "You have no right to be jealous; I can look at any man I want, with or without your approval."

"Soon as he leaves here, we're settlin' the matter of me and you . . . I'm gonna have me a talk with your father, an' he'll make you marry me b'fore the year is out."

"He *won't*, Edward. Don't get your hopes up. Papa loves me too much to try and force me into a marriage I don't want."

"If he says you gotta, you ain't gonna have much choice. There's nothin' else you kin do, Kate. This island an' this life is all you're ever gonna have."

"True, but I don't have to share it with *you*." Too tired to argue any more tonight, Kate headed for the doorway. If she stayed any longer, Edward might get to shouting, and then Jonas Irons would hear every horrible word. "I'm going to bed, Edward. I advise you to do the same."

"I'd be happy to go to *yer* bed." Edward's thick lips curved upward in a leer. "Once I did, you'd be *eager* to marry me. What you need is a real man between your thighs, Kate. Then you won't be makin' calf-eyes at every stranger who washes up on the beach."

"Good night, Edward!" Kate marched past him and swept up the stairs.

"All right, I'm leavin'!" he shouted behind her. "But you ain't heard the last of this—not by half!"

As Kate neared the top step, she heard Edward yanking open the front door of the house. As soon as he did, an animal yowled. A second later, a black shape came hurtling up the stairs toward her. It was Whiskers, searching for Jonas. She intercepted the cat with her foot, reached down, and snatched it into her arms, where it struggled for a moment before quieting and succumbing to her soft croons.

"Well, little beastie," she whispered into its silky ear. "If you want him so badly, I suppose you might as well have him, or I'll be stuck listening to your complaints all night long. Come along, I'll just slip you inside his room."

123

Kate walked quietly down the hallway, bypassing her parents' closed door, and came to the door of the guest room. Not wanting to disturb Jonas—or more accurately, not wanting to *be* disturbed *by* him—she put her hand on the doorknob, intending only to open the door a crack and let in the cat. But the door suddenly flew open, and she found herself face to face with the very person she had hoped to avoid. He was standing there with an oil lamp in his hand, his bronzed features brightly illuminated, his blue-green eyes filled with surprise.

"Miss Montgomery! Ah, I see now why you've come." His gaze dropped to the cat, then came back to her face. "For a moment there, I was hoping it was to say good night and tuck me into bed."

"We already said good night downstairs," she reminded him, her attention abruptly drawn to the deep cleft in his clean-shaven chin.

It was such a manly cleft—such a masculine chin and jaw in comparison to her father's or Edward's. Her gaze plunged helplessly downward; she couldn't seem to control her eyes. She had given him one of her father's largest, most voluminous shirts, but it was still way too small. He had opened it to relieve the tightness across his chest muscles, and this close to him, she could see the texture of his chest hair— curly and springy. Crisp-looking. She wanted very much to touch it and move her hand over the smooth, firm muscles beneath.

Instead, she held out the cat. "If you don't take this animal, he'll yowl all night. Better he should curl up on the foot of your bed than carry on right beneath your window."

He took the cat by the scruff of its neck and tossed it in the direction of the bed, which was, she knew, very near the door in this tiniest of rooms in the house. "It won't be so bad to have a cat in my bed," he said softly, "providing it keeps its claws sheathed and

124

minds its manners. In fact, I rather think I might enjoy having a small soft creature to keep me company in my cold, lonely bed."

The comment held a wealth of double meaning; he wasn't talking about Whiskers. His eyes invited her to enter the room, sit on the bed, talk and . . . and maybe do more than talk. He stood so near that she could smell the soap she had given him to bathe with that afternoon; it had been scented with an extraction of the fragrant, reddish-orange blossoms that grew on a small tree called a frangipani in the front yard.

Her mother liked sweet-smelling soap, and so did she—but on Jonas, the distinctive fragrance had undergone a subtle change. There was nothing feminine about it. She inhaled deeply, her nostrils flaring at the unmistakable odor of *man*, an exciting combination of soap, sea, and his own indefinable essence.

"Tomorrow, I probably won't see you," she blurted, suddenly desperate *not* to see him, for fear of what his presence did—or *could* do—to her. "I—I have to go over to one of the other cays," she improvised, something she *had* been meaning to do for the past week. "I promised to take some of Bell's medicines to a plantation owner there, whose workers have been suffering from a mysterious ague."

"Then I'll go with you . . . I'd like to explore the Abacos a bit while I'm here. Will the sea be calm enough for the journey?"

"I'll be approaching on the leeward side of the cay. The waves won't be as high as on the open sea, and the journey's not all that far. But no, you can't go with me. You might catch the malady, you see. Besides, I may have to spend the night, and the O'Hallorans won't know you're coming. They have limited accommodations . . . and . . . and . . ."

"Then I'll just have to stay here, won't I?" The

more flustered she became, the more amused he seemed. "While you're gone, I'll explore *this* cay . . . I'm sure I can keep myself occupied until you return."

She wondered whether it was wise to leave him on his own for a couple of days; she would have to tell Edward to watch him every minute. Yet, it was certainly wiser for her to leave than to stay. Edward was so bloody worried that something might develop between the two of them, he would probably welcome the chance to keep Captain Irons busy. Maybe he could show him the salt ponds or something. The ponds were at the opposite end of the cay. Hiking there and back would use up more than half the day, and they could spend the other half touring the ruined cotton fields, examining the devastation wrought by the chenile bugs.

Eager to escape the man's dangerous presence, she stepped back from the doorway. "Then good night again. Feel free to sleep late. I'll be leaving quite early in the morning, but after your ordeal, I'm sure you'll want to rest. If you need anything, please ask my father—or Edward. Meals are usually announced by the ringing of a bell that stands out back by the cook shed. I think I've covered everything, so if you'll excuse me, now . . ."

"Wait a minute." Still holding the lamp in one hand, he clamped his long, strong fingers around her wrist. "What about your mother?"

She jerked in surprise, having forgotten all about her mother. "My mother? What do you mean?"

"Would you prefer I avoid her? Aren't you afraid my presence in the house will upset her further—especially since she thinks I'm someone else, whom she obviously hates?"

Kate had to scramble mentally to recall the lies she'd told Jonas about John Merrick, who in fact, was a balding, potbellied planter, who lived with his wife and six children on Green Turtle Cay. He did have blue eyes, however, nearly the same color as Jonathan's and Jonas's, and that was why he'd popped into her head when she was searching for an imaginary suitor to explain away her mother's wild behavior when she first saw Jonas.

"Yes, I would rather you avoid her . . . It shouldn't be too difficult. She prefers taking her meals in her room to joining Papa, Edward, and me at table. Lately, she hasn't been leaving her room much at all. I fear she's declining rather rapidly. The only person she seems to want to have around her is Bell, her maid. For the most part, she ignores the rest of us."

Jonas Irons raised a dark brow, as if perplexed. "Why do you put up with that? Seems to me you should insist that she join you at meals and take more of an interest in her surroundings. Locked away in a room, almost anyone would soon lose their grip on reality."

Kate guiltily shrugged her shoulders, never having asked herself that question or even thought of it. Yet his suggestion seemed eminently sensible; she ought to have insisted that her mother join them for dinner, at least. Why *had* she permitted Mama to withdraw from life and retreat more and more into her own, secluded, little world? By doing so, she had probably made her mother's problems worse, instead of better.

"I . . . I don't know," she said. "I guess I've been too busy to notice much what Mama's been doing."

"Too busy wrecking." Jonas's tone dripped disapproval.

The warmth and invitation in his voice and eyes was suddenly gone, fled in the space of a heartbeat. Kate felt his withdrawal as surely as if he'd suddenly thrown up a wall between them. He emanated icy aloofness as he moved back into the room and began to shut the door. "Have a safe journey, Miss

Montgomery. Undoubtedly, I'll see you when you return."

Then he actually closed the door in her face!

She spun around and almost ran into Mattie, nearly invisible in the gloomy hallway. "Mattie! What on earth are you doing up here at this hour? Everyone's gone to bed for the night. You should be home in bed yourself."

"Why, Miz Kate, honey, I jus' 'membered I hadn't tol' Ruthie t' put soap or towels in Cap'n Irons's room. All I wuz doin' wuz bringin' 'em up to 'im."

Kate couldn't see Mattie clearly in the darkness, but the towels in her arms stood out whitely against her dark skin and faded clothing. "Here, give them to me. Captain Irons has retired for the night. I'll just put them outside his door, where he'll be sure to find them in the morning."

"You sure he won't need 'em t'night, yet?"

"I'm sure," Kate snapped, remembering how he had still smelled of soap from his bath earlier. "Go home, Mattie. See that Cal gets a good night's rest, too. The two of you can accompany me when I go over to Man O' War Cay tomorrow. I'll have to take Cal or Benjamin in any case, and you might as well go along in case we have a lot of workers to dose with Bell's ague remedy."

"You doan want me t' stay here an' look after things?" Mattie questioned, a slight tremor in her voice.

Mattie was usually glad of a chance to visit with friends on Man O' War Cay, not to mention escaping the hot confines of the cook shed for a day or two. What was her old friend, confidante, and faithful servant up to? Kate wondered. Why was she so reluctant to leave Conch Cay all of a sudden?

"No, I want you to go with me; didn't I just say that?"

"Yes, ma'am, y'all surely did," Mattie responded

128

in an uncharacteristically defeated, servile tone.

"Then be ready at sunup—you and Cal, both."

"Yes, ma'am, ah'll be ready."

I'd better keep her away from Jonas, Kate thought, watching Mattie turn around and go back down the stairs. I have a feeling she came up here for another reason besides soap and towels.

Chapter Nine

Jonas rose early the next morning and descended the stairs to find a house as silent as a tomb. He had to look long and hard before he finally discovered someone in the cook shed, preparing breakfast. Two dark-eyed, dusky-skinned females were languidly cutting up fruit and baking something that smelled as if it were burning.

Wrinkling his nose at the charred door, Jonas stuck his head in the door and greeted them. "Good morning ladies . . . I don't suppose there's any tea to be had, is there?"

"Oh, yessir, Cap'n Irons . . . We done gots tea a-steepin' an' breakfast, too, in a few minutes," the older and chubbier of the two women answered. "Cassie, git the cap'n a cup of tea."

The young woman named Cassie moved swiftly to obey, her huge doe eyes wide as saucers. "Here y'all are, Cap'n . . ." She handed him a steaming pewter mug, then dropped a quick, embarrassed curtsy, as if fearing he might smack her for her troubles.

"Thank you," he responded gravely, then leaned against the doorjamb to sip the hot, oddly flavored brew, which he guessed had been made from a local plant, instead of real tea leaves.

His presence clearly discomfited the two women

who started rushing about the cook shed, nearly running into each other in their eagerness to look industrious. Jonas couldn't help smiling behind his mug. It seemed as good a time as any to start asking questions; the women were too flustered to do a good job of lying.

"What are your names?" he asked innocently, as if he hadn't just heard the one call the other Cassie.

"Ah'm Cassie, sir, an' this here is Daisy. We're in charge o' de cookin' now dat Mattie's gone off wid Miz Kate t' pay a visit t' Man O' War Cay," the younger one babbled.

"Hush up, Cassie," the older woman said. "The cap'n only asked our names. He don't need t' hear all your chatter 'bout things that don't concern you or him."

Jonas immediately interpreted Daisy's remarks to mean that she and Cassie had been warned not to talk to him. He sought to put them at ease in hopes that they'd let slip something if they weren't so wary and frightened.

"I already know that Miss Montgomery left for Man O' War Cay this morning," he assured them. "She told me last night she was going—and also invited me to make myself at home while I'm here. I intend to do just that. I thought I'd spend the day exploring Conch Cay and wondered if I might take soom food and water with me."

The two women stared at him a moment, and then Daisy said: "If y'all jus' give us a minute, ah'll fix a sack fer you t' take along. Cassie, you run and wake up Massah Edward so's he can go wid de cap'n. Ah know Miz Kate would want someone t' keep de cap'n company."

Jonas prevented the girl from leaving by stretching his arm across the doorway. "It won't be necessary to awaken Master Edward. Let him sleep. I can find my own way around the island. Truth to tell, Edward

132

and I aren't agreeable companions. I don't much care for a man who mistreats the people he's supposed to be overseeing."

Jonas watched the two women carefully to note their reactions to that statement. Daisy narrowed her eyes at him before exchanging glances with the wide-eyed Cassie. Neither disputed his assertion that Edward mistreated the slaves, which Jonas had only suspected by Edward's manner and by listening to the way he spoke to those he considered his inferiors. Jonas hoped he could win the women over to his side by letting them know that he didn't approve of Edward's behavior.

"We's sposed t' make sure Massah Edward knows where you is all de time," Daisy finally muttered. "We could git in a peck o' trouble if'n we don't wake him."

"Then pretend you never saw me this morning," Jonas suggested. "I'll just help myself to some food and water, and you can claim you thought I was still in bed."

"We cain't do dat, Cap'n . . . Miz Kate deserves better from us." Shaking her head determinedly, Daisy resumed punching down the bread dough in her bowl. "Whatever *she* tell us t' do, we gonna try our best t' do, 'cause dere ain't no finer mistress den Miz Kate. Cassie, go wake Massah Edward right dis minute."

"Aw, Daisy . . ." Cassie pouted, hanging back and darting a pleading glance at Jonas. "Don't send me t' Massah Edward's cabin while he's still in bed. Ya'll know whut he'll try t' do t' me."

"Not if you tell him de cap'n is up here waitin' fer 'im." Daisy was adamant. "Go on, Cassie—git!"

"But I'm not up here waiting—I'm already gone." Jonas straightened from the doorjamb and handed Daisy the pewter mug. "You wouldn't want Cassie to *lie* to Master Edward, would you? I'll see you two charming ladies at supper, or whenever I get back from my ramblings."

"Tarnation!" Daisy exploded, raising exasperated eyes to meet his. "Here . . . If'n y'all's bent on doin' things yer own way, y'all better tek dis."

She snatched a crusty, slightly blackened loaf of bread from the table and thrust it at him. "But doan you tell Miz Kate ah gave you dis when you refused t' wait fer Massah Edward."

"Better tek dis, too, Cap'n." Cassie extended a stoppered water gourd to him. "I wuz fixin' t' give it t' Fish who's guardin' de salvage down on de beach, but ah can fill another one quick enuff."

The gourd had a strap around it so he could sling it over his shoulder, and Jonas happily did so. At least he wouldn't starve or go thirsty, even though the bread didn't appear too palatable. Too bad Kate hadn't left Mattie and taken the loyal Daisy with her instead, he thought as he left the cook shed. Mattie's bread had been delicious.

Heading for the northerly end of the cay, Jonas ignored the light drizzle falling from a sky only a little lighter colored than Whiskers who followed behind him, meowing for a piece of the burnt bread. When he didn't stop to feed the cat, Whiskers gave up and began stalking a toad hopping into the under-brush. Soon, toad and cat were gone from sight, and Jonas was alone as he started a methodical search of the island, looking for he-knew-not-what.

Jonas spent the entire day exploring the north end of the cay. Except for the forest, it was desolate and barren. Wind and waves had sculptured a large saltwater marsh, but not much could be done with it, not even salt raking, for it was far too exposed to the elements. The water apparently never dried up in it, leaving behind the salt. He returned to the house, ate a solitary, unappetizing dinner in the candlelit dining room, and then sat awhile in the parlor before retiring. Neither William, Edward, nor Sybil appeared, and for that small blessing, he was grateful, being reasonably certain that their conversation would be less than stimulating or informative.

The next morning, he got to the cook shed before Cassie and Daisy, helped himself to bread, fruit, water, and a wedge of cheese, and then set out in a southerly direction. The sky was still overcast, and it misted on and off most of the morning, but that day, he discovered the ruined cotton fields, a patch of sparse guinea corn, and the indigo experiment, where the plants looked too weak and spindly to survive. He also caught a glimpse of a small herd of horses running in the distance on a deserted stretch of beach.

That night, he dined with William who fell asleep during dinner, confronted Edward who demanded to know where he'd been for two days, and ran into Sybil in the upstairs hallway. Kate's mother instantly began shrieking and had to be led back to her room by the short, plump Bell, who glared daggers at him for upsetting her mistress.

Thereafter, he sought to avoid meeting any of Kate's family or Edward, and spent his entire time either on the beach, exploring the island, or in the cook shed, trying to get information—any information—out of Daisy and Cassie. The two women told him nothing of importance, and when he visited the slaves quarters, no one would speak to him there, either. The slaves, even the children, gazed at him with wary eyes and avoided all but the most trivial pleasantries.

The weather continued to be gloomy, though occasionally the sun came out, transforming the cay into a place of rare beauty, with its many blooming bushes, trees, and flowers, its gorgeously colored ocean, and its pristine beaches. Jonas discovered brilliantly plumaged parrots congregating in large flocks to eat pinecone seeds and wild fruits, white-crowned pigeons, woodpeckers, hummingbirds, and a yellow-striped bird which one of the slave children told him was called a banana bird.

Jonas had expected Kate to return in two or three days, four at most, but she did not. After several days of intermittent gloom, there came a day of high winds, making sailing impossible, so Jonas did not look for her then—but on the sixth day, he did. That day started out with a glorious sunrise and kept getting better as it continued.

The air had never smelled so fresh or sweet, and the sea never looked so blue as Jonas set off across the island to investigate the coves and inlets on the lee-ward side. If Kate *did* return today, she would land on the leeward side, and he hoped to be there to greet her. He hated to admit it to himself, but he was growing hungry for the sight of her.

Was she really as striking as he remembered? It didn't seem possible that her eyes could actually be that golden; no one really had gold eyes, did they? And her hair couldn't be the closest color to a fiery sunset that he'd ever seen . . . and her figure. Did she or did she not have the most perfect pair of legs—and the sweetest bottom—that God had ever seen fit to bestow on a woman? And what about her bosom? Was it as full and luscious as he recalled, or was he merely so foolishly besotted that he was inventing attributes she didn't even possess?

The one thing about Kate Montgomery that he had no difficulty recalling was her haughty, self-confident attitude—the way she could appear so imperious and queenly even when dressed in trousers and an oversize shirt. Her nose should have graced a monarch, he decided, for despite the freckles sprinkled across it, it was truly regal. She expected to be obeyed when she gave commands and resented it when she wasn't or when anyone so much as questioned her. Yet for all of her imperiousness, she didn't seem to realize when she was being manipulated or taken advantage of by people who were supposed to want what was best for her.

To his enormous surprise and dismay, Jonas found himself eagerly anticipating his next encounter with the intriguing, contradictory Kate. He was still ashamed of himself for having nearly lost his head kissing her, but at the same time, he couldn't seem to stop fantasizing about the *next* time he might steal a kiss . . . or she might offer one. He still wasn't certain who had instigated the first kiss, or exactly how it had happened, but he *was* positive that they had both enjoyed it—and would enjoy the next one, even more.

Having gone kissless for so long, he couldn't seem to quell his desire to kiss Kate Montgomery again. No matter how much he tried to convince himself that kissing her was a stupid, dangerous thing to do, given his present circumstances, he still wanted to do it—badly. In fact, he wanted to do much more than merely kiss the haughty Miss Montgomery. His dreams had become downright erotic, filled with the most vivid images of himself making love to Kate. He wished he didn't feel as he did, but no amount of self-flagellation—how could he possibly desire the person responsible for his brother's death?—seemed to make a bit of difference in the way his body responded to the mere thought of her.

Every muscle and nerve ending seemed to be quivering with excitement; today, she would *surely* return!

The leeward side of the cay turned out to be mostly rock. Exploring along the length of it, Jonas did find a small sand beach, and the discovery of it was almost enough to make him stop thinking of Kate altogether. The sand beach sloped gently into the sea, where, a short distance out, the water darkened from a brilliant turquoise to a bluish-purple, suggesting a sharp descent. Jonas stripped off his shirt and waded out to check, laughing out loud when waves lapped his bare chest barely a half-dozen yards offshore. Another five yards, and he had to swim; he couldn't touch bottom even when he dove for it.

Shaking his head to clear wet strands of hair from his eyes, he studied the rim of trees crowding the beach. He could not have wished for a more ideal spot to build a ship. Or dozens of ships. The area was large enough to accommodate a wooden cradle for supporting a vessel during its construction, and the downward slope of the beach would aid the craft's descent on skid logs into the waiting sea. It was a perfect setup!

Stroking back to shore, Jonas could hardly wait to examine the trees closest to the beach. They, too, turned out to be ideal. He didn't have to go far into the forest to find nearly any kind of tree he wanted; both pine and hardwood abounded. Neither building nor launching a vessel would be a problem—not with enough men and the proper tools.

His enthusiasm ebbed a bit when he remembered that he had neither—but Kate did. At least, she had several able-bodied men who could presumably take direction. Her family also owned the wood, which meant that any project he undertook would have to be a joint one. A small ship, a handy little sloop perhaps, would be the best place to start. If their first effort sold for a profit, they could then think about hiring enough men to build a bigger vessel.

Jonas's excitement suddenly spiraled to a fever pitch. In the back of his mind, he had always wanted to build his own ships, rather than converting older, less suitable vessels to the Caribbean trade. Now, the opportunity had fallen right into his lap! Kate must be made to see what a golden opportunity it could be for both of them. He must convince her to sink the profits from the salvage into the venture. His cargo had included saws and augers he could use, but he *would* need more tools, and some temporary labor, too. There were probably freedmen for hire in Nassau, who'd be willing to work for a short time, doing the heavy job of felling trees, then cutting and stripping them.

If none of Kate's workers were skilled with their hands, he'd also need a decent carpenter to direct the labor and a good shipwright, too. He himself could provide the design, assist, and oversee most of the work, but there were a few important details he didn't trust himself to handle alone.

Kneeling down, Jonas took up a sliver of driftwood and began to sketch his ideas in the sand. He traced a modest-size vessel with a single mast, a miniature cabin, and a deep hull, then erased it, and drew something bigger. The craft would be negotiating fairly wide stretches of open ocean and carrying a good-size cargo. He wanted a vessel broad enough in the beam to accommodate lots of crates and barrels, but not so broad that it couldn't easily ride large waves or was as slow as a turtle.

Oblivious to his surroundings now, he sketched fast and furiously—considering and discarding ideas almost as fast as they came to him. Eventually, he settled on a trim, deep-hulled, double-masted schooner, smaller than either the *Patriot* or the *Liberty*, but big enough to carry cargo and plenty of sail between the islands in this part of the world.

That's it, he thought—the perfect size, shape, and design. It was roughly drawn, of course, and needed to be refined and redrawn to scale, but he had captured the general idea.

Just then, a shadow fell across his sketch. Startled, he looked up to find Kate Montgomery—hands on skirted hips, sunbonnet pushed back from her wind-blown hair—gazing down at his sketch. "Whatever are you doing?" she inquired in her husky voice.

Giving himself time to calm his galloping heart, he glanced toward the beach where a simple boat, larger than a dory and possessing a short mast and rudder, was nuzzling the shore. He hadn't seen it approach nor heard anyone disembark, but there were Kate's two servants, Mattie and Cal, preparing to haul the boat up on the sand, and here was Kate herself, apparently fascinated by his artwork.

Jonas sat back on his haunches. "Can't you tell what it is?" he countered. "I'll be greatly disappointed if you can't."

She wrinkled her sun-burnt nose and squinted her eyes. "It's a boat, of course."

"A ship," he corrected. "But that's not all it is . . . It's a . . . a lifetime dream, a chance at a new beginning. It's the ship we're going to build right here on this very beach."

"Not we," she said. "And not here . . . Not on Conch Cay will you build such a ship or any ship."

"Yes, we," he insisted, getting to his feet. "And yes, here. You couldn't find a better place to build a vessel. Everything that's needed is close at hand."

"Forget it," she said crisply, reaching out a dainty bare foot to erase the drawing.

"Don't do that!" He grabbed her arm but it was already too late. The drawing was ruined—not that it mattered, because it still existed in his mind. Nevertheless, he stared at her in rising anger, noticing for the first time the pallor that tinged her cheeks and the blue smudges beneath her eyes. Also, she looked thinner than he remembered.

"You've come down with that bloody ague you went off to treat," he accused, pushing the issue of the ship aside in the face of this more immediate concern. "Is that why you took so long to come back? You got sick?"

140

She seemed amazed that he cared about the state of her health or how long she had been gone. "I stayed because most of the family and their people all had come down with it. They aren't over it yet, but at least, they're doing better now, and I don't anticipate anyone else dying because of it."

"You mean someone *did* die?"

She nodded. "First, a slave child and then, Granny O'Halloran . . . a lovely old lady whom everybody dearly loved. She was simply too old to fight it, on top of everything else that's gone wrong in recent years."

He could tell by her expression that something more was bothering her than just these senseless, tragic deaths. "What is it?" he probed. "Tell me about it."

She averted his gaze, but not before he saw the sheen of tears in her beautiful golden eyes. "It's . . . it's just that Granny's death—and the child's—was the final blow to the family. They've had to endure so much, you see. Once, like us, they were rich and had everything. But over the years, they've been reduced to the most wretched poverty. They can't go on any longer. As soon as everyone is fit enough to travel, they're returning to America—giving up, as it were—and throwing themselves on the mercy of relatives they haven't seen in two decades. I can't help wondering what sort of reception they'll receive," she added bitterly. "For myself, dying would be a better alternative. But I suppose I don't really understand the depths of their despair or how weak and shattered they've become."

She spun around and flung her arms wide. "To leave this place!" she cried, her pale face coloring with passion. "To actually abandon all this loveliness! I don't see how they can bear it, how they can simply walk away and not look back. But I suppose they feel they have no choice, not when it's

141

impossible to live here with any degree of comfort or security. My mother feels the same way they do, and Papa, too. Maybe when you get old, you no longer have the will to fight, or the pride, or the energy . . ."

"Or the stubbornness," he inserted, admiring the quality which Kate herself possessed in abundance. "It takes a great deal of stubbornness to persevere in an endeavor nearly everyone else views as a failure."

Emotions chased each other across her lovely face, like clouds racing across the sky. Despite himself, he was deeply moved. Her sorrow sprang from her great love for the island. Overshadowing everything was the fear that she would one day lose it, regardless of her efforts to hang on and make a success of the place. Wasn't she too young to bear such a burden—one normally borne by the men of a family? Jonas thought of her useless, self-pitying father and wanted to boot the man right off the cay into the ocean. How dare he spend his days in a sodden stupor while his daughter struggled to put food on the table?

Kate glanced down at her bare toes digging a small hole in the sand. "For the first time," she whispered, "I've had to consider—admit, actually—that we may not make it either. It might be better for Mama and Papa both if we went back to Georgia and begged Mama's relatives to forgive us and take us in. Surely, they'd do that—and see that Mama gets the medical help she needs."

Jonas had a vivid mental image of this proud, stubborn girl appealing to relatives she could hardly remember, relatives who had taken a different side in the war. They apparently hadn't done a thing to help the Montgomerys in all the years since, and he desperately wished he could spare her that final, ultimate humiliation. It would break Kate's spirit to have to admit defeat and beg help from strangers. And what if they refused their help?

He knew of a Loyalist family in Salem, who had

tried to return and take up their lives where they had left off. People shunned them, refused to do business with them, never invited them to social gatherings, and treated their children like lepers. Resentment and bitterness still simmered beneath a veneer of distant politeness; by her own admission, Kate still hated Americans, and he himself didn't much care for Loyalists, though he'd finally come around to doing business with them.

"Kate . . ." He slid his arm around her slender waist and tilted her chin, so he could see her eyes. "Kate, listen to me . . . I don't want you to say no before you've heard my entire proposal. I believe we could make a go of building ships here on this island. With your trees and workers, and *my* knowledge we could start with something small and modest, then progress to more ambitious projects. In three to five years, we'd have a new business established, one that would enable all of us to live comfortably, if not luxuriously. Think of it. We could build ships and boats of all sizes, to fit every need. In time, we could build them to order. I haven't got all of the details worked out yet, but I've made a proper beginning. Let me tell you what I've been thinking."

"I've already said no," she insisted, but her eyes said she was interested.

So he took her hand, pulled her after him to walk along the beach, and told her anyway—confided all his hopes, dreams, and plans. They grew as he explained them. The shadowy parts took form and substance. He knew he was spinning moonbeams, exaggerating what could be accomplished, but the way she listened, the way the light kindled in her eyes, drove him onward. He had the unnerving sensation that together, they *could* accomplish anything.

When he had finished and stood waiting for her answer, his heart slammed against his rib cage, and

143

he felt as if he'd just run a circuit of the entire cay. Incredibly, doubt and rejection crept across her face. "I don't know," she said. "I wasn't planning on you staying here . . . I don't know how well we'd work together."

"You mean because I'm an American and you're a Loyalist?"

"Yes . . . That and the matter of your brother. You still think we had something to do with his ship going down, don't you? That's the *real* reason you want to stay—to find out what happened to him."

Her forthrightness caught him off guard. Yes, it *was* the real reason, but somehow, in the past few hours, he had forgotten all about his brother. The shipbuilding project, in and of itself, had consumed his attention and made him want to stay almost every bit as badly. Then there was Kate herself. He recoiled from the idea that he wanted to remain because of her, but the thought did occur to him, filling him with unease and a deep disgust at himself for succumbing so easily to a pretty girl's attractions.

"At this point in time, my brother is not the issue," he warily responded. "I'll always wonder what really happened to him, and if it could have been avoided, but the proposition I've just made to you is strictly a business deal, one that would benefit both of us. In considering it, I've set personal concerns aside, and I hope you will do the same . . . What we're trying to do here, Miss Montgomery, is survive—and hopefully, prosper. That's the main reason why I made the suggestion. We both have perfectly good reasons for *not* entering into a joint business venture—but I think the reasons *for* doing so far outweigh the reasons against."

"Yes . . . You're right," she said slowly. "We've tried everything else—cotton, salt raking, indigo, and so on. The one thing we haven't tried is shipbuilding. Do you really think we can get enough

144

money from the salvage to buy tools and hire competent men?"

"We'll never know unless we try, now will we?" Excitement and elation once again surged through him. He felt like shouting and singing but kept his tone carefully neutral. "Am I to take it we have a deal?"

She darted him a shy, hesitant smile. "I'll have to speak to my family and Edward, of course . . ."

He was immediately jealous that she would mention the overseer. "Oh, does Edward own any of the trees or slaves we'll be using?"

"No, but I'll expect him to devote his full effort to the project, so of course, he must first be consulted."

"Overseers should be *told* what their work is, not asked if it suits them," Jonas huffed.

"Edward has worked for my family many years, Captain Irons. He's stood by us in good times and bad, and they've most all been bad. I can't do this without including him in the decision."

"Then I suppose we can't celebrate until you've spoken to everyone you need to speak to."

"No, I suppose we can't," she agreed, but then she abruptly spun away, half dancing across the sand. "Ships!" she crowed. "We're going to build ships and become very rich, the envy of everyone! We're going to build the best ships in the world!"

Swept up in her sudden joy which echoed his own submerged excitement—and also enchanted by the change in her—he grabbed her around the waist. Lifting her off her feet, he, too, spun around. "Yes, ships! The best damned ships that ever sailed the Atlantic or the Caribbean."

"Little ships, at first," she said laughingly. "And then bigger ones . . ."

"Yes, ships that can cross the sea to England! See that forest? See those trees?" He set her down and pointed. "That's what they're going to become—

wonderful, beautiful ships! Ships built by the Irons-Montgomery shipbuilding firm of Conch Cay, Bahamas."

"Montgomery-Irons," she immediately corrected. "My family's name should come first."

He was too exhilarated to argue. "Call it whatever you like. I don't care."

"You really don't?"

She glanced up into his eyes, and he stopped talking, stopped thinking, stopped breathing even, as he gazed down into her radiant face. She was breathtakingly beautiful. More than beautiful, she was exquisite. He looked at her lips and wanted more than anything to kiss them, to see if they were as soft as they had been that first time.

But even as he was reaching for her, the smile disappeared. The radiance faded, and she regarded him somberly. "This *is* going to be strictly a . . . a business arrangement, isn't it?"

"Yes," he said, drawing back from her. "It would be better—and safer—for all concerned, if we made it a point not to . . . to become personally involved with each other."

"We won't," she said softly but coolly. "I promise you; I shall see to it."

Chapter Ten

It's the most wonderful idea, Kate thought to herself as she brushed her hair that evening in preparation for dinner. Why hadn't *she* thought of it first? All this time that particular beach and all those trees had been waiting there, but she had never seen the potential for them until Jonas pointed it out to her.

Oh, she and Papa had once discussed the possibility of starting a lumber operation on the cay, but they had been daunted by the problems associated with shipping the wood to market in Nassau or other ports. Besides, wood was plentiful on many islands in the Bahamas, including New Providence where Nassau was located. Lumbering would not have been profitable—but building ships right here on Conch Cay was altogether a different prospect entirely.

She could hardly wait to talk it over with Papa and Edward—and Mama, too, of course, when the time was ripe. She had already mentioned the idea to Cal and Mattie, both of whom thought it a splendid oppportunity. Mattie, especially, had been enthusiastic, again suggesting that Kate tell Jonas the truth about his brother, whereupon Kate had threatened Mattie with the direst consequences should she let slip a single word about Jonathan Irons.

147

Kate's only problem with the venture was Jonathan Irons. Now, more than ever, it was important that Jonas never learn about his brother's fate, never discover that Kate had been lying right from the start, and never realize that both shipwrecks had been caused by Edward's overzealousness in augmenting their slim resources.

In order for the shipbuilding project to succeed, Edward and Jonas must work closely together. They would *all* have to work long and hard, cooperating to the utmost, and harboring no grudges or smoldering resentments. If Jonas ever learned the truth about his brother, he probably would no longer be interested in joining forces with the Montgomerys; more likely, he'd set out to destroy them. Kate couldn't bear to see this dream, too, crumble to dust, not now, when it seemed she might have found a way out of their financial difficulties.

She needed Jonas to help her. She certainly couldn't build ships without him, and if she were honest with herself, she had to admit that she would be equally devastated if he came to hate her. She wasn't falling in love with him—most definitely not!—but she couldn't deny that she was attracted to him. Also, being at least partially responsible for his losses, she wanted to make it up to him for the grief and economic setbacks he had suffered.

Pity. That was the only emotion he aroused in her, Kate told herself. Then she brushed her hair until it crackled, tied it up with a precious bit of ribbon, dressed in a favorite apricot-colored gown that, while worn and faded, still managed to impart an amber gleam to her eyes, and pinched her cheeks until they pinkened. She stared into the cracked looking glass that she consulted only on rare occasions and checked her appearance. Would Jonas find her pretty? Or would he compare her to the more fashionable young women of Salem and think her hopelessly unsophisticated and plain?

Jonathan had claimed that she outshone them all, but Jonas did not seem the type to pay glib compliments to a girl, no matter how much she longed to hear them. One kind word from Jonas would be worth a whole bushel basket full of flattery from Jonathan, but she might wait forever to hear it. Jonas sorely lacked his brother's easy charm, Kate thought critically, but then she remembered Jonas's kiss and his dazzling, carefully hoarded smiles, and realized that whatever Jonas lacked in charm, he made up for with his own brand of sensual magnetism. Both his kisses and his smiles were unforgettable.

Sighing at her own foolishness—and also her fickleness in placing greater value on any of Jonas's attributes over Jonathan's—Kate poked one last stray hair back into place, then hurried to join Edward, her father, and Jonas, already waiting downstairs in the front room. When she arrived breathless in the doorway, all three men turned to look at her. Papa and Jonas rose to their feet, and Edward awkwardly followed.

"Dear girl, you look enchanting this evening," Papa gallantly said, offering his arm. "May I have the honor of escorting you into the dining room?"

She smiled and curtsied, catching sight of Edward's scowl as she did so. "Of course, you may, Papa."

"What're you all dressed up for, Kate?" Edward grumbled, scanning the rather revealing gown with unconcealed disapproval. "It ain't somebody's birthday, is it?"

"No, but we do have something to celebrate. I'll tell you all about it at dinner." She swept past him en route to her father's side. "Shall we go in at once, Papa? Mattie probably has everything ready; I'm afraid I've kept you all waiting while I tried to do something fashionable with my hair. Alas, it resisted my efforts as usual, so the waiting was all for naught."

"Why'd you want to do something different with it anyhow?" Edward sulkily inquired. "Ain't nothin' wrong with it the way you always wear it."

Edward's peevish questions and comments did not deserve a polite response, Kate decided. She allowed herself one small peek at Jonas's face, since he had thus far said not a word. He was staring at her with a gratifyingly stunned expression, as if words had failed him. Kate smiled to herself; the look on his face spoke louder than any shallow compliments he might have made. *He*, at least, approved of her appearance.

"Mattie promised to start the meal with conch chowder, tonight," she gaily chattered as they marched into the candlelit dining room. "Do you favor conch chowder, Jonas?"

Edward's face grew even darker at her use of Jonas's first name, but Jonas himself—scrubbed clean and shining but still wearing the same shirt and breeches as that afternoon, the shirt her father had lent him—gave her one of his spine-tingling grins. "Never had it, sorry to say. Conch is never served in Salem. I'm not even sure what it is."

"Papa, tell him about conch," Kate urged as they all sat down. Tonight, she wanted her father relaxed and sober. If she kept him talking, he wouldn't drink as much.

"Well," William began, "A conch is a snail-like creature that lives in a large, rose-colored shell. During the breeding season, mainly during the summer months, the female produces an egg mass you can sometimes see resting on the sea bottom. In a few days, the eggs hatch into baby conchs, but they are so small you can't find them right away. In time, they become more visible, developing a snout with a

150

mouth at the end and a foot with a claw. As the conch grows, so does its shell, at first being round like a spiral, and pink in color with pink or yellow inside the lip . . .''

"He don't wanna know all that," Edward protested, as Mattie entered and began serving the chowder in the fragile, old chinaware with the pattern of blue willow leaves that Kate's mother had brought with them to the island. "Just eat the damn soup. It ain't as tasty as conch fritters but it's good enough."

"On the contrary," Jonas corrected. "I do want to know about conch and anything else you care to tell me, Mister Montgomery. Please continue."

"William . . ." Kate's father said, delighted to have so attentive an audience. "Please call me William. Well, about the time conchs are three or four years old or thereabouts, their shells are full size, and they start to grow a broad lip on them, a sign of approaching maturity. If they aren't harvested from the sea and turned into conch chowder or fritters or some such other tasty dish, they live to be ten or twelve years old. Their shells darken as they age, and the meat, of course, toughens a bit."

"*This* meat isn't tough," Jonas exclaimed. "It's a delicacy, like good lobster or crawfish. I've never eaten such a fine soup."

He was savoring the chowder as he ate and listened to Papa. Mattie, eavesdropping in the doorway, wore an expression of deep pleasure.

I wish he would compliment me the way he does Mattie's cooking, Kate thought wistfully.

"Delicious as it is, conch does get tiresome if you have to eat it day after day," she observed. "Mama is always begging for red meat, 'real food,' as she calls it, instead of seafood, but we very rarely get a taste of beef. When we do, it's usually salted and has been in a barrel much too long."

151

Jonas looked up from his soup and caught her eye. "I won't miss beef if I can eat soup like this everyday."

"We'll see how much you like it after you've been eating it for a year," she retorted before she thought.

Both Edward and her father noticed the slip. "Fortunately, you'll be tasting good fresh beef soon enough, I should imagine," William said with false heartiness. "Now that the weather's clear, Edward can take you to Nassau anytime you wish. There, it should be an easy matter for you to find passage back to your home in Salem."

"I'll take 'im tomorrow," Edward promised, glowering at Jonas. "We can leave after breakfast, first thing."

Kate had intended to wait until the meal was finished before imparting her news, but now, she saw she might as well say something immediately.

"Papa, Jonas won't be returning to America just yet, nor will he be leaving for Nassau in the morning. He has made me a business proposal, and I've . . ."

Edward threw down his spoon with a clatter, splashing chowder all over the cloth Mattie had dug up to cover the rough tabletop. "I knew it! Damn it t' hell an' back, I jus' knew it! What sorta business proposal was it? Did he offer t' keep ya' warm at night, in exchange fer . . ."

Kate pushed back her chair and sprang to her feet. "Stop it, Edward! Stop it, at once! If you care a whit for your own position here, you won't *dare* say what you're thinking!"

"Now, now . . ." William placated. "Edward didn't mean anything, Kate dearest . . . It's only that he's jealous of any man spending time talking to you alone—and why shouldn't he be? After all, you're practically betrothed to Edward."

"We are *not* betrothed, never were and never will be. I don't know what Edward's been telling you, but he very well knows that we'll never marry . . . I've told him so myself. I had rather marry a codfish, then bind myself to Edward for life!"

"A codfish! Is that how ya think of me, when all I wanna do is keep you safe and happy—look after you like I been doin' since you was practically a little girl?"

"You've *never* looked after me! You've only lusted for me . . . I've mostly looked after myself, and I . . ." All at once, Kate realized that Jonas had stopped eating his soup, calmly laid down his spoon, and was watching and listening with an almost bored expression, except that his eyes were anything but bored. They had turned the most chilling color of blue she had ever seen, and she was suddenly afraid—terrified, actually. In this kind of heated exchange, anything could be said, and once said, could not be recalled. She had to regain control of the situation. Right now. This very minute.

"Sit down, Edward," she ordered quietly but forcefully, for Edward, too, had risen. "I refuse to discuss this any further. We will finish our dinner, and then I will tell you and Papa about Jonas's proposal. Whatever you may think of it, you will *not* draw the ridiculous conclusion that anything personal exists between Captain Irons and myself. Nothing does exist, except . . . except a mutual desire to profit from a commodity that Conch Cay possesses in abundance."

"What commodity? Ya mean conch?" Edward sneered. "Are we gonna start sellin' conch to folks who can get it free jus' by rowin' out t' sea in a dory an' divin' overboard?"

With great effort, Kate clung to her dwindling patience. "No, Edward, we are not going to start selling conch to our neighbors, who are probably just as sick of it as Mama."

"It would sell well back in Salem," Jonas drawled,

his face as inscrutable as a piece of driftwood. "If you could think of a way to keep it from spoiling on the journey."

"Sorry, but I can't," Kate snapped. "Mattie, serve the rest of the dinner, will you please?"

After they had all sat down again and eaten—what, Kate had no idea—she reopened the topic of Jonas's proposal. "Jonas—I mean, Captain Irons—has suggested that the beach on the leeward side of the island would be an excellent site for building ships . . ." she began, and then went on to explain why Jonas thought so and how he envisioned the partnership working between them. After she added her own opinion of how such a joint venture could benefit all of them, she paused and impatiently awaited their reactions. "Well?" she prompted. "Doesn't it sound like the answer to all our prayers?"

Her father sat frowning at his empty plate, which Mattie had not yet removed. "It . . . ah . . . certainly seems like a project we ought to consider."

Edward tilted back his chair and began picking his teeth with a sliver of wood taken from his pocket. "T' me, the idea stinks like a bucket of week-old fish guts."

"It does not," Kate calmly denied, determined not to lose her temper a second time. "I probably shouldn't have asked your opinion, Edward, inasmuch as the trees don't belong to you, anyway. I did so only out of politeness and consideration for the many years you've worked for us."

"And I'm tellin' you the blunt truth—the idea stinks."

Kate waited a moment for Jonas to defend his proposal, but Jonas merely sipped his tea, saying not a word. Kate wondered if he thought it beneath him to defend himself to one such as Edward. Edward's crudity—his lack of manners and refinement—had never been so glaringly apparent.

"Could you be a little more specific regarding your objections, Edward?" she inquired, deliberately using a tone of voice and sophisticated manner that she knew would infuriate Edward and remind him of the vast differences between them, social and otherwise.

"Don't none of the slaves—or me or you, neither, for that matter—know a tinker's damn 'bout buildin' ships."

"Ah, but that will be the captain's contribution. His knowledge," Kate explained.

Edward leaned across the table to glare at Jonas. "How many ships have ya built, Cap'n? An' didja build 'em with your own two hands, or didja have carpenters t' do the heavy work?"

"In point of fact, I haven't built any," Jonas coolly announced. "But I've directed the overhauling and renovations of a half dozen . . . And I grew up in shipyards. I assure you I can design a seaworthy vessel and make certain everything is done as it should be."

"We plan to hire carpenters and shipwrights in Nassau. I've already told you this, Edward," Kate hastened to point out. "And while I would appreciate your cooperation in this endeavor, I don't absolutely need it in order to proceed. What do *you* think, Papa?"

Kate turned to her father and touched his fingers imploringly, for she did so want him to approve—and become as excited as she—over the possibilities.

Her father raised a hand to his eyes, as if he were suddenly terribly weary. In the candlelight, his face had turned more sallow than usual. "I think I should like a bit of brandy to settle my stomach after that large meal. Maybe then I can think more clearly."

"No brandy, Papa! Brandy will only muddle your thinking—not make it clearer. Don't you realize what this proposal means to us? Captain Irons is

155

offering us a chance—perhaps our very *last* chance—for survival. More than that, it's an opportunity to use what precious few resources we have on this cay to achieve more than mere survival. If we can build and sell even one ship, I can afford to plant a new crop of cotton or indigo. I can afford to buy you and Mama new clothes and shoes. Maybe I can even afford to take Mama somewhere to see a new doctor who can cure her, once and for all. Oh, Papa! If we succeed in this, it could mean a whole new life for us—the one you always dreamed we would have!"

"There ain't no future in shipbuildin'," Edward insisted. "Why, it's plain as the nose on yer face, Kate; the cap'n is just usin' this as an excuse to stay here an' spy on us."

"And why would I want to spy on you, Edward?" Jonas asked in a deceptively quiet tone that vibrated with a sudden intensity.

Kate shot Edward a warning glance, but Edward chose to ignore it. "I ain't got the slightest idea, Cap'n, but it's either that or you got yer eye on Kate, here."

"On Kate?" Jonas's chilly blue gaze flicked over Kate, then lingered a moment, warming as he studied her. "I might have my eye on her, at that," he conceded. "Now that you mention it, she's clearly worth a second glance."

Kate felt herself flushing from head to toe. As compliments went, this was a modest one, but as precious as a sparkling jewel to her.

"Well, yer all done lookin' over my property, Cap'n. We don't want or need you here," Edward challenged, rising and hitching up his trousers. "You can go back where ya come from, 'cause we been managin' jus' fine without ya. Haven't we, Will?"

Edward's presumption—his lack of respect in addressing her father and his referral to *her* as his "property"—infuriated Kate. "No, we haven't, Edward. We've been managing miserably. And regardless of what you and Papa think of this enterprise, or of Captain Irons himself, *I* intend to pursue it. Are you going to help or not?"

Edward faced her across the table and folded his arms across his chest. "I ain't buildin' no ships, Kate—specially not with some snot-nosed sea-cap'n who never even built one b'fore."

"Good, then you will now be in charge of the garden, the fields, and filling the cookpot. Every other man, woman, and child who can possibly help will be assigned tasks associated with building our first ship . . ."

"The hell you say! Will, are you gonna let her git away with this?" Edward appealed to her father who still sat at the table, clutching the cloth with visibly trembling hands.

Papa avoided looking at Edward. From past experience, Kate knew that her father hated confrontation, and when backed against a wall, would timidly acquiesce to whoever pushed the hardest. She always made certain that she did, but her father's spineless hesitation nonetheless exasperated her. Just once, she wished he would do something decisive and masculine, even if it meant denying her.

"Kate, d—dearest . . . Perhaps you should at least talk with your mama. You know how much change upsets her. To have Captain Irons living with us for an extended period of time would be quite impossible."

"I don't intend to live here, Mister Montgomery," Jonas interjected. "I'll first build myself a hut on the beach—and a shelter for the other male workers. That way we won't have to waste time walking so far everyday to and from the site. We'll cook and eat our meals there, too. One man can take off early to catch fish or dive for conch."

"Cassie and Daisy can do the cooking," Kate said. "Or Mattie. I'll have the women take turns. Mama need not be inconvenienced at all. Only Bell must stay here all the time. Bell is the only one she cares about anyway."

"It's too much for me to think about." Papa sighed. "No matter what I say, Kate, you'll do as you please regardless."

"Don't worry about it, Papa, leave all the worrying to me," Kate soothed, despising his weakness, but at the same time anxious to spare him suffering or unhappiness.

"This ain't gonna work," Edward groused. "You're gonna be sorry ya gave in t' her again, Will . . ."

"*Why* will he be sorry, Edward?" Kate demanded. "What does he have to lose? What do any of us have to lose, at this point? You haven't raised a single valid objection as to why this won't succeed. Why can't you stop being difficult and stubborn, and join us? We desperately need another set of hands."

Edward grimaced. "Never. I don't want nothin' t' do with this. It's the biggest mistake you'll ever make, Miss High and Mighty Kate Montgomery—an' I don't have t' tell you or your daddy or your mama why, 'cause you already *know* why."

With that, Edward rose and stomped from the dining room. A moment later, the front door slammed.

Jonas watched her from his end of the table. "Would anyone care to tell *me* why?" he inquired into the silence.

Chapter Eleven

Jonas never did get an answer to his question. Kate adroitly brought the meal to an end and hurried her father off to bed almost before the old man knew what was happening. Jonas lingered in the front room for a bit, waiting to see if she would return, and when she didn't, he finally gave up and went to bed himself.

The next day, Kate provided him with a quill pen, ink, and paper, so he could get started on a proper set of plans for the first ship they would build. She then disappeared, leaving him alone with only Whiskers for company, and he didn't see her for the rest of the day. Mattie brought him lunch—bread, fruit, and tea—and he kept working, scattering his drawings on thick sheets of precious parchment across the dining-room table.

Late in the day, the tread of soft footsteps in the hallway interrupted his concentration. He looked up, and to his great surprise, found Kate's mother, Sybil, ethereal in a voluminous dressing gown, standing in the doorway watching him. He dared not move a muscle, lest the woman start screaming again. Instead, she astounded him by walking calmly into the room and peering at his sketches.

"These are quite good, Captain Irons," she said, as

159

politely as if she'd never in her life exhibited anything other than perfect behavior. "Did your family in Salem build ships?"

He looked at her carefully. Her graying hair was artfully arranged in a style that had been fashionable twenty years ago, but it wasn't her hair alone that commanded his attention. He searched her hazel eyes for the look of madness he had seen on the two occasions when they had last met; it wasn't there. For once, she seemed lucid and rational, and slightly impatient for his answer.

"Did they?" she repeated.

"My father didn't build them, but he sailed them— and knew them from bow to stern. He passed his knowledge along to me, and I, too, know a great deal about ships."

She nodded. "Then perhaps this venture can work. You needn't look so surprised that I know about it. Neither Kate nor my husband, William, have seen fit to inform me yet, but I know everything that goes on in this house, and even beyond, in the slave huts and elsewhere on the cay. People try to keep secrets from me, but they usually don't succeed."

Jonas had no response to that, so he merely leaned back in his chair, watching her, wondering what she would do or say next.

"I understand you'll be staying with us for a while. Certain people aren't too happy about that. Is it your habit to insinuate yourself into other people's lives?"

"I'm only here because my ship wrecked off your island . . . and I'm only staying because I see a way to recoup my losses," he responded levelly.

"So I've heard," she said. "Well, one never knows what will happen next in life, does one? You can plan to your heart's content, only to have all your lovely dreams shattered in an instant."

She fingered one of his sketches, and he kept a close eye on her, in case she suddenly became violent or destructive. She coyly raised her eyes and gazed at him through the fringe of her lashes.

"I'm really not mad, you know ... I'm only occasionally confused. But Bell explains matters to me, and then I accept them. That's all one can do, isn't it? Accept and be docile about things?"

Nodding his answer, Jonas decided to take advantage of her lucidity, which might, after all, be temporary. "Who is it that I remind you of, Mrs. Montgomery? Why were you so upset and afraid the first time you saw me?"

She smiled guilelessly. "Do you remind me of someone, Captain? Did I actually say that? Dear me ... I've forgotten. My memory always has been deplorable."

"Your daughter says I look like someone named John Merrick," Jonas prompted. "Are you acquainted with a John Merrick?"

Sybil wrinkled her fine brow, which was crisscrossed with a web of delicate wrinkles. "Now where have I heard that name before? Yes, it is familiar ... I'm sure I know it. But I simply can't think who John Merrick might be at the moment."

"He must have been someone very important, to have elicited such a reaction from you when you thought I was him."

"If he was, I shall remember him shortly. That sometimes happens, you see. I remember things a day or two later. If I do recall him, I'll come and see you. I'd like to know why I despised you, at first, too. You seem a nice enough man. I only hope you don't upset my daughter's plans to marry Edward. Dear Edward is quite worried and distraught; he thinks you may be competing with him for Kate's affections."

"I'm not competing with anyone for anything ..." Jonas denied. "Are you absolutely certain your daughter *wants* to marry Edward? She said at dinner last evening that she didn't."

"That's merely a young woman's last-minute fears, Captain. Why, Kate and Edward have been planning to marry for several years, now. They're going to live here on Conch Cay and take over the hard work of running the plantation; it's all been decided a long time ago."

Jonas debated whether or not to refute this. The matter had nothing to do with him. Yet he did find it strange that Kate's parents would willingly consign their only daughter to a crude, boorish opportunist like Edward. "You think Edward is a fine enough man for your daughter?" he couldn't help asking.

"Oh, you mustn't let Edward's rough ways turn you against him! He's a rare gem that only needs a bit of polish to render him a perfect husband for our dear Kate. Until Edward came, my poor William had to do everything himself. He never was cut out for this sort of life, making do with little or nothing. Edward got the slaves properly in hand—something for which neither William, nor Kate either, has a knack—and began at once to make improvements. He repaired the house, cleared more fields for planting, and even built a wind-powered cotton gin, patterned after Joseph Eve's machine in Nassau. Why, for a short time before the chenille bugs became such a nuisance, our cotton crops promised to be considerable. What harvest we had could be ginned at the rate of three hundred and sixty pounds per day. Edward also introduced us to the unsavory but profitable business of wrecking. I don't know what we'd have done without him."

"That doesn't mean the man should be granted the honor of marrying your daughter."

"But there simply isn't anyone else suitable or deserving enough to become her husband. Don't you see? Kate has no desire to leave Conch Cay; unlike William and me, she loves it here. If she marries Edward, we can all remain, safe and secure, and the two of them together, with the drive and energy of youth, can make the plantation a great success."

"What you've mentioned are all monetary concerns, Mrs. Montgomery. What about Kate's happiness in her marriage? Don't you want her to love and be loved?"

"We can't have everything, Captain Irons. We must all make compromises. Life has taught me that harsh lesson, and now, Kate must try to learn it, too. It's far better to be safe and secure, than to be in love and hungry."

"I haven't noticed anyone starving as yet, Mrs. Montgomery."

"We eat slave food!" she snapped. "Whatever can be harvested from the sea or grown in our own poor excuse for a garden. And we dress no better than the slaves. Not that I'm complaining, mind you, for I've known worse hardship than this."

"If you aren't complaining, then what are you doing?" Jonas blandly inquired.

"I'm simply telling you why it's in Kate's best interests to marry Edward!" Sybil explained with an exasperated shake of her gray curls. "So you must *not* interfere, do you understand? I won't stand by and watch you break my daughter's heart, for that's what you'd be doing. One day, you'll be going home again, and when you do, Kate must remain here on Conch Cay—with us and Edward."

"Kate's choices may not be *your* choices," Jonas began, trying to be diplomatic, but just then, Bell stalked into the room, her feathers a-ruffle, looking exactly like a broody hen searching for a lost chick.

"Dere you is, Miz Sybil! I been lookin' all over fer you. It's time fer yer nap."

"My nap?" Sybil Montgomery blinked rapidly several times and then furrowed her brow. "Goodness, what time is it? Have I missed teatime, then?"

"No, first you gonna have yore tea, den you gonna

163

have yore nap. Old Bell's made you some lovely tea from an herb I picked jus' dis mornin'."

"Oh, I suppose I must go and get it, mustn't I? Will you excuse me, Captain Irons? I don't wish to be rude, but I must go have my tea and my nap . . ."

"You been real naughty, not lettin' ole Bell know where you wuz," Bell scolded, herding Sybil ahead of her out of the room. "Ah turn mah back on you for de blink of an eye, an' off y'all goes, gettin' inta trouble, no doubt . . ."

"Wait a minute," Jonas called out in his most commanding, sea-captain's voice. "Mrs. Montgomery seems to be feeling better this afternoon. Why must she be put to bed like a little girl?"

Bell turned to face him, her ample body rigid with affront. "Ah's de one tekin' care o' Miz Sybil 'round 'ere, Cap'n, 'cause ah's de only one who can deal wif her durin' her bad times. When ah say she needs a nap, she needs it bad, 'cause if'n she don't get it, she gonna have herself a screamin' fit b'fore too long."

"Bell? Come along now, Bell," Sybil Montgomery pleaded, her voice rising in agitation. "I want my tea . . . and it mustn't be cold. You know how I detest cold tea."

Bell rolled her eyes at Jonas, as if to say "see what I mean?" "Ah's comin', Miz Sybil . . . de good Lord knows, ah's comin'."

She left Jonas shaking his head, but still unconvinced. Something about Bell's manner and her relationship to Sybil Montgomery deeply disturbed him—but he couldn't explain why. He went back to working on his sketches, all the while pondering Sybil's remarks about Kate, Edward, and himself. Sybil needn't worry that he intended stealing Kate away from Edward. He was here to build ships and find out what had happened to his brother. That was all.

But even as he tried to convince himself of his

164

motives and intentions, he couldn't wait to see Kate again and to show her the sketches. He wanted her to approve of his designs and admire his creativity. He hoped she would realize what he was trying to do and applaud his efforts. He earnestly desired to see her eyes light up and sparkle, and her smile shine just for him . . . He couldn't stop himself from smiling when he thought of her, dancing with joy and excitement on the beach. Wait until she saw the ship he was going to build! *Then* she would have a *real* reason to laugh, clap her hands, and dance.

While Jonas busied himself with his sketches, Kate prepared to build huts on the opposite side of the cay. Because it was such a long walk to get there, she used a large dory to go back and forth, ferrying workers and tools around the tip of the cay to the calm, deep waters of the leeward side of the island.

There, she directed Cal, Benjamin, Fish, Daisy, Cassie, and several others, including Gilbert, Bell's husband, and Ruthie and Ernest, Mattie's children, to clean up a section of the beach near the forest, gather palm leaves for thatching, and commence felling trees suitable for corner posts and roof supports.

She hoped to surprise Jonas by having the huts all ready and built, so that work could begin immediately on the ship itself, as soon as he completed the sketches and they returned from selling the salvage in Nassau. For however many days it took Jonas to draw up the plans, she intended to work on the huts—a small one for him, and a larger one for all the workers.

As she worked, she thought about the trip to Nassau. It would be an awkward one, if Edward went along. Obviously still angry and determined to thwart the shipbuilding project at every turn, he had

165

stomped off in the direction of the indigo fields early that morning. She did *not* want him to accompany her and Jonas to Nassau to sell the salvage.

I simply won't invite him, she thought. Cal could go along to help sail the small, sturdy vessel they used for inter-island travel, and Mattie could come, too, both to oversee meals for them all, and for female company. It wouldn't be necessary for Edward to be there, scowling at everyone and behaving like a disgruntled mule.

Kate just wished she could figure out a way to disinvite Edward for meals at the house. He was accustomed to taking them with the family, usually joining her and Papa for dinner. She supposed Papa would put up a fuss if she told Edward to eat elsewhere, not to mention the fuss Edward would make. Then she remembered that once the project actually got started, she wouldn't have to share meals with Edward and her father anymore; she could eat them on the beach, with Jonas and the workers.

That thought made her work all the harder to get the huts underway. The day flew by and before she knew it, it was time for the return trip around the island to the other side of the cay.

Cal came to get her. "Miz Kate," he said in his slow, patient way. "Ah done took all de women and chillun an' ole Gilbert back to de windward side; is you ready t' come, now? Ah imagine Mattie gots suppah ready, and Massah William an' Massah Edward'll be waitin' on ya."

"I'm coming, Cal. Now, tomorrow morning, bright and early, I want you to fetch the *Zephyr* and anchor her near the salvage. We'll load her with as much as we can, so she's ready for the trip to Nassau, then we'll sail her here and anchor offshore until it's time to go."

"Yes'm, Miz Kate. You think we'll get all dat salvage aboard? We got a lot dis time."

166

"If we don't, we'll just have to leave some and make a second trip—but we'll try. I don't know how soon Captain Irons will be ready to go. With this good weather we're having, I hope he doesn't wait too long."

"Who you gonna tek wif you, an' who you gonna leave t' work on de huts, Miz Kate?"

So she told him as they sailed the dory back around to the other side of the cay. "Old Tom can help, too," he reminded her. "Once we load de salvage, he an' Fish won't have t' take turns guardin' it no more. He good at thatchin', and he gonna have plenty o' time."

"That's wonderful, because I'm hoping the huts can be completely finished before we return from Nassau. Oh, dear, I just remembered something. Captain Irons wants to hire a carpenter and a shipwright in Nassau. I suppose they'll be wanting their own separate hut."

"Won't be dat much more work t' build three, Miz Kate. Ah'll jus' tell Benjamin not t' let Fish sleep half de day while we're gone . . . Den it'll all git done."

"Thanks, Cal."

Dinner that night was a much calmer affair than it had been on the previous evening; Edward did not appear. Mattie told Kate that Edward had eaten earlier, then gone off to sulk in his own house. Kate was grateful for his absence. Having no time to dress in anything fancy, she came to the table in her faded, homespun skirt that had seen years of service on top of the afternoon's labors. But at least, her face and hands were clean, and she had run a brush through her tangle of hair.

They ate quickly and quietly—Kate again hardly noticing what was on her plate—and afterward, Papa, yawning, excused himself. As soon as he left the room, Kate jumped up and began clearing away the china and cutlery.

"Now, show me what you've been drawing so far,"

167

she begged Jonas. "I must see your plans! But wait until I make a clean spot."

Jonas chuckled, his scarred face much softer and less sinister-looking in the candlelight. "You seem very eager."

"I *am* eager! I've been waiting for this all day."

Jonas tipped back his chair, making no move to retrieve his rolled-up parchments piled high on the wooden sideboard. "What were *you* doing to-day?"

"What I always do—work!" Tossing her head with impatience, Kate hurried to the sideboard, picked up one of the scrolls, unrolled it, and held it beneath the overhead chandelier of candles illuminating the table. "Oh, Jonas!" She sighed. "This is beautiful! What is it?"

He stood and peered over her shoulder. "That's the design for the keel ... I'm drawing each part separately and including all the measurements, so we'll know exactly how to build each one."

"But how will it look, when all the parts are put together?"

"Well, that sketch isn't finished, but I suppose I can show you what I've got so far."

He went to the sideboard, rummaged around a moment, and returned with another scroll. "Here, this should give you some idea ..."

He unrolled the scroll and held it out for her inspection. The vessel depicted therein looked more like a skeleton than a ship. "Explain what I'm seeing ..." she demanded. "Tell me everything there is to know about this ship."

So he did. She listened with only half her attention. The other half focused on his face, so young and animated, so mesmerizing, not merely handsome or attractive, as he told her in great detail about the design, the measurements, the advantages, and disadvantages of the ship they were going to build.

When he talks about something he loves, something that excites him, his whole expression changes, she thought. She felt dazzled and slightly breathless; not another man alive could compete with him in compelling presence, enthusiasm, or raw energy.

It occurred to her that no other man she had ever known had shown such passion and excitement over a mere idea—except perhaps, her grandfather. Grandpa Montgomery had radiated excitement and energy; he had always been busy, involved, opinionated . . . and critical of people who were overwhelmed by life, rather than determined to meet it head-on.

Grandpa would have approved of Jonas . . . but Kate wasn't so certain of his reaction to Jonas's brother. Jonathan had seemed content with his lot—had mentioned several times that his elder brother was the one with all the discipline, ambition, and brains.

How can I be so disloyal to Jonathan's memory? Kate agonized, even as the fire of Jonas's dreams ignited in her own breast.

"I was thinking of calling her the *Phoenix*," Jonas was saying, gazing deeply into her eyes. "That is, if you approve. What could be more appropriate, inasmuch as this vessel symbolizes our own resurrection from the ashes of failure and despair?"

"I think it's a wonderful name—perfect, for our first endeavor."

They stood for a moment, unmoving, the drawing temporarily forgotten. Kate could not glance away from his sea-blue eyes.

"I feel like a phoenix rising from the ashes," he huskily admitted. "I didn't now how much I wanted this, until I actually sat down to design this ship. I felt I was *meant* to be doing this, that I had been waiting all my life for just such an opportunity. But why didn't I realize it before? Why was I content to do what my father had always done, expanding upon his accomplishments, of course, but never really asking myself if I didn't have my own vision to pursue?"

The moment spun out between them, shimmering and perfect, like a skein of gold thread flashing in the sunlight.

"I don't know why," she whispered. "But I feel the same excitement you do. We're going to build something special, new, and beautiful. A proud little ship that will take to the sea like a dolphin. Just thinking of it makes my heart beat faster."

She laughed a little, self-conscious under his scrutiny.

Or maybe it's you yourself who causes this reaction in me, she thought ruefully. A hot yearning rose in her—a longing to be as close to Jonas physically as they were emotionally for that single, glowing instant. She looked at his lips—those expressive, finely chiseled, sensual lips! How she longed to kiss him again, to seal their partnership with a gesture that expressed faith and hope in the future—and in each other!

As if he had read her mind, he slowly set the scroll down on the table. "Kate . . ." he said, making her name sound like an invitation.

She leaned toward him, inhaling his scent, aware of the heat his body gave off. Reaching out, he drew her into the circle of his arms. She felt the pressure of his hand on her back, felt the hardness of his chest grazing the fullness of her breasts. Her knees began to quiver, and she found it impossible to breathe properly.

"Lovely Kate . . ."

The ceiling suddenly creaked overhead, and a querulous voice floated down the stairwell. "William? William!"

It was Mama.

"Where's Kate? I want to see Kate before I go to bed."

Papa's voice—low and muffled—answered. "Don't fret, Sybil . . . Kate will be coming up shortly."

"But she's downstairs alone with that . . . that great lout of a sea captain who's trying to take her away from Edward. I want to see her, now! I'll become quite distressed if I can't see her."

Kate gently disengaged herself. "I'd better go say good night to Mama and reassure her that I'm all right."

Jonas quirked an inquiring eyebrow at her. "Will you also reassure her that she needn't worry about my taking you away from Edward? She expressed that very same concern to me earlier today. Paid me a surprise visit while I was working."

"She did? What did you say—about Edward and me?"

"What will *you* say?" he countered, his jewel-bright eyes studying her intently.

"I'll say that you can't take me away from Edward because I never belonged to him in the first place."

He touched his index finger to her lips and gently drew it along the lower one. "I'm glad . . . I don't like to think of Edward kissing you . . . touching you . . . holding you tight against him . . ."

She shivered, and he dropped his hand.

"Go and see your mother, Kate . . ." His tone was only slightly regretful, but firm and unyielding. Turning from her, he reached for his sketches.

Mortified by what seemed like a rejection—reluctant but still a rejection—on his part, she fled the room.

Chapter Twelve

Four days later, they were ready to leave for Nassau. Jonas's designs were completed, not as skillfully rendered as he desired, judging from his complaints, but the important figuring was done, with accompanying notes, measurements, and drawings which Kate thought were as detailed and carefully executed as they could possibly be. The weather held fair. If it continued to do so, there was no reason why they couldn't sail immediately. While they were gone, the huts could be finished, and as soon as they returned, the ship started.

Bearing in mind that Jonas as yet had no idea she was having the huts built, Kate had Cal and Benjamin sail the *Zephyr* around to the windward side of the cay, so he wouldn't see how much had already been accomplished. There, bright and early the next morning, she, Jonas, and Mattie climbed in a dory and braved the perils of the reef in order to board the *Zephyr*. The little boat had no cabin and only two sails, but her hull was broad and deep; all of the salvage fit inside, pleasing Kate—but apparently not Jonas.

"This old bucket is going to get us to Nassau?" he queried, surveying the *Zephyr* as she wallowed beside them in the blue-green swells outside the reef.

"She's gotten us there many times. Don't insult her; she's a good little boat." Kate caught the line Cal tossed down to them and held the dory steady against the *Zephyr*'s side, while Mattie seized Cal's hand and clambered aboard. "As long as we don't encounter a sudden hurricane, we should make it without any problems," she assured him.

"She's barely seaworthy," Jonas snorted, taking the line from her. "And she's overloaded besides."

"The more loaded down she is, the better she sails." Brushing a strand of wind-blown hair from her eyes, Kate gave him a sidelong look. "If you don't approve of her, you can always build us a bigger and better one . . . when you have time."

"I can see you intend to keep me busy everyday including Sundays for the next twenty years or so," Jonas grumbled sarcastically, but he smiled as he said it.

Watching them over the side of the *Zephyr*, Mattie and Cal traded grins. The two servants looked inordinately smug and gratified, Kate thought, as if this trip had been staged for the sole purpose of granting them a holiday. They were leaving their children behind, in Daisy's care, and also escaping Edward, whom they mutually disliked. But there was something more—some other reason—for their obvious pleasure in the journey. Kate suspected they were matchmaking, eyeing Jonas the same way they had eyed his brother, Jonathan, as better husband material than Edward. If so, they were doomed to disappointment, because thus far, Jonas had been doing an excellent job of keeping their relationship strictly business.

"We gotta good wind, Cap'n Irons," Cal called down to them. "If it holds steady, we oughta make Nassau by t'morrah night."

"If we don't reach it by nightfall tomorrow, we'll have to anchor outside the harbor until daybreak."

174

Kate grabbed onto Jonas to keep her balance as the dory suddenly tilted in the water.

"Be careful," he admonished, clamping one arm about her waist and holding her steady against him.

The unexpected contact with his body brought a hot flush to Kate's cheeks. Gazing into his eyes—those incredibly blue and piercing eyes!—Kate found it difficult to remember what she had been going to say next. "I . . . I don't want to negotiate the harbor entrance after dark," she stammered. "If we're not careful, we could miss it altogether."

"I doubt we'll have much of a problem. Where are your navigational instruments?" Jonas casually released her and glanced up at Cal. "You at least have a compass, don't you?"

Cal cut a wide grin and pointed upward. "Ah always use de sun, moon, and stars, Cap'n. But doan worry, ah'll git us t' Nassau."

"Either that or we may wind up in Cuba," Jonas muttered, this time without smiling.

They finished boarding the *Zephyr* and sailed all that day before a brisk wind, under sunny skies—Cal handling the tiller and Jonas expertly managing the sails to coax the most speed out of the heavy-laden vessel. Toward evening, the wind died down, nearly becalming them. There was nothing to do but sit and wait for it to pick up again. Mattie served cold food, then went astern to pass the time with Cal, leaving Kate alone with Jonas in the bow.

It was a beautiful evening. Dolphins played in the water beside the boat, and as usual, the colors were gorgeous—the ocean and sky a pure, brilliant turquoise, and the horizon streaked with pink, gold, and purple, as the sun slid downward into the sea. A sense of peace and tranquillity hung over the scene; the only sound was the gentle lapping of the waves against the hull.

Kate sat atop a barrel across from Jonas who

175

lounged on a crate, relaxed but alertly watching for the distant rippling of the ocean's flat surface that signaled the return of the wind.

"What are you thinking?" she asked, when he seemed loathe to break the silence.

He grinned lazily. "I guess I'm dreaming of our sleek, little ship, the *Phoenix*. Too bad we'll have to sell her in order to get money to continue. I'm going to hate traveling in this sorry excuse for a ship every time we have to go to Nassau."

Kate tilted her head to one side and regarded him with a teasing grin. "As I said before, if you don't like this one, you can always build us another."

He frowned and exhaled a long sigh. "It'll be a long while before I can spare the time to work on a ship for us, Kate. We need money—and men, not to mention navigational instruments. And the nicer the ships we want to build, the more money and men we need. How are we going to pay for brass trim? And canvas to make sails? I lie awake nights asking myself these questions."

"We'll find a way. There's always wrecking," she offered, gauging his reaction from beneath her lashes. "We may be able to salvage the brass and canvas we need."

He gave her a long, smoldering look. "You know how I feel about wrecking. If you and Edward insist on doing it, go ahead—but don't expect me to join you."

She drew up her knees and wrapped her arms around them. "Could you actually stand there and watch a ship go down, Jonas, without lifting a hand to save anything? It's a tragedy, of course, but there's no sense letting a valuable cargo go to waste."

"I'll help rescue the crew, but I won't raise a hand to take salvage off somebody else's ship," he stubbornly insisted. "I know how it feels to lose everything you own."

176

She sighed, wishing she hadn't raised the issue. "You talk as if we're *stealing*, and I resent that. We're just keeping the sea from claiming everything."

"Call it what you will . . . You don't return the goods to their rightful owners, so it amounts to the same thing."

"You're the only one who thinks so," she sniffed. "We risk life and limb to save what we do; we're entitled to compensation . . . and we have to pay duty on what we sell in Nassau. You already know that. So the government benefits, too."

"Let's abandon this subject, shall we?"

Jonas shifted his position so he was facing away from her. She could only see his profile, but his expression seemed morose as he stared over the darkening sea. She laid her head on her skirted knees and brooded—hating it that they continued to disagree on this issue. The silence stretched long and heavy between them. Finally, she couldn't stand it anymore.

"Won't you miss Salem while you're here in the Bahamas?" she blurted. "Perhaps you should post a letter home from Nassau, so your friends know where you are."

"I might do that," he agreed. "Only I doubt anyone will care where I am or why—except perhaps my creditors."

This struck her as a very harsh—and revealing—statement. "But surely there are people who worry about you, for your own sake, not just for the money you owe them."

He swung around to look at her. "No . . . Now that my brother's gone—assuming he's dead—there's no one. I was always too busy to cultivate close friendships in Salem. My oldest crew members were the nearest I had to friends, but now, they're dead, too. So I guess my best friend is Whiskers." He flashed another one of his self-deprecating grins. "I hope Daisy and Cassie take good care of him while we're gone. I'd hate to lose the one creature on earth who enjoys my company."

That cat isn't the only creature, Kate thought—no indeed, Captain Jonas Irons.

"You don't have any *female* friends?" she probed incredulously. "No one trying to entice you into marriage?"

"Entice *me?*" Amusement shone in his eyes. "Not that I know of. The husband hunters were all interested in my handsome, charming brother, not me. I'm thought to be too dull and surly to make a good husband. Jonathan, on the other hand, has—or had—women pining over him, bringing him presents, flowers, and pastries every time he went to sea. I suspect he had women in every port. Many were the dainty packets he received from abroad, smelling of jasmine or some other exotic scent. He used to laugh and toss the letters in the dustbin, usually without reading them. It was a sore point between us; I never could understand how he could be so heartless and still have women falling at his feet."

Kate swallowed hard and almost choked on her tongue. This wasn't *her* view of Jonathan; if anything, it was the exact opposite. Jonathan had managed to convince her that—before her—he'd had no interest in or experience with other women. He had sworn he was "dedicated only to the sea," until he met her . . .

"Your brother doesn't sound like a very nice person," she mumbled, her voice gone huskier than usual with shock. "Surely he wasn't as bad as the picture you're painting of him."

Jonas laughed. "Where women are concerned, he was worse! Salem is littered with the broken hearts of naive, young women who thought he was going to marry them just because he stole a few kisses. However"—he paused and abruptly sobered—"Jon-

178

athan was one hell of a fine brother. Generous, loyal, trustworthy, the best friend I ever had. Not a day goes by that I don't miss him. So perhaps you can understand my obsession with finding out exactly what happened to him—and why. If he died as a result of foul play, I want to know it and avenge his memory. I can't accept the fact that he's just another statistic on the long list of men and ships lost off the coast of the Bahamas . . ."

Kate averted her face, anxious that he not see how his words were affecting her. She had to stifle the urge to weep. She was losing Jonathan all over again, not the man himself, but the image she had created, and the wonderful memories she had clutched so closely to her bosom. Jonathan had probably never loved her at all! He had only mentioned the possibility of marriage because he felt confident she would never say yes or actually leave Conch Cay. Undoubtedly, he had only wanted the same thing Edward wanted—only he was more adept at getting past her defenses.

Tears welled in her eyes, but she held them back with a terrible effort of will. Gradually, anger submerged her grief and humiliation. Never again would she allow a man to get as close to her as Jonathan had done—oh, never again would she be so foolish and vulnerable as to believe anything a man claimed while he was busy trying to get her clothes off . . . Thank God he hadn't succeeded! She wouldn't so easily be taken in a second time . . . not by any man, particularly one with a handsome face. Jonas himself could take his blue eyes and his dazzling smile and . . . and find some other gullible female on whom to practice them!

This should put an end to wishing that he would look at her as a woman, instead of a partner. The *last* thing she wanted was to fall in love again, and certainly *not* with another man named Irons!

179

"You're so quiet. Have you gone to sleep on me, Kate?"

Kate looked up and was astounded to discover that it was almost dark. She could barely see Jonas. When she didn't answer, he continued in a dry, faintly mocking tone.

"I'm sorry if I've bored you, Miss Montgomery. If you didn't want to know about my personal life, you shouldn't have asked."

"You didn't bore me . . . I'm just sorry I pried into your affairs. Talking about your brother must be painful for you. It's painful for me to listen, and I never even knew him."

That, at least, wasn't a lie; she never really had known Jonathan Irons, not the Jonathan whom Jonas had just described.

"I'd better go light a lantern," she said, sliding down off the barrel. "It's gotten too dark to see properly."

The wind picked up again about midnight, and Cal and Jonas set their course by the stars. Kate stood for a long time in the bow, letting the welcome breezes whip her hair about her cheeks. She never did weep, but her throat grew raw from unshed tears. Toward dawn, she curled up beside Mattie on the spare canvas spread out to protect the salvage and fell asleep, not awakening until Jonas gently shook her shoulder.

"Kate . . ." he said urgently. "Wake up. You have to spell Cal at the tiller. He's dozing where he sits, and it takes two of us to sail this boat efficiently."

She awoke in an instant. "Oh, yes, of course . . ."

Anxious to get away from Jonas, she bolted for the stern. It was a brilliant, fresh morning—too beautiful to nurture gloom and despair. Determined to forget about Jonathan and Jonas, she focused on the lovely, dawning day. Off the port side, a huge green turtle was keeping pace with them, and to starboard, silvery flying fish eluded a diving, white-tailed tropic bird.

"Cal, I've come to give you a rest," she announced, seating herself beside the big black man. "Go lie down beside Mattie and sleep for a few hours."

Cal blinked and shook himself, like a dog coming out of a stupor. "Ah ain't tired, Miz Kate," he denied.

"Nonsense, you're exhausted . . . Go on. Captain Irons will make certain I don't get us lost." She took hold of the tiller and held it steady, as Cal had been doing.

"Thanks, Miz Kate . . . Might be ah could close mah eyes a bit aftah all."

Cal was asleep almost as soon as he lay down, and with him and Mattie lost in dreamland, Kate realized she was once again alone with Jonas. He gave her a cheery little salute and came to join her at the tiller.

"Perfect morning, isn't it?" he asked, lifting a foot onto the bench beside her and leaning forward on his raised knee. "I'm half tempted to go after that turtle over there. He'd make good eating, I bet."

"He would, but I don't think *he'd* like the prospect," Kate said. "If you're hungry, there's food left from yesterday."

"I'll wait 'til Mattie awakens; I'm not sure where she put it. Why don't you want me to kill that turtle? I could toss a rope over him, first, and . . ."

"Can't you just enjoy the morning, Captain Irons?" she snapped. "Must you spoil it with the grisly prospect of blood, gore, and a death struggle?"

"My, my . . . Out of sorts, this morning, aren't we? Guess I'll let the old boy live, after all . . . anything to make you smile again."

She ignored him for several moments, then curiosity got the better of her. "How do you know it's a boy?" she asked. "I've never been able to tell the

181

difference between boy and girl turtles."

He shaded his eyes with one hand and studied the turtle, gliding through the water in their wake. "He's too ugly to be a girl, that's how. I wonder how he attracts a mate. What girl turtle would look at him?"

"Maybe girl turtles are more interested in qualities other than his appearance . . ." Kate primly retorted. "You must admit he's an excellent swimmer. On land, he's probably awkward and ungainly, but in the water, he's completely at ease."

"You mean a girl turtle would like him because of his gracefulness in the water? Hah! Not bloody likely . . . I wonder if he's a good provider. Maybe that's the secret of his appeal; he brings home pearl necklaces and diamond ear bobs to his lady love."

"You have a very jaded view of women; we aren't all fortune seekers, you know. Men are the greedy ones, only they want sexual favors. They'll say or do anything to get a woman to do something she shouldn't."

"Now, who's jaded? You mean to say men are only interested in a woman's body, not her mind or her character?"

"A man professes to love a woman—may even ask her to marry him, but all he really wants is to bed her. You said yourself that your brother was like that."

"My brother, yes! But not me. I don't regard every woman I meet as a potential conquest. I have the greatest respect for women. I laud and revere them. I applaud their sensitivities . . . I . . ."

"Then why have you never married, if you love women so much? You can't love them as much as you say you do, since you've obviously shunned marriage."

Jonas flung his hands wide. "I haven't *shunned* marriage! I simply haven't yet found a woman who understands my dreams and goals in life. Women all want to control their men. They carry on like fishwives when they don't get their way, dictating to their husbands at every turn—or trying to, anyway. If I married, the first thing my wife would want is for me to leave the sea. She'd expect me to stay home all the time and entertain her. Never mind what makes *me* happy or satisfies my ambitions; she'd have all sorts of needs and demands to create upheaval and unhappiness in my life."

"*Some* women, maybe, but not *all* of them!" Infuriated by his unfair attitude, Kate thumped her chest with her clenched fist. "I, for example, am not at all like my mother, who's been criticizing my father ever since they were wed. Nothing he's ever done has been good enough for her. However, when *I* marry, instead of criticizing, I intend to support and help my husband. I'll put *his* interests before my own. That's what marriage is, or ought to be—a partnership where two people care more for each other than they do for themselves."

Kate and Jonas were now eye to eye, both so intent on winning the argument they had forgotten all about the turtle. Suddenly, Jonas started to laugh. He straightened, threw back his head, and guffawed.

"Look at us!" he bellowed. "We started out discussing a turtle and ended up debating issues that have plagued men and women and destroyed relationships since the dawn of time."

"I don't see what's so funny," Kate sputtered, though her own lips were starting to twitch. "You're just trying to change the subject because you know I'm right."

"Of course, you're right! We're both right! We've each seen a side of the opposite sex—and the same sex—that has soured us on love and fidelity. No wonder neither of us has ever married or *wants* to marry. You'll never find a man to live up to your ideals, Kate . . . nor will I find the perfect woman. It's impossible."

"I thought I'd found such a man once," Kate admitted. "But then I learned he wasn't what I'd been so sure he was."

"John Merrick broke your heart, did he?" Jonas's voice became surprisingly gentle, almost tender. He cupped her cheek in his warm, sun-browned hand, and his blue-eyed glance caressed her face. "Don't grieve too much, sweetheart . . . No man is really worth it. And whatever you do—don't let your family pressure you into marrying Edward. He'd only make you miserable."

"I'll *never* marry Edward," she said vehemently, and wished she could tell him about that other man, the one who had really broken her heart. His last name had been Irons, the same as Jonas's, not Merrick.

Jonas leaned closer and brushed his lips across hers, a sweet, gentle kiss meant to console, not arouse. She sat very still, resisting the feelings that swept through her as their mouths met. The hurt from finding out about Jonathan was still too raw, too new . . . and this man was Jonathan's brother. She already knew that Jonas was capable of arousing her passions the same as Jonathan had done. She couldn't risk losing her head—and her heart—a second time.

I've suffered too much for having lost them the first time, she warned herself.

Chapter Thirteen

The *Zephyr* reached Nassau too late at night to attempt entering Providence Channel, so Jonas lowered the sails and anchor, and he and Cal took turns standing watch while Kate and Mattie slept. They sailed into the fine, sheltered harbor shortly after sunrise, and by midmorning had tied up at the public docks beside Bay Street.

Jonas had been to Nassau many times, but he never failed to admire the quaint, picturesque, little town, which the Loyalists had vastly improved upon since the days when pirates and buccaneers roamed filthy, rat-infested streets. The Loyalists had built new streets, laid out in the old gridwork pattern, but now kept clean and free of debris. They had also constructed a new jail, workhouse, and roofed marketplace, as well as adding to the total number of charming houses and shops built of wood or whitewashed, coral limestone.

In town, thatched roofs were prohibited, and the English Georgian style of architecture predominated. Houses consisted of two or three stories, many with balconies or timber verandas enclosed by delicately designed wooden hand railings and louvered shutters called jalousies. High peaked roofs, dormer windows, decorative brackets, latticework, and distinctive stone corner pieces, called "quoins," characterized Nassau's homes and public buildings, many of which were overhung with hibiscus or bougainvillea. The air smelled of fish, cooking spices, and the tangy scent of the orange and lemon trees grown in hidden gardens.

Jonas was eager to start exploring the alleys and taverns in search of workers—and he also had a private matter to attend to while in Nassau. But first, he wanted to be certain that Kate was capable of disposing of the salvage by herself.

"Do you want me to stay here and help unload—or start looking for buyers?" he asked, as they walked toward Vendue House, where Kate had insisted they must go first.

"No, I've done this often before and usually by myself. Mister Pilkington at Vendue House will assess the value of the salvage, determine the amount of duty, and arrange for buyers. We have a long-standing relationship," Kate told him. "Later, I'll hire workers to do the unloading. Edward is always so eager to taste the pleasures of town life that he disappears as soon as we arrive."

"Then I'll stay with you," Jonas insisted, put off by the image of Kate doing all the work while Edward went off to play.

"No, really, you mustn't . . . Let's not waste time. Go ahead and find your workers. They may need several days to arrange their affairs before they can leave. Let's meet again at suppertime. I'll be staying with a family on Charlotte Street, across from the cemetery. Edward always found his own lodgings, but I'll see if my friends can accommodate you, as well as me. Mattie and Cal will probably sleep on the boat."

"I'm sure I can find my own lodgings," Jonas said. "Only I have no money."

Kate smiled at him, her beautiful, golden eyes

bright with amusement. "Then you see why we must meet at suppertime. Perhaps by then, if all goes well, I'll have a portion of the proceeds from the salvage and can give you some pocket money—and also funds to start purchasing supplies. In any case, you can stay with my friends—the Culpeppers. They're lovely people."

"Loyalists, I presume . . ."

"Of course."

"So why would they want to shelter a homeless, shipwrecked American?"

"Because I'll tell them you're my friend—and also my new business partner. However, it would be wise if you didn't mention that you were bound for Nassau when your ship went down off Conch Cay. They think little enough of Lord Dunmore as it is, without finding out that he's been encouraging American bottoms to trade here. The Culpeppers only approve of British bottoms using the port."

"I shall try not to make them angry, inasmuch as I'll be very hungry for supper by then."

"Good luck until this evening." She lifted her hand in farewell, and Jonas watched her a moment as she threaded her way through the street traffic toward Vendue House.

Her shining red-gold hair, tumbling free down her back, erect carriage, and unusual height made her stand out from the crowd, though she was as poorly dressed as any of the mulattoes and Negroes passing to and fro. Several well-dressed white women strolled by Jonas, and he wondered how Kate would look done up in the latest fashions, her hair piled high on her aristocratic head. Kate rarely wore a hat or bonnet, much less a spangled turban, such as one of the women sported. But then Kate seemed to have little interest in clothes, or perhaps, little money to buy them. All that would change once their ship-building venture proved successful. When it did,

Jonas promised himself, he would take her shopping in Nassau and make sure she bought herself some pretty gowns with slippers to match.

Chiding himself for standing there gazing after her like some love-struck schoolboy, Jonas pivoted on his heel and headed back down Bay Street. Before he began his search for carpenters and shipwrights, he intended to pay a visit to the little shop where Jonathan's watch had turned up so unexpectedly. The proprietor might remember it—and could tell him who had brought it in to sell. He hoped with all his heart that it hadn't been a red-haired, golden-eyed female . . .

He found the gem shop exactly where his friend, Captain Talbot Daniels, had said it would be, but the balding, potbellied proprietor, while recognizing the watch, denied remembering anything about it.

"Sorry, but I can't recall who first brought it in—man or woman. We handle a large volume of items in my shop, more than half of them retrieved by wreckers. Things often come in and go out again on the same day. I can't be bothered with keepin' records of every single transaction and who was involved in it."

"Perhaps Lord Dunmore would be interested in hearing of your lax record-keeping," Jonas threatened, hoping to jog the man's memory. "I imagine he'd want to make certain that duty has been properly paid on all your merchandise."

The fat little shopkeeper paled. "Now, don't go stirrin' up trouble, Captain . . . I'm tryin' to earn an honest living here. I haven't done anything wrong. I'll think about the watch a day or two and see if I can tell you anything then. Maybe it'll come to me who brought in the watch."

"Forget it." Jonas sighed, knowing the situation was hopeless. "I want the truth, not some story concocted to make me feel better."

Feeling disheartened, but also relieved, he left the shop. The worst thing would have been to hear that Kate had indeed brought the watch to the shop. The incident reminded him that he still couldn't trust Kate *not* to have been involved in his brother's shipwreck. He mustn't allow himself to become so charmed by her that he lost his initiative to discover the truth. Yet it was damn difficult to keep his hands off her when she so much resembled a ripe, fresh peach, waiting to be plucked from the branch and enjoyed to the fullest.

Turning up a side street, he trudged in the direction of a grog shop he remembered as being a haven for seamen. There, he might find a carpenter or shipwright for hire—or hear of someone available. Stepping aside as a black child skipped down the street, he almost ran into a man walking in the opposite direction. The fellow had his head down and wasn't looking where he was going.

"Watch yourself," Jonas barked. "Before you knock somebody down."

"Right . . . sorry, sir." The man looked up, his eyes widened, and he let out an excited yelp. "Glory be, sir! Is it really you? Why, I thought you was dead and drowned, Cap'n!"

Recognizing his voice, Jonas held the man at arm's length and took a closer look at his faintly familiar, beard-stubbled face. "I'll be damned! . . . Musket Jones. How in hell did you get here?"

Musket Jones had been Jonas's first mate, clean-shaven then, whom Jonas had thought dead along with the rest of his crew that fateful night of the shipwreck. Overcome with emotion, delighted to see the man alive again, he seized Musket by the lapels of his frayed seaman's jacket. "Where are the others? Are you the only survivor? How did you get here?" he demanded huskily.

"Hold on there, Cap'n . . . I kin only answer one

189

question at a time. Here, let's go get ourselves a mug o' rum an' trade stories. I jus' got paid fer unloadin' a boatload of cotton, so I'll see ya t' the first mug, but after that, yer on yer own."

They made their way to the groggery—the two of them grinning like idiots and periodically clapping each other on the back. When they got there, Musket gallantly stepped back and gestured toward the heavy wooden door, which stood open, propped by a large stone. "You first, Cap'n . . . An' when you get inside, take a good look around. Might be you'll find a few more surprises . . ."

"Surprises?" Jonas echoed, stepping through the doorway into the cool, dark interior of the limestone building.

As his eyes adjusted to the change from bright sunlight to shadow, he saw several empty wooden tables, and then a table where four men sat drinking from tin mugs. Excitement flared in his chest; he couldn't believe his eyes. The men at the table spotted him at almost the exact same moment. Chairs fell over as they leapt to their feet.

"By God!" Jonas breathed, when he recovered from the initial shock. "It's a bloody miracle . . . That's what it is."

Before him were four more of his long-lost crew members—alive and in the flesh!

"Pinch me, Donald, am I seein' a ghost?" one of them, Nimble Clayton, asked.

Nimble, a tall, stringy man with a prominent Adam's apple, had been Jonas's shipwright, as well as an excellent all-round seaman, unafraid to take to the shrouds, no matter what the weather—hence, his name, Nimble. Donald Fell, Jonas's helmsman, rushed forward and caught Jonas in a hearty hug. Bearlike in appearance, Donald sported a bristling copper beard, and bushy hair to match.

"Cap'n Irons! I never thought I'd lay eyes on you

190

again! Where've you been? We thought you was dead like everybody else off the *Liberty*, and we was the only ones who made it!"

Nimble, Donald, and the remaining two men, John Ferguson and Orville Hammet, surged around him—pumping his hand and exclaiming over his unexpected appearance, until Jonas protested.

"All right, everybody—sit down and tell me what happened. The last thing I remember was the ship breaking apart on the reef and myself being thrown into the water and sucked under. By then, I thought most of you were already overboard and gone. There wasn't time to lower a longboat. How did you escape that undertow?"

Big Donald Fell righted two chairs and gestured Jonas into one, then ordered more rum all around the table. "Hell, Cap'n, it happened like this . . ."

The five survivors then explained how each of them had managed to escape the foundering ship. All had been tossed into the sea, but Nimble found a large piece of timber and clung to it, kicking and paddling to keep himself from being dashed onto the reef along with the ship. Eventually, the four other men made it to the timber—first, Donald, whose superior strength stood him and Nimble in good stead, as they jointly propelled the timber farther out to sea and away from the treacherous reef and undertow.

Musket had been the second man to make it, and Orville the last, the first four having rescued him just as his strength gave out, and he would have drowned. For a full day and another night they clung to the timber and drifted in the sea, exhausted and half delerious, believing themselves doomed. Then they saw land—one of the other cays that made up the Abaco chain.

"Green Turtle Cay it was, Cap'n," Musket said. "An' we all pulled t'gether t' get there. Once we did, we met some wreckers who lived on the cay, and a few days later, they brought us t' Nassau."

"An' here we bin ever since, tryin' t' make enough money t' git home again, but so far without success," Donald grumbled in his deep bass voice. "Hell, we can't even hire out as seamen. There ain't that many American ships comin' through here yet, an' what there is don't need us. We sure as hell didn't want t' sign onto a British bottom, so we bin takin' whatever odd job comes along. There ain't many that pay good, 'cause the freedmen'll work for almost no-thin'."

"What about you, Cap'n?" John Ferguson asked.

John was the youngest of Jonas's crew, a likable, sandy-haired lad, who had sailed with Jonas for the last three years. John and Orville both, had been young and green when they came to him, little more than boys, but they had been willing and eager to learn. He was overjoyed to find them alive and well—and words couldn't describe how he felt to see Musket, Donald and Nimble. They were Jonas's three best, most reliable hands—friends of long-standing. Seeing them again was like discovering gold pieces where he least expected them.

"I somehow made it across the reef," Jonas explained. "Don't ask me how, because I haven't any idea. I thought I was going to die—almost did, in fact. A young woman found me washed up on the beach, like a dead mackeral. She and several others were out wrecking. We saved some of my cargo, and that's why I'm here—to sell it."

Silence greeted this statement, as all five men watched him in amazement, tinged with envy. From their expressions, he could tell, that to them it seemed as though he was the only one to land on his feet, still in charge, still a step above them, not really having suffered as much as they had, or the rest of the crew.

"What about that light?" Donald gruffly inquired.

"Did you find out what it was?"

"No," Jonas said. "The light remains a mystery. So does my brother's death. I've tried to find out what happened to the *Patriot*, but no one I've talked to so far seems to know."

"Pity, that . . ." said Musket Jones. "I'd give a lot t' git my hands on whoever put that light out there an' probably sunk your brother, too."

"So would I," Jonas agreed. "But let's talk of the future, not the dismal past. Now that I've found you, I have a business proposition to make to you gentlemen . . ."

Jonas outlined his plans, and by the time he was finished, all but Orville agreed to work for him on Conch Cay.

"Cap'n, I'm sorry," the young man apologized. "But I gotta go home . . . See, I left a little gal waitin' for me there, an' it'll take too long t' build all these ships you're talkin' about an' make some money. I don't want t' live the rest of my life on a little, bitty island. It's back t' Salem for me, sir, just as soon as I can earn enough money t' get there."

"I understand," Jonas said. "Though I can't say I'm not disappointed. I had intended to hire freedmen to do the work, but I prefer men whom I can trust, men who already know which end of a ship is the bow and which the stern. Why, with Nimble here in charge of the actual construction, I only need to find another plain carpenter to oversee the work of making boards and timbers."

"Sorry, Cap'n, but I jus' can't stay," Orville insisted.

"Ah, but you'll take letters back for the rest of us, won't you, lad?" asked Donald. "You can assure our families that we're safe, an' tell 'em we'll send back our wages as soon as we can."

Donald and Musket both had wives and children back in Salem, Jonas knew. Nimble did not, but he

193

had a sister who lived alone and took in washing to make ends meet.

"You better tell Emmaline where I am, too," Nimble urged Orville. "She'll be frantic when the *Liberty* don't return, and word gets out that we sank off the Abacos."

"I'll give you letters for my creditors," Jonas added. "They'll have to sell the ships I have in dry dock undergoing repairs, in order to collect the money I owe them. I won't be able to pay my bills for a long, long time."

"Damn shame, Cap'n," Donald muttered. "Seems you've lost plenty, too, haven't you? But at least, you got this chance t' make a new beginning."

"It's a chance for all of us to make a new beginning," Jonas assured him. "Now, let's drink to our first ship, the *Phoenix!*"

While Jonas was toasting his first ship and Kate making arrangements to sell the salvage from the *Liberty*, Edward, Bell, and Sybil sat on the front veranda of the Montgomery house on Conch Cay and plotted how they might protect themselves from the interloper who had washed up on their beach. William was upstairs, sleeping off the effects of too much rum shared with Edward at the noon meal, and Daisy and Cassie were out in the cook shed cleaning up the remnants of the meal.

"Miss Sybil, we gotta do somethin'," Edward was saying. "It ain't right that Kate went off alone t' Nassau with that Irons fellah. She's supposed t' be marryin' me, but here she is, cookin' up deals with that damn American an' spendin' all the money we made from wreckin' on a cockeyed scheme t' build ships."

"Doan upset Miz Sybil," Bell cautioned. "She's doin' right fine t'day, takin' her meals in the dinin' room with you and de massah . . . Ah doan want her upset, y'hear?''

In point of fact, Bell had made certain that Sybil had come downstairs today, just so that Edward could talk to her and ply her fears. Neither Bell nor Edward liked the way things were going—what with this new project that meant Captain Irons would be staying on the island, and also meant that everyone would be busy building ships, now, instead of planting cotton or raking salt, activities that in the end, better served their own best interests.

Edward and Bell both agreed; Sybil must be made to understand what was happening and furthermore, consent to their plans. They dared not proceed without the tacit approval of someone in authority, even if that authority had eroded over the years.

"But what can we do?'' Sybil asked plaintively, fanning herself with a palmetto fan. "I had Bell put a charm under Kate's mattress—a little sack of sweet-smelling herbs, wasn't it, Bell? It was supposed to soften Kate's heart toward you, Edward, but nothing's happened that I can see. There's been no effect on her . . . As for the shipbuilding, I can hardly stop that. Neither Kate nor William consult me about anything.''

Edward poked an accusing finger at Sybil. "Hell, Miss Sybil, you can tell Will t' tell Kate she's gotta marry me, whether her heart's softened up or not! We gotta stop this nonsense about formin' a partnership. It's time Kate quit lookin' at other men an' realized what's best fer her an' everybody else on Conch Cay. Marryin' *me* is what she oughta do, an' as soon as possible.''

Sybil paused in fanning herself and gave Edward her full attention. "I agree, dear Edward. Why, you're the only one in the whole world I trust to take care of all of us here on Conch Cay. You'd *never* take Kate away from us, and if you and Kate started working

195

together, instead of arguing all the time, I *know* you could make us all rich and happy. The problem is how to make Kate fall in love with you. I fear you've put her off, Edward. Despite the love charm, she doesn't seem to recognize your excellent qualities."

Edward glowered and rose from his chair. "It's true I ain't a fine gentleman, like your husband, Miss Sybil, but I know how t' treat women of quality, like you an' yer daughter. I wouldn't beat her or nothin'. And once we got rich, I'd buy her whatever she wanted. What more does a man haveta do?"

He ran one hand through his shaggy blond hair. "If she'd ever let me git close enough, I know I could . . . *satisfy* her, if ya know whut I mean." He darted a sidelong glance at Sybil, testing her reaction. "I got me a little experience with women, Miss Sybil. A man's got his needs, ya know. I kin be real tender an' gentle when I wanna be; I'd never hurt her. Then, after we got t'gether, maybe she'd see that I'm the only man fer her."

Sybil Montgomery didn't seem in the least shocked by these revelations, nor disapproving. "Yes . . ." she said, languidly waving the fan. "It's true . . . Once a woman develops a carnal taste for a man, she'll go anywhere with him, do anything he asks. Is that what you're saying, Edward? That if you could just— *convince*—Kate, in your own way, *then* she'd be willing to marry you?"

"You bet she would!" Edward boasted. "But she won't even let me kiss her! I've tried, and all she does is fight me."

"Maybe what she needs is somethin' stronger than a love charm, Miz Sybil," Bell said slyly, pouncing upon the opportunity she had been awaiting.

"Why, what could that be, Bell? You told me before that all we had to do was put that charm under her mattress. I suggested either a potion *or* a charm. And you said we should try the charm, first. Is a potion stronger?"

Lowering her eyes, Bell smiled in a coy, secretive way. The hook had been taken; now all she needed to do was reel in the fish—and while she was doing it, she'd get the most out of Sybil that she possibly could.

"Yes'm, Miz Sybil . . . a potion is lots stronger. But ah gots t' go over t' Big Abaco jus' t' git de ingredients. Dat's why ah didn't suggest it in de fust place. An' ah gots t' trade somepin' valuable t' a slave girl ovah dere, b'for ah gits all ah needs. An ah ain't got nothin' t' trade."

"Well, I could come up with something . . . a few hairpins, perhaps, or some bright bits of ribbon and lace."

"More valuable den dat," Bell scoffed. "Dis gal likes pretty things—an' more t' eat den jus' guinea corn. Ah'm gonna have t' pay dear t' git whut ah needs."

"Flour? Sugar? Molasses? Edward will give you whatever's necessary . . . Plus I've got a small cameo broach she might fancy."

"Yes'm. Dat might do it," Bell bargained. "But it's also gonna tek a jug o' de massah's rum . . . No, make dat *two* jugs," she added, seeing Edward hold up two fingers out of Miz Sybil's line of vision.

One jug would go to Edward and one to Ole Gilbert, Bell's nearly useless husband, for whom she'd developed a grudging affection over all the years they'd shared a bed. She smiled to herself, imagining her and Gilbert drinking rum under the sheets together in the dark of night. The rum would make Ole Gilbert mighty randy, the way he'd been as a young man, able to satisfy all her cravings and then some.

"This potion . . ." Sybil said worriedly, wrinkling her brow. "It's safe, isn't it? It won't harm Kate in any way, will it?"

197

"No, m'am," Bell hastened to assure her. "All it'll do is give her a powerful itch . . . and de fust man she sees aftah she drinks it is gonna be de lucky one who'll get t' do de scratchin'."

Bell winked at Edward who grinned and clamped a hand over his crotch.

"But what if she sees someone other than Edward?" Sybil clutched Bell's arm, her voice rising in panic. "What will happen then?"

"Doan you worry none, Miz Sybil. Dat ain't gonna happen . . . Y'all jus' leave everythin' t' Edward an' me. We'll make certain de man is Edward. An' aftah de deed is done, Miz Kate ain't gonna be able t' fergit all de pleasure she done had. Why, she'll be *beggin* t' marry Edward."

"Oh, I hope so!" Sybil cried. "Just remember to be gentle, Edward. A woman doesn't like a man to be too rough with her."

"Oh, I'll be gentle . . . I promise."

Edward turned away a moment to adjust his breeches, which were, Bell saw, bulging in anticipation. "Now, if ya excuse me, Miss Sybil," he said. "I jus' remembered somethin' I gotta tell Cassie."

As Edward left the veranda, Bell wondered if he'd be gentle with Cassie. She didn't think so—but then, Cassie was not her problem. Cassie herself would have to come to her, pleading for relief from Edward's unwanted attentions, before Bell would do anything to help the girl. Unless forced to take matters into her own hands right from the start, as in the case of Edward and Kate, a good Obeah woman waited for potential clients to recognize that they had a problem and come to *her*. Of course, it didn't hurt to help create the problem, in the first place.

Chapter Fourteen

One week to the day after they arrived in Nassau, Kate and Jonas were ready to return to Conch Cay. They did so loaded down with tools, chains, and other necessary paraphernalia, plus the four former crew members Jonas had hired, two black freedmen he had found, one of whom had carpentry experience, and several barrels of precious flour and other items Mattie needed at the cook shed, in order to be able to feed so many people.

As each new person boarded the *Zephyr*, Mattie privately took his measure, deciding in an instant whether she liked the man or not. To her delight, she liked all of the men Jonas had hired—but then, she very much liked Jonas himself. She and Cal had decided on first meeting Jonas, that he was the perfect man for Miz Kate to marry.

True, he was sometimes gruff and bossy, and he could look as stern and forbidding as a church preacher or a slave-catcher. But a lesser man—a softer-spoken, more polite man—wouldn't have been *enough* of a man to win the respect of their fiery Miz Kate. Given time, Kate and Jonas would surely discover for themselves just how well matched they were. Mattie believed it was destiny—pure destiny— that had brought Cap'n Irons to Conch Cay just in

199

time to prevent Kate from succumbing to family pressure and marrying Edward.

However, Mattie continued to worry about the fact that Jonas might one day learn about his brother. Reluctantly, she conceded that it wasn't *her* place to tell him, after all. If anyone should tell him, it was Miz Kate, and as soon as a private moment again presented itself, Mattie intended to keep urging the young woman to do so, before Jonas found out on his own. Now that Jonas was definitely going to be staying at Conch Cay, he *must* be told; someone was bound to talk sometime, and if Jonas heard it from anyone else, he'd be furious with Miz Kate and probably never marry her.

The journey home seemed to take no time at all. Mattie happily fed the boat's occupants and spent time sitting beside Cal, watching the sea's colors change as the boat sped over sandbars, deeply submerged reefs, and the dark valleys between them. Soon, the journey was over, the boat unloaded, and she was back in the cook shed again, while Cal and Benjamin sailed the *Zephyr* around to the leeward side of the cay to check on the progress of the hut-building and to anchor in the shelter of the little cove where the boat was kept.

Mattie knew that the huts were supposed to be a surprise for Captain Irons, and she dearly hoped that he'd be so impressed by Kate's initiative that he'd hug and kiss her. Romance would finally blossom between the two, and everything would happen just as Mattie and Cal had discussed it in low whispers in the night, wrapped in each other's arms. In one stroke, Kate would gain the husband she needed and deserved, and they themselves would be rid of Edward, the hated overseer who made their lives— and everyone else's—so miserable. Cap'n Irons would never put up with a troublesome lout like

Edward—not when Edward had once had his own plans for Miz Kate's future.

On the morning after their return to Conch Cay, Mattie was quietly stirring a kettle of fish chowder, when she chanced to hear voices whispering outside the cook shed. It should have been silent as a tomb near the house at this hour. Cap'n Irons, Miz Kate, the other workers, and all the men from Nassau had already set out for the beach on the other side of the cay. Daisy and Cassie had gone off to the pond to do laundry, and it was still too early for Miz Sybil or Massah William to be out of bed, which meant that neither Edward nor Bell had any excuse for being nearby.

Wiping her hands on her faded apron, Mattie stuck her head out of the door to see what was happening. There was no one outside, but she glimpsed Edward and Bell standing near an open window of the house. They were in the back hallway, through which one passed on the way out to the cook shed.

Mattie couldn't hear what they were saying, but their low voices and intent expressions aroused her suspicions. What could they be discussing? Edward had no authority over Bell; Bell answered only to Miz Sybil. Why wasn't Bell at home, as she usually was in the morning, working on the charms, spells, and potions for which she had gained a reputation of respect and fear among the island Negroes and even beyond?

Mattie thinned her lips in disgust and disapproval. No good could come from a whispered conversation between Bell and Edward. Everyone knew that Edward opposed the shipbuilding project; he hadn't been too happy about Miz Kate's orders that everyone had to work on the huts while she was gone, either. From all accounts, Edward had been particularly

201

nasty during their absence; one afternoon, he had called Cassie from the cook shed, taken her down to her hut, and there used her brutally, right in front of her small children.

The next day, Cassie had two swollen eyes and a cut lip, which Edward had told her better be healed before Miz Kate came home—or else Cassie must think up a good excuse for how she'd gotten them. Massah William, drunk on rum or brandy every night, never knew a thing about the incident—or would have cared, if he had known. Edward had been spending a great deal of time in Massah William's company lately, and once, he'd sat on the veranda talking with Miz Sybil. That was the same day he'd been so terrible to poor Cassie.

Swept with unease, Mattie slipped around the side of the cook shed and tiptoed nearer to the window, pressing herself against the wall of the house, where they couldn't see her unless they leaned out and turned their heads in her direction. Their voices were clearer, now, and she could hear every word they were saying.

For several moments, she stood there listening, and her mouth dropped open in shock. Lord have mercy! Edward and Bell were two wicked, evil creatures! Mattie had never in her life heard such a vile, horrible plot—and the worst of it was, they would surely get away with it, if she and Cal didn't do something to stop it. But, what? Slaves didn't go around making accusations against white men; Kate might believe Mattie, but what about Massah William and Miz Sybil? No, those two would believe Edward and Bell, who'd deny everything and see that Mattie and Cal were severely punished, perhaps even sold.

Shaking with fear, dreading the consequences should she be discovered, Mattie stayed plastered to the wall of the house until Bell and Edward parted, then she dashed back to the cook shed as fast as she could run, arriving there bare seconds before Edward himself barged through the doorway.

"Fix me a basket of food, Mattie," Edward ordered without preamble. "An' fetch a bottle of Will's good wine outa the cellar—you know, one of those he don't take out unless it's Christmas or some other holiday."

Mattie mustered all her courage and self-control to pretend she didn't know why he wanted these things. "Whut you gonna do, Massah Edward—have yurself a picnic?" she inquired breathlessly.

"Yeah, a picnic . . ." He grinned unpleasantly. "Gonna be a full moon t'night, a perfect night fer a picnic on the beach. But don't you tell nobody . . . Jus' put the basket where I can find it later on—right there on the table, with a cover over it. Oh, an' I want a nice green coconut . . . The kind Miss Kate is fond of. Put that an' a big knife inside the basket, too."

"Miz Kate know about dis picnic?" Mattie croaked, trying to sound as if *she* didn't know all the details— or the purpose—of the picnic, and especially the nice green coconut.

Edward stopped grinning. "That ain't yer concern. I'll invite her when I'm good and ready. Whatsa matter? Don't you think she'll come? I bet you think she's too good to picnic on the beach with ole Edward when the moon is full."

Mattie tried but couldn't quite stop herself from agreeing with that assessment. "Only time I know Miz Kate t' go out alone on de beach wif you, Massah Edward, is when she's spectin' a wreck t' happen. An' it don't look like no storm'll be a-blowin' in t' night."

"She'll come," Edward growled. "She *likes* bein' alone with me. Miss Kate's gonna marry me—an' when she does, the first thing I'm gonna do, is git rid of you an' yer uppity husband."

Clamping her mouth shut, afraid she'd already said more than she should have, Mattie lowered her eyes and attempted to look servile. "Yes, sir, Massah Edward . . . Ah'll have the basket ready jus' like you done tol' me."

"Good, you better. I'm still overseer around here, and if you don't jump when I say so, yer gonna live t' regret it."

After Edward had gone, Mattie leaned her hands on the worktable, the better to still their trembling. She *had* to think of a way to foil Edward's and Bell's evil plans. There must be something she could do— without getting herself and Cal in trouble. She raised her eyes to the ceiling, seeking inspiration and guidance from a higher power . . . and that was when she saw the dried herbs dangling from the rafters.

Bell was the acknowledged expert on Conch Cay, but she wasn't the only one who knew a thing or two about herbs; Mattie used them to enhance her cooking, and she knew the ingredients of many of the teas and nostrums Bell concocted to dose Miz Sybil and the workers when illness plagued them. She could never devise an antidote to Bell's love potion, of course, but maybe she could find a way to dull Edward's lustful ardor, at least temporarily, without him knowing it . . . and maybe, if she thought hard enough, she could even manage to figure out a way to get Miz Kate and Cap'n Irons alone together on that moonlit beach . . .

Jonas couldn't keep the grin off his face as he surveyed the site where he intended to build his first ship. Three sturdy huts now stood in a copse of palm trees—well back from the sea and the area where the ship's cradle would stand, but close enough that weary men wouldn't have to walk too far to find rest and shelter. Turning to the golden-eyed young woman beside him, he laughed and shook his head.

"You're full of surprises, aren't you, Miss Montgomery?"

"If you knew me better, you wouldn't be at all surprised," she retorted saucily. "I don't believe in doing anything by half measure; once I commit myself, I jump in with both feet and give everything I have."

"So I see . . ." Jonas said, wondering what it would be like to make love to a woman who gave nothing in half measure. In a desperate effort to distract himself from the tantalizing thought, he strode forward across the sand. "Do you mind if I inspect the huts? How did you decide that three was an appropriate number? I'd have been more than satisfied with one to keep the rain off our heads."

Kate had to break into a run to keep up with him. As she did so, she lifted her skirt, affording him a delightful view of a well-turned ankle—a view that further eroded his aplomb. "One for my people, one for yours, and one for you alone . . ." she chattered. "The boss should always have his own quarters, just as a captain on a ship has his own cabin. The huts are quite modest, I regret to say. As yet, they don't even have doors . . . and one still lacks part of the roof. There wasn't enough time to finish the thatching."

Jonas kept going until he reached the huts—two of which were fairly large. The third was smaller, and stood off by itself; it was just big enough for one person—or two, if they were friendly.

"I take it you'll be returning each night to the house," he said, stooping slightly to enter the smallest hut. "I don't see separate bedchambers in here."

205

"Oh, that doorway isn't high enough for you, is it?" Pointedly ignoring his jibe about the bed-chambers, Kate entered beside him. "I'll ask Benjamin to fix it; it won't be any trouble. I'd hate to have you banging your head against the doorjamb some dark, rainy night when you're coming or going."

Peering into corners, Jonas moved awkwardly about the hut. There was nothing to see inside the empty structure, but it was pleasantly cool, dark, and shadowy after the bright sunlight outside. Flaring his nostrils, Jonas was certain he could smell the sweet, clean scent of Kate's wind-blown hair. Feigning concentration, he pretended to inspect the workmanship of the hut. Four stout saplings formed the corners, and other timbers had been lashed together to support the roof. The walls were a whitewashed daub and wattle, and the whole was covered over with thatched palms. A good storm could blow the whole thing down, Jonas suspected, but the hut would serve admirably until he could build the wooden house and office he envisioned having for himself.

"If you do decide to sleep over one night, I suppose I could always bunk in with my men," he speculated. "Unless you'd trust me enough to let me hang a blanket down the center of this hut to make a wall."

She lifted her chin, responding finally to his teasing. "I can't imagine *any* reason why I'd want to spend the night here with you, Captain . . ."

"Jonas," he breezily corrected, wanting to hear the sound of his first name on her lips. "I thought we were past the formality of using our last names to address each other."

"Jonas, then . . . No, I'll go home every night and sleep in my own soft bed, thank you, which reminds me . . . I'll have to see about having pallets or sleeping mats made up for your men. You can have a bed from the house, but the others will have to make do with something more modest."

"A mat or pallet will be fine for me, also, Kate . . . I don't need anything fancy. This hut itself is a luxury—more than I expected on such short notice. How can I repay you for all you've done to get this project underway as soon as possible?"

She smiled radiantly. Sunlight filtering through the thatching dappled her lovely face, causing the breath to catch in his throat. "Start building our ship tomorrow!" she cried. "That's what I want you to do. Better yet, start building it today!"

Her enthusiasm ignited a fire deep in the pit of his belly. Lord, but she was a beauty! He wanted to grab her and press his mouth down upon hers, then grind his pelvis into her soft belly. Each day, it was becoming more difficult to keep his distance. Each day, she seemed to give him more reason for abandoning his reserve and allowing raw instinct to take over. Did she realize how enticing she was, standing there in her plain, faded clothing, with her bare feet peeking out from beneath her skirt, and her hair tumbling wildly down her back?

"Kate," he rasped, barely able to keep himself from reaching for her.

Something in his tone startled or alarmed her. She colored and stepped backward slightly. "Come outside, Jonas, and I'll show you where the cooking will be done. I've also had a necessary pit dug farther back in the woods. It's for—waste," she informed him, reddening even more.

"I know what a necessary pit is for," he mocked.

Taking a deep, steadying breath, Jonas removed himself from the tempting confines of the little hut. Kate followed close at his heels, so that he almost ran into her when, safe in the glare of the sun, he spun

207

back to face her. "What about the women? Will you let the wives of your workers come to visit and spend the night here at the project?"

"Oh, no! They'll come and go when I do. Any man who wants to sleep the night at home has only to ask permission, and I—or you—can grant it. I'll be coming every day, of course, and Mattie, Daisy, or Cassie will be accompanying me."

Jonas frowned. "It might not be a good idea to permit the women to spend much time here. They'll only divert the men from their work—and may cause other problems, as well. As a sea captain, I've found that men get along much better together and work harder, if there isn't a woman in seeing, hearing, or smelling distance."

Kate regarded him soberly, her clear, honey-colored eyes unwavering. "Does that include me, too, Jonas? If it does, I must tell you that I don't care a fig for what the men may be thinking. They will just have to get used to me—and unless they want to do their own cooking, they'll conduct themselves like perfect gentlemen around whatever females I bring with me."

"I wasn't suggesting that you never come near the place," Jonas began tactfully. "But I do think that you . . ."

"I intend to help build this ship!" Kate interrupted. "I plan to work side by side with you and the men. If anyone has a problem with that, they had better resign themselves to my presence; that includes you, Jonas. All of my money—and my hopes and dreams—are going into this venture, and I'll work as hard as any of you, if not harder, because I have the most to lose if it fails."

"You do? And just what will you be losing, if I may be so bold to ask? You'll still have a home, an island, and a family—not to mention a would-be husband.

I'm the one who'll be left with nothing. So if I say I don't want women here because women cause problems, then I damn well don't want women here! And *that* includes *you!*"

Drawing herself up like a spitting cat—like Whiskers confronted by a large lizard outside the house—Kate glared at Jonas with fury in her magnificent eyes and a red stain creeping up her aristocratic cheekbones. "I can't believe we're having this distasteful conversation!" she spat. "Here, I surprised you with these wonderful huts, and instead of thanking me, you insult and provoke me beyond endurance. May I remind you that this is *my* island, my trees, my money that bought all the tools and supplies, and hired these men."

"The island's *not* yours, it's your father's. Unless he's already deeded everything to you, before his death. Likewise the trees, the slaves, and the huts they've built. As for the money . . . ah, that we can dispute. May I remind *you* that you got it selling the salvage from *my* ship. So in actuality, it's really *my* money."

"Oh, you are unbelievable!" she cried. "And despicable!" Her eyes sparkled with a combination of anger, indignation, and unshed tears.

Glancing past her, Jonas saw that their raised voices had attracted the attention of the men unloading supplies from the *Zephyr*. Immediately, he grew embarrassed and chagrined. He found it difficult to remember how the argument had started. Of course, Kate had the right to spend as much time here as she wanted; she was his partner, wasn't she? He had agreed to that. He just hadn't foreseen all of the complications of that relationship.

"I guess I am," he conceded sheepishly.

"You guess you're what?" she demanded, her tone laced with suspicion.

"I guess I'm unbelievable . . ." he repeated patiently. "I can't believe me, either—standing here fighting with you. Only a moment ago I was thinking myself the luckiest man on earth to have you for a partner."

"You *are* lucky to have me as a partner—and I'm lucky to have you. Neither of us could do this without the other. And I don't think you should forget that ever again."

"I won't," he assured her. "Do you forgive me?"

She flashed him a tiny, reluctant smile. "I suppose so . . ." It was like the sun reappearing from behind a dark cloud bank. In that moment, he would have done anything to keep her smiling.

"There's going to be a full moon, tonight, which means we can work late," he placated.

"I'll help," she promised.

"Not at night!" he started to argue, then stopped and grinned ruefully. "If you do, I insist upon seeing you home safely, since you refuse to stay in my little hut with me."

She tossed her red mane, half coquette, half exuberant, high-spirited filly. "Well, maybe I won't help tonight. This particular evening, I may be busy."

They stood eyeing each other, both aware that every word they spoke was a kind of challenge. Advance and retreat. Invite and discourage. It was a sort of dance—a mating dance, Jonas realized with sudden sharp insight. We're as drawn to each other as a hen and a cock, a bull and a cow.

Their meeting and mating suddenly seemed inevitable, written in the stars, or some other such silly, romantic notion. He sensed that she felt it, too—the explosive tension. The scintillating vibrations. Any moment, he expected lightning to shatter the air between them.

210

"Shall we get to work then, Kate?" he dryly inquired.

"By all means, Jonas. I'm ready when you are."

He led the way back to his men, all the while asking himself if she meant more by her last comment than her expression suggested. He hoped she *would* work late that night; seeing her safely home might prove to be a richly rewarding experience.

Chapter Fifteen

Kate debated whether or not to work late that night all through the afternoon. When Cassie served her a bowl of fish chowder that Mattie had sent for supper by way of Fish in the dory, she still had not made up her mind.

"Miz Kate, ah gotta talk t' you privatelike," Cassie whispered as she pressed the wooden bowl of savory-smelling fish chowder into Kate's hands.

"What about, Cassie? Mmmmm . . . this looks wonderful. Don't let me forget to thank Mattie for preparing such a fine meal for our first work night. Maybe by tomorrow, we'll be ready to do the cooking right here."

Kate sat down cross-legged in the sand to eat, while Cassie hovered anxiously nearby. "Ah cain't say right in front of evahbody," the girl murmured. "Please, can we walk down the beach a little ways?"

Having just settled herself, Kate was loath to rise again. "Wait until I'm finished eating, Cassie, and you're done serving. Then we'll find someplace quiet to talk."

"Yes'm, Miz Kate." Cassie moved on to the next person, who happened to be Jonas.

Jonas took his bowl of soup from her and joined

Kate on the sand. "What was that all about?" he asked, nodding in Cassie's direction. "The girl looks upset."

"I've no idea," Kate blew on the soup to cool it before she ate. "She wants to talk to me about something, but didn't say what was wrong. Don't let Cassie's problems spoil your appetite; go ahead and eat. Cassie's prone to building every little difficulty into a major crisis. Whatever it is, I'll find out soon enough."

They sat eating in companionable silence. Jonas seemed as starved as she was, and Kate swallowed the last mouthful with a long sigh. "I hope there's enough for seconds. Mattie makes fish chowder every bit as well as she does conch; I can't get enough of it."

"It's delicious," Jonas agreed. "Here . . ." He reached for her bowl. "Let me fetch you another."

"No, that's all right, I'll get it . . ." She took his bowl from him, instead. "I might as well find out what's wrong with Cassie. She's finished serving the others. Wait, here."

She smiled at Jonas as she rose to her feet. How handsome and muscular he was, lounging indolently in the sand! Sometime during the afternoon, he had removed his shirt, revealing the darkly tanned torso she had first admired when he swam in the pond. During the afternoon, she had had ample time to view not only his torso but the faint remnants of the bluish-purple bruises he had sustained from the shipwreck. They ought to have faded completely by now; that they hadn't was proof of the severity of the injuries he had suffered.

Fortunately, his brush with death had in no way impeded his ability to work. He could wield an ax as well as Cal and Donald. Jonas had wielded it for hours at a time today, moving with a rhythmical grace that struck a deep chord within her. Watching

214

him fell trees was like watching a beautiful animal—Neptune, perhaps—stretching his muscles as he galloped along the beach. Like Neptune's, Jonas's movements were a joy to behold, and after each tree had fallen, he had let out a boyish whoop of triumph. His excitement and energy rubbed off on all of them, so that everyone was inspired to work to their utmost.

"Wait here . . ." she repeated, almost tenderly. "I'll be right back."

"Don't worry. I'll wait." Jonas's blue eyes lazily caressed her face, but with an intensity that made the blood rush to her cheeks and her heart pound in her chest. Unnerved by her own reactions, she rushed quickly away.

Kate found Cassie near the small cookfire they had built to reheat Mattie's soup. Cassie was setting the big iron pot back on the embers to keep it warm, in case someone wanted more later. When Kate tapped her on the shoulder, she jumped like a frightened rabbit, her round face startled and etched with fear.

"Oh, Miz Kate, it's jus' you!" she panted, relaxing a bit. "You done me a turn, tappin' my shoulder like dat."

"Are you all right, Cassie?" Kate studied the girl more closely. Cassie's eyes seemed puffy and swollen; somehow, she had split her lower lip—but nobody had mentioned anything about Cassie getting hurt while Kate had been in Nassau. "What did you do to your face? You look like you've been in a fight."

"Oh, it's nothin', Miz Kate—nothin' a-tall. Ah stubbed mah toe one night an' fell down an cut mah lip, dat's all. Why, it don't even hurt anymore. Bell give me a salve t' put on it, an' it was better by de very next mornin'."

"So what did you want to see me about, Cassie?"

"Well, Miz Kate . . . it's . . . um, Massah Edward. B'fore ah left de house wif Fish t' bring de chowder,

Massah Edward done give me a message t' tell ya. He said he has t' see y'all about somethin' mighty important, an' he wants ya t' meet him on de beach t'night, about an hour aftah sunset at de place where you an' him always watch fer shipwrecks."

"He wants me to meet him on the beach!" Kate exclaimed. "Whatever for? Did he tell you the reason?"

"No, Miz Kate." Cassie shook her turbaned head and twisted the corner of her apron in her dark hands. "He jus' said I wuz t' tell ya dat it's real important an' not somepin' he kin talk about up at de house . . . Dat's why you gotta meet him on de beach."

Kate clucked her tongue with impatience. Why tonight, of all nights, did Edward have to make such a strange request? And whatever did he want to talk about? Speculating, she narrowed her eyes; maybe he just wanted to get her alone with him again, so he could continue to press his unwelcome suit.

"I won't go," she said aloud. "Edward can say whatever he wants to say in daylight, in front of others. This is just another one of his transparent schemes to convince me to marry him."

"Ya gotta go, Miz Kate!" Cassie quavered, hiccuping on what sounded like a huge sob. "'Cause if ya don't, if ah cain't convince ya, Edward says he's gonna . . . he's gonna . . ."

"He's going to what?"

"Oh, Miz Kate, ah cain't tell! Please doan make me tell!"

"Did he threaten to beat you?"

Cassie's terrified silence answered the question. Kate jerked as if she herself had been struck, which indeed, she felt she had been. Horrified, she stared at the girl. "He said he'd beat you, didn't he? He threatened you with bodily harm."

Two big tears dripped down Cassie's cheeks.

216

"Massah Edward, he . . . he ain't always such bad a man, Miz Kate, but . . . but when he git mad, when we don't do whut he say, he git back at us somehow . . . Oh, ah shouldn't even be tellin' you dis. But ah couldn't think of no reason t' convince ya t' go. Ah knows ya'll doan like Massah Edward half as much as he likes you."

"His behavior is outrageous!" Kate sputtered, stalking up and down the sand in her agitation. "As usual, he's gone too far and must be put in his place."

"Den y'all gonna go t'night, Miz Kate?" Cassie gushed hopefully. "But please doan tell 'im ah tol' you he wuz gonna beat me, 'cause den he gonna beat me fer sure. Ah never said nothin' like dat, now did I?"

Kate stopped pacing and laid a comforting hand on the girl's shoulder. "Don't worry any more about Edward, Cassie, because he isn't going to touch a single hair on your head. I'll handle this matter. I'm just glad you finally told me the truth about Edward. It's what I've suspected all along."

"Miz Kate!" Cassie wailed. "Massah Edward gonna say ah lied. He gonna say he would nevah beat or hurt me, an' yore Papa an' Mama are gonna b'lieve 'im, jus' like dey always do. Den ah's gonna get in terrible trouble!"

"The *first* thing I'm going to do is talk to my father," Kate informed the girl. "Once and for all, we're going to settle this matter of Edward's ambition and his awful brutality. Papa's going to see what a bully Edward truly is. I said not to worry, Cassie. Leave everything to me. Now, dry your eyes, and let's get this supper mess cleaned up. We'll be leaving shortly in the dory."

Forgetting that she had promised to fetch another bowl of soup for Jonas, Kate handed the bowls to Cassie and stalked off to find Fish. In less than twenty

217

minutes, she was prepared to depart with Fish and Cassie. Brooding on her fury, she never thought to say goodbye to Jonas, until he confronted her on the way to the dory, her arms filled with pots and cooking utensils brought earlier from the house.

"Where are you going?" he demanded, glowering at her. "Have I offended you in some way—or are you always this rude to people?"

"Oh, Jonas, I'm sorry! I really am . . . It's just that a problem has come up at home, and I must leave immediately."

His fierce expression softened. "Can I help with anything? I'll go with you, if you like."

"No, it—it's just a . . . a . . . domestic matter, but something I must deal with right away. I'll see you tomorrow . . ." She hurriedly stepped past him on her way to the dory.

Cal came up beside Jonas as he stood on the beach, watching her departure. While Fish was rowing the dory away from shore, Kate realized that the big black man might have wanted to go with them to see Mattie. It should really be Fish who stayed and Cal or Benjamin who returned to the house and slave quarters. Almost as if Cassie had read her mind, the black girl turned around on the narrow wooden seat.

"Oh, Miz Kate, ah done almos' fergot. Mattie said she wuz hopin' Cal would be comin' home wif us t'night."

"Stop the boat, Fish," Kate ordered. "Cal! Come trade places with Fish. There's only room for one of you, so it ought to be the man who's married."

Then she saw Benjamin, looking as hopeful as Cal, ambling down to the water's edge. "I'm sorry, Benjamin . . . but you'll have wait until tomorrow night to visit Daisy. This dory is too small for all of us."

Eager to take the oars from Fish, Cal splashed

218

toward the little boat, while Fish grumbled as he swung his legs over the side. Soon, the dory was once again gliding through the blue-green water. Kate glanced worriedly at the sun sliding slowly downward toward the sea; she still had a couple of hours before she was supposed to meet Edward on the beach. That should be plenty of time to have it out with her father and gain his backing to fire Edward—and if it wasn't, then she would take all the time she needed, and Edward could fry in hell. She was done being cordial to the man; from now on, it was war.

Jonas watched the little dory until it disappeared from sight around the edge of the cay. He couldn't help wondering what was wrong at the house. Though none of his business, he wanted to know. It suddenly occurred to him that Edward, Kate's father, and Cal were the only three men remaining on that side of the island. If the problem proved serious, only Cal or Edward would be much help, and truculent, difficult Edward would use any opportunity available to make Kate feel indebted to him.

Turning to the disappointed Benjamin, Jonas said: "I don't suppose you'd consider accompanying me on a long walk tonight, would you, Ben?"

"A walk to where, Cap'n? I wuz hopin' t' git home t'night, but dere wasn't room in dat dory for both me an' Cal."

"If we set a fast pace, we could reach the windward side of the island by moonrise, couldn't we?"

"Yes, Cap'n. We shore 'nuff could."

"Give me a minute to leave some instructions with Big Donald, and then let's get started. Something tells me we might be needed there tonight, and when I can, I always obey my hunches."

"Ah'm wid you, Cap'n . . . Dat chowder give me

back mah energy, an' ah' shore 'nuff would like t' see mah woman on a night when de moon's gonna be full."

So would I, Jonas thought, picturing Kate's hair and eyes shining in the moonlight. He shook his head to clear his vision; he had a long walk ahead of him, and he doubted that it would lead to a moonlight tryst with Kate.

"Papa, are you awake?"

Kate stepped onto the veranda and peered down at her father, who appeared to be sleeping where he sat, his chair tipped back and leaning against the outside wall of the house. In the fading light, he looked frail and wan; maybe he *wasn't* sleeping. Maybe he was ill!

She leaned over and brushed his arm, catching a strong whiff of spirits as she did so. Her father didn't stir until she shook him slightly, then he roused, righted the chair, and glanced groggily about him. "Edward? That you, Edward? Have another drink . . . I like a man who sits down and drinks with me; that's a man I know I can trust."

Papa's speech was slurred, his motions jerky, and Kate knew she would have no meaningful discussion with him, this night. "Papa . . . Edward's not here. It's me, Kate."

"Kate?" He glanced blearily up at her. "What happened to Edward? He was here a minute ago, havin' a drink with me. Where did he go off to?"

"I'm sure I don't know, Papa. What did you and Edward talk about while you were drinking to-gether?"

"Why, we talked about you, Kate. That boy is determined to marry you; he loves you like I once loved your dear Mama—and still love her, no matter that she's changed some since then. Why don't you pay more attention to poor Edward and smile at him once in a while?"

Exasperated and disgusted, Kate groaned to herself. "Look, Papa, we have to talk about 'poor' Edward—but not now, not tonight, when you can barely see straight and certainly can't think properly. Why don't you go to bed, and we'll talk first thing in the morning?"

"Don't wanna go to bed, yet," her father said stubbornly. "I'm not done drinkin'. You go to bed an' I'll just sit here a spell."

"Come on, Papa." Kate took the empty glass from her father's hand, hooked an arm around his waist, and dragged him upright. "Let's go upstairs while you can still walk."

"I'm not so drunk I can't walk!" he protested angrily, but he clung to Kate and leaned on her heavily as she maneuvered him into the house and up the stairway to the room shared by both her parents.

Mama was deeply asleep in the darkened chamber where a single candle beneath a glass guttered on the table beside the bed. Her slow, heavy breathing told Kate that she had probably drunk one of Bell's drugging teas before retiring. Normally a light sleeper who awoke at the slightest noise, Sybil was unable to get any rest unless she downed one of those powerful concoctions. Bell's teas had the same effect on Mama as being struck across the head with a mallet. Someone could be screaming right in Mama's ear, and she wouldn't awaken.

Not worrying about the noise they were making, Kate helped her father remove his boots, vest, and pocket watch, and climb into bed. She covered him with a light blanket. He was snoring before she left the room. On her way out, Kate took the candle with her, then continued down the hallway to her own bedchamber. She wouldn't meet with Edward, after all, she decided—not alone on the beach. Whatever he wanted could wait until morning. If he dared come into the house after her, he'd find a locked and barred door standing between them.

Kate stripped off her clothing, donned a night-dress, and lay down on her own bed, but sleep eluded her. She was still too incensed over Edward's threats to be able to relax. She *had* suspected that Edward was mistreating the slaves behind her back, but then dismissed her suspicions when no one would admit to it. A sudden, chilling thought made her snap upright; what if Edward got so angry when he realized she wasn't coming, that he went straight to Cassie's house to take his revenge on her this very night?

Damn, but that was just what he might do!

Kate leaped off the bed, grabbed the clothes she had just removed, and struggled back into them. Much as she detested the idea, she'd *have* to meet Edward on the beach. While she was there, she might as well tell him what she thought of a man who used threats and intimidation to force people to do his bidding. Then she'd order him to leave Conch Cay. If he refused to go—and Papa refused to make him—then *she* would go. She'd leave the house for good and move into Jonas's hut. Jonas would just have to sleep with his men until another hut could be built for him.

Surely, Papa and Mama wouldn't side with Edward; it was long past time to force the issue and find out exactly where they stood. Papa and Mama had a choice to make. It was either get rid of Edward or lose their own daughter.

Mattie and Cassie crouched wide-eyed and silent behind the house, keeping a solitary vigil in the dark shadows that cloaked the yard. "Listen, gal," Mattie whispered. "You think dat's Miz Kate stirrin' upstairs, gittin' ready t' meet wif Edward? Ah hope she ain't changed her mind. Den ah won't haveta lie an' tell 'er a ship is passin in de ocean, jus' t' git her down dere t' meet wif de Cap'n, instead."

"Is you positive Massah Edward's gonna stay sleepin' an' cain't hurt Miz Kate?" Cassie asked softly. "She wuz all riled up 'bout him, an' if she do see him, she gonna blister his ears good. Den he might do what he an' Bell cooked up in de fust place."

"Ah'm positive . . . Ah mixed de wine wif de same recipe Bell uses on Miz Sybil," Mattie answered. "Ah jus' hope Cal runs real fast t' fetch de Cap'n back here . . . Poor Cal. Ah didn't hardly have time t' explain everythin'. Ah jus' sent 'im off as soon as he walked inta de cook shed. Doan know whut de cap'n gonna think about Cal tellin' *him* dere might be a wreck t'night."

"If de Cap'n don't come quick, all he'll be likely t' find is Edward passed out on de beach behind dem trees where you dragged him aftah he drunk de wine. Oh, Mattie, ah hope dis works! If it don't, we may nevah git another chance. Worse yet, we may git a whuppin'."

"It'll work," Mattie promised with more confidence than she was feeling, considering all that *could* go wrong.

She ticked off the possibilities on her fingers. Miz Kate might refuse to go to the beach for any reason— either to meet Edward, or to see if a ship was really out there, heading toward Dead Man's Reef. That was the excuse Mattie planned on giving her if she changed her mind about meeting with Edward. Even worse than that, Edward *might* wake up too soon, before Miz Kate and the Cap'n found the picnic all

223

laid out for them, and Miz Kate saw her favorite treat—the green coconut—and drank the love potion hidden inside.

What if Miz Kate didn't have any appetite to enjoy a coconut tonight? Or what if she drank the love potion, but it didn't work? Or what if it did work, but she encountered Edward or some other man *before* she saw the Cap'n? There was so much to worry about. Cal might fail to convince the Cap'n to accompany him back to the windward side of the island . . . Or the two men might get lost in the forest. Mattie tormented herself with these potential disasters. Only one thing so far had gone absolutely right; Edward had drunk the wine while waiting for Miz Kate to join him on the beach.

With her own eyes, Mattie had seen him do it. Within minutes, he had stretched out on the blanket and gone to sleep. Then all Mattie had to do was roll him up in the covering and drag him behind the trees. After that, she had spread out a new blanket and left everything for Miz Kate to find.

She hoped Miz Kate would drink the coconut and fall in love with the Cap'n while Edward snored uncomprehendingly in the bushes. Mattie figured it was too much to hope for that Miz Kate and the Cap'n would commit to marriage tonight, but at least Edward's plans would now be ruined. And the best part of it was he would never know what had happened or why.

Mattie intended to drag Edward back out to the beach and substitute a new coconut just as soon as Miz Kate had gone, and it was safe to do so. Edward would assume Kate had never arrived. Later he might try and get her to drink from the new coconut, but if she did, nothing would happen, and his fury would turn on Bell. Mattie had laughed over that possibility earlier in the day, but now that she had succeeded in getting this far, she had a bad case of nervousness. Cassie's fear fueled her own, so that she almost leapt from her skin when she saw Miz Kate herself come around the side of the house and head toward the beach.

It was too soon! Cal hadn't come back yet with the Cap'n; how could she keep Miz Kate down on the beach long enough for Cap'n Irons to arrive?

"Cassie, stay here!" she hissed. "I gotta go talk wif Miz Kate."

Chapter Sixteen

"Mattie, what are you doing out here this late at night?" Kate asked when Mattie suddenly popped in front of her. If not for the light from the rising moon, Kate might have run right into her friend. She had thought Mattie fast asleep by now with Cal in her own little house.

"Miz Kate, ah was jus' comin' to de house t' fetch ya . . . Cal an' me—we went down to de beach t' watch de moon rise, an' we saw lights out on de water."

"Lights? Ship lights?" Kate asked stupidly, then chided herself for posing such a dumb question. What other kind of lights could there be? Unless Edward was once again laying a trap for some unwary sea captain. Maybe *that's* why he wanted her to come down to the beach tonight! He was hoping to lure a ship onto the shoal.

"Yes'm, dey was ship lights shore nuff."

"Did you happen to see Edward down there?"

"No, ma'am, but ah spect Massah Edward gonna come lookin' fer Cal or Fish or somebody t' h'ep him, if he's seen dose lights same as me an' Cal. 'Course, he doan know Cal come home t'night, yet. But he'll be along shortly, lookin' fer someone t' go out in a dory wif a lantern."

"You and Cal had better go for a walk in the woods then," Kate ordered. "That way, if Edward does come looking, he won't find your husband or anybody else to help him except Cassie and Daisy . . . and those two won't be much help."

"Yes'm, Miz Kate . . . Cal an' me will do dat. But whut you gonna do?"

"I'm going down to the beach to check on those lights—and to try and stop Edward if he plans to sabotage a ship by himself."

Mattie's white teeth flashed in the moonlight. "Dat's a good idea, Miz Kate. Ah know y'all doan like it when Massah Edward causes shipwrecks."

"I certainly don't! And I'll stay down there all night if I have to, just to stop him!"

Again, Kate saw the white flash of Mattie's teeth as she grinned. "God bless y'all, Miz Kate . . . Now, ah better hurry an' hide me an' Cal."

Mattie headed for the slave quarters while Kate continued in the direction of the beach. By the time she arrived there, the moon was well up in the sky, lighting a path across the sea and flooding the beach with molten silver. The waves curling on the shore flung diamond-studded droplets of spray onto the wet sand, and it was almost as bright as day.

Kate scanned the ocean but saw no lights or glimmers of white sail. That struck her as odd; perhaps the curve of the cay itself was causing the lights to be concealed from view, she speculated. She started hiking north toward the lookout point where she and Edward had an unobstructed view when watching for shipwrecks. Even before she reached the spot, she found the outspread blanket and picnic basket, where Edward had obviously been waiting for her. Edward himself was nowhere to be seen, but a green glass wine bottle—more than half empty— gave mute evidence that he had been there.

Snorting contemptuously, Kate pulled the cork

from the bottle and emptied its remaining contents onto the sand. Papa wouldn't be too happy to learn that Edward was raiding his carefully horded stock of salvaged vintages. Surprisingly, her father drank only rum or brandy to sate his cravings; any wine recovered from shipwrecks he saved for festive, family occasions.

"Edward!" Kate called out. "Where are you?"

The only sound was the breaking of the surf onto the beach. Had Edward already gone in search of a slave or two to help him haul salvage—but salvage from what ship? Kate still could not see any lights. She walked farther up the beach until she came to the spit of rock where she and Edward usually maintained a lookout. She climbed the boulders, retrieved the canvas sack from its hiding place in a rocky crevice, and took out the long, narrow case containing the spyglass.

With the spyglass, she examined the entire land and seascape all around. There were no vessels out on the ocean, and no Edward upon the land or sea . . . unless Edward had already launched a dory and was out there somewhere, waiting to flash a lantern light as soon as a suitable quarry came into sight. The blanket and food basket were proof that Edward had been there, and Mattie and Cal couldn't be mistaken about what they had seen. But where was Edward, now? And what had happened to the lights?

Tucking the spyglass under her arm, Kate returned the canvas sack to its hiding place, and then climbed back down to the beach. For however long it took, she must wait here until she knew what was happening. Maybe there was a clue in the food basket as to Edward's whereabouts! She ran back to the blanket and rummaged through the basket, finding nothing but a large green coconut, a hunk of bread, bananas, and some of the pastries Mattie made with bits of conch, crawfish, and tiny shrimp.

229

Defeated, she sat down on the blanket, pulled up her knees, and hid her bare feet under her skirt. There was nothing further she could do; she would have to wait until Edward revealed himself and told her what this was all about. Fortunately, he could not sneak up and surprise her, for the moon lit the beach all the way back to the line of forest, a good distance away.

She gazed up at the sky, simultaneously reviewing her grievances against Edward and marveling at the moon's perfect symmetry and lustrous, opulent light. Tonight, the stars were mere, distant pinpricks, unable to compete with their brilliant sister. The breeze kissing her cheek was sweet and gentle as a baby's breath. After a while, she grew thirsty and her thoughts went to the coconut.

She loved the stringent, refreshing elixir of a fresh, green coconut far better than wine or ale. It was a cherished treat. How thoughtful of Edward to have provided it, she thought with some irony, still not trusting his motives for insisting she come to the beach, tonight. Pulling the basket over to her, she lifted out the coconut with both hands; had Edward thought to include a knife to cut the top off, so she could drink the liquid trapped inside?

In the bottom of the basket, she found a knife, but when she went to cut the coconut, she discovered that it had already been cut—quite expertly. A small, square hole had been sawed through the thick flesh, so that the top of the coconut could be removed and then replaced after one had finished drinking. The precious contents were thus protected from spoilage and dirt.

Glad that she didn't have to do the hard work of battling the rind, Kate removed the top, lifted the coconut to her lips, and drank a mouthful. The milk tasted sweeter than usual, given the hard green shell. Still, it was as refreshing as she had anticipated, and she drank again, savoring the cool liquid as it slid down her throat.

She stopped short of draining the coconut dry; if the night proved long and tiresome, she would relish having more later. Carefully, she replaced the sawed-off top and set the coconut back into the basket. Then, after a cursory check of her surroundings, she lay back on the blanket and again turned her attention to the moon. A night such as this was made for lovers. On just such a night, she and Jonathan had traded kisses beneath the moon. But that memory brought only pain and sadness, so she thought instead about what it would be like to trade endless, sweet kisses with Jonas . . .

When Jonas and Benjamin encountered Cal bounding toward them on the narrow path worn through the forest, Jonas felt only a momentary surprise. He had been expecting trouble, and Cal's presence only confirmed it. Recognizing the big black man in a shaft of moonlight spilling through the tall trees, he sprinted forward to meet him.

"Cal, what is it? What's wrong at the house?"

Cal stopped in his tracks and caught his breath before answering. He was breathing hard from running, and his dark face shone with rivulets of sweat. "Cap'n, Miz Kate sent me t' get you. She says t' tell you t' hurry fas' as you can, 'cause dere might be a wreck t'night."

"Tonight? With a full moon lighting the cay? Why in God's name would she think that?"

"Ah doan know, Cap'n, but it's happent b'fore. Jus' cause it's easy t' see de cay doan mean it's easy t' see de reef. On a night like dis, folks git careless. A'fore dey realize de danger, dey's ripped a big hole in de bottom of dere ship."

"Then it's a good thing I was coming anyway; we must be more than halfway there by now. Come

231

along, gentlemen. Let's see who can get there first."

Jonas bolted along the path, outdistancing his two followers with ease. Cal was already tired, and Benjamin didn't seem to want to leave his friend behind. By the time Jonas reached the vicinity of the house, he himself was winded and gasping for breath. He stopped to rest a moment and leaned against a tree trunk, before taking the path that led to the windward beach. As he stood gulping air, a dark figure materialized on the veranda.

"Cap'n?" Mattie's voice called softly. "Dat you, Cap'n?"

Jonas stepped out into the wash of moonlight. "It's me, Mattie. Where's your mistress?"

"She done gone down to de beach, Cap'n . . . She waitin' fer y'all t' come."

"Where's Edward?" Jonas asked, not liking the idea of the overseer being alone with Kate, which he probably was, if a wreck was expected.

"Ah doan know, Cap'n . . . Ah ain't seen 'im. But if ah do, y'all want me t' give him a message?"

Jonas considered a moment. Wreck or not, if Edward wasn't already down on the beach, Jonas didn't want him to show up. Whatever already had— or was about to—happen, he and Kate could handle it fine without Edward. "Yes, tell him we won't be needing him. There's no sense in all of us losing sleep, tonight. If we do need him, we can always send for him."

Mattie laughed softly—at what, Jonas wasn't sure. "Oh, ah'll tell 'im dat, all right . . . What happent t' Cal?"

"He'll be coming along shortly. Benjamin's with him. They might as well stay here, too, until I find out what the situation is. There's been no shipwreck as yet, has there?"

"No, Cap'n, not dat ah know of. Miz Kate said she'd come an' git me, Daisy, an' Cassie, if de ship ran

232

onto de shaol, an' we had t' help rescue survivors an' pick up de salvage."

"I'll come and get all of you if it becomes necessary," Jonas promised. "Which way on the beach was Kate headed?"

"N'oth, Cap'n. Jus' start walkin', an' ya'll surely gonna see her."

"Thank you, Mattie."

Jonas set off down the path to the beach, and when he got there, turned left and walked a parallel line along the curl of frothy surf. To his surprise, no lights winked on the ocean; there was only the moon, bathing everything in glowing luminescence. He wished he had thought to get a drink of water at the house; his mouth felt dry as bone . . . but he put the minor discomfort out of his mind and kept walking, searching the silvery beach for any sign of Kate or Edward.

Kate spotted Jonas before he saw her. Thinking he was Edward, she stood up, and abruptly realized that the figure striding toward her was too tall to be Edward. Recognizing Jonas, she ran to greet him. At the same moment, Jonas broke into a run and sprinted toward her. Moonlight etched the planes of his face, and his chest muscles—visible through his open shirt—rippled with liquid light, causing Kate to inhale sharply. The man was too handsome by far, she thought, or maybe she was moonstruck, the way her flesh prickled at the mere sight of him. They stopped mere inches apart, on the verge of throwing themselves into each other's arms, or so it seemed to Kate.

Embarrassed by her own eagerness, she abruptly drew back. "What are you doing here, Jonas?"

The question apparently puzzled him. "What do you mean, what am I doing here? You sent for me.

Cal met me and Benjamin in the woods and told us to come quickly; you needed us.''

"You and Benjamin were out in the woods?'' Kate asked to cover her own confusion. "What were you doing there?''

"Before Cal came to get me, I had already decided to return to this side of the island. I thought I might be of some use in solving whatever problem provoked your hasty departure. I guess you could say I was worried about you.''

Having someone worry about her was a new experience for Kate, resulting in a jolt of pleasure. She had the unnerving sensation that she could feel Jonas's presence through the pores of her skin.

"Thank you,'' she whispered, still not certain why Cal had gone in search of Jonas, but glad that he had.

Jonas nodded toward the moon-washed ocean. "So where is this ship that's supposedly headed this way?''

Kate swallowed hard. Cal must have told Jonas about the ship, but she didn't understand why he would have done so on his own, without instructions from her. "I don't know . . .'' she answered honestly. "I've been waiting here for over an hour, and I've seen no trace of any ships.''

"Did you see lights earlier?''

"No, but Mattie and Cal both claim they saw them.'' Kate avoided mentioning Edward and his puzzling request that she meet him on the beach, which might or might not have something to do with the ship lights the two slaves had seen.

"That's strange . . . But then this isn't the first time mysterious lights have appeared and disappeared in this vicinity, now is it?''

"It isn't?'' Kate asked with a sinking feeling. Jonas had never come right out and accused her and Edward of luring him onto the shoal, but several times, he had seemed on the verge of doing so. She had often wondered why he *hadn't* made that specific accusation. Neither had his men mentioned the light, and this, too, struck her as odd, now that she thought about it.

While she pondered the situation, Jonas watched her intently. "On the night my ship sank, I could have sworn I saw a light out on the water, but then it disappeared. Have you any idea what it could have been?"

"Not in the least," she assured him, averting her eyes lest he see the lie in them. Turning, she began to stroll back in the direction of the blanket. "Perhaps it's a natural phenomenon of the moon and stars reflecting off the sea," she suggested out of desperation.

"Ah, but it was dark that night—and stormy," he reminded her, falling into step at her side.

"Then perhaps lightning can also produce such an unusual effect. There's much we don't understand about nature, Jonas. We live very close to the earth, sea, and sky here on our island, but we don't have ready explanations for everything we experience. That's one reason why I love it so; it's always the same but also different . . . challenging . . . a feast for the senses and also for the mind. I'm always learning something new."

She glanced at him side-long, hoping she had distracted him from his original question. He was still watching her, but his expression had subtly altered. A slight flare of the finely chiseled nostrils and a parting of the sensual lips alerted her that something had changed between them. Jonas was indeed distracted; he now wore the look of a man suddenly hungry for a woman. His eyes roamed—or was it devoured?—her face and hair, then moved lower to linger on her bosom. An answering hunger leaped in the pit of her stomach. He wants me, she thought, thrilled by the revelation . . . and dear

Lord, how I want him!

"I plan to stay out here a bit to watch for that light," she informed him breathlessly. "Will you join me? Maybe we can discover more about this strange phenomena that's fooled us into thinking we see ship lights, when there's nothing out there." She walked faster toward the blanket spread on the sand. "Are you hungry? Would you like something to drink?"

Dropping to her knees at the edge of the blanket, she seized the first thing she saw and offered it to him. "Have you ever tried coconut milk? Actually, the liquid inside hasn't turned to milk, yet; the coconut is still too green. But this is the way I like it best—slightly prickly on the tongue."

Never taking his eyes from her face, Jonas accepted the coconut, his fingers brushing hers as he did so. "I must admit I'm thirsty . . . and I'll try anything once."

She patted the blanket beside her. "Sit down and make yourself comfortable. You must be tired after such a long walk across the island."

"Run . . ." he corrected. "I ran most of the way."

Sitting down beside her, he tilted the coconut to his lips and swallowed several times. When he lowered it, he was grinning. "You're right . . . the liquid's wonderful when the shell is still green. I thought it would be tart or bitter—but instead, it was wonderfully refreshing."

"This one is sweeter than usual," Kate commented. "I don't know why—another unexplainable, natural phenomenon, I suppose."

He set the coconut down between them, then picked it up again and moved it to the other side of his body, so that nothing separated them but a small patch of blanket. The significance of the gesture wasn't lost on Kate; her pulse began to pound. Breathing deeply—she felt as if she herself had just

236

sprinted across the island—she tilted back her head and studied the brightly lit vault overhead. The sky was so vast and limitless; she and Jonas might have been the only two people in the world, tonight. No one but the two of them existed beneath the brilliant moon. The only sound was the surf murmuring at their feet and the cries of several seabirds wheeling overhead.

She waited for him to make the first move—and prayed that he would. Then she tossed her head in disgust at herself and stared determinedly out to sea, where there were still no ship lights.

"You're very beautiful, do you know that?" Jonas's voice was so low and husky she could barely hear it.

She angled her head to look at him. "I've never thought of myself as beautiful. My hair is too red, my eyes too yellow. I have my grandfather's unusual coloring—and his faults, too," she added with an awkward laugh.

He leaned back on one elbow. "Tell me about these faults. Maybe they will help me forget about your beauty, so I can be virtuous and think about mysterious ship lights, instead of . . . other things."

She didn't have to ask him what the "other things" were; she already knew and was finding it every bit as difficult to keep from thinking about them, too. "I'm too quick-tempered, too impatient . . . and too self-absorbed," she blurted out.

"Self-absorbed? I wouldn't use that term to describe you."

"Oh, I don't mean I'm always thinking about myself, but I tend to concentrate so hard on this or that, that I sometimes ignore—or don't notice—what's happening right beneath my nose."

He nodded. "Yes, I can believe that. It explains why you allow your parents to behave as they do—and permit Edward to overstep his bounds."

The criticism was mild, but still stung. "I do the best I can!" she flared.

He chuckled at her reaction. "Of course, you do . . . and your best is most impressive, I assure you. I've never met a woman quite like you, Kate."

The huskiness had returned to his voice. She shifted position to face him and found herself closer than she had anticipated. "I haven't met any men like you, either," she admitted, adding silently: *Not even your brother made me feel the way you do.*

"Of course, I don't know you very well yet," she backtracked. "But that can be quickly remedied. Tell me about *your* faults, now."

"Me? I don't have any—unless you count lusting after a beautiful woman a grave fault."

"You're an American . . . In my opinion, that's a worse fault. And you are a bit of a tyrant; you like to boss people about and expect to be obeyed instantly. You are also quick-tempered."

"I am not!" he exploded, then grinned sheepishly. "Well, only when people aren't performing to my expectations—or like you, have a habit of saying things that sorely prick me."

She, too, leaned back on one elbow, resting on her side as she gazed into his eyes. "I don't say such things on purpose, Jonas. Normally, I'm very careful of people's feelings. I don't like to hurt or anger them. Only when I lose my temper do I let fly and damn the consequences."

"What will you be like when you love a man?" Jonas asked softly. He raised his free hand and rested it lightly on the curve of her hip. "That's something I've been wondering since the day I first met you. I suspect there's a wealth of fiery passion lurking beneath that haughty, controlled exterior. What will you be like when you *lose* control?"

As Jonas spoke and touched her, Kate could feel her much-vaunted control slipping away. In an almost idle fashion, he caressed the curve of her hip, running his hand down the length of her thigh almost to her knee, and then back up again to the indentation of her waist. Kate could hardly keep from sighing; he aroused the most wonderful, fluttery feelings inside her. She longed to melt against him and offer her mouth for his kiss, but feared he might find that too wanton a gesture. Unlike Jonathan, Jonas moved slowly and cautiously—as if he didn't want to commit himself but couldn't help having gone this far.

His hand traveled from her waist to the curve of her breast and paused there. Could he feel her heart leaping against his hand? she wondered in a delicious panic.

"You are so soft—so womanly," he whispered, moving nearer and nuzzling her hair. "A man could lose himself in your softness, Kate . . . He could forget everything but the need to touch and possess you. Would you then unsheath your claws and slash him to ribbons?"

"Some men, I would . . . but not you, Jonas. Never you . . . You make me want to give myself to you . . . to surrender everything . . . and finally learn what a maiden only dreams about." She gasped as his tongue suddenly flicked inside her ear, stealthy as a serpent about to strike—a serpent whose strike she most ardently wanted.

"I myself would like to know what maidens dream about, lovely Kate. Do you ever imagine a man doing this to you?"

He commenced nibbling on her earlobe while his fingers explored the shape of her breast. His thumb encircled its tip—once, twice—gently teasing it into a hard nub. She moaned and rolled onto her back, opening her arms to enfold him. He moved over her and lowered himself onto her body with great care, fitting the planes and angles together—pressing hard against soft—pushing the hot, hard bulge at his thighs into the hollow, aching nest between her own legs. Then—only then—did he start to kiss her.

He lowered his open mouth to hers and kissed as if he were consuming her alive and whole. But he did it with such great gentleness, such sweet expertise, that she wanted to weep with the pleasure of it. His tongue danced with her tongue, his lips mated with hers, his breath became her breath, his taste and scent drowned her senses. He kissed her until she couldn't think, talk, or breathe. Then he drew back, planted a knee on either side of her belly, and began to unfasten her clothing. She tried to assist, but her hands were trembling so badly that she fumbled helplessly.

"Hush, hush, love . . ." he crooned, as if she had spoken, which she had not, nor could she have. "Let me do it . . ."

He bared her breasts and knelt, gazing down at them, as though he had never seen anything so pure and perfect. The naked adoration in his eyes made her sudden embarrassment trickle away. With casual grace, he removed his shirt, and she did what she had been wanting to do since first she had seen the gleaming expanse of pectoral muscles and curly hair. Fingers outspread, she placed both hands on his chest—on the sculptured magnificence that was so distinctly, blatantly male. Savoring each moment, she let his maleness seep through her fingertips.

"You are beautiful," she said at last, and he laughed deep in his throat.

"You haven't seen all of me yet. Wait until my hairy legs are revealed."

"I *have* seen them—that day at the pool."

"Then you have a ridiculous sense of beauty. *These* are beautiful . . ." He placed his palms over her breasts and making a handful of each one, gently squeezed. "God forgive me for my presumption, but

240

I've been wanting to do that . . . and much, much more."

"What more?" she gasped, clinging now to his shoulders. The urge to writhe against him came upon her, but she resisted it, half afraid to move lest the sensations his hands were awakening somehow slid away from her.

"This, for one thing . . ."

Letting go of her breasts, he bent over her and rubbed his own pebbled nipples against hers. His chest hair grazed her full mounds, causing the sensitive peaks to quiver in anticipation of more touching—more knowing. He rested the weight of his lower body against her belly for a moment, and the heat and hardness of him pricked her through the several layers of fabric separating them. When he drew back, he left a damp, aching void, and she longed to recapture the pleasurable pressure of his body rubbing against hers.

Dipping his head, he captured one of her nipples in his mouth. Unable to stop herself, she arched her back. He bathed the aching bud with his tongue, suckling her with relish, and sighing deeply, turned to the other breast. By the time he had finished, she was tossing her head from side to side, moaning, and trying to pull him closer. She wanted more . . . more . . . and yet more . . .

As he levered himself to one side, her eyes flew open in dismay. But it was only a momentary respite, long enough for him to strip away the remainder of her clothing and his. She watched him through slitted eyes, all her muscles, bones, and joints liquified, and she lay shamelessly outspread . . . unable to move, uncaring that he saw her revealed in her entirety beneath the light of the moon. That glowing orb shone directly down upon them, etching his contours, as well as hers, in bluish silver.

She gazed upon his body with awe, desire, and

utter fascination. He was magnificently endowed, and she knew a moment's terror that he might not fit inside her. He saw where she was looking and with one hand, lifted himself for her closer inspection. "Tell me now if you don't want me, Kate . . . or if I frighten or repulse you. Once we begin, I doubt I'll be able to stop."

Kate herself was already past the point of stopping. No words could gain passage through her passion-clogged throat, so she did the only thing she could think of to communicate her desire. She reached out and closed her hand over the rigid proof of his splendid masculinity. Immediately, his hand covered hers, holding it down upon the long, hard shaft. He groaned her name and flung back his head. For the first time in her life, Kate sensed the full power of her femininity.

Moved by instincts as old as time itself, she raised herself and kissed his nipples—suckling and teasing them—giving him the same pleasure he had earlier given to her. Rolling onto her side, she trailed a line of kisses down his hard, flat belly, dipping her tongue in his navel, then continuing down to her own hand, still covering the part of him she most wanted to know. As she moved her hand to kiss him there, he grasped her shoulders and hauled her up against him.

"No, Kate . . . no. If you do that, I won't be able to stand it. Our lovemaking will end before it's barely begun."

He pressed her back into the blanket, nudging her knees apart as he did so. "Open to me, Kate . . . open to me."

She did as he begged. The tip of his shaft probed between her thighs, slicking and lubricating her. She lifted her hips to grant him easier access. He kissed her mouth, her cheeks, her hair, rubbing himself against her, yet still not entering. Again, he fondled her breasts. Again, he stroked, petted, and played with her body. He slid his hand down between them and caressed the throbbing nub hidden between the pink folds of tender, engorged flesh. She thought she might die of her need for him.

Finally, she grasped him and attempted to guide him into her. Quickly, he rose up on his elbows, positioned himself, and plunged into her—a single, deep, penetrating thrust. As her maidenhead tore, she cried out, her body involuntarily stiffening from shock and discomfort. He remained still above her, except for the kisses he lavished on her face and mouth.

"I'm sorry, sweetheart," he murmured into her ear. "I didn't know how to spare you this, other than never loving you at all."

She hugged him to her, fighting the tears that gathered in her eyes and threatened to spill over. After a moment, the sharp pain subsided. He waited until she was once again breathing normally, then began to move within her. This should hurt, she thought, but it didn't. A marvelous pressure began to build. The friction of his thrusting was exactly, perfectly *right*. It was what she had been wanting all along.

Instinct again taught her what to do; she caught his rhythm and rocked with his thrusts. The tempo increased. The wonderful pressure built. She imagined herself soaring with him on silvery wings, rising majestically into the night sky. They exploded together in a shower of starlight; she became Jonas and he became Kate. Their fragments intermingled, blended, became indistinguishable, one from the other, then drifted slowly downward . . .

They lay together a long time, wrapped in the splendor of their mating, neither wanting to break the enchantment that enfolded them like a shimmering cloak . . . then Kate heard an alien sound.

She pulled away from Jonas and sat up, grabbing for her clothing. So closely attuned to her had Jonas become over the past hour, that he wordlessly followed suit and had his trousers on before she had finished tugging her skirt over her hips.

She struggled to fasten her bodice over her bare breasts and finally gave up and fluffed her hair over herself instead. Someone was walking toward them from the line of trees. The figure stumbled and almost fell, then righted himself and kept coming. Kate recognized him even before he spoke, his voice quivering with outrage as he stomped up to the very edge of the blanket.

"What the hell's goin' on here? What've you two been doin'?"

Jonas sounded almost bored as he calmly answered: "A better question would be—what are *you* doing out here, Edward?"

Chapter Seventeen

"I got as much right as *you* t' be out here—maybe *more* right!" Edward bellowed. "I wuz watchin' fer ship lights, but somehow, I fell asleep."

"Yes," Kate said dryly. "I found the half-empty wine bottle. You still look groggy and disoriented, Edward. Why don't you leave us alone and go sleep it off?"

"Jus' how long you two been alone out here?"

Edward's expression was ugly and accusatory as he took in their dishevelment and Jonas's discarded boots and shirt. Then he did something completely bizarre and unexpected. He bent down, grabbed the coconut, and held it up in the moonlight to examine it. Noting that the top was missing, he turned it upside down and shook it; a single, glistening pearl of liquid dribbled out and plopped on the sand.

"It's gone . . . You guzzled every last drop!" he shouted. The realization seemed to infuriate him. Glowering, his face congested with hatred, he advanced on Jonas. "You dirty, whorin' son of a bitch . . . I'll kill you fer this. By God, I swear I'll kill you."

In one lithe movement, Jonas rose from the blanket and stepped aside as Edward launched his attack. The coconut rolled away, and the two men circled each other—Edward panting with fury, and Jonas cool and controlled.

"What happened here is none of your business, Edward," Jonas said reasonably. "But if you're determined to fight about it, then fight we will."

"I'll *kill* you, damn you! You got what was mine—what I been waitin' fer all these years." Edward swung a meaty fist that glanced off Jonas's shoulder.

Jonas drew back his own fist and landed a solid blow squarely on Edward's jaw. Instead of stopping him, the blow only goaded Edward to greater effort. He seized Jonas in a bear hug, striving to crack his ribs, but Jonas jammed his knee in Edward's belly and shoved him backward. Kate scrambled out of the way and began searching for a weapon. Jonas was taller than Edward, but not as solidly built, plus Edward had raw fury on his side. Undoubtedly, Edward *would* kill Jonas, if he got half a chance.

Thuds and grunts sounded behind her as the two men went at it; afraid to look, Kate concentrated her attention on finding something with which to hit Edward. She briefly considered the discarded coconut, but decided it wasn't heavy enough. A short distance from the blanket, she found a hunk of driftwood, damp, heavy, and waterlogged from the tide.

Brandishing it in both hands, she returned to the battling men. Opportunity presented itself several moments later. Planting her feet wide apart, Kate took one huge swing and broke the piece of driftwood over Edward's head. For the space of several heartbeats, he remained upright and swaying, then slowly toppled to the sand and lay still, the sound of his breathing the only assurance he was still alive.

"Didn't trust me to get the job done, did you?" With the back of his hand, Jonas wiped a trickle of blood from his mouth. "I *am* capable of defending us both, you know."

"I didn't want you to get hurt!" Dropping the remnant of driftwood, Kate rushed toward him. "Are you all right?"

Jonas shrugged off her concern with typical masculine disdain, his manner surly and impatient. "I can take care of myself, Kate . . . I don't need a female to fight my battles; you should have let *me* handle Edward."

"But you were fighting over me!" she cried, flinging her arms around his neck. "Oh, Jonas, please don't be angry over my interference! I *know* you could have handled it; I just lost my head, that's all! Don't let Edward do this to us! Don't let him destroy the beautiful experience we just shared!"

Jonas disengaged himself, went to the coconut, and thoughtfully picked it up. "Was it really so beautiful, Kate?" He turned the coconut in his hands, studying it, then lifted it to his nose and sniffed the inside. "Or did we only imagine it so because we had drunk something calculated to heighten our passions and make us irresistible to each other? Or rather, should I say, calculated to make Edward irresistible to *you*? Where did you get this coconut? Was it here when you came down to the beach or did you bring it with you?"

"Well, it was here on the b—blanket," Kate stuttered with dawning awareness. "All cut and ready to drink beside the food basket, but . . . but . . ."

"But what? Why were you so surprised to see me when I first arrived? Were you, perhaps, expecting Edward? What were you doing on the beach in the first place?"

Kate wet her lips, suddenly nervous, because she didn't know how to explain. The truth might only make matters worse, but she had to take the risk

247

because nothing else she could think of seemed remotely plausible. "Cassie told me I had to meet Edward on the beach tonight, because if I didn't, if I failed to show up, he was going to beat her."

Jonas's disbelieving scowl caused Kate's heart to twist painfully in her breast. She rushed on, determined to be truthful in this, since the lies she had already told Jonas lay heavy as an anvil in her stomach. "That's why I came home—to have it out with my father and Edward. Papa was too drunk to discuss the matter, so I put him to bed, then went to bed myself, having decided *not* to meet Edward, after all. But then I got to worrying about Edward beating Cassie because I didn't appear, and I got up again. That's when Mattie told me about her and Cal seeing ship lights, and I *knew* I had to come. I found the coconut and this food basket here, but I never did see Edward or the ship lights. And then you came along . . ."

"I came along? You never *sent* for me?" Jonas's look could have felled a tree.

"No, I . . . I . . . Well, of course, I *wanted* you to come, and I was glad when you did . . ."

"But you didn't actually send Cal to fetch me."

Kate shook her head, too worried about his reaction to say the words. "I . . . I guess Mattie was so excited about the ship lights that she took it upon herself to send for you. Also, she despises Edward, so she probably didn't want me in a position where I'd wind up alone with him."

"Which is exactly the position he had planned for you—being alone with him on the beach in the moonlight, drinking God-only-knows what sort of evil concoction from a tampered coconut. Bah!" He threw the coconut to the ground with such force that it shattered and split in pieces. "I've heard of such things, but I never counted Edward resourceful enough to think of using them."

"Wh—what things?" Kate quavered, not at all sure she wanted to know. "What things are you talking about?"

"Aphrodisiacs . . . Certain substances that can arouse and stimulate a person sexually, far beyond the realm of what's usual and expected. I know of shipping firms who do a brisk, private business in such substances; there's also a sea captain who peddles amulets from Jamaica and another who sells packets of a powder that can be slipped into a teacup when a lady isn't looking."

Kate felt sickened; her stomach turned over with dread and nausea. "Do you . . . do you think that's what happened to us? We . . . we drank something that made us . . . made us . . ."

"Lose all our inhibitions and fall into each other's arms like two lust-crazed wantons?" He smiled, but it wasn't a pleasant expression. "I never planned on making love to you tonight, Kate . . . Nor could I have imagined—not in my wildest fantasies—that you would respond so wholeheartedly, with such exquisite abandon. You are—were—a virgin, and virgins are notoriously shy lovers. Only with experience do they gain the kind of passion *you* exhibited tonight. As for my behavior, I shocked myself with my own lustfulness. Women have *never* affected me as you did; I could never understand what my brother was talking about when he raved about the 'joys of the bedchamber.' I thought of those joys as a pleasant diversion, more or less, but nothing like the madness that came over me, tonight."

"Oh, God!" Kate covered her face with her hands. It was all too much, not just the reminder about his brother's profligacy, but the realization of what had happened between *them*. "Edward meant to seduce me, but instead, you and I . . . we . . . we . . ."

She couldn't say it; it was too awful. She had just given herself to a man who was all but admitting he

249

didn't want her—had only taken her because he was under the influence of some horrid drug or powder! When she thought of what they had done, what she had done to him and allowed him to do to her, she couldn't breathe for the shame of it. It hadn't been love at all . . . It had been moonlight, sorcery, and a tampered coconut!

"Don't worry," he said, prying her hands from her face. "If you're pregnant, I'll stand by you. I'll marry you if I have to."

"If you have to!" She jerked away from him. "Do you think I'd marry any man, if he was only marrying me because he *had* to? I'll marry Edward, first! I was going to send him away; I'd planned to make my parents choose between me and Edward. But now, I've changed my mind. He can damn well stay for as long as he likes. Because if I *am* pregnant, I *will* marry him! At least, I'll be getting a man who loves me, who thinks enough of me to *want* to feed me aphro . . . aphro . . ."

"Aphrodisiacs . . ." he supplied, with chilly helpfulness.

"Edward is a bully! He's cruel, selfish, ambitious, and vain, to ever think I'd marry him! But at least he loves me!" Kate could feel herself losing control, teetering like her mother on the brink of no return, but it had somehow ceased to matter. "What he tried to do tonight is base, detestable, and underhanded— but not half as terrible as you saying that you only made love to me because you couldn't help yourself, and you'll only marry if you *have* to! Damn you, Jonas Irons! I wish I had never met you. I wish I'd never lain with you! I . . . I . . . thought I had fallen in love with you . . . Well, thank God, Edward found us, and we discovered the truth about that coconut. If he hadn't, we might have acted on impulse and rushed into marriage because of what we thought we felt, and it would have been the worst mistake of our lives."

"Yes," Jonas agreed. "We might very well have done something as foolish as pledging undying love and commitment. I'm sorry if I've hurt you, Kate, but it's best we face facts: It wouldn't have worked out between us. I'm still an American, and you're still a Loyalist. I've offered you a way to survive here honorably, yet you still can't resist the temptation of profiting from a wreck. I'll never understand how you can justify the behavior of a vulture picking over a carcass. Maybe you and Edward deserve each other. You can spend the rest of your lives wreck-watching on the beach together. As for me, I'll build my ships, take my profits, and leave here as fast as I can. I'll go back to Salem where I belong, and you can stay on Conch Cay where you belong, and we'll just have to forget each other and what happened on this damn beach tonight!"

"I've already forgotten it!" she screamed, then, more calmly, in a voice that shook with the effort to keep it from shrieking: "I'll send Cal down to take care of Edward. Don't bother to see me back to the house; I prefer returning home on my own."

Spinning on her heel, she stalked away, head held high, keeping the tears from falling through sheer willpower and determination . . . plus a dose of plain old stiff-necked pride. She was, she told herself, far too angry and upset to cry—and she would never, under any circumstances, let Jonas Irons know how much he had hurt her.

Jonas watched Kate go with a mixture of consternation, guilt, and blessed relief. He *hadn't* meant to go as far as they had, tonight. Yes, he had wanted to kiss her and dally a bit in the moonlight, but he had never planned on the utterly devastating and shattering experience that had resulted! Making love to

Kate had exceeded all his expectations; it had completely destroyed his long-held, preconceived notions that a man needed a woman only for sex. *This* had been more than mere sex. It had been more than a mere dalliance in the moonlight. It had been something primitive, elemental, and as necessary to his happiness and well-being as *breathing*. It had, he frankly admitted, scared the hell out of him.

He didn't want to want a woman as much as he had desired Kate, tonight. He didn't want to be that enchanted and beguiled by one . . . or to become that vulnerable. Such wondrous ecstasy, such moonstruck madness, could only end in acute pain, agony, and disappointment. She *couldn't* have wanted *him* that much, either . . . It *had* to have been some spell or potion that made her respond to him as she had. Even the memory of her sweet, burning kisses had the power to turn his knees to water! The contents of that coconut must be affecting him still, he grimly decided.

Glancing down at Edward, still out cold, Jonas felt another jolt of disgust and fury. The man was a swine, not fit to look at Kate, much less lust after her and plot her downfall. What had he put in the damn coconut? Jonas seized one of Edward's arms and began dragging him toward the surf. Halfway there, Edward regained consciousness and groaned pitifully. Disinclined toward mercy, Jonas maneuvered him to his feet and half carried him into the shallows.

There, he dunked Edward's head under the water and held it submerged until the overseer's struggles became desperate. "St . . . stop! Yer drownin' me!" Edward yelled as he came up gasping.

"That's exactly what I'll do to you if you don't tell me what was in that coconut!"

"What're you mad at me for? I didn't do nothin'! Yer the one who oughta be ashamed of yerself!"

252

"I didn't do anything, either," Jonas lied, loathe to think of Edward assuming the worst of Kate and maybe telling others what had happened. "You arrived just in time to stop me. But you sure as hell put something in that coconut to make Kate behave like a loose woman! Now, damn it, what was it?"

He shoved Edward's head beneath the water again, and Edward came up blubbering. "I don't know! I swear I don't know! It was some kind of love potion I got off Bell, but she didn't tell me what wuz in it, an' I didn't ask!"

Jonas moved around behind Edward, placed his foot in the center of the overseer's backside, and shoved as hard as he could. Splashing and waving his arms like a startled porpoise, Edward sprawled headfirst in the waves. Satisfied that he had his answer—all he was going to get out of the man, anyway—Jonas waded out of the water.

It *had* been a love potion, just as he suspected. Neither he nor Kate were responsible for their actions, tonight. They hadn't been able to help themselves. The things he had felt, the emotions he had never known he possessed, the incredible passion—they had all been a lie. Caused by a potion. What a relief! What a crushing disappointment!

If he truly wanted to recoup his losses and become a rich man, he ought to bottle the stuff and sell it. People would eagerly spend fortunes to experience what he had known—for a single, glorious hour!—this night. Scintillating passion. Incredible desire. Total satiation. Oneness and completeness. The perfect blending of self with another human being. For an hour, he had had it all, what poets wrote about, maidens sighed for, and ordinary people sought in the darkest hours of the night.

Having known it once, how could he now live without it? He felt cheated and deprived; at the same time, relief overwhelmed him. It had only been a potion. He threw back his head and laughed. The laughter poured out of him; he howled with grim amusement. Crawling out of the water on his hands and knees, Edward stared up at him as if he'd gone crazy.

"Yer daft," Edward said. "Yer daft as a hound dog bayin' at the moon."

That only made Jonas laugh harder. Leaving Edward to his own soggy company, Jonas walked slowly down the beach, convulsed with laughter, but the more he laughed, the more the joke seemed a tragedy from which he might never fully recover.

After a sleepless night in which Kate lay alone in her bed, as still and cold as a dead woman, she rose with the dawn and padded in her bare feet into her parents' bedchamber. Arriving at the foot of the four-poster, she called their names. "Mama, Papa . . . wake up. I have to talk to you."

Neither figure moved, and she had to repeat herself, half shouting, until at last, they both stirred. Her mother's frilly, lace-trimmed nightcap had fallen down over her eyes, and Sybil pushed it upward with a slender, trembling hand. "Kate? What is it? What are you doing here in the middle of the night?"

"It's not night, Mama, it's morning . . . and I need to talk to you and Papa . . . Papa, are you awake?"

Her father sighed, coughed, and cleared his throat. "Is something the matter, Kate? Why can't this wait until we've risen? Your mama needs her rest—and so do I."

"No, Papa . . . What Mama needs is to get up out of this bed, leave this room, and start living life again. And you need to stop drinking and be the man you've always wanted to be, the father I've never really had."

That statement got their full attention. William and Sybil emerged from the bed covers like two creatures awakening from a long hibernation. On Conch Cay, animals didn't hibernate, for the winters were warm, but Kate had read about animals in northern climates who slept through the cold parts of the year, and she vaguely wondered why her parents had chosen to spend so much of their own lives escaping reality. Perhaps because it was so painful and disillusioning to be wide awake and aware, as she was discovering for herself.

"Dearest Kate, whatever has happened?" her mother asked. "You look so . . . so sad and pale."

"I'm not sad, I'm angry. And I've reached a decision. Last night, Edward did something completely unforgivable. If he had succeeded in his wicked plan, I'd be standing before you now, a shamed and fallen woman, a woman with no recourse except to marry the man who took her virtue and claimed her virginity. Never mind that she didn't love him, and indeed, despised him with all her being."

"Kate!" Sybil gasped. "You aren't . . . you haven't . . . Why, if you have, then you must, of course, marry Edward at once!"

"No, Mama . . . I'm not and I haven't," Kate said, at least not with Edward, she added silently. And if Edward should claim otherwise, she would just deny it. He couldn't prove anything; she and Jonas had finished by the time Edward appeared on the scene.

What she would do if she were pregnant, Kate had not yet decided. Despite what she'd told Jonas the night before, she *still* wouldn't marry Edward. Did an innocent child deserve a father like Edward? Never. It would be better for Kate to drown herself and her baby in the sea than to marry Edward.

"However," she continued. "The fact that I'm still intact, is only pure luck and good fortune. Edward didn't succeed in his plan to compromise me, thereby forcing me into marriage. That he dared *try* is reason enough for dismissal. I plan to send him away—permanently, but in order to do so, I need your consent. He'll never go unless he knows that you, too, want him gone."

"But . . . but, Kate, dear . . ." Running his fingers through his thinning hair, her father sat up in bed. "Whatever he's done, you can't just dismiss a man who's given us the best years of his life. Edward's like family; one doesn't discard family, especially when everything Edward's done—or tried to do—I'm sure he's done only because he loves you."

"Papa, he intended to rape me, while I was under the influence of some . . . some potion he hid in a coconut!"

"Oh, Kate darling, I'm sure he didn't mean to *hurt* you," Sybil demurred. "He probably only hoped to soften your heart toward him. You're so cruel to Edward, daughter, so very cruel and intolerant. The man *loves* you; that's his only fault."

"It's *not* his only fault! He bullies and mistreats our workers. He threatens them and punishes them behind our backs. He threatened to beat Cassie, if she didn't cooperate in his plan. And he's made her do things as well . . . Why, Cassie's youngest, little Ollie, looks enough like Edward to be his son. I know you don't see anything wrong with the way Edward treats the slaves, but I do! And I can't stand it anymore. You *must* make Edward leave the cay!"

Her parents glanced helplessly at each other; between them passed the first real communication and silent agreement Kate had witnessed in years. "No, Kate," her father said. "We need Edward too much. If you don't want to marry him, we'll be disappointed, of course, but we'll try to understand.

256

And I'll convince Edward that from now on, he must leave you alone. But we won't make him leave. Despite what you say, he's been a good, loyal employee—a fine overseer. He's stood by us in good times and bad. The few good times we've had have been largely the result of his efforts."

"What about *my* efforts, Papa? I've done every bit as much as Edward; some people might say I've done more. Doesn't *my* opinion count for anything? Don't you and Mama even care what I think?"

"Of course, we care, dearest Kate! You mustn't ever think we don't care," her mother protested. "But we must do what we feel is best for all concerned—and keeping Edward at Conch Cay is vitally important. A plantation is doomed if it doesn't have a capable overseer."

Kate tried one last time. "*I* can function as overseer, Mama. I already direct most of the work, and the slaves readily obey me. They work better for me than they ever did for Edward."

Amazingly rational, considering her usual state, Sybil sadly shook her head. "No, daughter. It isn't proper for a woman to be an overseer. Your duty is to marry and bear children, heirs to our estate. I can't imagine whom you plan to take for a husband, now that you've so adamantly refused Edward. Surely, you couldn't be interested in another American. Remember what tragedy and heartache the last one caused. I oppose that sea captain's continued presence here. I oppose his using our island and resources to build his ships. Despite our feelings on the matter, you've gone ahead and offered him your help and the services of all our slaves. Have you done it because you're in love with him? Tell us now, Kate . . . Do you plan to abandon us and run away with him, once his ship is built?"

Tears spilled down Sybil's parchment-thin cheeks, her mouth quivered, and an alarming look came into her eyes. "Kate, could you really do that to us? Is that what this is really all about? Saints preserve us, I knew it! I shall die of grief and sorrow if you do this to us again, Kate!"

Then her mother began to sob. Her frail shoulders shook, and she gasped for breath. "Oh, I can't breathe! William, help me, I can't breathe, I tell you!"

"Don't just stand there!" William cried, showing a gumption that was all too rare. "Run and fetch Bell! Hurry, before your poor mother expires on the spot!"

Kate wheeled and ran out of the room. As she hurried downstairs and raced for Bell's hut, guilt almost suffocated her. *This* was what always happened every time she challenged her parents. This was why she could never leave them, never have a life of her own, or even choose her own husband. If she knowingly upset her mother beyond her slim endurance—thereby causing her death—how could she live with herself afterward?

Each time these attacks occurred, they became more violent and destructive, more difficult to overcome. Her mother sometimes turned blue, and once, Kate feared her heart had stopped beating. It had taken Bell pounding on Mama's chest and alternately pouring strange remedies down Mama's throat, to bring her out of it . . . and then, Mama had sunk into one of her spells. For weeks, she had made no sense, speaking not a single coherent sentence.

Not one of the doctors they had consulted over the years had been able to help her. One had claimed it was all a result of losing her dearly loved son on Tynbee Island. Whatever the reason, mental or physical, Mama's attacks were the worst things Kate had ever had to face. She dreaded them with all her heart—and dreaded even more, being the cause of them. She never should have awakened her parents and issued this ultimatum . . . Dear Lord! She had thought of demanding they also get rid of Bell, who had undoubtedly given Edward that potion.

Now, Kate promised herself to give Bell anything she wanted, do anything the slave woman desired, if only Bell would use her dark powers to save her mother one last time!

Chapter Eighteen

Sybil Montgomery didn't leave her bed for a week. When she finally did leave it, she hardly knew where she was or what she was doing. Only Bell could communicate with her. Only Bell could get her to eat, wash, dress, comb her hair, or do any of the normal, routine activities taken for granted by most people. Kate's guilt all but destroyed her own appetite—and her father's reproachful looks didn't help matters any. William began to drink earlier in the day and stay up later at night, usually with Edward for company, and the two of them would consume enough rum to inebriate five men.

If Kate chanced to see Edward during the day, he would only glare at her, grunting when she spoke to him, or ignoring her altogether. If Kate had not had Mattie's silent sympathy at night, and the hard work of stripping trees to keep her busy during the day, she would have plunged completely into despair and self-pity. As it was, she found it difficult to keep those emotions at bay, especially whenever she chanced to glance at Jonas, who never seemed to look her way.

The rift with Jonas bothered her every bit as much as the rift with her family—perhaps more so. It may have been a potion that caused her to yield to him, and to feel the way she had that night on the beach, but it wasn't potions, black magic, or love charms that made her heart ache with loss, and caused her to yearn for a kind word, gesture, or smile from him. Her grief was as great as it had been when she lost Jonathan.

Jonas was the last thing she thought about before she fell asleep at night, and the first thing she remembered when she awakened. Sometimes, she awoke drenched in perspiration, her body throbbing with unfulfilled need, the result of having dreamed that he was holding her, loving her, possessing her once again.

She couldn't seem to control her physical responses to him even in broad daylight. Whenever he came near, her flesh burned as if consumed by fire. She had only to look at him, wielding an ax, or rolling a huge log toward the spot on the beach where they were building the ship's cradle, and her breath caught in her throat, her limbs began to shake, and something hot and liquid uncurled in the pit of her belly.

She named the weird malady Jonas fever, and blamed it on the contents of the coconut she had drunk that night. But how long did aphrodisiacs last? And why had *she* been more affected than Jonas? He didn't seem to be suffering in the least. His sea-blue eyes looked past her with a chilly disinterest that froze her to the marrow of her bones. He spoke to her only when necessary or unavoidable—and then only about business matters.

He went out of his way to avoid being alone with her. When he could, he used intermediaries to convey messages. She got to know his men almost as well as he did, and she admired them for their many talents and cheerful enthusiasm for the back-breaking work. They were making excellent progress. The ship's cradle was nearly finished; soon, they would lay the keel and begin actual construction of the ship.

Jonas had either marked or already felled the trees they would need for the vessel. Maderia, wild tamarind, dogwood, pine, and horseflesh had felt the bite of the ax or would in the near future. Building the cradle, preparing to start work on the ship, kept Kate going when the long, sunny days seemed dark and gloomy. But there were a few times when her emotions overwhelmed her, and she had to escape and go off by herself, until she could handle things again. Those were the times when she suddenly dropped the small ax given her by Big Donald to strip branches off the big trees, and with no word or apology, fled into the forest. She always headed in the same direction—to that end of the island where the pool offered a refreshing swim, or Neptune was apt to trot up to her in welcome and nuzzle her hand, searching for a treat.

Neptune was the fine, small stallion who had somehow made it to shore one night following a shipwreck during a terrible storm; the storm had been so bad that she and Edward had been unable to save any salvage, much less any lives. The morning after, she had found the horse roaming the beach, snatching mouthfuls of sea grass here and there, but apparently unsatisfied. He had come right up to her, whinnying a welcome, and she had looped her arm around his proud, arched neck, stroked his velvety muzzle, and led him inland to the pond, where he had lapped the fresh water with obvious relish.

Neptune might have wound up a plow or saddle horse, but Kate was the only person Neptune would allow to touch or catch him. Edward had tried to toss a rope around his neck and subdue him, only to be dragged across the sand by the snorting, wild-eyed creature. Edward promptly decided that their old mule could continue doing the menial labor, and his own two legs or a dory were good enough for getting around the island.

Several weeks later, another shipwreck yielded two mares, and in time, the small herd grew to three mares, all ruled by the little stallion, whose chestnut-colored coat was nearly the exact same shade as Kate's hair. Without benefit of saddle or bridle, Kate learned to ride Neptune—so named because he came from the sea—but for the most part, she simply visited him on occasion, admired his newest foal, and went away again, refreshed and happy, simply from having spent time with her independent friend.

On this hot, sunny afternoon, Kate was once again swept with the need to escape. The Jonas fever hit her with stunning force when she happened to see Jonas stripping off his sweat-soaked shirt and bending to lift a maderia log. As Jonas rose, holding one end of the tree trunk while Big Donald hefted the other, the muscles of his upper arms bunched and stood out like thick cords. Likewise his chest muscles.

Kate achingly recalled how the moonlight had gilded those very same muscles, as Jonas knelt over her and reached down to fondle her breasts. Suddenly, her ears were ringing, her heart hammering, and her body drenched with perspiration. She rose from her knees beside a felled pine, only half stripped, dropped the axe, and headed into the woods. Breaking into a run, she ran until her side cramped, and her chest heaved as she fought for breath.

She walked the rest of the way to the pond, and there found Neptune and his little band, grazing near the marshland. Neptune nickered in greeting, kicked up his heels, and galloped toward her, stopping just short of running her down. It was a game they played—Neptune's lighthearted way of reminding her that he was master of all he surveyed. But today, Kate had no patience with games. Sobbing in misery, she walked up to him, clutched his red-gold mane, and buried her face in it.

"Oh, Neptune, what shall I do? I want him so much, and I can never have him! I don't know what's wrong with me; it's as if I'm bewitched."

Neptune blew through his nostrils, enduring her tears with quiet dignity. When she had finished crying she grabbed a hold of his withers, swung her leg over him, and pulled herself aboard. He tossed his head as her legs closed around him, then stood listening for a moment, his head held high, waiting for the little click of her tongue that signaled she was ready to go.

She had no means of guiding him, other than her legs, which he obeyed only when he felt like it. Today, he didn't feel like it. He rolled into the easy, comfortable canter that could take them both across the island in one-fourth of the time it took to walk it, and Kate merely hung on, not caring where he went. For now, it was enough that he was taking her anywhere; maybe on his back she could forget about Jonas, her family, and the solitary hell of the past few weeks.

Jonas was aware of the precise moment when Kate left the work site. He didn't need to see her go to realize that she had gone. He had developed a sixth sense that alerted him to where she was and what she was doing, nearly every minute of every hour of every day. Some strange, inexplicable instinct told him when she was tired, hungry, or thirsty, and what her mood was—deeply unhappy—which she had been ever since the night they'd made love on the beach in the moonlight.

He waited to see if she would return; her sudden departure could mean a call of nature, or it could once again be an overwhelming desire to escape his presence. It was probably the latter. This wasn't the first time she had fled the beach and disappeared for hours, without saying a word to anyone; what other reason could there be, if not a burning urge to flee from the sight of him?

Whatever love—or lust—she had felt for him had turned to hatred and revulsion; he could read condemnation in her beautiful, golden eyes, shadowed now with acute pain and sorrow. She wore the look of a mortally wounded fawn, and he cursed himself a thousand times a day, for not having had the good sense and willpower to resist the effects of that love potion.

Hard work had been the saving grace for both of them, but for Kate, it was sometimes not enough, and he wondered if she knew something he didn't yet know, such as whether or not he had made her pregnant. Would she tell him if she had conceived his child? Somehow, he doubted it. And if she had, would she really marry Edward, as she had threatened?

These were questions that tormented him day and night—that and the memory of their lovemaking, the sweet yielding of her mouth to his invading kisses, the way she had laid her hand so boldly upon his manhood and would have kissed him there, if he had let her! A hundred times since then he had pictured her doing that, pleasuring him as he had only imagined whores would pleasure a man, not decent women—and certainly not innocent virgins!

A hundred times he had damned himself, her, and most especially Edward, for introducing him to sensual delights and possibilities that he found himself craving with a helpless desperation. He spent his days trying not to look at her, because if he did, he feared he might suddenly drop ax or saw, sweep her into his arms, and carry her into the forest—there, to tear off both their clothing and

266

take her on the forest floor, like a stag mounting a doe.

But even when he wasn't looking at her, he knew she was there, watching him with those wounded eyes. Sometimes, he was sure he could smell her. Her hair had been scented with wild mint and salt-sea air that night, and her skin had borne the faint, tantalizing odor of citrus. Their lovemaking had yielded a muskiness that clung to both of them, and the recollection of it caused a swelling in his snug breeches, so that the seams threatened to burst apart.

He finished helping Big Donald place the huge timber next to the wooden skeleton of the ship's cradle, then excused himself and headed for the forest. "I want to look for another maderia about the same size as this one," he called over his shoulder. "This one won't yield enough boards for our purposes."

"I thought ya had already found one," Big Donald called after him.

Jonas waved and kept on walking. "I want a better one!"

Soon, the forest gloom encased him. He found it easy to follow Kate's trail; the dry, sandy soil bore the unmistakable imprint of her delicate-boned feet. She had an unusually long stride, he noticed, or else she had been running. He, too, started to run, seized by a dark premonition of impending danger or disaster. Maybe Kate was pregnant and had decided to end the pregnancy in some foolish, desperate manner that would negate the need for marrying anybody.

Refusing to debate the wisdom of pursuing her, when she so obviously wanted to be alone, Jonas hurtled through the woods at top speed and was totally unprepared for a near collison with a galloping horse. The animal suddenly burst through the trees and low brush, heading straight for him. As surprised as he was, the horse reared to avoid him, and a slim figure astride its back toppled sideways and fell to the ground with a resounding thud.

The horse immediately took off again and disappeared into the forest, but the figure lay there, still and silent, her burnished red hair covering her face. Jonas swore under his breath and hurried to Kate's side, having no doubt it was she; he would have recognized her at any distance, even in the dark of night. Why was she riding the horse, bareback yet, without even a bridle? On his journeys around the island, he had several times caught sight of the little band of horses, and in response to his questions, Cal had told him the animals were wild and untamed. Miz Kate was simply letting them breed, and planned one day to sell the offspring to folks on neighboring cays; but first, she needed to find someone with the expertise to break them to saddle or harness, and she must also obtain the proper equipment.

What in God's name had possessed her to attempt riding a dangerous, wild stallion? Checking for broken bones, Jonas ran his hands over Kate's slender body. He found nothing amiss, but Kate didn't stir— not until his hands explored her rib cage and skimmed lightly over her breasts. Then she moaned. He patted her cheek and called her name. Her only response was another deep moan.

"Kate . . . Dear God, don't let her die . . . Don't let her be badly hurt," he prayed without thinking.

The words came naturally to his lips, though it had been a long time since he had conversed with the Almighty. Gently, he gathered her into his arms. As he was lifting her, her eyelids fluttered open, and she gazed up at him with a dazed, bewildered expression.

"Jonas?" She raised her hand, and her fingertips grazed his jaw. "What happened to me? Why are you here?"

"You fell off a horse, Kate . . . I can't find any

broken bones, but you struck the ground hard. You may have hurt your head; you lost consciousness for several minutes."

"Oh . . ." she said, wincing. "Now, I remember . . . I was riding Neptune. We were galloping; I wasn't watching where I was going. Then suddenly, he reared and threw me. You can put me down now. I think I can stand."

Loathe to let go of her so quickly, Jonas eased her down the length of his body, until her toes touched the ground. She leaned against him, trembling, and he kept his arms around her, lest she collapse. "Are you all right? How does your head feel?"

"I'm a little dizzy. Other than that, I'm fine. The dizziness will pass in a moment."

He continued to hold her, and she neither moved nor pulled away. Her acquiescence emboldened him; he couldn't help himself. He kissed the top of her head, then her temples, and finally her closed eyes. She stood very still, pale as a sheet, making not a sound. He cupped her chin in one hand and tilted her face upward, so he could reach her lips. She opened her eyes. They brimmed with tears, shimmering gold in a shaft of sunlight penetrating the forest gloom.

"Don't do this to me, Jonas. If you don't really mean it, if you're only succumbing to the urges of the moment, please don't touch or kiss me . . ." Her husky voice lanced him like a spear.

"I haven't drunk any potions lately," he whispered. "None that I know of—but still I want you, Kate. You're like a fever searing my brain and heart . . . I can feel the heat of you from ten feet away. My body trembles at the sight of you. I can't eat, can't sleep, for want of you . . . I don't know what's happened to me. I only know I must have you . . ."

"Jonas . . ."

His name came out as a languorous, throaty sigh. With the pink tip of her tongue, she traced the shape of his mouth and the contours of his lips, as if she were starved for the taste of him. It was the most erotic thing he had ever had done to him. For a moment, he couldn't speak or move. She put her hands on his shoulders and licked along the column of his neck. Her hands slid lower and wrapped around the muscles of his upper arms. Her head dipped, and he felt her warm breath on his chest and her soft, wet mouth on his nipple.

Desire swept him from head to foot, shredding his self-control. He longed to clamp her to him, thrust deeply inside her, and bury himself in the hot, throbbing core of her. With his last remnant of logical thought, he refrained from obeying the clamorous demands of his body. It was wrong to take Kate out here in the woods; he couldn't lay her down on this bare, uneven ground, where the trees stood too close and patches of rock erupted through the thin soil. Nor did he want to take her standing upright, with her back ground into a tree trunk.

Mustering all his strength, he waited until she had finished suckling his other nipple and now sought his mouth with passion-swollen lips. "Wait . . . Wait, Kate," he begged.

Her eyes held anxious inquiry, but he soothed her with a long, deep kiss that simultaneously drugged and inflamed him more than any love potion ever could. Again, he lifted her into his arms, cradling her like a precious infant, and began walking in the direction where he hoped to find the pool. This time, she did not resist, but instead snuggled against him, winding her arms around his neck and nipping at his earlobe.

The pool wasn't far away, but it seemed like the longest walk of Jonas's life. When he got there, he set her down; no sooner had he done so when she suddenly danced away from him—her golden eyes merry and teasing. "I'm hot, Jonas . . . so very hot. I want to go swimming."

"Swimming! But your head! You shouldn't go near the water."

She paid him no heed. Already, she was tearing off her clothing—tossing garments left and right. Her lack of shame or shyness entranced him, but there was little time to savor the sight of her emerging nudity. He had only a moment to admire the perfect roundness of her pert, rose-tipped breasts, her slender waist, and her long, golden legs—then she ran splashing into the pool, her laughter floating behind her like the tinkle of silver bells.

He nearly tripped and fell trying to pull off his boots and trousers. When he was naked, he pursued the naked nymph cavorting in the placid water of the pool. She eluded him by diving underwater; he managed to grab a slippery ankle, but she broke free, rising to splash him in the face. The pool was too small and shallow for serious swimming, but he chased her around its perimeter, finally catching her near a sandy bank. She did not resist as he pulled her half out of the water, half onto the sand, and fell upon her.

"Kate, I don't understand this madness or what causes me to feel and act this way . . ." he gasped by way of apology for his driving need.

She cupped a hand over his mouth to stop his speech. "Does it matter why or how, Jonas? If you were to find a gold sovereign buried in the sand, would you spend the rest of your life agonizing over how it got there and who might have lost it? Some treasures can only be enjoyed, my love. It's senseless to toss them away, merely because you didn't earn them or they might belong to someone else . . ."

A wrecker's philosophy, he thought dryly. Some distant part of him strongly disapproved, but he could no more have let her go, than he could have cut off his right arm and tossed it away. "When I'm near you, nothing matters but that I should be nearer still . . ." he grumbled, despising his weakness and fearing this dark, unmanageable side of himself.

"Then come nearer, Jonas . . . Come into me, my darling . . . I love you . . . Yes, I love you, Jonas—more than my life, more than . . ."

He didn't wait to hear what more. He filled her mouth with his kisses and her body with his turgid shaft. He rammed his very essence into her, all the while kissing and caressing her, squeezing her full breasts, trying to subdue and possess her totally. In the end, it wasn't he who possessed her, but she who possessed him. He poured himself into her, shattering and exploding into a million dazzling pieces. He felt that he no longer existed; the old Jonas—the disciplined, ambitious, coolly calculating Jonas—was gone forever. In his place was a man he didn't know, a man who could be controlled with the simple crook of a woman's little finger, a sweet smile of invitation, or a come-hither glance from a pair of golden eyes. He knew even as he ravished her and was ravished in return that he couldn't live without this woman—at his side, in his bed, beneath his body, enfolded in his arms. She had bewitched him utterly.

"Marry me, Kate," he begged. "Marry me, and I'll stay here with you forever."

"Yes," she murmured. "Oh, yes, my darling Jonas."

She wrapped her arms and legs around him as if she would never let him go. They stayed beside the pool for the remainder of the afternoon, reveling in their nakedness and the joy and pleasure they brought to each other. They sported in the water and on the sand, discovered how to couple in the water without drowning, and taught themselves the subtle nuances of lovemaking that could drive each other wild with renewed desire, when both were already sated.

They had no awareness of anything or anyone, until quite suddenly, the voice of Big Donald came booming through the woods. "Cap'n! Cap'n, where are you?"

While Kate cowered in the pool, trying to cover herself with hair and water, Jonas scrambled for the shore and his trousers. "Stay here!" he hissed over his shoulder. "I'll go meet him and see what he wants."

Within seconds, he had struggled into his clothing and was headed in the direction of Donald's voice. He met Donald himself a few minutes later. The big, copper-bearded man was excited and breathing hard. "Where've you been, Cap'n? I been lookin' all over. We got a visitor down on the beach. Says he's from a neighborin' cay an' he's come t' see what we're doin'."

Silently bemoaning the visitor's bad timing, Jonas wondered if the man was merely curious or had come, perhaps, in search of employment. "What's his name?" Jonas inquired, debating whether or not this was important enough to leave Kate.

"Merrick . . . Said his name's John Merrick."

The name was a mule kick in Jonas's gut. "John Merrick!"

"Yeah . . . do you know him, Cap'n? From your expression, I would guess you do, an' it's someone you got reason t' hate."

"Go back to the beach and tell him to wait . . . I'll be along shortly. I . . . I left my boots back by the pool; it's so hot today I decided to jump in and cool off."

"By yourself, Cap'n—or did ya have company?" Big Donald's grin was sly and knowing. "You an' Miss Montgomery both have been missin' fer hours. I wuz startin' t' git worried."

"Better you should worry about getting your work done," Jonas snapped. "What Miss Montgomery and I have been doing is none of your business or anyone else's. Anyone who thinks otherwise can go back to Nassau."

"Sorry, Cap'n . . . There'll be no gossip. I'll see t' that."

"Good, then get going and tell Mister Merrick I'm on my way."

Chapter Nineteen

Kate knew as soon as she saw Jonas's face that something was wrong—something bad had happened. He was looking at her strangely, as if he hadn't seen her clearly before and now disapproved of what he saw. Suddenly aware of her nudity and half embarrassed by it since he was now clothed, she rose from the water and placed one hand across her breasts, and the other over the thatch of curly hair between her thighs.

"Jonas, what has upset you so? Whatever it is, we'll face it together." She hurriedly left the pond and reached for her clothes.

Jonas came up to her and helped her dress, holding up her wet hair so she could close the fastenings at the nape of her neck. "We have a visitor—someone drawn by the activity on the beach."

She wrinkled her brow, failing to see why that should be so disturbing. "Who is it? Did Donald say?"

He turned her around to face him before he answered. "Your old lover has returned to Conch Cay, Kate . . . You remember him, the man who wanted to marry you and take you away with him."

Kate could feel the blood draining from her face. "I assume you mean John Merrick," she said, finding

275

her wits after a moment's hesitation. "He was never my lover," she hoarsely denied. "You, of all people, should know that."

A glint of fierce jealousy gleamed in Jonas's blue eyes. "Nevertheless, he meant a great deal to you— enough to terrify your mother that he might one day succeed. Now, it seems he's returned. Shall we go and find out what he wants?"

Kate didn't know what to say. As soon as Jonas saw John Merrick, he would know she had lied. There was no resemblance whatever between Jonas and the short, balding, potbellied, little planter, except for the blue of their eyes, yet she had claimed that Jonas and John looked exactly alike. John might even have his wife with him, or a couple of his sons; why, oh why, had he left Green Turtle Cay and come calling, today of all days?

"Jonas, I . . . I . . ." The lump in her throat made it difficult to talk. More difficult still was to admit that she had lied, for what explanation could she give for the lies, except the truth? And what would happen if she told it? Disaster, she was certain. Now, Jonas would never marry her; she had destroyed all chance of trust and communication between them. She should have followed Mattie's advice and admitted everything long ago!

"Jonas . . ."

"Yes, Kate? Do you want to tell me something?"

His eyes were implacably cold, without warmth or compassion, the eyes of a stranger. She could scarcely believe they had spent the entire afternoon locked in each other's arms, their bodies joined together, their spirits united in perfect harmony and oneness.

"Yes, I . . . I suppose I must. But I don't know if you'll be able to understand, much less forgive me."

"Perhaps when I meet John Merrick, I'll understand. You never expected him to return here, did you? His sudden arrival has caught you off guard.

Tell me about him, Kate. Tell me every last intimate detail. I have the feeling this will change things between us—and not for the better, but maybe it's better to learn the truth now, than to have it sprung on me when it's far too late to do anything about it."

"Oh, Jonas, I should have told you when you first arrived here! But I was so afraid of what you'd do that I couldn't. There was nothing to be gained by telling you; it wouldn't have changed anything. Anyway, I was sure you'd be leaving shortly. I never dreamed you'd be staying—or that we would fall in love. And after we did, after I knew how I felt about you, I still couldn't bring myself to tell you, because . . . because I knew it might spoil things, just as you fear."

"You'd better start at the beginning, Kate. Meeting John Merrick can wait. This can't. Start now, and don't quit until you've finished."

And so Kate told him—not all of it, of course, for there was no point in upsetting him needlessly or stirring up violence, which she was sure would result if Jonas knew that Edward had been responsible for his brother's shipwreck, as well as Jonas's. She stated only the bare facts: that Jonathan's ship had indeed gone down off Conch Cay, all hands had been lost except Jonathan, whose life she had saved, much as she had saved Jonas's, and that Jonathan had later died while fishing during a sudden, violent storm. Not knowing whom to contact, they had buried him deep in the forest, where no one would ever find his grave if they had no knowledge of it.

With each word she spoke, Jonas's face grew paler, his lips more compressed, his eyes more shadowed and haunted with pain. "So . . ." he said at last, when she had finished. "That's what happened to my brother. After all this time, I finally know." Then he gave her a look that nearly cut her in two. "Why didn't you tell me before? Why did you lie and try to keep his death a secret?"

"Because you hated wreckers! That was obvious from the start. I had saved your life, but you were ready to believe the worst; you *wanted* to believe the worst. I had to protect my parents, myself, Edward, and my workers. You might have sought revenge against us for something that was accidental. You would have blamed us for his death. At that point in time, you wouldn't have accepted that his death was as great a tragedy for me personally as it has been for you."

"Ah, yes . . . That's what so disturbed your mother, wasn't it? In the brief time he was here, Jonathan exerted his legendary charm and nearly convinced you to go away with him—or to bed with him, which is probably all he wanted in the first place."

Jonas's tone made a mockery of her feelings for Jonathan; yet, they had been the most beautiful experience of her life—until Jonas himself came along. "I *loved* him!" she cried. "And I grieved for him as a wife would grieve for her husband! I hadn't yet lain with him, no—nor had I decided to accept his proposal—but I had *wanted* to do both. I yearned to do both."

As soon as the words left her mouth, Kate knew she had said the wrong thing. Jonas's beautiful, sea-blue eyes darkened to the color of slate. "How gratifying to discover that I was your second choice, your consolation prize, as it were, for never having lain with or married my brother."

"That's not t—true!" Kate choked. "You're no substitute for Jonathan. What I felt for him has nothing to do with what I feel for you."

"I don't doubt I'm *not* a fit substitute for Jonathan. Where women are concerned, I never could compete—and until now, I never wanted to. Just how does one compete with a dead man? Dear God! If it would bring him back again, I'd gladly cut out my

278

heart. Strange as it may sound, I feel as if I already have. If Jonathan were standing here now, which of us would you choose, Kate?"

"Stop it! Why must I choose at all? Why do you bait me like this? Is your jealousy worse than your sorrow? I've just told you that your brother is dead and buried, yet you don't weep, don't grieve, don't pray . . ."

"Never think I'm not grieving, Kate—or weeping. I weep and grieve for Jonathan all the time, on the inside where it doesn't show. As for praying, I regret to say I do that rarely, if at all . . ."

"Then maybe you should do it more often!" Ashamed of her snappishness in the face of Jonas's suffering, Kate sighed and laid her hand on his arm. "Please forgive me, Jonas. I'm sorry I didn't tell you sooner . . . but I had hoped to avoid a scene like this. Nothing you can do, say, or feel will bring Jonathan back again. I've had time to accept that; you haven't. Let me go and say hello to John Merrick. Then I'll come back here and . . . and take you to Jonathan's grave, if you wish."

"You're right; I haven't had time to accept this," he said. "I must think about things . . . I'd like to be alone for a while. But first, there's something I must get from my hut."

"What? I could get it for you and bring it back here."

"No . . ." He shook his head, his face and eyes still cold and distant. "I'd rather get it myself. It's something that belonged to Jonathan. I want to show it to you. Perhaps you'd even like to have it for a keepsake. It was something that meant a great deal to him."

"Then you should keep it, whatever it is," she quickly insisted. "He was your brother. To me, he was only . . . a candle flame that flared brightly for a brief time, and then, sadly, went out."

"And what am I?" came the faintly sarcastic question. "Another candle flame?"

"No, Jonas," she answered with all the sincerity and truth in her heart. "You are a fire that will burn forever. *Forever*," she repeated, but he only looked at her as if he didn't believe her, as if every word she said was a bitter, cruel lie.

By the time Kate had visited with John Merrick, showed him the plans for the ship, inquired after his wife and children, and bade him goodbye so he could get home before dark, it was already early evening, and the shadows were lengthening on the beach. She herself had to leave in the dory with Daisy and Fish, or she would not get home before nightfall.

She went searching for Jonas. Instead of returning to the pool to wait for her, he had disappeared into his hut and not come out again. She found him sitting alone on the woven mat that served as his only furnishings, other than the bed, trunk, and chipped washbasin she'd brought from the house.

"He's gone, now, Jonas," she said by way of greeting, then she perched warily on the edge of the bed. "It's time for me to leave, too, but I won't go if you want me to stay. I don't care what anyone thinks. I'll spend the night here with you . . . but only if you wish it. Tell me what you want, Jonas. Tell me what you're thinking."

He hadn't moved since she had entered the hut, and he barely moved now, and didn't look at her. His attention centered on a small, round object he held in his hands. "This belonged to Jonathan," he said quietly, his voice edged with emotion. "It was a gift I gave him when he became a man, and he swore to keep it always with him. You may already have seen it; perhaps he showed it to you."

He extended his hand and held out the object to

her. Even before she took it from him, Kate knew what it was—Jonathan's round brass watch in its engraved case, which was etched with an anchor and the inscription: *To my brother and my friend . . . a true man among men.* It was signed with the letter J and dated, but Kate could not remember the date.

Her fingers trembled as they closed over the precious memento. After she had found Jonathan's body on the beach, she had searched his pockets, looking for the watch, because she knew how much it had meant to Jonathan. It had not been anywhere on his person, and she had credited its loss to the hungry sea. How had Jonas found it? She herself had seen Jonathan tuck it into his breast pocket just before he left to go fishing.

"I know the watch," she admitted, smoothing its rounded contours, then tracing the engraved anchor on the lid. "It was Jonathan's most precious possession."

"Then he must have told you about me."

Realizing she was caught in another lie, Kate bit her lip in chagrin. Earlier, she had told Jonas she had made no effort to contact Jonathan's family, because she didn't know he had one or still lived with his brother.

"He did mention you, when he showed me the watch, but he never gave me your address or even stated if you were still alive. We had more important things to discuss besides you, Jonas," she said defensively, aware that she was stoking his jealousy, but preferring him jealous to furious over her continued lies.

Amazed that the watch bore little evidence of damage by sand or salt water, Kate examined it more closely. "Where in God's name did you find this?"

"Look at me, Kate . . . I want to see your face when I tell you."

She raised her eyes to meet Jonas's and saw the

281

faint trace of tears on his cheeks; his handsome face looked ravaged. While she had been visiting with John Merrick, Jonas had sat alone—mourning his brother.

"A friend of mine—and of Jonathan—discovered the watch in a Nassau shop."

"But that's not possible!" she blurted, riveted with shock. "I mean—I can't believe Jonathan was so anxious for money that he would have sold the watch," she desperately backtracked. "He might have done it when he accompanied Edward and me to Nassau to sell the salvage from his ship, but I find that hard to credit. He never said anything to me about it, and I know how much he valued the watch."

"Then how do you account for it being found in Nassau?" Jonas inquired in a deadly calm voice.

As Kate tried to sort out the mystery, thoughts tumbled violently in her head. She didn't dare tell Jonas that Jonathan had had the watch in his pocket when he left to go fishing; Jonas would immediately conclude there had been foul play. *Had* there been? *Edward.* Edward must somehow be involved in all this; could Edward have found Jonathan's body on the beach before she did, and callously searched his pockets in hopes of retrieving some item of value?

It would be very like Edward to do that; thinking about it, Kate realized that Edward hadn't seemed as shocked and surprised as everyone else to hear that Jonathan's body had washed up on the beach. *Damn Edward!* There was apparently no end to his greed and selfishness. But what good would be served by telling Jonas that Edward had probably robbed Jonathan as he lay dead, and then sold the booty to a shop in Nassau?

"I can't account for it," Kate admitted with a small sigh of anguish. "Jonathan *must* have sold it to the shop; that's the only explanation. Did you visit the

282

shop when *we* went to Nassau?"

"Yes . . . I did. But the proprietor didn't remember who had brought the watch to him. It seems he handles all kinds of salvage and never questions where it comes from. You wreckers aren't the only ones to whitewash your filthy business."

Despairing that he would ever forgive her, Kate lifted the watch and held it out to him. "I'm so terribly sorry, Jonas . . . I don't know what more I can say. I've lied to you and deceived you. I've done things you roundly condemn. You've made me see myself as I really am, and I'm not sure I like what I see. I can justify what I've done—I'd probably do the same things again, if I had to—but . . . but . . . I realize that you may hate me for them. You certainly have no respect for me. Tomorrow, I'll show you your brother's grave, and then you can decide if you still want to marry me. I'll understand if you don't."

Without saying a word, Jonas took the watch from her hand and Kate jumped nervously to her feet. "I have to go now. It's getting late. Good night, Jonas."

She hesitated, hoping he would rise and stop her, take her in his arms, and tell her it didn't matter—that nothing mattered except their love for each other. She prayed he would at least look at her. But Jonas said nothing. He didn't even glance at her. His eyes remained on the watch, which he held as if it were a sacred talisman, a reminder of all he had lost because of her and Edward.

She had never felt so rejected and helpless. Choking on sobs she couldn't quite suppress, she fled his hut.

In the morning, Kate took Jonas to visit his brother's grave. It was located in the thickest, most remote part of the forest that covered the island, mute testimony that no one on Conch Cay wanted the outside world to know that a young man had died and been buried there.

Kate had transplanted wildflowers to the area around the grave and marked the spot with a small, white cross, but there was no headstone or marker containing Jonathan's name or any information about him. That was the first thing Jonas noticed—and the first words he spoke to Kate since the night before.

"There's nothing to say who lies here. It could be a pauper's grave—or a slave's. It's the resting place of a man of no consequence, someone no one wishes to remember." His voice vibrated with anger.

"I had planned to get a headstone eventually. But I've been preoccupied trying to see that we all get enough to eat. Also, there's been no money to purchase a proper headstone."

"Any stone at all would be better than nothing; it shouldn't be too hard to find someone to carve a few words or a date on it."

"I'm sorry . . ."

The phrase was beginning to sound repetitive, but Kate didn't know what else to say. In reality, she had planned on placing a fine, white piece of coral limestone on the site, with Jonathan's name, the dates of his birth and death, and the phrase, *I shall love you through all eternity,* carefully chiseled upon it. Such work could be done in Nassau, but stonemasons and carvers cost money, and the needs of the plantation had had to come first.

"If I suddenly died, would you bury me here, too—in an unmarked grave beside my forgotten brother?" Jonas demanded, his eyes shooting sparks.

"Of course not! You would *both* have markers—just as soon as I could afford them."

"When I finally leave here, I'm taking his remains with me. I'll have him reburied in the family plot in Salem, where he belongs."

This then, was her answer as to whether or not he still wanted to marry her. Obviously, he did not. Yesterday by the pool might never have happened. He no longer loved her; the truth had destroyed his love.

"Whatever you think best," she replied tonelessly. "I won't fight you on it. Doubtless, you know where Jonathan would prefer to lie far better than I."

"Leave me," he commanded, his gaze fastened to the modest grave. "I want to be alone with him."

Nodding silently, she withdrew and returned to the work site. Big Donald Fell, Musket Jones, Nimble Clayton, and John Ferguson were all hard at work, as were her own workers and the extra men they had hired in Nassau. No one said a word to her, and she wondered if Jonas had told his men what had happened to his brother. It seemed to her that they took pains to avoid looking her way or speaking to her, and were only working because of Jonas.

It didn't really matter to her what they thought—if they were angry or upset or blamed her for both shipwrecks. Nothing could make her feel more miserable than she already did. She supposed someone would eventually accuse her of luring ships onto the reef with lights; when the accusation finally surfaced, she would have to decide whether or not to continue protecting Edward. He was the last person she wanted to protect. If anything, she *wanted* him to be punished for the sly treachery that had caused so much suffering, including her own.

Yet there was no way Edward could be punished without her parents, too, paying the price. No matter what Edward did, her father continued to defend him; so did her mother, when she was lucid. The three of them were such staunch allies that Kate had become an outsider in her own home. With Jonas now rejecting her, Mattie and Cal remained her only friends.

285

I will build this ship, she thought with a vengeance, attacking a fallen pine tree as if it were a living being. And after I finish, I will build another. I won't think about anything but work. Somehow, some way, I'll get through this. I will because I must. This place, this island, is all I have—and I'll do anything I must to keep it.

Chapter Twenty

Three weeks went by with agonizing slowness—three miserable, unhappy weeks during which Jonas buried himself in the work of shipbuilding and spent as little time as possible in Kate's company. The keel was now laid and the hull going up, one laboriously fashioned board after another. The difficult, painstaking labor blotted out Jonas's pain and enabled him to get through each grief-racked day. For he was grieving not only for the loss of his brother, but also for having lost Kate, or more accurately, his love and desire for Kate.

When he thought of her now or caught a glimpse of her from the corner of his eye, Jonas felt nothing—only a curious numbness. But then, how could he love a liar? Not only a liar, but a wrecker, who might very well have *caused* his brother's death and his own near destruction. The answer was he couldn't. He and Kate had been as intimate as two people can be, but she still hadn't told him about his brother. No wonder he felt nothing for her now; maybe his former passion *had* been the result of some long-lasting aphrodisiac. If so, the potion had finally worn off. He should be relieved that he wasn't pining for her. But he wasn't relieved. Instead, he had a grim suspicion that the numbness was only a coating;

beneath it, lay a raw, bloody wound that might never truly heal.

Reviewing his impossible situation, Jonas suddenly looked up from putting a new edge on his ax to find Kate standing a foot away from him, her pale face determined, her mouth opening to speak. Since she hadn't spoken to him or approached him directly since that day in the forest when she had taken him to his brother's grave, Jonas was startled and immediately set down his ax beside the whetstone he'd been using to sharpen it. "What is it?" he growled, resenting the interruption.

She wet her lips before answering. "I won't be able to help you tomorrow," she said. "Everyone's getting tired of fish and conch. We're short of food anyhow, with so many people to feed, so I thought I'd go over to Big Abaco and hunt boar."

"Boar!" His voice rose in disbelief. "You're going off to hunt boar by yourself?"

"Not by myself . . . I know you can't spare Cal or Benjamin or any of the others, so I've asked Edward to help me. He has little enough to do these days."

"Edward!" Jonas almost choked on the name.

"Edward and I have hunted boar together many times. We often do so at Christmas."

"And how do you kill the beasts—with your bare hands?" Jonas's fury knew no bounds. He wasn't sure which enraged him more: the thought that she, a mere fragile woman, would dare face such a dangerous creature, or that she'd do it in company with Edward.

"My father owns several Brown Bess muskets, and Edward also has one. The guns are old but still serviceable. I'm a competent marksman, and can load and fire as fast as any man. Indeed, I'm usually the one who waits in ambush and does the killing, while Edward drives the beast into my path. However, he and Cal do the butchering. I confess I

288

have no stomach for that."

"You will not go boar hunting on Big Abaco alone with Edward!"

Heads swiveled in Jonas's direction; a sudden expectant hush fell over the work site.

"You can't stop me. Nor do you have anything to say about it. But if you wish to join us, I have no objection, especially if you know how to shoot. Boar hunting is a challenging sport, and I'd be foolish to turn down the offer of a man who can handle a musket. The slaves cannot. Also, they panic when the boar makes his charge and sometimes don't stand their ground."

Jonas felt faint with fear for her. He had a vivid mental picture of a huge beast with wickedly curving tusks bearing down on Kate, who stood all alone, facing him with nothing but an old, temperamental musket in her slender hands. "You actually provoke the beast into charging?" he asked, filled with horror and incredulity.

"Provocation is hardly necessary. Do you know of a better way to do it? If you do, we'd be glad of your advice."

"I've never hunted boar," he admitted. "But I know well enough how to handle firearms, though it's been some time since I fired a Brown Bess. I insist upon accompanying you."

"Good." Kate gave him a wintry smile. "We'll be leaving quite early. Edward and I will meet you here at dawn tomorrow morning."

"Why does Edward have to come at all?" Jonas challenged.

"Because he knows boars in general, and Big Abaco in particular. I doubt we'd succeed without him. As long as my father insists that Edward continue working for us, he might as well earn his keep. When you are eating fresh pork tomorrow night, you won't mind that he came with us."

"I'll mind," Jonas assured her. "And I'll keep a close watch on him to make sure he doesn't doctor the meat first."

"A good idea," Kate agreed. "We certainly don't want a repeat of what happened before with a coconut."

Jonas stared at her, all his senses roaring to life in an instant. She steadfastly returned his gaze, and memories shimmered invitingly between them. He could recall every detail of her body, the feel of her satiny flesh beneath his hands and mouth, the warmth of her lips, the shape of her breasts and buttocks filling his eager palms.

"I'll be ready," he promised, his voice roughened with sudden, intense desire.

She nodded, turned, and walked away. He couldn't keep his eyes from following her. The gentle sway of her hips sounded a siren's song in his brain, and he wanted her with a passion that matched or exceeded everything he had felt for her in the past. The numbness had magically disappeared, and in its place, was a ravenous hunger too powerful to ignore or deny.

Two hours after sunrise the next morning, Jonas, Kate, and Edward dragged a sturdy, flat-bottomed skiff ashore on Big Abaco. The craft on which they'd made the journey from Conch Cay had been slow and unwieldy in the surf, but it was amply suited for carrying two or three hundred pounds of pig, which was the size of some of the boars that roamed the island, Kate had informed Jonas.

Having secured the skiff beyond the reach of the sea, Jonas glanced at his surroundings with interest. Big Abaco or Great Abaco as it was also called, was huge compared to Conch Cay. Though not overly wide, its length was remarkable, consisting of seemingly endless stretches of deserted beach, marshland, and forest that bore no signs of human habitation.

"Not well settled, is it?" Jonas asked Kate.

"Oh, there are people living here, most of them on the east coast at Carelton and Marshes Harbour, but not near here. We came to this area purposely, because we're more likely to find boar away from the settlements."

"I see there's plenty of pine trees and maderia." Jonas nodded toward the thick forest set back from the sandy beach.

"Yes, the vegetation is similar to what we have on Conch Cay, and there are good harbors here, too. Boats could as easily be built here as there." Her tone implied that if things didn't work out at Conch Cay, Jonas might consider a change in location, which he just might, Jonas thought to himself, if worse came to worst.

Edward interrupted his speculations by thrusting a musket into his hands. "Ya know how t' load this thing?" he sneered. "Or do I haveta show ya?"

Jonas would have given much to ram his fist down the other man's throat. Instead, he calmly took the musket and other items Edward handed him and wordlessly began loading the old ten-pound piece with powder, ball, and paper—all rammed down tightly into the muzzle with a ramrod.

The discharge from a Brown Bess could inflict a grievous wound, but at a range greater than 125 yards, the ball fell harmlessly to the ground. The rate of fire was two or three shots per minute, and the weapon often misfired. In rain, it was totally useless. For all of these reasons, British soldiers and others who swore by the muskets, relied more on the 21-inch bayonet usually affixed to the musket's muzzle, than they did on the gun itself.

None of the four muskets they had brought with

them contained a bayonet, and in any case, Jonas couldn't imagine killing a charging boar with a mere bayonet. A hunter would have but a single opportunity to shoot the beast, and if it didn't go down, the penalty was being slashed to ribbons. By the time a man—or woman—could reload, the animal would be on top of him or her. No wonder the slaves were afraid to withstand the charge of a maddened boar; there was precious little room for error.

Jonas glanced toward Kate and saw that she had been expertly loading her musket at the same time he had been loading his. When she had finished, she slung the straps of both powder horn and leather cartridge case over her shoulder and gave him an inscrutable glance. She might be wary of sending messages with her eyes, but he could sense her excitement from ten feet away. She ought to have been terrified, but she wore the expression of a determined hunter—huntress—already on the trail of her prey.

"What is the plan?" he inquired. "Would either of you care to enlighten me?"

"We'll stay together until we find a spoor and determine which way the boar is headed and how far behind it we are. Then we'll split up," Kate explained. "You and I will set a trap for the animal, and Edward will try to drive him into it."

"What if he charges Edward, instead?" Jonas asked.

"Then Edward will shoot it. Since we each have a musket, and there's two of us, he'll keep the extra. Fortunately, Edward's quite good at confusing wild boars and getting them to run in the right direction. They don't see or hear very well, but their sense of smell is excellent. He takes advantage of that by crisscrossing his own spoor, so that the poor beast often runs in circles trying to locate him, growing more maddened and confused in the effort. You'll

292

see. It will be quite easy."

"But what happens if he drives the boar to one of us, and we miss it or don't kill it with our first shot?"

"For obvious reasons, we mustn't let that happen." Kate grinned, for a moment setting aside their estrangement. "The trick is to wait until you *can't* miss. There's danger, but there's also a strange, heady exhilaration. It's like looking into the face of death, but escaping at the last possible moment. Boar hunting is actually quite stimulating."

Jonas felt admiration, as well as fear for her safety—and his own. He already knew that Kate possessed courage, but this was a reckless side of her character he hadn't yet witnessed. He wasn't sure he approved of such brashness in a female—but then, Kate was no ordinary woman. She had already demonstrated that in countless ways, not the least of which was her uninhibited, unself-conscious love-making.

Today, as another example, she was again dressed in male clothing—worn leather breeches, a coarse linen shirt, and a man's striped woolen vest. Her lovely hair was stuffed under an old cocked hat of a style popular thirty years ago, and on her feet she wore heavy leather sea boots. Yet, despite her masculine attire, she exuded a potent femininity that made both him and Edward glare at each other, like two male dogs scenting the same bitch in heat.

"Let's git goin'," Edward grumbled. "Sometimes it takes hours to find a spoor—and then hours more of trackin' 'til we catch up with the pig."

He took the lead and headed into the forest. Kate followed, with Jonas at her heels. Never having hunted boar, Jonas was uncertain what they were looking for, but less than an hour later, Edward let out a quiet whoop of triumph. "Here!" he hissed. "Droppings . . . and they ain't very old."

"How can you tell?" Jonas asked, eyeing the droppings with mingled curiosity and distaste.

Edward touched a finger to them, then unconcernedly wiped his hand on his trousers. "They're still warm, Cap'n . . . Don't you know nothin' about huntin'?"

In point of fact, Jonas didn't know a great deal. One didn't hunt on the deck of a ship, but he wasn't going to admit his inexperience to Edward. "So what do we do, now?" he demanded.

Edward lifted his head and sniffed the fresh wind, as if trying to locate the boar by its smell. "We'll run into marshland if we keep goin' in this direction. I remember it from las' time . . . an' hogs don't like swimmin' any better'n I do. I'll go up ahead, find him, and circle him a few times. Then I'll head him toward the beach. You stay here in case he backtracks; let Kate go down by the water an' wait fer 'im."

"Kate's going where I go," Jonas disputed. "Or else I'm going where she goes. Take your pick."

"It will be all right, Jonas," Kate whispered beside him. "The boar can't very well corner me on the beach, right out in the open."

"There's no protection out there! Not a tree or a bush. I think we should take him right here in the forest."

"That's stupid," Edward argued. "Maybe there ain't no pertection on the beach, but out there, he can't surprise her neither. All she has to do is aim the musket, wait 'til he gets close enough, and then blow out his brains."

"If it's so damn easy, I'll take the beach, and she can stay here," Jonas said frostily.

"Suit yerself. Don't make me no difference if it don't bother Kate."

Jonas and Edward both looked at Kate. Shrugging her shoulders, she nodded. "It really doesn't make a difference one way or the other. There's danger in both places. But I do think we should split up. Otherwise, he might get past us."

Grudgingly, Jonas conceded the point. But he vowed to stay close to the forest so he could rescue Kate if she needed help. The plan decided, Edward crept ahead, crouching as he studied the ground, and pausing now and then to listen. Kate, meanwhile, sought the protection of a huge tree with outspread branches that hung down low enough for her to grab hold of and swing herself up and out of harm's way, if necessary. Appeased by the nearness of the tree and the ease with which Kate could climb it, Jonas silently made his way back toward the beach.

Broad, shallow dunes dotted the area, an unexpected discovery, and clumps of sea oats waved in the offshore wind. Fragrant white bay lilies dominated the tops of the dunes, while the gentle valleys between held plants with small, bright yellow flowers. Jonas did not have the unobstructed view that Edward had proclaimed, and he was glad he had taken the beach and left Kate in the relative safety of the forest.

He explored the dunes, walked a bit farther in the direction from which the boar would most likely come, then crouched down near a huge piece of driftwood, the remnant of a fallen tree. It was scant protection, but better than nothing. Then began the waiting . . .

The sun climbed high overhead, but thankfully, fleecy clouds held back the heat, which could be intense in the middle of the day. Jonas wished he had brought along one of the small casks of fresh water they had left in the skiff. He considered whether or not green coconuts might be found nearby, but in view of his last experience, he wasn't eager to resort to coconuts to quench his thirst.

Then he heard an alien sound—a grunting, snuffling sort of sound, accompanied by the swish of sea oats as a large body forced itself through them. Straightening, he swung the musket into firing position, placing the butt firmly against his shoulder. He still didn't see anything, but the noises grew louder and seemed to be coming from around the side of the nearest sand dune.

He aimed the musket, sighting carefully down its muzzle and trying at the same time to scan the surrounding area with his peripheral vision. Then he saw it—an enormous beast, standing all of three feet high at the shoulder, with a head and body length of at least five feet, and curving, upturned tusks, a good ten inches or longer.

The boar had tiny eyes for such a large creature, coarse, black, bristly hair, and yellowish underfur. The animal's tusks protruded from either side of its flat, naked snout, and its ears were flattened, as if listening for sounds behind it. At the sight of Jonas, the beast's ears snapped forward, and it skidded to a stop in midrush. Pausing a moment, it squealed defiance and charged straight for Jonas.

Jonas never thought of running; there was no place to escape or hide. Fully aware of this, he stood silent and unmoving to meet the charge and leveled the muzzle of the musket at the boar. The hard part was trying to decide when to pull the trigger. A shrill scream shattered his concentration.

"Jonas! He's headed your way! Jonas!"

The voice belonged to Kate, but Jonas dared not glance away from the red-eyed beast with its long, glinting tusks. As the boar thundered toward him, he caught a whiff of its rich, gamey odor. Taking his time, he slowly squeezed the trigger. For the space of a long, drawn breath, nothing happened. Finally, the musket issued a weak, ineffectual pop and a puff of smoke too small to stop a butterfly.

It took another moment for Jonas to realize what had gone wrong. The powder in the musket hadn't fully ignited, giving little or no impetus to the ball, which had spun harmlessly out of the gun's muzzle and dropped to the ground right in front of the boar's flat nose. Onward the animal came, grunting its outrage.

"Jonas!" Kate screamed.

Jonas leaped to one side, and the boar charged blindly past him. But it didn't go far. Wheeling on its short, stubby legs—showing a speed and agility remarkable for its enormous bulk—the boar charged again. Jonas swung the musket high over his head and brought it down with a crash across the beast's snout. The impact of the blow deflected the charge sufficiently that the boar's tusk missed Jonas's thigh by a scant whisker.

But now the musket was broken in two. Disgusted, Jonas hurled the remaining piece after the boar as it skidded to a stop in the sea oats.

"Jonas, I'm coming! Hold on, I'm coming!"

Jonas could hear Kate's labored breathing as she raced toward him, but he still didn't dare glance away from his snorting adversary. Moving slowly, he inched toward the driftwood. The boar appeared momentarily dazed, but then it spun toward him, four hundred pounds of porcine fury bent on destroying him. This time, the animal smashed into the driftwood, splintering it into pieces that showered Jonas's abdomen and legs. On the next pass, it would surely gore him. He could never outrun it. Those vicious tusks would tear into flesh, tissue, and blood vessels, like a hot knife slicing through butter.

Determined that he wouldn't die running away like a coward, Jonas braced himself for the final, fatal impact. The boar again made his turn and came hurtling toward him, but the impact never came. A movement off to the side alerted Jonas to Kate's presence as she raised her musket to firing position. A moment later, the animal's head exploded in a huge

297

puff of blood, smoke, and flying bone fragments. The earsplitting concussion knocked Jonas flat on his back. He lay there stunned, while the acrid-smelling gunsmoke writhed sinuously around him, making his eyes water and causing him to choke. His head spun when he tried to lift it, so he lay back panting and attempted to gather his scattered wits.

Tossing her musket aside, Kate flung herself on top of him. "Jonas! Oh, God, Jonas!" She sobbed hysterically. "I thought I wouldn't get here in time! I thought you were as good as dead. When I saw your musket misfire, I knew there was nothing you could do to stop him, nowhere you could go to escape. Oh, Jonas, my heart stopped beating! If that boar had killed you, I don't think I could go on living."

Her words were sweet as honey to Jonas; eagerly, he lapped up her attention and devotion, holding her tight against him and reveling in the sweet weight of her trembling body. "It's all right, Kate . . . I'm all right. He didn't hurt me, thanks to you. I can't believe you got him, but you did. For the second time, you've saved my life."

She leaned back to gaze at him with tear-bright eyes. "I have, haven't I? Don't you think you owe me something for that, Jonas?"

"What is it you want, Kate? You know I don't have a shilling to my name. I possess absolutely nothing of value to give to you."

"Yes, you do," she insisted, her voice softening so he had to strain to hear it. "Forgiveness . . . You can forgive me for lying to you about your brother, for not telling you what happened to Jonathan until John Merrick's unexpected appearance forced the issue."

Yes, he thought, I can do that—or can I?

He cupped her face between his hands. "You mean I can *try* and forgive you. Whether or not I'll succeed is another question. Feelings can't be controlled by merely deciding to stop feeling a certain way. It still hurts me to think that you lied, Kate—and kept on lying though you claimed to love me. What kind of love permits deceit and subterfuge?"

The tears spilled over and rolled down her cheeks. "I don't know, Jonas . . . But surely, if you love me, you ought to be able to find it in your heart to forgive me."

Yes, he thought, I ought to be able to do such a simple, but so terribly important thing.

"Maybe forgiveness is the very essence of loving," he mused aloud, wiping the tears from her cheeks with his thumbs. "Is that what you mean?"

"Yes," she whispered. "After all, neither of us is perfect; we might have to make a habit of forgiving each other."

"What an interesting notion," Jonas murmured, distracted from the philosophical debate by the nearness of her lips to his. He drew her face closer and tasted the salt of her tears when he pressed his mouth to hers.

She responded eagerly, kissing him back with a fervor and enthusiasm that was pure, unadulterated Kate. They might have gone further, forgetting everything, including the dead boar nearby, but a shout from Edward caught their attention.

"Kate!" he was bellowing from somewhere in the forest. "Ya got the boar, didn't ya? Where'n hell are you?"

"I notice he isn't worried about where I might be," Jonas said dryly.

Kate laughed, scooted to one side, and offered Jonas her hand to help him rise. "We had better get up. It wouldn't do to be discovered rolling about in the sand beside our dead quarry."

In answer, Jonas only grunted, resenting Edward's presence with every fiber of his aching body. The man's timing was impeccable. So was his hunting prowess. He had driven the boar straight to the beach, exactly as planned. Jonas wondered if Edward could have known beforehand that the musket he had given Jonas would misfire; if not, then why had he assumed Kate had shot and killed the boar, and not Jonas himself?

Chapter Twenty-One

The success of the boar hunt gave Kate the perfect opportunity to plan a pig roast for the evening of the following day. It wasn't difficult to convince Jonas that since everyone had been working so hard, it was time to celebrate and have a bit of fun. The fact that Jonas hadn't said he *wouldn't* forgive her and had kissed her besides, seemed reason enough for a celebration all by itself. The future was indeed looking brighter, so gleefully, Kate ordered a pit to be dug near the work site, in which the boar could roast all through the day. Then she enlisted Mattie, Daisy, and Cassie in cooking and baking other delicacies, and in a high fever of anticipation, invited Edward and her father, mother, and Bell to join them for the evening's festivities.

She so wanted everyone to make peace and get along. She hoped to gain her parents' approval of the shipbuilding project, and prayed that once they saw the progress being made, they would become supportive, and so would Edward, despite his black looks, disparaging remarks, and initial resistance. To her great surprise and gratification, Papa and Edward agreed to come—not so, Mama, who claimed that the evening would be far too exhausting and the trip there in the dory too perilous. Bell, of course, agreed with this assessment, but Kate was so happy to have her father's acceptance, that she scarcely minded that her mother had refused.

Papa even offered to supply a cask of his precious rum and had Edward bring it to the work site beforehand, while the women and children were busy setting up makeshift tables to hold the bounty from Mattie's cook shed. Work quit early that day, and everyone helped to make pitchpine torches and plait palm fronds into mats where people could sit. As darkness fell, the torches were lit, and the pit uncovered, whereupon the delicious odor of roasted pork drifted tantalizingly over the work site.

Men, women, and children lined up with wooden trenchers and waited to be served by a shining-faced Mattie and Cal, who were doing the honors of carving the luscious meat. Kate served her father a heaping plateful and left him sitting on a mat with Edward for company, while she fetched a trencher for herself and Jonas. Jonas had undertaken the job of cutting open green coconuts for the women and children to drink, explaining to Kate that he wanted to be sure Edward got nowhere near them. Jonas was, however, perfectly willing to quit by the time Kate went to fetch him.

The pork, roasted yams, guinea corn, and other accompaniments proved as delicious as Kate had imagined they would be, but the best surprise occurred later, after the meal was finished. Nimble Clayton produced a sailor's hornpipe, and Cal fetched a gombey drum made of goatskin. Along with several other primitive instruments, including a whistle and a cowbell, brought out by the slaves, a cacophony of sound resembling music echoed forth beneath the torches. The slaves demonstrated the intricacies of John Canoe—or junkanoo—a kind of shuffling dance named after an African slave prince, and the seamen performed sailors' jigs.

The only thing that spoiled the night was that Papa, Edward, and most of Jonas's workers got drunk. A few became loud and boisterous, to the point that Kate sent Cal and Benjamin home early in the dories, along with the women and children, so that no one would get hurt if things got out of hand. By midnight, all of the drunken revelers, including Kate's father and Edward, had fallen asleep on the mats; only Kate and Jonas remained awake and sober.

Taking her hand, Jonas wordlessly led her toward his hut. In its welcoming, inky-black interior, they melted into each other's arms, eager to sate the hunger awakened on the previous day. Breathlessly, they kissed, shed clothing, and fell to the bed, entwining arms and legs around each other. Passion exploded in the darkness, and the only sound was their heavy breathing and moans of pleasure as they sought and found mutual fulfillment.

"Oh, God, Jonas . . ." Kate sighed as ecstasy ebbed and the power of speech returned. "If anything better than this exists in life, I can't think what it might be . . . When you are inside me, loving me with all your being, I feel transformed, made whole and new, and I know that I'll never be lonely again."

Silence met her impassioned comment, and she strained to see his face in the humid darkness. "Jonas? Are you listening?"

"I'm listening, Kate," Jonas finally answered. Then he lifted himself above her, maintaining the union of their bodies, but letting the cooler air circulate between them and dry the dampness of their flesh.

"I want you to promise me something, Kate," he said, his voice low and intense.

"What, Jonas?"

"Promise me that there will be no more lies between us—no more secrets, deceit, or subterfuge."

303

She lay still beneath him, wondering if now was the time to admit that Edward had sent Cal and Benjamin out in the dory with lights to lure his ship and Jonathan's onto the reef . . . and that she had seen Jonathan put his watch into his pocket just before he left to make that fatal fishing trip. Did suspicions count as lies? And was there anything to be gained by announcing them or by telling the truth about the lights, when he hadn't mentioned that specific issue, tonight?

She didn't think so; yet if she refused to make the promise he sought, she had no doubt she would lose Jonas. "In the future, I'll always tell the truth," she said softly, hoping he wouldn't probe any further into the past.

To her enormous relief, he didn't. Instead, he began to move within her. "When we are together like this," he murmured between slow, deep thrusts. "It doesn't matter that you've lied. You could be a murderess, and still, I would want you . . . would hunger to do this with you."

Though her desire had just been satisfied, it reawoke as a result of his exquisitely controlled thrusts. "But if we're going to build a life together, Kate, there must be more between us than just this madness. Another man's body could give you this pleasure. Another woman's could squeeze my seed from me . . ."

His voice trailed off as he made long, slow strokes that plumbed the depths of her and compelled her to lift her hips frantically to take more of him into her. She didn't think she could feel this way with any other man; only Jonas could arouse this frenzied, glorious urgency to have him thrust deeper—and deeper still, into the very core of her.

All reality, all sight, sound, smell, and feeling, narrowed to the small space where their bodies joined together, he giving, she receiving. "Jonas!"

she gasped. "Only you . . . I want only you. There will never be anyone else for me . . ."

"Give to me, Kate," he groaned. "Give me everything. Promise me I have it all . . ."

"All . . ." she cried, arching under him.

It was three days after the boar roast, and Sybil Montgomery was in a foul, unforgiving mood. She had heard how well the event had gone; everyone had had a marvelous time. There had been feasting, singing, and dancing by whites and blacks alike, and drunkenness among the whites. Edward and William had been so incapacitated that they spent the night on the beach where the new ship was being built, and later the next day, when William returned home, he had commented on how much progress had been made, and how Captain Irons seemed to know exactly what he was doing.

When she had questioned Edward about the project, Edward had expressed reluctant admiration and allowed as how there might be money to be made from shipbuilding, after all. His acceptance of the project—however grudging—had incensed Sybil; didn't Edward realize the dangers to his own best interests if this ship were actually built and sold for a profit? Didn't he understand what was happening?

A person had only to look at Kate to know that the girl was building not only a ship, but a future for herself, a future in which her parents may or may not play a prominent part . . . probably not. Sybil herself could well recall how she had defied her own parents to marry into a staunchly Loyalist family. Once a young girl fell in love, all was lost. And if Kate wasn't already in that hopeless condition, she soon would be.

These days, Kate positively glowed with energy, happiness, and enthusiasm. It was the same glow she

305

had worn when she had thought herself in love with that other rascally American. Edward and William might be too naive and stupid to recognize that dazzled look, but Sybil wasn't. She knew her daughter well—and the next time, Kate wanted to celebrate something, it would probably be her betrothal or wedding to Captain Jonas Irons!

The situation was deteriorating fast. If something was to be done, it must be done soon, before it became too late. Sybil had thought long and hard on the problem and come to the conclusion that despite Bell's past failures to rescue matters, only Bell could change things now. To that end, Sybil called the servant into her bedroom one morning after Kate had left the house, and bade her close the door and listen carefully.

"Yes'm, Miz Sybil?" Bell inquired, cocking her turbaned head. "Is you wantin' somepin'?"

Bell's expression revealed her awareness that Sybil was herself this morning and not ill or confused, as she so often was. While her strength held out, Sybil knew she must impress upon Bell that she wouldn't accept any more failures from her—such as what had happened with that disastrous episode involving the love potion. This time, there must be no mistakes.

Sybil raised her head from her plumped pillows and gestured for Bell to come closer. "Don't make me shout, Bell," she scolded. "What I have to say is for your ears alone."

Bell came up to the side of the bed and stood there with a humble attitude that Sybil found most annoying, considering the powers the woman possessed. "Now then, Bell," Sybil continued. "Have you come up with a suitable antidote for that love potion my daughter drank?"

Bell's face hardened into lines of defensiveness and resistance. "No, Miz Sybil . . . I done tole you already dat was my bes' potion Edward put in dat coconut, an' it ain't mah fault dat de fust person Miz Kate seed after she drank it was Cap'n Irons."

"I concede it isn't your fault, Bell, but you know I've been waiting for you to come up with an antidote we can slip to her."

"Ah'm sorry, Miz Sybil, but dere ain't one," Bell stubbornly insisted.

"Come, come, now, Bell! There must be! I've already told you I'll pay handsomely for it, just as I did for the potion itself. Don't you believe me?"

"Sure ah b'lieve y'all, Miz Sybil. But dat ain't de problem. De love potion done already worked; leastaway, Miz Kate has de look of a woman who's given her heart t' a man. T' change dat is gonna tek some doin'. Ah can't guarantee mah magic is strong enuff 't turn love into hate. Love is allus stronger den hate."

"Well, you must do *something*, Bell! We can't let things continue as they are. Kate's already spending every waking moment in the captain's company, helping to build that ship. Why, poor Edward's so discouraged he's practically given up on winning her. He's even making approving noises about the potential to be found in shipbuilding. And if Edward goes over to the enemy, all is finished, Bell! Kate is as good as lost to William and me. She'll marry Captain Irons, and eventually, he'll want to take her away from here, and . . . and . . ."

Sybil paused to catch her breath. Her heart was thudding so hard it felt as if it might burst. She sensed the presence of something dark and evil—those awful snakes!—and shivered with fear.

"Ah knows . . . ah knows, Miz Sybil," Bell sought to calm her. "But y'all gotta relax, or de sickness is gonna tek hold again. You want ah should fetch you a cuppa tea?"

Sybil tossed her head restlessly on the pillows. "Lord, no, Bell! I want to plan, not sleep. You think tea is the answer to everything, and this time, it isn't! If you can't find a way to solve this problem, then I'm just going to have to send for someone who can. After all, you aren't the only Obeah Woman in all of the Bahamas.''

Bell's eyes widened at that, and Sybil could almost see her mind working, as she wondered what would happen to *her*, if Sybil invited some other practitioner of the black arts to take up residence on Conch Cay. There was a freedwoman in Nassau, both women knew, whose fame was slowly but surely spreading to rival Bell's own reputation . . .

"Awright, Miz Sybil . . . Awright. Ah'll come up with somethin', ah surely will. But whatever it is, will cost plenty. Ah'll haveta mek special offerin's t' the spirits.''

"I'll provide whatever's necessary, Bell. You should know that by now. When William's drunk, he'll give me anything I ask; he'll usually do so even when he's sober.''

"Yes'm, Miz Sybil. Dat man is yore devoted slave, or de closest thing to it ah ever seed in a white man.''

"He *should* be!" Sybil snapped. "I've given up enough in my life for *him*. Now, leave me, I wish to rest. In an hour, you can bring my breakfast.''

Bell retreated toward the door, plainly glad to be dismissed. "Yes'm, Miz Sybil . . . Ah'll spend de time until y'all needs me again, thinkin' what ah can do t' git rid o' Cap'n Irons b'fore he up and marries Miz Kate.''

One week after the boar roast, Jonas had just sat down outside the door of his hut to eat the evening meal Kate had left for him, when Nimble Clayton approached him with a worried expression on his lean, dark face.

"Cap'n, can you come right away an' take a look at

them boards from that last maderia tree we cut? We've damped 'em down to bend 'em some, an' we measured 'em right when we cut 'em, but I can't see as how they're gonna fit as tight as we was hopin' they would."

Jonas sighed and glanced down ruefully at the trencher full of food—his favorite, grouper fingers— that Mattie had fried, at Kate's request, which echoed his own request made earlier that week. He was so hungry his mouth was already watering, though he hadn't yet taken a bite. Worse yet, he'd made plans with Kate to meet later that night, after he finished eating and everyone had settled down to sleep. Kate had already gone home in the dory, but had promised to slip out of the house and escape to the pool, while he did the same from the work site. They hadn't had an hour alone together since the night of the roast, and he was as hungry for her as he was for the grouper fingers.

"It's real important that we get the fit right," Nimble reminded him, his Adam's apple bobbing with worry. "I was gonna start puttin' 'em in place first thing, t'morrow, but I can't if they ain't gonna fit."

"Wait here a minute. I'll set this inside, first, then I'll come and look before it gets too dark." Jonas rose, entered his hut, and started looking for a place to set down the trencher where Whiskers wouldn't be likely to get into it.

The cat promptly wound itself around his leg, meowing in protest and gazing hopefully up at him. "Be patient, Whiskers," he admonished. "You'll get your share."

There really wasn't any spot in the hut inaccessible to a hungry, determined cat, so Jonas stuffed the entire trencher inside a burlap knapsack and set it carefully down on his trunk. Then he scooped the cat into his arms. "You come with me, Whiskers . . . I

309

don't trust you not to steal the whole thing."

With one last longing thought for the grouper fingers, Jonas followed his shipwright over to the hulking skeleton of the ship's cradle where the vessel itself was well underway. His conference with Nimble lasted three-quarters of an hour. They discussed several ways of solving the problem, decided on one, and then Jonas excused himself to return to his dinner. It was getting dark by now, and as he trudged back to his hut and lit an oil lantern, Jonas suddenly realized that Whiskers was no longer with him. Sometime during his discussion with Nimble, he had set the cat down.

Immediately, his eyes went to the knapsack, and he growled an obscenity. Remnants of fish lay scattered across the top of his trunk, but Whiskers was nowhere to be seen.

"You damned little sneak!" he cried, searching the hut with his eyes. "Where are you? Crawled off with a bellyache, I don't doubt, since you left hardly any for me!"

He looked under the bed, but saw no cat. Then he heard a pitiful sound, a thin, high meow just outside the doorway of the hut. Quickly, he shone the lantern there. Whiskers lay stretched on his side, his swollen abdomen and rigid body mute testimony of his suffering, the probable result of overindulgence.

Hanging the lantern on the hook he had devised for it inside the hut, Jonas picked up the cat and laid it gently upon his own bed. The creature meowed a second time, then twitched its tail and shuddered. Jonas no longer cared about the loss of his dinner; the cat was in a bad way. He and Whiskers had survived the shipwreck together, lived together, and shared their food for quite some time, now. He couldn't let the poor thing die, but didn't know what he could do to save it. Could a cat die from overeating?

He examined the remainder of the fish and

discovered that Whiskers hadn't eaten as much as he had initially feared, certainly not enough to have resulted in such disastrous consequences. Maybe the fish hadn't been cooked properly or was tainted to begin with. Stroking Whisker's belly, Jonas wondered whether he could make the animal expel the food by massaging its stomach or sticking his finger down its throat. While he was debating this, Whisker's whole body stiffened, he made a sound almost like a squeek, then suddenly, relaxed and went limp beneath Jonas's hand.

It took a moment for Jonas to realize the animal was gone. His throat clogged with emotion, and tears gathered in his eyes. It's only a cat, he told himself. It's only a cat . . . and then it struck him; it could have been him! If he had eaten at the same time as Whiskers, he, too, could be ill or dying. Tainted food could drop a man as well as an animal. He had known of sailors suffering the tortures of the damned and sometimes dying from eating food gone bad aboard ship—not, thankfully, his own. Whisker's original master, Oatcake, had always paid scrupulous attention to the food he served, because maggots in the meat or flour did not bode well for maintaining a crew's health or efficiency.

I'll have to warn Kate, he thought. Others may have eaten the fish and even now, might be getting sick.

First, he would check the men outside. Leaving the cat where it lay, Jonas hurried from the hut, shouting for everyone to come at once. They came, yawning sleepily, most already having retired to their huts for the night.

"Is anyone ill?" he barked. "Do any of you have an aching belly?"

The men glanced at each other in puzzlement.

"Did you eat grouper fingers for dinner?" Jonas bellowed.

"We all ate fish stew, Cap'n," Big Donald announced. "That's what the women prepared fer us."

Jonas breathed a sigh of relief. "Then I guess the meal Miss Montgomery brought for me was special—prepared for me alone, thank God."

The men exchanged sly glances of amusement, and a few cracked a joke or two among themselves. Jonas caught the tone, if not the actual words, and barked at them again. "There will be no comments of disrespect where Miss Montgomery is concerned!"

Big Donald cleared his throat. "I already told 'em I'd bash in the head of any man who gossips about you and Miss Montgomery, Cap'n."

"Good, then you had all better remember that. I'll be leaving now to go and see her. That damn cat who always follows me around just died after eating the fish Miss Montgomery brought for my dinner. I've got to find out if anyone else at the house has gotten sick from eating it. Fortunately, I myself never got a chance to taste the fish, because Nimble came and asked my advice about something. Nimble, the cat's lying in on my bed. See that it's disposed of, will you? I have a feeling I'd better hurry."

"Yes, sir . . . Will you be walkin'?"

"No, this time, I'll take a dory." Then, Jonas remembered that by now, Kate would be waiting for him by the pool. "On second thought, I'll walk, after all . . . Rather, I'll run. Don't worry if I'm not back before morning. Get to work, and I'll rejoin you as soon as possible."

"Aye, aye, Cap'n," the men chorused, and Jonas set off into the woods at a run.

Chapter Twenty-Two

"Jonas, what is it? What's happened?" Kate stepped out of the darkness into a patch of moonlight, where she knew Jonas could see her, just as she had spotted him, his face drawn with worry, as he hurried toward the pool and their secret rendezvous.

"Kate!" He rushed up to her, but instead of embracing her, held her at arm's length. "Damn! Why didn't I bring a lantern? Are you all right? Did you eat any of those grouper fingers you sent for my dinner?"

"I'm fine, Jonas—and no, I didn't eat any grouper fingers. Mattie made only enough for you; everyone else had fish stew tonight, and the fish wasn't grouper . . ."

Jonas's sigh shafted the night. "God be praised for that small mercy. There was something wrong with the fish, Kate. Whiskers ate it before I did and died before I could do anything to save him."

"Oh, no! Poor Whiskers. But thank God, you're safe!" Kate flung her arms around Jonas and hugged him tightly. "Oh, Jonas, if anything had happened to you . . ." She couldn't complete the sentence; the possibility was too terrible to contemplate.

He rubbed her back and shoulders, soothing away the tension with his warm, strong hands. "Then you're positive no one else ate the grouper fingers, and there was no grouper in the stew, tonight."

"I'm positive . . . Benjamin and Fish only caught one grouper this morning. The rest were grunts, I believe, and more suitable for stewing than frying, especially when there's so many mouths to feed." Struck by another horrifying thought, Kate drew back slightly. "Have any of your men fallen ill? Were there other victims besides Whiskers?"

Jonas shook his head. "Not yet, and I hope there won't be. Whiskers got sick almost immediately after eating the fingers."

"But why didn't you eat them, too, Jonas? Weren't you hungry? That's why I had Mattie make them—because they're a favorite of yours."

"They are—or were a favorite, and I was more than hungry, I was starved. But Nimble came to consult me about a carpentry problem, and I didn't get a chance to eat right away. I hate to think what might have happened if I *had* eaten them. Fortunately for me, poor Whiskers got there first."

"You'd have had fish poisoning, too, I imagine—and you might even have died from it."

"Is fish poisoning a common ailment in the Abacos?"

"It's not terribly common, no, but it does occur throughout all of the Bahamas, especially if you eat the wrong kinds of fish."

"I thought everybody ate grouper, when they're lucky enough to catch them."

"They do—providing the fish aren't too big. For some reason, the bigger fish aren't as edible as the smaller ones, although we once caught a huge sea bass that was delicious and had to be salted because we couldn't eat it all before it spoiled. There are all kinds of fish in these waters, Jonas. Through trial and error, we've learned which ones make the best eating and are unlikely to cause illness, and which

314

ones can't be trusted. Of course, we continue to learn every time we go fishing. Even among groupers, there must be a dozen varieties; some we never eat, no matter what their size, because of the possibility of fish poisoning."

"What sort of fish had my brother gone after, when he got caught in that storm?" Jonas suddenly asked.

At the mention of Jonathan, Kate started, then got hold of herself so she could answer calmly. By unspoken agreement, she and Jonas avoided discussing his brother; the subject was still too painful, but apparently Jonas's curiosity had won out over his reticence to introduce a topic that had almost ruined everything between them—and could still do so.

"Jonathan had gone bonefishing," she said, then rushed on to continue the lesson on Bahamian fish. "Bonefish aren't as good eating as groupers, but they are far more challenging to catch. They grow to about the length of a man's arm and possess a wonderful, fighting spirit. They live in the shallows, mostly, and feed on the tiny crabs and other crustaceans there."

"It would be just like Jonathan to go fishing for the feisty ones," Jonas said with a chuckle. "When fishing for women, he always did have an eye for whatever was hardest to catch."

"I don't think I wish to discuss that aspect of Jonathan's character," Kate primly retorted, wondering why Jonas didn't yet seem to realize how much it had hurt her to learn that Jonathan had been a rake and she herself only another one of his conquests.

Sobering, Jonas lifted his hand and idly caressed her cheek with his fingertips. "Yes, it's probably wiser to go on pretending I never had a brother. Will his shadow always stand between us, Kate? Will we never be able to talk about him without stirring up anger, hurt, and suspicion?"

315

"That depends upon you, Jonas," Kate informed him. "Will you ever get over being jealous of your brother and upset because I didn't tell you about him, in the beginning?"

In the moonlight, Jonas's eyes were dark and shadowed. "I think I am over it, Kate . . . I'm hardly brooding on the subject when I'm kept awake at night thinking about you. When I lie in the dark, imagining you in my arms, anger and jealousy are the furthest things from my mind."

Kate stepped closer to him—close enough to feel the heat of his body radiating through his clothing and hers. "What is on your mind at such moments, Jonas?" she boldly questioned.

"You . . ." he said simply. "And the soft, breathy, little sighs you make when I touch you in a way that particularly pleases you . . ."

She smiled at that, hoping they were safely past the subject of Jonathan. "Everything you do pleases me, my love—and I, too, lie awake at night, wishing I were in your arms."

He slid one of those self-same, iron-hard arms about her waist and hauled her up against him, so that she could feel every ridge of muscle on his lean, trim body, as well as the pulsing evidence of his arousal. "Marry me, Kate," he said huskily. "Marry me as soon as possible. Then we won't have to sneak around to protect your reputation . . . Nor will we have to worry that a child might be conceived before we're ready to have one."

She laughed softly, brimful of joy at the suggestion. "I haven't yet conceived, my darling . . . Believe me, I'd tell you if I had."

"I want to do right by you, Kate Montgomery. I'm not a man who can callously use a decent woman and then walk away from her, leaving her to face the consequences alone. That was my brother's way, not mine. Had he lived, he might have done that to you. I

316

know it hurts you to hear me say it, but it's the truth. You've told me the truth, and I've had to accept it and learn to live with it. Now, you must do the same. I pledge to always tell you the truth, Kate, no matter how wounding it might be.''

"Oh, Jonas!" Wrestling with her fears and worries, Kate rested her forehead on Jonas's shoulder. For him, everything would always be black and white and simple. But for her, life was habitually shaded with varying tones of gray. Aside from the secrets she still kept from him, the idea of immediate marriage presented a host of new problems. He thought it would all be easy; she knew better. She needed time to accustom her parents to the idea, especially her mother. If she marched into Mama's bedchamber and announced plans for a precipitous wedding, her mother would probably swoon—and not come out of it for weeks or months.

What kind of beginning for their new life together would that be? And how could Kate bear the guilt that would surely ensue? Mama must first be convinced of Jonas's intention to remain on Conch Cay; she must realize that after this ship was completed, there would be another . . . and another, and another. Jonas must spend time getting to know her parents better, for indeed, they were an important part of Kate's life.

And what if the shipbuilding venture should fail? Kate forced herself to consider that unhappy possibility. If the profits from the project proved too meager, Jonas might *not* wish to remain on Conch Cay. She could easily imagine him growing restless and despondent, and finally deciding to return to Salem. Part of her own commitment to Conch Cay derived from the fact that she had nowhere else to go. Jonas did. He wasn't a Loyalist like William Montgomery, a man without a country to call his own.

317

Her joy trickled away as she recalled a proverb she hoped would never apply to her and Jonas: *Marry in haste, repent in leisure.* During her childhood, her grandfather had many times quoted it to Papa, when her own parents argued over things and disagreed. As the daughter of two people repenting for half their lifetimes, she could not refute the wisdom of that warning statement.

"Kate, sweet, why are you so silent?" Jonas tilted up her chin so she was forced to look him in the eye.

On this, at least, she could be truthful. "I want to marry you more than anything in the world, Jonas, but . . . but I think we should wait a bit. We mustn't rush into anything, or you might later come to regret it."

"Do you think I don't know my own heart, Kate? Do you doubt my love for you?"

"No! Oh, no, I don't, Jonas. And I'm as positive as I can be that I love you. But we have to consider— other things. My parents hardly know you. At this point, they will oppose our marriage . . . and I so much want them to accept it."

"Kate, you won't let your parents talk you out of marrying me, will you? Because that's what they'll try to do, I'm afraid, if for no other reason than that I'm an American."

She tightened her arms around his waist. "There's nothing they can say to dissuade me, Jonas. I, too, know my own heart. It's only that I hate to hurt them, if I can avoid it. In time, they'll come to accept you. In time, after they get to know you, a marriage between us won't come as such a shock to them."

"How *much* time, Kate? It could be years before they decide to accept an upstart American for a son-in-law."

"When the ship is done!" she exclaimed impulsively. "When we've made a tidy profit and have begun work on the next one, then maybe they'll be able to see that you're here to stay, and they won't mind so much that we marry."

"But Kate . . ." he murmured, embracing her tightly. "The success of the *Phoenix* should have no bearing on whether or not we marry. I love you and want to marry you, whether we make a profit on her or not."

"So do I, Jonas, but we must be practical! Our future happiness depends upon it. We must find a way to live and prosper, if not by building ships, than by some other means. I've seen what poverty can do to destroy love, and I don't want . . ."

"Practicality be damned!" Jonas interrupted. "I've bowed to practicality and necessity all my life, but I won't let them rule me now. You and I can do anything we set out to do, Kate. We have youth, energy, and determination to succeed; what more do we need?"

He crushed her to him and plundered her mouth with his kisses. In the brushfire of rising desire, Kate couldn't think clearly anymore—except to marvel helplessly: *He's right. Together, we can overcome any obstacles in our path.*

A moment later, Jonas drew back breathlessly. "I want to love you under the stars and moon again, Kate—not here in the darkness of the forest. I want the whole of the universe to witness how I love you. Let's go to the beach and love each other where the surf curls upon the sand."

"It's too far to the beach," she protested shakily. "I can't wait that long."

"Then we'll ride your horse," he suggested. "Will he come when you call him?"

"I don't know . . . Sometimes, he comes . . ." Catching Jonas's ebullient mood, suddenly certain that anything *was* possible through the power of their love, Kate grinned. "We'll try calling him and see."

Turning from him, she cupped her hands around her mouth and shouted: "Neptune! Come here, boy, come to me, now . . ."

There was a rustle in the trees and the muffled sound of hoofbeats striking the sandy soil. A moment later, Neptune appeared, shaking his gilded head in a splash of star shine. The horse made a low, whuffling sound as he came closer, neck outstretched, his velvety muzzle searching for her hand. Lacking a reward to give him for his obedience, she scratched behind his pricked ears, a gesture he had always appreciated. He blew softly through his nostrils and nudged her.

Stepping to one side, she mounted him easily, with a boost from Jonas, then invited him to join her on the horse's broad back. To her surprise, Neptune stood perfectly still, and Jonas had no difficulty getting up behind her. "I used to ride our neighbor's old nag bareback all the time when I was a lad," he explained, threading his arms around her waist. "When my father was gone at sea, Jonathan and I hadn't much else to do but get into trouble, and stealing rides from our neighbor's horse was only one thing we did together."

"Now, we'll see if Neptune will obey my leg commands," Kate commented dryly. Cautiously, she squeezed both legs, and Neptune obligingly set off at a smooth trot, avoiding trees and other obstacles with the grace of long practice.

With little urging from her, the stallion kept to the path that wound through the woods and down to the beach. When he came out onto a clear stretch of sand, clearly illuminated by the half moon and the stars, she urged him to greater speed, and he broke into the easy, rocking canter that made him such an unexpected pleasure to ride.

"This is far enough," Jonas muttered behind her. "How do you get him to stop?"

"I don't!" Kate cried laughingly over her shoulder. "He'll stop when he wants to or not at all."

Neptune pounded down the deserted beach, then stopped so suddenly that both Kate and Jonas tumbled off his back and fell in a heap of tangled arms and legs. Fortunately, the sand cushioned their fall, and they sat up, laughing and unharmed. Neptune stood nearby, his head raised, his nostrils flared, then he trumpeted—a high, shrill whinny of excitement and welcome.

"Look," Kate urged Jonas. "It's one of his mares, and from Neptune's reaction, I'd say he's very glad to see her."

Farther down the beach, a smaller horse lifted her head from the sea grass and watched the stallion approach. She neither shied away nor trotted forward to meet him, but when Neptune came up to her and touched his muzzle to hers, she squealed and swung around, flicking his face with her tail. Then they were galloping together up and down the beach, stopping, snorting, spinning . . . kicking up the sand with their flashing hooves.

Kneeling behind Kate, Jonas slid his arms around her. A moment later, his hands found her breasts. As they watched the stallion and the mare cavorting together, Jonas fondled Kate and undid the fastenings of her clothing, baring her upper body. He nipped at her ear, rolled her nipples between his fingers, and breathed hotly down her neck. In the pit of her stomach, Kate felt the uncoiling of something mysterious, elemental, and wondrously stimulating . . .

She turned to Jonas and pulled at his shirt. Their mouths came together, their lips molding in a fiery kiss. Jonas gripped her buttocks and pressed her to him, rubbing his chest against her bare breasts and pushing his lower body into hers. For a moment, Kate lost herself in the wonder of being skin to skin with him. Her body flooded with heat, responding to his sexuality with every muscle and fiber. Her head spun with anticipation of the next glorious intimacy he might demand.

"Look over there," Jonas growled, breaking the kiss and nodding toward the beach.

Kate did and saw Neptune rising on his powerful hind legs to cover the mare, who stood quietly now, hind legs outspread and tail raised. The stallion sheathed himself in the mare's body and began pumping, his powerful hindquarters thrusting with grace and power in a wild, primitive mating . . . a thing of beauty and power that touched Kate's soul and thrilled her, as if she herself were the mare, and Jonas, the stallion.

Then Jonas was bending her backward into the sand. He tore at her clothing and his own, spread her legs, and mounted her. His powerful thrusts echoed Neptune's, and Kate could do nothing but cling to him and hold tightly as the splendid pressure built within her and threatened to explode.

"Kate!" he cried in mingled awe and ecstasy.

She squeezed and held him, finding her own explosion at the same time he found his. Dimly, she heard the pounding of receding hoofbeats, or maybe it was her own heart beating in her ears. Afterward, they lay together in perfect peace and contentment for a long, long while. Then they rose, went down to the surf, washed themselves and each other, strolled the beach, and made love again near the curl of surf.

After that, they spoke of nothing and everything—how horses mated versus how people did it, how cats, dogs, and chickens did it, and then they experimented and played together like wanton, curious children, trying this position and that, using previously discovered techniques and learning new ones for rousing bodies already sated and sluggish with repletion.

They sported on the beach in their nakedness until dawn pearled the sky, then reluctantly dressed and kissed good night.

"Marry me, Kate," Jonas begged one last time. "If not today or tomorrow, then very soon. I can't bear to say goodbye to you like this."

"But I'll be seeing you in a couple hours, if I can stay awake to work today," Kate smilingly protested.

"Yes, but then I'll have to pretend I didn't just spend the night in your arms, taking you over and over, like Neptune mounting his mare."

"I'll think about it," Kate agreed, as loathe to part as he was.

"No, Kate . . . Don't think. Plan. Plan when and how we can marry the soonest. I'll come and talk to both your parents. I'll reassure them and soothe their fears. I'll . . ."

Kate stopped his impassioned speech by pressing her palm to his mouth. "Hush . . . I said I would think about it, and I will, Jonas. We certainly can't spend every night meeting on the beach like this, and still have energy to build a ship the next day. If we don't marry soon, we'll never get any sleep!"

His smile crinkled his sea-blue eyes and erased the lines of fatigue from his face. "I'm going to take that as acceptance. Good night, my love . . . or rather, good morning."

Jonas headed for the forest, while Kate continued down the beach toward the path that led up to the house. Mattie might already be in the cook shed by the time she arrived there, but no one else should be up and about. She had no fears of being unable to sneak into the house unobserved and make her way quietly upstairs to her own room.

The sun was rising as she neared the house and stepped onto the veranda. It creaked beneath her bare feet, and suddenly the door flew open, and Bell rushed out, followed closely by her distraught-looking father.

"Oh, Miz Kate, dere you is! We ben lookin' all over fer you . . . Oh, Miz Kate, somepin' terrible has happened!"

"Where have you been?" her father thundered, taking in her dishevelment with disbelieving eyes and frowning suspiciously.

"I bet I kin tell you where she's been," a voice said from behind her.

Kate spun on her heel to face Edward, who stood slouched against a tree in the front yard.

"Only it ain't the right time t' talk about such things, when a person's mama is dyin' and callin' fer her," he finished with a smug, self-satisfied smile.

"Dying!" Kate spun back to her father. "Is Mama really dying, Papa?"

"*She* thinks she is, and this time, she may be right," William stiffly replied. "She became ill during the night and wanted to see you. Edward's been everywhere but he couldn't find you—or Captain Irons, either. Your absence made your poor mother worse. She lay awake all night, calling for you and weeping. Now, she seems to have slipped into a coma."

"Oh, dear God! I'll go up to see her at once!"

Kate raced past her father and Bell, and dashed up the stairs. She was almost to the top when she realized that she could never mention marriage, now—and maybe not for a long time to come. She was practically in tears when she reached her mother's room, but whether her tears were for the sake of her mother or because of Jonas, she could not decide. All she knew was that the present and future looked very bleak, indeed.

Chapter Twenty-Three

Four days passed before Kate again had an opportunity for a private conversation with Jonas. She met him beside the pool in the late afternoon, having sent a message with Cal because she herself had been unable to visit the work site. They embraced wordlessly, reveling in each other's presence, and then Jonas drew her to a large flat rock overlooking the pool and bade her sit down and tell him everything.

"Cal has kept me informed," he told her. "But I want to hear it all from you. How is your mother? Has she made any improvement over the past few days?"

Kate entwined her fingers in his before answering. She badly needed the comfort that simply touching him brought to her, for she felt strained to her limits and guilty to be taking even this much time away from her mother.

"I've never seen Mama this bad, Jonas. Half the time, she doesn't know me and keeps calling for me, even when I'm right there beside her. She refuses to eat, rarely sleeps, except when Bell administers her teas, and won't get out of bed at all. She keeps saying she has nothing to live for now that I've deserted her, and when she isn't calling for me, she's weeping over my dead brother, Robin."

"I'm so sorry, Kate." Jonas gave her hand a squeeze. "Isn't there anything your father can do to comfort her? If not, then perhaps she should be taken to Nassau, where a physician might be able to help her."

"Doctors haven't been able to help her in the past, Jonas . . . so I doubt they can help her now. They've bled and purged her, dosed her with strange remedies, used leeches to suck out the bad humours, and tried several other things that didn't work. The final choice is to lock her up or confine her in some way, in case she becomes a danger to others. I could never do that to my mother, and in any case, she's already locked up, so to speak, since she prefers her bedchamber to any other place."

Jonas bent and gently kissed Kate's forehead. "My poor, brave Kate. The situation must be unbearable. Does she listen to you at all when you try to tell her that you *haven't* deserted her—and that you don't intend to?"

"No, Jonas . . . She seems to be living in a place where no one can reach her. This has happened before, but she always came out of it eventually, and I've always been careful never to do anything to alarm her and *put* her in that place—until now. That's what I did the other night. I wasn't there when she panicked and needed me, so in a way, I'm *responsible* for her present condition. Had I been at home, instead of on the beach with you, I could have prevented this occurrence."

"Kate, you mustn't blame yourself for your mother's illness, and you mustn't let her illness become a tool to control and manipulate you . . ."

Swept with a wild panic of her own, Kate blurted: "But what else can I do, Jonas? What choice do I have? I am her only child; I'm all she has, really, since my father is so little help to her. I *can't* abandon her to live my own life. If I do, I'm as good as killing her. I'll be forced to watch her die, all the while knowing I'm the cause."

"Kate, stop it! You're talking nonsense. You owe your parents love, respect, and help in their old age, but you don't owe them the right to make all your choices and live your life for you. You carry filial responsibility too far . . . You also have an obligation to yourself and to me and to any children we might one day have."

"You can't expect me to marry you when my mother is in this condition, Jonas," Kate said bitterly. "If I married right now, it would be the final blow to her. She'd probably die within a month—or else she'd become such an unmanageable lunatic that it would be the same thing as dying, a kind of horrible, living death."

Jonas kissed Kate's forehead again, then kept his lips close to her hair, as he quietly murmured: "Sweetheart, you must think me a most unfeeling, insensitive man to demand that you marry me now, this instant, when you are so desperately worried, fearful, and preoccupied. I'm willing to be patient and give you the time you asked for the other night, Kate, but I'm not willing to wait forever to make you my wife. One day, when your mother improves, you will have to tell her about us and reveal our plans. You'll have to ease her into accepting them."

Kate grasped Jonas's hands and held them tight against her breast. "But what if she doesn't improve, Jonas? What will we do then?"

"Then it won't make much difference if you tell her or not, will it? She won't realize what's happening. I'll ask your father to sell me some land so I can build a house close enough to your family's that you can visit your mother everyday. Maybe then, she'll finally realize that she hasn't lost a daughter, but gained a son."

"Papa may not want to sell you the land, Jonas. He still has his heart set on my marrying Edward. He told me so the other night and scolded me for 'plunging my mother into despair' as he called it," Kate reluctantly revealed. "There was no question in *his* mind that my mother's lapse into madness is all my fault."

Jonas's mouth thinned in anger. "Your father is trying to manipulate and control you, too, Kate. I'm finding it increasingly difficult not to call him out and punch him silly, not just for being a drunkard, but for sacrificing his daughter's happiness to make up for his own failures. If he were any kind of man at all, he'd have found a way to deal with your mother's problems years ago, instead of dumping them all on you. And the fact that he would hand you over to a man like Edward, only gives me all the more reason to despise and pity him—maybe even to hate him."

"But I can't hate him, Jonas! No matter what he is, no matter how weak and manipulative, he's still my father. Just as Sybil is my mother. When you marry me, you get my family in the bargain. I know that a woman is supposed to foresake all others and cleave only to her husband, but for me, that's clearly impossible . . ."

"If he won't sell any land to me, then perhaps I can buy some on a neighboring cay. It will mean that he and your mother will see you less often, but at least, we'll still remain in the same vicinity."

Suppressing a sob, Kate buried her face in her hands. "Oh, Jonas! I don't know what's right or wrong anymore! Sometimes, I feel as if I, too, have come to hate my parents and the heavy burdens they've placed upon me. Then I feel so guilty for having such shameful feelings that I don't know what to do with myself."

Jonas gently pried her hands away from her face. "Kate . . . Kate . . . Sweetheart, you mustn't agonize over this so much. It will all come right in the end; we'll *make* it right. This is only the first of many problems we'll probably have to face in our lives together. What matters is that we *do* face them together—that we don't let them tear us apart . . ."

He stood and gathered her into his arms. She tilted her face to receive his kiss, but before their mouths could meet, the crackle of brush told Kate they were not alone.

"Well, now . . ." Edward said, coming toward them from the opposite side of the pool. "I had a hunch this was where I'd find the two of ya—gone off alone again t' be by yurselves."

Turning toward the intruder, Jonas stepped in front of Kate, as if to shield her. "Somehow you always manage to show up when I least want to see you, Edward. If you have something to say, say it and be gone, but have a care that you don't get too personal. I particularly don't wish to hear any criticism or speculation regarding Miss Montgomery's conduct."

Jonas's tone held a steely note of warning. The atmosphere suddenly grew tense and charged with danger as the two men faced each other silently across the pool.

"What do you want, Edward? Why are you here?" Kate demanded, moving out from behind Jonas.

"Bell sent me t' fetch ya. Yer ma finally et something and is lookin' better. Bell thought ye might want t' know—'specially since Miz Sybil is askin' fer ya, again."

"Thank you, Edward. I'll come at once. You can accompany me back to the house." Kate glanced toward Jonas whose hostile expression revealed his willingness to tangle once again with Edward. She touched his arm in silent supplication. "I have to go now, Jonas. If Mama is truly better, maybe I can return to the work site tomorrow. I trust that everything is going well there?"

Jonas answered without taking his eyes from Edward. "We're making excellent progress. Soon, we should be ready to hoist the *Phoenix*'s mainmast into position."

"That's wonderful! I hope I can be there to see it . . . I'll try." She stood on tiptoe to give Jonas a light kiss on the cheek, taking the opportunity to also whisper: "I love you," into his ear.

That brought his eyes back to her. Immediately, the tension eased from his body, and the corners of his mouth turned up in a grin. "I love you, too," he mouthed silently back at her.

Neither of them looked at Edward to see what he thought of their affectionate display. Kate no longer cared in the least what Edward thought or didn't think. Her heart belonged only to Jonas; whether or not they could ever marry, she loved no man but him.

To Jonas, it sometimes seemed as if time was slipping through his fingers like sand through an hourglass; it went so quickly. At other times, he felt that the days dragged by with leaden feet, and he only came alive every couple of days or so, during those precious minutes when Kate came to visit the work site. Now and then, she worked the entire day, but then it would be two or three days before she returned. Sybil Montgomery's health fluctuated daily—worsening every time Kate left her for a day, then improving only after Kate spent long periods at her mother's bedside, reading to her, brushing her hair, or otherwise tending her needs.

To Jonas, the pattern was perfectly clear; Sybil was using her illness to keep Kate and himself apart. But to Kate, her mother's illness was merely capricious—striking without warning, triggered perhaps by Kate's devotedness or lack of it, but certainly not deliberately controlled.

Jonas struggled to be patient, trusting that in time, Kate would realize what was happening, confront her parents, and put an end to their blatant, often whining manipulation. As if the constant pendulum-swing of emotion wasn't bad enough, there was also the continuing problem of Edward, hovering always in the background. Edward contrived to turn up unexpectedly nearly every time Jonas sought privacy with Kate—and the surly overseer always had a reasonable excuse. Kate's mother was taking a turn for the better or worse, Bell had a new tea she wanted to try on Kate's mother, William must consult with Kate regarding the business of running the plantation, or the horses had gotten into the guinea corn and eaten themselves sick on it.

Sometimes, it was even Edward who brought Kate to the work site in the dory, because Benjamin, Cal, and Fish were already there—and often, it was Edward who took her home again, because the slaves were too tired from the heavy physical labor to make the twice-daily trip. A hundred times, Jonas had to bite his tongue to keep from insisting that Kate finally choose between him and her parents. But every time he opened his mouth to say something, the pleading look in Kate's golden eyes stopped him.

Quite obviously, the conflict was tearing her apart. Her aristocratic bone structure had never been more apparent than now; the flesh had melted away from her face and figure like candle wax eaten by a flame. She was reed-thin—almost wiry, her eyes abnormally large and her feminine curves more sharply pronounced. An air of fragility had replaced the vivid impression of blooming health and vibrancy she had possessed when he first met her; he feared she might break under the strain of being forced to choose between him and her family.

So he didn't insist. Instead, he gazed after her with

331

helpless longing whenever she was near, and buried himself in work whenever she wasn't. They did not meet secretly in the forest or on the beach, not because Jonas didn't want to, but because he knew that Kate feared a repeat of what had happened before when she was gone all night. He didn't want to pressure her—but hoped that *she* would make the first move, which to his great disappointment, she didn't.

The only salve to his bruised and battered feelings was work piled on top of work. He drove himself and his men to their limits, finding his only satisfaction in seeing the vessel rise in the ship's cradle, until its structure towered over the beach. On the morning of the day that he intended to place the tall, heavy mainmast into position, he made sure Kate was aware of what they'd be doing that day. She arrived about midmorning, with Edward in tow, but Jonas was so glad to see her that not even Edward's glowering presence could diminish his elation.

Kate was wearing trousers and boots today, her bountiful hair done up in a single, long, fat braid that fell down her back, but to Jonas, she was the epitome of feminine grace and beauty. Ignoring Edward completely, he took Kate's arm and all but dragged her over to see the hoist they had built to raise the mast. "This is how we're going to do it," he told her enthusiastically, then described the process while the men attended to last-minute details, stopping only to greet her or nod in her direction.

"I'm most impressed by your ingenuity," Kate exclaimed, smiling up at him. "But won't raising the mast be dangerous? What if it should break free of the ropes and chains you've rigged up to hold it?"

"It won't," Jonas assured her. "I have perfect confidence in my men's strength and dexterity. It'll take most of them to raise the log, but only one or two of us to actually position it."

"It's too bad Neptune and his mares aren't broke to

harness," Kate mused. "Their strength would be a wonderful asset. Neptune alone might be able to raise that log." Kate eyed the long, tapered, and carefully planed maderia log that lay waiting to become the mainmast.

"Maybe by the time we're ready to raise the mast on the next ship, I could have him trained to harness," Jonas suggested. "He didn't seem to object to our riding him bareback that night."

The mention of "that night" brought back memories to Kate, as well as to Jonas. She blushed a charming rose color and lowered her lashes flirtatiously. "I don't think I'll ever forget that ride—or what happened afterward," she whispered.

"Nor will I . . . Perhaps we should repeat the experience, just to see if there's any way it could be improved upon over my recollection of it."

Her mouth slanted downward at the suggestion, and she glanced uneasily away from him. "Not yet, Jonas . . ." she pleaded softly. "We dare not chance it just yet."

He wanted to shout at her—shout and shake her—and demand to know *when*, if ever again? But instead, he shrugged aside her refusal and continued explaining how the mast would be raised. Kate nodded and listened attentively, as if she had not just driven a stake into his heart and poured salt in the wound besides.

A short time later, all was in readiness to begin. Jonas and Nimble climbed up the side of the cradle and took their positions on the newly finished deck of the vessel, that smelled strongly of raw wood and pitch. Then Jonas signaled to Donald, and all the workers grabbed hold of the stout rope wound around the winch and began to haul on it. Chains and hawsers creaked and groaned under the strain, as the mighty log lifted and swung into the air.

From the corner of his eye, Jonas saw Edward join

Kate on the beach below. The two of them watched intently, though Edward seemed more interested in being close to Kate than in observing the hoisting of the mast. Jonas knew a moment of anger; Edward could have volunteered to help with this, at least, when strength was more crucial than know-how. Another man on the main rope would have eased things for all of them.

He turned his attention back to the swaying log as it raised high into the air. Big Donald moved quickly to lock the winch in place, then assigned the workers places on the guide ropes, so that the log could be maneuvered into position as it was lowered into the waiting socket on the ship's deck. In Salem, things were done a bit differently, with more care for safety, but Jonas had had no choice but to proceed with this more primitive method. He lacked the equipment and manpower available in conventional shipyards, but perhaps in time, he and Nimble might be able to devise better ways of doing things.

Donald gave the signal for the men to haul on the guide rope controlling the upper half of the mast. They did so, and the mast tilted, enabling Jonas and Nimble to grab the bottom half and begin guiding it toward the socket. This was the most critical moment; properly seated in the first socket, the mast should slide downward through the bowels of the ship into another socket, and be held firmly in place between the upper deck and the hull.

Jonas and Nimble nearly had the massive timber in place, ready to be lowered, when Jonas heard a shout. "Hold on there! Keep it steady!" Donald boomed in his big voice.

"We can't, Donald! The rope is fraying! Look out, 'cause she's gonna go!" John Ferguson shouted.

"Cap'n! Nimble! Watch out!" Donald cried.

It all happened so quickly that Jonas had almost no time to react. One moment, he and Nimble had the mast resting against the lip of the wooden socket, and the next, it was teetering above them, then crashing downward. Jonas dove to the right and Nimble to the left. The huge log fell crossways, catching on the ship's railing and smashing it and the uncompleted sides to smithereens. Jonas rolled when he hit the deck; wood chips pelted his head and shoulders, and something sharp drove into his side.

He kept on rolling, felt something hard and heavy brush one leg, and then he was out from under the mast and wedged underneath the capstan, along with Nimble.

"Godalmighty, Cap'n! It nearly crushed us flat!" White-faced, Nimble raised his head to look at Jonas. "Are you all right, Cap'n?"

Jonas groped with one hand for his side and found a long, narrow sliver of wood imbedded in it. He pulled it out and flung it away before answering. "I guess we're both still alive, Nimble—though I can't believe our good fortune."

"There's gonna be damage—lots of it," Nimble darkly predicted. "And we're gonna haveta find another log to serve as the mast. I think this one's broken."

"Let's take a look," Jonas said. "And make certain no one else got hurt."

As they were struggling to their feet, they heard the screaming. It was Kate, and she sounded hysterical. "Jonas! Jonas! Get out of my way, Edward, I've got to get to him!"

Favoring his bad leg which was suddenly throbbing, Jonas limped to the side of the vessel and peered over it. Kate was trying to climb the cradle, while Edward attempted to restrain her. "Let go of me!" she screamed, delivering a huge clout to Edward's ear. "I'm going up there!"

Jonas called her name, but she had clawed halfway

335

up the side, before she heard his repeated bellows. "Kate! Damn it, woman, look up here! I'm alive and well; I didn't get hurt."

Her golden eyes held a glint of wildness. She narrowed them as she searched him anxiously. "There's blood on your shirt!" she announced and continued climbing with a vengeance.

Startled, Jonas looked down at himself. He did indeed have blood on his shirt, at the spot where he'd pulled out the big splinter. He lifted the shirt and discovered a small wound, oozing red, but not hurting in the least. By the time he'd tied his shirt around his waist to staunch the flow, Kate was at the top of the cradle and clambering into the ship.

"It's nothing, Kate—not worth the effort of being upset."

She ignored his effort to put the injury in its proper perspective and untied the makeshift bandage to see for herself. Then she ran her hands over his body, frantically checking for broken bones. He caught her by the wrists. "I swear to you, Kate . . . The mast missed us—only by inches, but then, that's all we needed."

Kate darted a glance at Nimble. "You're both unharmed?" she questioned tremulously.

He drew her into his arms. "We're safe and sound, Kate. You can quit worrying. Today wasn't my day to die."

She made a funny little sound, a cross between a squeak and a sob, and flung her arms around his neck, paying no heed to anyone, though every last man on the beach was watching, and probably green with envy. He patted and soothed her. "There, there, sweetheart . . ."

She was trembling and quaking like a leaf in the wind, and Jonas didn't know what to do to help her. Not that he minded having her in his arms again, but he hated to see her so upset for his sake. A shout from

Big Donald made her head snap up, as she turned to listen.

A moment later, Donald swung a leg thick as a tree trunk over the shattered railing beside the fallen mast and stomped quickly over to them. "Cap'n! Cap'n, I examined that rope, and I can't find what went wrong. It was a brand new rope we bought in Nassau; it shouldn't have let go like that—unless somebody tampered with it beforehand."

"Tampered with it!" Kate exclaimed. "What do you mean—tampered with it?"

"Well, Miss Kate, somebody might've cut it partway through, for example, so it would come apart with the first stress placed upon it."

"Who would do such a thing?" she demanded, bright flags of color staining her high cheekbones.

Looking down at the assembled workers, Jonas locked glances with Edward. *Edward might do it,* he thought. He's the only one who has a reason.

"I doan know, Miss Kate. It's jus' a suggestion," Big Donald explained. "Because as I said, it's hard t' believe a new rope could be so faulty it would break the first time we used it."

"Don't you check your ropes before you put men's lives at risk, Donald?" Kate challenged. "Captain Irons and Nimble could have been killed. You were in charge of hoisting the mast; you should have checked the ropes first."

"I *did* check 'em," Donald grumbled. "But I didn't see a blamed thing."

"Then it *must* have been an accident," Kate concluded with a little sigh.

Obviously, she had shared his suspicions and was now relieved to discover they were false. However, Jonas didn't share her relief, until he suddenly remembered something. "I myself checked the ropes this morning—every inch of them," he informed her and Donald. "Like you, Donald, I would have noticed had they been partially sawed in half."

Then Jonas also recalled that Edward hadn't appeared until Kate herself arrived. Edward had brought her in the dory, so the overseer *couldn't* have cut the rope. It would have had to be done between the time Jonas and Donald had examined them, and the time the mast had been raised. And if Edward had done it then, surely someone would have questioned what he was doing near the hoist and equipment. Jonas had been watching the man closely the whole time he had been on the beach; Edward simply had not had the opportunity to indulge in foul play.

Kate swung around to face him with a determined gleam in her golden eyes. "Promise me you'll be more careful in the future, Jonas. Swear to me nothing like this will ever happen again. Next time, *test* the ropes before you use them for the first time."

"I intend to," Jonas replied. "Now, if everyone has calmed down sufficiently, let's see about assessing our damages and fixing them."

Chapter Twenty-Four

Three weeks after the incident involving the mast, the damages were completely repaired, and a new mast stood proudly in place. This time, there had been no accidents; everything went smoothly, according to plan. Elated by the success of the mast-raising, Jonas talked Kate into another celebration, using the logic that they had two things for which to be thankful and rejoice: First, only the finish-work remained to be done on the vessel, and while time-consuming, it wasn't as dangerous as the primary construction phase had been, and second, Kate's mother was showing marked improvement.

While it could never be said that Sybil Montgomery had returned to normal, she was at least lucid most of the time, knew where she was, and most importantly, no longer seemed so dependent on Kate. Bell was able to meet most of Sybil's needs, and Kate no longer had to spend the major portion of every day with her mother, though she was careful to visit her both morning and night.

Prodded by Jonas, Kate had begun insisting that her mother leave her bed and spend time downstairs each day—and even go for short walks outside to see the trees and flowers or sit on the veranda, if she felt too weak to venture into the yard. Kate's father was so pleased by Sybil's progress that he no longer drank quite as much in the evenings, though he still spent an inordinate amount of time in Edward's company, bemoaning the many failures of the plantation system in the Bahamas and reminiscing about the way things had been when he was a boy in America.

All in all, Kate had much to celebrate, Jonas told her, not the least of which was the possibility that they could again find time alone together.

"If your father would agree to donate another cask of rum to the festivities, there's a good chance everyone will fall asleep early like they did the last time, and you and I can then retire unnoticed to my hut . . ." he murmured in her ear.

"You're wicked!" she scolded, but her reddened cheeks and merry eyes revealed her excitement and anticipation. "Maybe I could convince him to donate *two* casks," she speculated. "And I'll tell Bell to give Mama a double dose of her nightly tea, so I won't have to worry about her waking up and calling for me."

"*I'm* wicked?" Jonas teased. "I can't begin to compete with *you*, my dear."

They giggled together like two naughty children, and then made plans for a celebration to be held two nights later. That would give them time to make all of the arrangements, including having Fish dive for conch and Benjamin and Cal fish for gray or yellowtail snapper, both highly esteemed food fish. Neither Kate nor Jonas wanted to take time to go boar hunting, but Kate hinted that she might have Mattie wring the necks of a couple chickens and surprise Jonas with some special poultry dishes.

Jonas worked hard the day before the party, and by nightfall, was glad to seek the comfort of his bed. He lay awake for a short time, imagining Kate in the narrow bed beside him. It had been so long since they'd been together that he was half afraid he wouldn't know how to act when he finally did get her alone. Then he grinned into the darkness; he'd remember soon enough. How could he forget? The times he had possessed her sweet body were forever burned into his brain—each sweet, tender kiss, each wondrously exciting caress, each slow, rapturous stroke as he plumbed the depths of her and made her his.

Tomorrow night, he intended to love her so thoroughly that she'd be unable to say no when he insisted that they speak with her parents and settle the matter of their future once and for all. Sybil Montgomery may be as strong now, as she was ever going to get; to wait longer would only invite another relapse and another long period of waiting . . . and Jonas didn't think he could be that patient. Nor could Kate. They had both endured the agonies of the damned over the past few weeks, and Jonas was determined to put an end to the painful separation. The sooner the Montgomerys accepted the inevitable, the better.

He fell asleep dreaming of the joys to come, but his dreams soon became tormented and frightening. He dreamed he was trapped in the midst of a fiery circle, flames leaping all around him, and smoke filling his lungs. The intense heat made him writhe on the bed; he was so hot—so terribly hot! The crackling sounds indicated the fire was coming nearer, but he couldn't seem to find the energy to escape. Weariness and fatigue kept him chained in place, unable to move, scarcely able to breathe.

He told himself he was having a nightmare, but he couldn't make himself wake up . . . Then suddenly he did awaken. Someone was shouting, calling his name, but when he opened his eyes, all he could see was a sheet of flame. Both the walls and the thatched roof of the hut were on fire, the flames consuming the dry palm fronds with sickening speed and a noise

341

that reminded him of popping muskets.

"Cap'n Irons! Cap'n, are you in there?"

Jonas recognized Nimble's nasal tones, and then Donald's big, booming ones. "Hell, he can't be in there and still be alive! By now, he'd be roasted like a Christmas goose."

Jonas sprang to his feet, his eyes tearing so badly he couldn't see to find the door. He made a wild guess and dashed for safety—and a single breath of pure, sweet air before he suffocated. Nimble and Donald caught him as he stumbled and fell outside the burning hut. Gasping in a futile effort to fill his clogged lungs, he couldn't speak, but Nimble guessed what he wanted anyway.

"Water! Somebody git the Cap'n some water!"

Then Nimble was pounding him on the back and making him cough. Someone—Cal?—shoved a tin mug into his hands, and Jonas drank deeply, the cool liquid like a balm sliding down his throat. A few minutes passed before he regained his voice, but even then it had gone all raspy, as if he had a fatal congestion in his chest.

"What happened?" he finally managed to mutter. "How did my hut catch fire?"

The men around him exchanged blank, puzzled looks. "We don't know, Cap'n," Nimble said. "We was hopin' you could tell us. Yours was the only one t' burn; neither of the other two caught fire."

Had he left a lantern or a candle lit? Jonas wondered, but no, he distinctly remembered lying in the dark, thinking about Kate. Quickly, he scanned the faces of the men bending anxiously over him, and then studied the line of figures hauling buckets of water in a hastily formed brigade on the beach. He spotted all of his former crew members, as well as Kate's workers. He didn't see Edward, but the overseer's name was the first to pop into his head.

Edward must have set his hut ablaze.

342

Who else would have done it? And who else would have "arranged" the accident with the mast? Maybe Edward had also poisoned Whiskers!

As soon as he could rise from his knees, Jonas did so. His chest hurt when he breathed, and he felt weak and shaky from his near brush with death. But nothing could have stopped him from leaving to search for Edward. Somehow, Jonas was sure he would know the truth as soon as he saw Edward's face; Edward could give any excuse he wanted, but his eyes would reveal the lie.

"I was sleeping, so I can't tell you how my hut caught fire," he growled. "At least, not yet. But maybe I can tell you by morning. I'm leaving to pay a visit to the Montgomerys. Finish putting out the fire, and try to get some rest."

"You want ah should go wif you, Cap'n?" Cal asked. "Ah'd relish de chance t' check on Mattie an' make sure de other women is all right. Ah gotta go in de mornin' anyway, t' he'p bring food fer de celebration."

"If there is a celebration," Jonas muttered. "Right now, I don't much feel like dancing and singing."

So Cal had his suspicions, too, he thought, noting the black man's worried eyes.

"I'd be willin' t' go with you, too, Cap'n," Big Donald volunteered.

"No, the rest of you men stay here. I'll be back by morning. If I'm not, then you *can* come after me."

On that grim note, Jonas took his leave, accompanied by Cal.

Kate wasn't sure what had awakened her; she lay listening in the darkness, and male voices drifted through her open window—Edward's and her father's. The men were apparently down on the veranda, probably polishing off a jug of rum. She couldn't hear what they were saying, but Edward sounded excited—almost breathless. Kate rolled onto her stomach and impatiently punched her pillow. She wished they would go to bed, or barring that, be a little more quiet.

Tonight, especially, she wanted to sleep, because if everything worked out as she hoped, tomorrow night she wouldn't get any sleep. She would be with Jonas in his hut on the beach, or maybe they'd steal off through the woods to the pool. Either way, she didn't intend to spend the night in slumber, unless she and Jonas slept *afterward*, wrapped in each other's arms.

She sighed; thinking about Jonas made her wide awake. It was something she tried not to do after she went to bed, for she needed her rest in order to put in long days of hard physical labor, or even just to deal with her mother. But she was awake, now, so she might as well get up and scold her father and Edward for having awakened her, and also warn them not to disturb Mama.

Rolling off the bed, she grabbed the dressing gown she kept handy in case her mother needed her during the night. Quickly, she slipped into it, finger-brushed her hair back from her face, and headed for the door and the staircase. Halfway down the steps, she heard sudden shouting, followed by a scuffle on the veranda.

She hurried to the front door and flung it wide. A candle burned in a glass on a small table between the two chairs where her father and Edward usually passed their evenings. Beside it was a jug and two mugs . . . but that wasn't all the candle illuminated. Jonas stood on the veranda, holding Edward by the front of his shirt. Papa, meanwhile, had gotten to his feet and stood swaying beside his chair, his bloodshot eyes blinking rapidly, as he tried to focus on what was happening.

"I want to know where you were earlier tonight,

344

Edward," Jonas was saying. His features had twisted with fury, but it was his voice that alerted Kate to the fact that something was terribly wrong. Jonas didn't sound like himself; she wouldn't have recognized his voice had she heard it before opening the door.

"Whatsa matter with you?" Edward grumbled. "Get your hands off me." He plucked ineffectually at Jonas's fingers, but the grip on his shirtfront didn't loosen.

"Not until you tell me where you were tonight."

Kate rushed onto the veranda, her stomach muscles clenching in dread. "Jonas, what's happened?"

Jonas's eyes briefly flickered over her, before returning to Edward's pale, but sullen face. "My hut burned down tonight—with me in it. I barely got out alive," he rumbled in his scratchy, unfamiliar voice.

"Burned down! But how could that happen? Did you forget to put out a candle?"

"No," Jonas gritted. "Someone had to have started the fire deliberately, which makes me wonder if the other two incidents which endangered my life were entirely accidental."

"You think Edward is responsible!" Kate cried. "That's the same thing as accusing him of murder."

Jonas gave Edward a shake. "If he set fire to my hut tonight, he intended to commit murder . . . Didn't you, Edward?"

"I didn't do nothin'!" Edward denied, pulling back and finally jerking his shirt free. "I been here all evenin' with Kate's daddy, haven't I, Will?"

Kate's eyes flew to her father's face. He wouldn't meet her gaze but straightened and cleared his throat. "That's right, Edward. You've been here with me—talking and drinking, like we usually do to pass the long nights."

"He never left here at all?" Jonas demanded, turning his attention to the older man. "Not even for an hour or two?"

345

William's mouth firmed, and for a moment, Kate glimpsed the man her father might have been had they remained in America and not been forced into exile. He tilted back his head to gaze at Jonas with a regal air that would have done credit to Kate's grandfather. "Didn't I just say that, Captain Irons? Edward has been here with me since late this afternoon. My own daughter can attest to that. Kate? Tell the captain; Edward was here when you got back from the leeward side of the island. You passed us on your way into the house."

When she didn't immediately answer, her father turned to her and bowed slightly. "Tell him, Kate," he urged. "Edward couldn't have set fire to the captain's hut, because he's been here with me the entire time."

"Kate, is that true?" Jonas's impatience showed in his face and body. He looked ready to throttle Edward.

"Well, yes," she admitted. "He was certainly here when I got home—and he was here through dinner and well into the evening. But I retired to my room sometime before midnight; what happened after that, I have no idea."

"But *I* do!" her father announced. "Edward was here all the time. He never left me, did you, Edward?"

Edward's face wore an irritating, triumphant smirk, as he gleefully agreed. "Nope . . . I didn't. Not that I'd be sorry if you'd fried to death in that hut, Cap'n. I don't like you, and I don't like Kate spendin' all her time with you, buildin' that ship. It ain't no secret how I feel about Kate. I still hope she'll eventually agree to marry me, so it wouldn't bother me in the least if you was suddenly t' disappear."

"*Edward!*" Kate spat, but before she could say more, Jonas said it for her.

"Kate will never marry you, Edward . . . You see, she's already consented to marry me, as soon as my

346

ship is built."

"Marry *you!*" William exploded. "By God, man, are *you* a murderer, as well as a seducer of innocent young women? Kate can *never* marry you! Why, it would kill her mother!"

"Papa . . ." Kate pleaded, not having intended to reveal her intentions in this hasty, blunt manner. "I hadn't meant to say anything until I was sure Mama had recovered enough from this latest episode of illness to be able to deal with my news. But now that it's come out, I'm glad. Papa, I love Jonas, and he loves me . . . We want to be married, but that doesn't mean I'm going to abandon you and Mama. We're going to live here on Conch Cay and build ships. Please believe me; I have no plans to leave you and Mama."

Her father merely stared at her, as if she had uttered the unspeakable. She very much feared she had. Her father's mouth was trembling, he had gone pale to the point of bloodlessness, and his eyes held a look of complete and total devastation. "I cannot believe you would do this to us, Kate . . . Marriage to . . . to an American, will finish your mother for good. Do you want her death on your conscience? Are you so selfish, ungrateful, and disobedient that you care nothing for your poor, unbalanced mother? And after she dies, what will become of me? Your mother is the only reason that *I* find the courage to go on living—because I dare not leave her!"

Tears rolled down her father's gaunt cheeks; he seemed to age right before Kate's eyes, his features resembling a skeleton's more than a man's. "What have we ever done to deserve such callous treatment from our only daughter, indeed, our only child, since Robin's death? I plead with you, Kate . . . I beg of you . . ."

To Kate's horror, her father grabbed hold of the back of a chair and sank down to the floor on his bony knees, which creaked as they bore his weight. "Don't *do* this to us, Kate . . . It is unthinkable. A Montgomery Loyalist cannot marry a traitor to the Crown. Your grandfather would rise up from his grave to condemn your faithlessness. Don't you remember what they did to him—how they stripped him naked, tarred and feathered him, and destroyed his manhood all in one blow? Oh, lord, I cannot bear it! I cannot! I cannot!"

Her father hunched over, gripping his chest with both hands. The chair fell over, as Jonas reached out a hand to grab him before he collapsed.

"Papa!" Kate sank to her knees beside her father and saw that he had gone rigid and white-lipped. His eyes had rolled back into his head, and she could not pry his hands from his chest when she took his arm. "Jonas! Edward! Help me get him inside. He's having some sort of fit or attack."

"Stand aside," Jonas said. "I can manage him on my own."

"Don't touch him, bastard!" Edward shouted, elbowing Jonas in the ribs. "He wouldn't want a filthy traitor t' lay a hand on him—not even if he wuz dyin'."

Jonas gave a long drawn sigh, then stepped back and allowed Edward the honors. "I won't argue with you now, or he's apt to die waiting for one of us to take him inside."

Grunting with the effort, Edward picked up the fallen man and carried him into the house ahead of Kate. "Take him upstairs to my bed," she told Edward. "And please be quiet so you don't awaken Mama. God only knows what *this* will do to her."

With a manner so calm that she amazed even herself, Kate spun to face Jonas who was following behind her. "Jonas, would you mind going down to the slave quarters and fetching Mattie and Bell? Tell Bell what's happened and ask her to bring any

348

medicines she thinks might be needed—and warn her to hurry."

"Of course, I'll go." Jonas caught her hand and squeezed it, his blue eyes searching her face. "He'll be all right, Kate. Don't worry. He's simply had a shock. I knew we should have told him about us before this . . ."

"We shouldn't have told him at all!" Kate was suddenly overcome with guilt. She realized now was not the time to discuss their future, but all her fears came spilling out regardless. "It will never work between us, Jonas! Don't you understand that, by now? We might as well give it up . . . I knew that loving you was futile from the very beginning; it just wasn't meant to be . . ."

"That's not true, Kate. You can't shield your parents from reality forever."

"But I can't kill them with it, either! Oh, leave me alone, Jonas! Please, just leave me alone . . ." She started to go up the stairs after Edward and her father, but Jonas grabbed her wrist, forcing her to face him.

His eyes held compassion and sympathy, but also hurt and confusion. "We can handle this, Kate . . . I promise you, we can handle it."

"*I* can't handle it, Jonas! What if my father dies because of this? What if my mother suffers another relapse? You can't ask me to build a marriage on the ashes of two people I love but have selfishly destroyed. I can't do it! Don't you understand? I . . . just . . . can't . . . do . . . it!"

She broke away from him and ran up the stairs.

"Kate!" he called after her, but she ignored him, ran into her room, and callously slammed the door behind her.

There would be time later to regret what she had said and to mourn the loss of Jonas's love and the life they could have had together. For now, all that mattered was saving her father. She would do anything to give him peace of mind and undo the harm she had already done. Always she had worried about her mother; somehow, it had never occurred to her that her father was every·bit as fragile.

As Edward laid her father on the bed, she grasped the old man's hand. "Papa . . . Oh, Papa, please don't die . . . I promise you I won't marry Jonas, if only you'll try to live and get better . . ."

Edward had the affrontery to grin, sure now that he had won her. Kate glared at him, then continued to stroke and hold her father's hand, her anxiety rising by the minute. "Papa, did you hear me? It was all a mistake. I realize now that you're right; a Loyalist can't marry an . . . an American. I haven't forgotten what happened to Grandpa—or to Robin on Tynbee Island, or to Mama, when she had to endure trials and hardships she wasn't strong enough to face . . . It's all right, Papa. I'm here now, and I'll never leave you and Mama. I won't break your hearts. Believe me, Papa; I've learned my lesson. After Jonas's ship is finished, I'll send him away and go back to wrecking. At least, wrecking is an occupation on which we can always count. And we don't need outsiders to help us do it."

A sob caught in her throat, and she fell silent, her eyes glued to her father's sunken face. He gave no sign that he had heard her, but Edward had. "'Bout time you came t' yer senses, Kate," he muttered with great satisfaction. "Now, if you really wanna set things right again, all ya haveta do is marry *me*."

Kate didn't answer; it was too much to ask of her in one day—to give up Jonas and to marry this despicable man, who very well might have set fire to Jonas's hut, tampered with the rope holding the mast, and poisoned the poor cat. There was also the matter of Jonathan and the mystery still surrounding *his* death. She concentrated on keeping calm and holding her tears at bay, even managing to feel a certain pride in her own strength and willpower. She had done what needed to be done, and somehow, she'd survive the pain . . . and the loneliness.

I excel at being a survivor, she desperately consoled herself. Surviving is what I do best.

And she knew then, as she had always known, that survival was all she would ever have; any chance of being truly happy and fulfilled was gone for good.

Chapter Twenty-Five

"Is we gonna celebrate de launchin' of de ship, Miz Kate?" Mattie asked Kate one afternoon as they sat together on the veranda. While waiting for Papa and Mama both to awaken from their midday naps, Kate was keeping Mattie company as she nursed Baby David.

It was six weeks after Papa had collapsed, and though Kate hadn't yet seen the vessel, she had heard from the workers that it was finished. The combined jobs of nursing her parents and running the plantation had taken all her time, so she had not visited the work site nor really spoken to Jonas. Papa had improved to the point of being able to leave his bed, but he trembled from the slightest exertion, walked with a kind of shuffling gait, and sometimes slurred his words, even when he hadn't had a drop to drink. Mama, of course, was still Mama—good one day, and bad the next—so that Kate never knew what to expect when she carried in her mother's breakfast tray, refusing even to allow Bell to perform that humble service.

"Seems we oughta do somepin', aftah all dis time and labor . . ." Mattie continued, switching her chubby-cheeked youngest child from one breast to the other. "It shore is a purty ship. Ah ain't never seed a ship so purty. Cal's as proud of it as Cap'n Irons . . ."

"I'm sure it's very pretty," Kate agreed, unable to suppress a spasm of longing to see the vessel—and most especially to see Jonas.

She had been fighting such urges for six long weeks of misery, but she still hadn't managed to totally conquer her rebellious desires. Jonas had come three times to the house, and three times she had refused to see him, because she knew if she did, she would only want to see him again . . . and again, no matter what the effect on her parents. Mattie and Bell had answered his questions about her mother and father, but she herself had hidden in her mother's room, thereby avoiding the possibility that she might throw herself into his arms, betraying both her parents and her long-cherished political beliefs, and beg him to take her away.

Finally, he had quit coming. She dreaded what was sure to happen now that the vessel was finished. Assuming it brought a profit in Nassau, Jonas would probably take his share and go build ships someplace else—or else he'd return to Salem. By now, he must want to leave Conch Cay as badly as she wanted him to go—except that she didn't *really* want him to go. However, considering the circumstances, there was no other choice. If he stayed, it would only be a kind of living hell for both of them.

"So whut y'all wanna do?" Mattie persisted. "De launchin' gonna be next week, Cal done told me, an' de men all wanna celebrate. But it won't be much of a doin' iffen y'all don't take part, Miz Kate."

"Mattie, you're like a dog worrying a bone; you just won't let go, will you?"

The black woman gave Kate a smile brimming with wisdom and sadness. "Ah spect ah is, Miz Kate . . . De truff is, me an' Cal is plumb worried about y'all. Don't tek no brains t' figure out dat you is

354

mighty unhappy—an' so's Cap'n Irons. De two of you ain't spoke a single word t' each other since Massah William done suffered dat fit. It ain't right t' treat de Cap'n like dat, Miz Kate . . . Dat man's heart is near broke in two 'cause y'all won't speak t' him or go down to de work site no more."

"Well, if you must know, Mattie, so is mine. But I can't do a thing about it. The reason Papa collapsed is that I told him I love Captain Irons and want to marry him. The shock of it nearly killed Papa, and God only knows what it would do to poor Mama. I had to promise Papa I wouldn't do it after all, just to convince him to get better."

Mattie rocked back and forth, hugging David and shaking her head. "Oh, Miz Kate . . . It ain't right. It jus' ain't right. Worse, it ain't fair. You deserve t' marry de man y'all loves. Why, ah'm a slave, but ah got t' marry Cal, de man o' mah choice."

"You might not have gotten to marry him, if it hadn't suited us as well as you," Kate reminded her. "Not that I would have stood in your way, but Papa or Mama might have . . . or Edward, except his opinion didn't have as much weight back then as it does now."

"But dat's whut ah mean, Miz Kate! Yore parents was right reasonable about me an' Cal; how's come dey can't be reasonable when it comes t' dere own daughter?"

"Mattie, on some plantations, you'd be whipped for saying what you've just said," Kate scolded. "It isn't your place to judge my parents. They can't help who they are and what they think. They hate Jonas because he's an American, and they're afraid he'll take me away from here . . . That's also why they didn't like Jonathan. They're entitled to their opinions—and as their daughter, I owe them obedience and respect, especially when I've seen how it can destroy them when I forget their desires and

355

seek only to please myself."

"Still doan think it's right, Miz Kate . . . Y'all ain't much better off den me. Fact is, you gonna be *worse* off, iffen you marry Edward. Den you gonna haveta obey him, too, an' ah don't think he gonna make any better husband den he is an overseer."

"Mattie! If we weren't such good friends, I'd never let you get away with such insolence."

"If we wuzn't friends, ah wouldn't speak so plainly, Miz Kate . . . But somebody gotta look after y'all's happiness, 'cause ah doan see you or yore mama an' papa doin' it."

"Let's drop the subject of my happiness, shall we? I'll think about the matter of a celebration for the launching. It does seem we ought to do something. Maybe we could send a special meal to the work site, provide a cask of rum, and possibly a bottle of wine to be broken over the bowsprit, though it's a shame to waste good wine like that."

"Fergit de wine," Mattie sniffed. "What would really make de men happy is for y'all t' show up an' admire dere work."

"I don't know," Kate said. "I'll have to think about it."

By launching day, Kate still had not made up her mind whether or not to attend the festivities she had helped to organize, but as it happened, the issue ceased to matter. After weeks of endless sunshine and blue skies, the day dawned blustery and stormy, with six-foot waves pounding the beach. Cal informed Kate that Jonas had decided to wait until better weather to slide his precious ship down the newly built skids and commit her to the sea. Even the water on the leeward side of the island was choppy, and everyone feared that worse weather might be on the way.

Mattie had prepared quite a lot of food in anticipation of the event, and realizing that the workers must eat, no matter what the sky looked like, Kate helped Daisy and Cassie carry baskets and kettles out to Fish, Cal, and Benjamin, who were going to tote it overland to the work site, since the sea was so rough. As she did so, the odd greenish hue of the sky worried her.

The wind was blowing so strongly that trees and bushes were bent to the ground, and Kate's own skirt billowed up around her waist. Growing more alarmed by the minute, Kate considered the possibility that a hurricane might be coming. It was the season for them, but it had been years since a storm of any real magnitude has passed through the Abacos. Today, somehow, the air felt different—charged with expectancy. There had been intermittent showers throughout the night, but no heavy rains had yet fallen, and she could smell more rain on the way.

"Wait, Cal . . . Don't take these things, yet. I have a better idea," she said as Cal reached out a large, calloused hand to relieve her of a kettle of chowder. "Remember that hurricane we had a dozen or so years ago—the one that destroyed the crops and almost blew down the house?"

Cal nodded, his eyes round and frightened with the superstitious fear all the slaves had of hurricanes and heavy storms. "Ah 'member, Miz Kate. Don't 'magine ah could evah fergit. Ah wuz pos'tive we wuz all gonna die."

"Before the hurricane came, it looked and felt just like this, didn't it?"

"Yes'm, Miz Kate . . . Now dat y'all mention it, ah 'member it did."

"We gonna have a h—hurricane, Miz Kate?" Daisy quavered, casting a wary look around her at the bent-over trees and bushes.

Cassie appeared too frightened even to speak. Her mouth worked soundlessly, but then she gave up and simply clutched her basket to her breast and stared at Kate like some terrified wild creature.

"Maybe . . . Maybe not," Kate answered. "But I think we should prepare for the worst. Cal, you better go get Captain Irons and the rest of the men at the work site. Tell them to tie down everything they can and come back here to the house. Benjamin and Fish, you stay here and start closing shutters, doors, and windows. Don't just latch them; tie or board them shut. Do the house, first. It's the strongest structure on the island, so we better plan on everyone sleeping here tonight. Daisy and Cassie, you'll have to make up pallets and fetch plenty of fresh water, just in case. I recall we had no water stored the last time, and our usual sources were contaminated with sand and silt for days afterward."

"Yes'm, Miz Kate . . . We'll do dat right away. What you want done wif all dis food?" Daisy asked. "Store it in de big house, too?"

"Of course . . . And tell Mattie to put out any fires she still has burning in the oven or elsewhere. During hurricanes, stray sparks can be dangerous. Also, she'll want to pick everything she can from the garden and the nearest fruit trees. Otherwise, the produce will only be destroyed."

As everyone scattered to obey Kate's commands, Kate realized that now she wouldn't have to decide whether or not she was strong enough to face Jonas again; she no longer had a choice. Unless he stubbornly decided to stay in a hut that might blow away, she would see him tonight. He'd be sleeping in the parlor. Excitement rippled down her spine, but she got hold of herself and resolutely went back to work. Facing the possibility of a hurricane, she didn't have time to think about Jonas, or what her reaction would be when she finally saw him. Maybe, after so long a time, she'd feel nothing at all . . . More likely, a hurricane would seem weak by comparison.

By midnight that night, Kate's suspicion that a hurricane was on the way had turned into certainty. The wind was howling like a pack of demented wolves, and the whole house was shaking on its foundations. No one could sleep. The slaves had gathered with their wives and children in the dining room, while Jonas's workers occupied the parlor. Edward had taken over the hallway, and Jonas sat on the stair with Kate. Only Kate's mother and father had gone to bed—lulled by a soothing tea prepared by Bell that was guaranteed to keep them both calm through any danger that threatened.

A single lantern illuminated the stuffy darkness. Kate kept it near at hand, so she could snuff it out in a hurry, and also because she felt safer from Jonas while it was lit. Not that she expected him to try anything with so many people in the house and in such a tense situation. But she had been doing her best to ignore him, or at least not catch his eye, and she knew from several furtive glances at him, that he was as miserable and unhappy as she.

He hadn't said much since he'd arrived—only that she was looking well, which she knew was a lie—and that everything at the work site was as secure as they could make it. Since the area was protected from the wind, Jonas felt perfectly confident that no harm would come to his newly built ship. Edward had scowled at that information, allowing that it was still a waste of time and money to have built the thing, because nobody could possibly want it anyway. It was too small for long sea voyages, such as crossing the ocean to England, and too big for use between the cays. Folks already had sloops and fishing smacks adequate for smaller journeys, so why would they want something so much bigger and harder to sail? he had sullenly asked.

"Because they sometimes get caught in storms like this one," Jonas had dryly responded. "My ship can handle mountainous waves, and while she's doing it, her crew and captain will be safe and snug inside a cabin, instead of out on a slippery, sea-washed deck. Tell me, Edward. Where would you rather be on a night like this—on the *Zephyr* or the *Phoenix*?"

"We only get storms this bad once every ten or twenty years," Edward had scoffed. "Maybe not even that often."

"That may be true, but you do get lesser ones with some regularity, and a man would still be safer on a bigger ship."

The discussion had ended there, and Jonas had been silent ever since. Kate blamed the tension in the house on the storm's intensity, but she was well aware that the tension between herself and Jonas had grown thick as porridge. So she sat on the steps, elbows on knees, her head supported in her hands, and listened to the fury raging outside. Occasionally, heavy objects banged against the walls or shutters, and water oozed around door and window frames as the rain searched out every crack.

She worried about the chickens shut up in a shed, and the horses, dairy goats, and the old, arthritic mule they used for plowing, running loose on the island. Where would the animals go to be safe?

A mighty bang! made her jump. Something large and heavy had struck the side of the house, and then Kate heard her mother shrieking upstairs in her bedroom, and Bell shouting over the storm's fury. "It's all right, Miz Sybil! It's jus' dis ole storm, dat's all! Ain't nothin' gonna harm ya'."

"Get away from me, Bell!" Sybil screamed. "This storm is all your fault! It's Divine Retribution, that's what it is—we're all going to die because of you!"

360

Kate jumped to her feet. This didn't sound like something Bell was going to be able to handle on her own. She couldn't avoid Jonas's startled, questioning gaze as he rose at the same time she did and stood several steps below her, ready to help.

"Divine Retribution for *what?*" he muttered.

"I've no idea," she answered. "I doubt if Mama even knows; storms sometimes make her hysterical . . . Stay here, Jonas. I'll go upstairs and try to calm her."

Kate whirled and ran lightly up the remainder of the steps. When she reached her mother's room—her father had taken up permanent residence in her room, and she was sleeping in the small guest bedchamber—Kate saw her mother struggling with Bell. The Negress was trying to push her back down on the pillows and prevent her from leaving the bed, while Sybil was doing her best to break free and escape.

"Get away from me! Don't you touch me, Bell!" Sybil's hair flew wildly about her face, which the lantern on the bedside table revealed to be as pale as her snowy-white nightdress, except for two feverish spots of color staining her thin, high cheekbones that were so similar to Kate's. Her eyes held the frightening and all too familiar look of madness. "God is punishing us, at long last! I knew it would happen eventually . . . You devil-woman! You handmaiden of Lucifer! You promised this would never happen. You swore to me we wouldn't be punished."

Bell cast a worried glance at Kate as she rushed into the room. "She's gone outa her head, Miz Kate! She doan know whut she sayin'."

"I can see that, Bell . . . Here, let me talk to her."

Bell let go of Sybil and stepped back, allowing Kate to take her place. Kate grabbed her mother's arm. "Mama! Mama, hush now! It's me, Kate."

361

Sybil stopped struggling a moment and narrowed her eyes at Kate. Recognizing her, she burst into tears. "Oh, Kate, my darling, my precious baby!" she bawled, throwing her arms around Kate's neck. "Whatever happens, whatever justice or calamity befalls us, just remember my dearest darling, that I did it all for you!"

"You did what, Mama?" Kate managed to gasp, as the fierceness of her mother's embrace nearly choked her.

"Oh, I can't tell you! I mustn't, because then you would hate me." She drew back and fixed Kate with a teary-eyed gaze. "But you wouldn't really hate your own mama, would you, Kate? You *couldn't* hate me, not when I only acted out of concern for your welfare and future happiness."

"What have you done, Mama?" Kate demanded. "What are you talking about?"

Sybil shook her head, sobbing and blubbering. "It's all Bell's fault, really. By myself, I could never have been so wicked." She seized Kate's hand and squeezed it so tightly that Kate's fingers crunched. "We must get rid of Bell, Kate . . . Yes, that's what we must do; we must take her to Nassau and sell her at once. Right now, this very minute . . . You'll do that for me, won't you? You'll get rid of that awful woman and her evil black powers?"

A cry of anguish and protest burst from Bell, but Kate dared not turn around to reassure the woman. "Mama, there's a hurricane coming, if it hasn't already arrived . . . We can't go anywhere. Listen, can't you hear it?"

At that moment, another heavy object slammed against the wall. A rending, splintering sound followed, and then wind and water poured into the room through the window opening, from which the shutter had disappeared. Bell screamed, and so did Kate's mother. The lantern flew against the wall,

362

shattered, and went out. Other objects became flying missiles, which struck Kate from every direction. At the same time, rain drenched her.

In the lightning's glare, both Sybil and Bell were white-faced and immobilized. Their fear had gone beyond the point of screaming; neither of them seemed capable of moving.

"We've got to get out of here!" Kate shouted, trying to shield her mother's slender body from the flying debris. "Bell, open the door!"

The door had blown shut, and moving like a sleepwalker, Bell attempted to open it. Her clothes had flattened against her large body, and her turban had been ripped from her head. She tugged on the doorknob, but couldn't budge the door. Suddenly, it was forced open from the other side. Jonas entered, took in the situation at a glance, and dragged Bell from the windswept, rain-lashed room. When he returned to assist Kate with her mother, Sybil recoiled from his touch and resumed screaming.

"No! No! You're supposed to be dead! Bell and I killed you! I saw you die! What are you doing here, again? No, don't touch me! I don't want to go with you! Kate, help me! He's a demon come to take me to hell!"

Jonas grabbed Sybil on one side and Kate took the other; together, they managed to drag the distraught, flailing woman from the room. No sooner had they reached the upstairs hallway, when the door to Sybil's bedchamber slammed shut. Trying to catch her breath, Kate leaned against the upstairs railing, while her mother sagged in her arms, moaning and weeping.

"It's over . . . all over. I knew we would have to pay . . ." She lifted defeated, accusing eyes to Jonas's face. "Oh, why couldn't you have stayed dead? I should have known you weren't really dead. You were so terribly hard to kill . . . Just when we thought we'd done it, you stirred, and we had to do it again.''

Jonas's perplexed face was barely visible in the light of the lantern still lit on the steps. ''Is she raving about me—or my brother, Jonathan?''

''Who will ever know?'' Kate helplessly shrugged her shoulders. She had to shout to make herself heard over the roar of the storm. ''Sometimes, she dreams about a pit, where snakes are waiting to devour her . . . Her rantings hardly ever make sense. Don't assume it's either you or Jonathan; it could be someone—or something—else entirely . . . Mama isn't capable of killing—or trying to kill—anyone. She doesn't even like to see a chicken have its neck wrung.''

''I'm sure she's talking about me or Jonathan, Kate, and I think I know how to find out which one.'' Jonas dug around in his pocket for a moment, then withdrew his brother's timepiece and held it up in front of Sybil's eyes. ''Do you recognize this, Mrs. Montgomery?''

At sight of the watch, Kate's mother's eyes widened, and she let out a piercing scream. Then she collapsed and would have fallen to the floor had Kate and Jonas not held her upright.

''What are you trying to prove?'' Kate angrily shouted. ''The woman is mad! Do you honestly think this poor, frail creature could have drowned and killed your brother?''

''She recognized Jonathan's watch!'' Jonas shouted back at her. ''And even if she had seen it sometime before he died, why would the sight of it now cause her to scream and faint—unless *she* was the one who took it off my brother's body and sold it in Nassau?''

''Mama hasn't been to Nassau in years! And she couldn't have taken it off Jonathan's body, because *I* was the first one to find him on the beach after the storm that killed him."

"But maybe it *wasn't* the storm that killed him. Maybe it was your mother or her devoted slave, Bell!"

Kate's gaze flew to the short, plump Negress cowering against the wall, a short distance down the hallway. Her expression revealed she had heard everything, and if anyone could look guilty, she did. Her kinky wet hair stuck straight up on her round head—the kinks had been blown askew by the wind—and her slackened lower lip was quivering.

"Ah doan know whut y'all's talkin' about!" she denied. "Ah didn't kill nobody! An' ah doan know nuffin' 'bout dat watch! Ain't never seed it b'fore in mah life."

Jonas abruptly let go of Sybil, leaving Kate to support her unconscious mother as best she could, while he advanced menacingly on the frightened woman. "Then why did Kate's mother claim that this storm was all your fault?"

"Ah doan know, Cap'n! Ah swear ah doan know!" Bell threw up her apron and dabbed at her tear-swollen eyes. "Dat woman is purely wicked! Ah doan care iffen y'all does sell me, Miz Kate—but ah ain't gonna tek keer o' yer Mama no more! Ah cain't h'ep her. Ah's done ever'thin' ah could, an' she still doan git no better. An' now, she's blamin' everythin' on me, when all ah evah did wuz whut she done told me . . . Gilbert! Gilbert! Oh, ah wants mah man, Gilbert!"

Bell launched herself past Jonas, Kate, and Sybil, and hurried down the steps, shrieking for her husband at the top of her lungs. "Gilbert! Gilbert, where is you when ah need you?"

At that moment, Kate's father, William, opened the door to Kate's bedchamber and stood there barefooted in his white nightshirt and cap. He cleared his throat, blinked, and peered uncertainly into the hallway. "What's going on out here? It's bad enough this storm is loud enough to wake a dead man—what's all the shouting?"

His speech was slurred, but his eyes were clear, which meant he'd drunk nothing but Bell's tea before he went to bed—a discovery that ought to have pleased Kate, but somehow didn't. All she needed was for her father to become involved in this ridiculous argument.

"You!" he cried, catching sight of Jonas. "What are you doing here in my house? You're not welcome, Captain! I don't want my daughter to have anything to do with you. She promised me she'd send you away—but here you are, as persistent as ever."

As he shuffled down the hallway toward them, he noticed Sybil, leaning weakly against the wall. "Dear God in heaven! What have you done to my wife?"

"She fainted when I showed her *this*," Jonas snarled, shoving the watch under William's nose.

Kate's father barely reacted, except to push Jonas's hand away with surprising strength, considering his bony, shaking fingers. "Get out of my way, Captain! Can't you see Sybil needs me? Kate, why do you permit this bully to even speak to your dear mama?"

Before Kate or Jonas could respond, the floor shifted beneath their feet, and the entire side of the house swayed from the impact of something large and heavy striking the outside wall. Kate lost her grip on Sybil, William careened against the railing, and Jonas had to grab hold of the old man to keep him from flipping over it. He, too, lost his balance and staggered against the railing, which, miraculously, held the weight of both men, until William slid to the floor, stunned and breathing hard.

Kate wound up in a huddle against the wall, with her mother half on top of her. There was a moment's pause, then a second reverberation shook the house to its very foundations. Wood splintered downstairs, and a collective scream arose from men, women, and children. The sound of rushing water drowned out their wails of panic and alarm.

"Cap'n! Cap'n!" Big Donald cried, as yet a third impact splintered more wood and caused more screaming, through which Donald's booming tones held the only note of sanity and reason. "Them are waves rollin' against the house! We're tastin' seawater down here!"

Seawater up to the level of the house? Seawater coming in waves to crash against the shutters and doors? Kate had never known such a thing to happen in all the years her family had lived in the Abacos. The house had been built on a sandy hill—the highest point on the cay—for the very reason that big storms were capable of flooding the island and driving waves across it. But the waves had never threatened the house, not even during previous hurricanes.

"God have mercy on us all," she prayed in a whisper, then raised her voice so Jonas could hear her. "Jonas, what should we do? If the house collapses, which it feels like it might, we've nowhere to go. We'll surely all die."

Jonas reached down a hand to help her rise. "We'll go to the ship," he said. "We'll have to leave at once, before the water rises any higher. The *Phoenix* is our only hope of surviving this storm, especially if the island floods."

Jonas's hand felt warm and comforting, but his suggestion struck terror into Kate's heart. It sounded impossible; she could not imagine how they might manage it. "The *Phoenix* is clear on the other side of the island! We'll never make it through the rain and dark; the cay might already be half submerged."

Jonas got a good grip and pulled her upright. "We can die huddled together in the dark, while the house falls apart around us, or we can die trying to get there . . . The choice is yours, Kate."

Put that way, there really wasn't a choice. "We'll try," she said, raising his hand to her lips and kissing his clenched fingers. "I think I'd rather die trying."

"That's my Kate," he said. "Come on, let's get your mother and father downstairs. The eye of the storm may reach us at any moment; when it does, that's when we'll leave. How long it'll last is anybody's guess. At least, we'll have a head start before the wind returns with a vengeance."

It won't be enough time, Kate thought to herself. But to Jonas, she offered a cheery grin. "Lead the way, Jonas. I'll gladly follow."

"I wish you meant that, Kate," he responded, his eyes locking with hers. "I really wish you meant that."

Chapter Twenty-Six

The roof had blown away and all the shutters had smashed or torn off before the eye of the storm passed over the house. By the time the roof departed, everyone but Sybil realized that they couldn't remain in the precarious structure; the water inside was already knee-high, and waves kept battering against the outer wall facing the beach. Kate suspected it was only a matter of minutes before the foundations crumbled, and the house itself collapsed.

Despite the panic, the chilling wetness, and the violent wind which destroyed everything it could reach, Jonas managed to keep everyone calm. He herded them into the long hallway leading out to the cook shed, where an absence of windows provided some shelter from wind and rain. Then, he quickly assigned tasks to everyone. Big William and Musket Jones were to take charge of Sybil Montgomery and carry her, if necessary, to the ship. Edward and Nimble Clayton were given responsibility for William. Each child was assigned to an adult, and each woman had to pick out a man to follow.

Mattie and Cal had already ventured down into the cellar before it flooded, and one of the things they had retrieved was a large coil of hemp rope, the kind kept on hand for a variety of purposes on the plantation.

Jonas cut the rope into sections, linking small groups together by tying people around their waists or wrists. This insured that no one would get lost—and no child be overlooked in the darkness. He put a man in charge of each section of rope and all the people attached to it.

Only Edward dared to argue with his selections. "I think Kate should come with me, Will, an' Musket . . . Will's a little groggy right now, but that's how he would want it, if he wuz awake enough t' say so."

Kate wondered if her father's grogginess was due to the tea he had drunk earlier or to the jug of rum she had seen both Edward and her father secretly swigging—to keep his strength up, her father had explained, when she confronted him. "I'm going with Jonas," she announced. "I'm responsible for Mattie's youngest—Baby David—because Mattie and Cal have their hands full with Ruthie and Ernest."

"You'd think yer own pa would be more important t' ya than a nigger-baby," Edward grumbled.

Kate kissed the baby—incredibly sleeping through all the din—and wrapped a tattered blanket more tightly around him. "The baby's name is David, and don't presume to tell me what to do, Edward."

She turned away from him to face Jonas, and that was when she suddenly realized that she hadn't had to shout to make herself heard. It was suddenly so quiet a mouse squeak would have been audible. "Jonas . . . !"

He nodded and lifted a lantern, the only light still left in the ruined house. "You're right, Kate. The silence means the eye has finally reached us . . . Listen, everyone. We're leaving now. Follow me as best you can. Things may look unfamiliar after this storm, and for several of you—my men, especially—the path isn't as well known as it might be to some. If you lose sight of me, follow Cal, Benjamin, or Fish.

And if the wind starts up again before we get there, keep going. It should be at our backs. Walk as fast as you can, but watch where you're stepping. You don't want to break a leg or twist an ankle—so don't run. Well, that's all I have to say. We'd better get moving."

"I have something to add," Kate burst out. "I love you all . . . I hope we make it. God willing, we will. May He watch over all of us."

"Amen," Jonas echoed.

He stepped forward, and Kate felt a tug on her right wrist, where she had tied the rope, then passed it around both herself and Baby David, binding the small, fragile body to her. She followed Jonas out through the cook shed, only one wall of which was still standing. The night air felt damp, warm, and incredibly heavy on her cheek—but mercifully, there was no wind! Instead, the silence hung thick as fog. She scanned the sky. In every direction, flashes of lightning still lit the green and purple underbellies of great, massive clouds rising like walls to enclose the cay. But high up—straight overhead—several stars were shining.

She had never seen such clouds or such a weirdly lit sky with its absurd sprinkling of stars, nor had she heard such a strange, foreboding stillness. No thunder rolled overhead. After the torrents of water that had previously poured down, no rain fell. In the yard, water lapped her thighs. Her skirt dragged like an anchor tied to her knees. Her feet sank into mud, and she wondered how she could walk at all, much less walk quickly. As Jonas entered the forest, heading away from the house and the beach it overlooked, the water receded, yet it was like walking through murky swampland.

Kate found herself unconsciously clutching with her bare toes every time she felt the firmness of rock. She wanted to hang onto it and not step forward into the unknown; what lay beneath the water was a mystery and therefore threatening. She and Jonas didn't speak. They simply walked—and splashed. Faint splashing sounds behind them indicated that Mattie and Cal and their remaining two children were keeping pace.

She was afraid to look back in search of her mother and father; both had sunk into a kind of bleary-eyed stupor in which they seemed unaware of what was happening. Kate supposed she should be glad, because if Mama's hysteria had continued, it might have become necessary to restrain her, in order to save her life. Nor would Bell have been any comfort in this instance; ever since the scene in Mama's room, Bell had kept her distance from her mistress. Bell and her husband, Gilbert, half crippled from old-age ailments, were somewhere behind Kate—exactly where she wasn't certain.

They were almost halfway to the ship, when Kate heard a noise like high-pitched singing in the distance. It started out as a thin, high whine—not like thunder—and not like anything else she had ever heard either. Jonas heard it, too, for he immediately began to walk faster, so that Kate had to run to keep up with him.

"What is it?" she gasped. Her side suddenly cramped, and she had to stop a moment. "What are we hearing?"

"The wind," Jonas said, pausing to wait for her. "The wind is returning. We haven't got much longer. If we hurry, we might still make it."

The distant whine was louder now—like a pack of vengeful spirits chasing them. No wonder the slaves were afraid of hurricanes, Kate thought. She couldn't remember ever having heard anything quite so ominous, scary, and seductive, tempting one to tarry and listen. They had reached an area of thick forest and tall trees, most of which were still bent over from the last onslaught of wind and water. A slight breeze shook the trees, disturbing the droplets gathered on the leaves, so that they pattered on Kate's face, arms, and hair.

She and Jonas resumed running, their feet making big sucking noises in the mud. The same noises could be heard behind them, as everyone struggled to match Jonas's pace. A human wail cut the night, stopping Kate in her tracks. "What's wrong?" she called out, whirling around and searching the darkness to identify the source of the anguished cry.

"Ah doan know, Miz Kate . . ." Mattie gasped. "Cal's gone back t' see."

Holding up the lantern, Jonas returned to Kate. "What's the matter?" he growled impatiently. "We can't stop now. We're almost there. We don't have but a few minutes at most, before the storm hits again."

The whine of the wind was louder now, and the breeze stronger, showering Kate and Baby David with a spray as heavy as rain. "You go on," Kate told him. "Take Mattie and the others. I'll stay and see what's wrong."

"No, you won't—we're tied together, remember?" Jonas held up his bound wrist. "Where you go, I go—and so does Baby David."

Mattie's Ruthie began to whimper in her mother's arms. "Mama, ah'se skeered," she quavered. "Where did Papa go?"

"Cal untied his rope?" Jonas interjected.

Mattie nodded miserably. "He slipped it off soon's he heard dat cry."

Jonas plucked at the rope around his wrist and hurriedly untied it. "Wait here, both of you. I'll send my men ahead with your parents, Kate. You follow them, while I go see what's wrong."

"No!" Kate cried, loathe to let him out of her sight. "I'll come with you."

"You can't! You've got Baby David," Jonas

reminded her. "Do as I say. Stay here and keep going."

He left her then, before Kate could think of any more arguments. However, she had no intention of going to the ship without Jonas. She had lost his brother to a storm, and she wasn't about to lose him in the same awful way. "Mattie, can you . . . ?"

"Ah kin tek him, Miz Kate," Mattie said. "It won't be dat hard t' handle two of 'em til Cal gets back."

Kate was already untying the ropes around the sleeping infant. Gently, she deposited him in his mother's free arm. "I'll be back as soon as I can," she murmured, then took off after Jonas.

The wail had come from Bell. The Negress sat in the mud, her back propped against a tree, about halfway back in the long line of people struggling to get to the ship before the storm's fury resumed. Bell's face was twisted in pain, but Kate couldn't immediately ascertain the cause, because Jonas's body partially blocked her view.

As Kate got closer, she heard the black woman moan: "It's mah ankle. Ah caught it in a tree root, an' now, ah cain't walk anymore."

"You've got to walk!" Jonas barked at her. "Gilbert and I will help you, but you've got to get up and try."

"No . . ." Bell thrashed her head from side to side. "Ah cain't mek it. An' ah cain't ask y'all t' risk yore lives tryin' t' save me . . . Gilbert, you an' de Cap'n gotta go on wifout me."

Old, grizzled Gilbert knelt down shakily in the mud beside his wife. "Now, Bell, honey . . . Ya'll know ah won't leave ya. Iffen you gonna stay, den ah'm gonna stay, too."

"Get up, both of you!" Jonas shouted. "This isn't the time to be stubborn or heroic. If you don't get up, you're both going to die out here."

Kate hurried to Bell's side, grabbed the woman's massive arm and tugged on it, but to no avail. Bell's weight defeated her efforts. "Bell, come on! We're almost there! I know you can make it, if you'll only try. Don't you hear the wind singing? Bell, it's going to be here soon."

Bell's dark eyes rolled upward in the lantern light. "Dey's comin' fer me . . ." she muttered in a tone heavy-leaden with guilt and superstition. "Gawd knows dey got reason . . . Dem spirits is comin' fer me shore enuff."

Snorting with impatience, Jonas held the lantern closer to Bell's ankle. "Maybe if we wrapped it good and tight, the ankle could better bear her weight. I don't think Gilbert and I alone can carry her. If anything, we might have to carry Gilbert. The old man looks exhausted."

Kate snatched up a handful of skirt. "I'll tear off a piece of cloth . . . It just might work."

While she struggled to rip the heavy fabric, Bell leaned her head against the tree trunk and closed her eyes. "It wuz me dat done it, Cap'n Irons," she said wearily. "It wuz me drugged yer brother so he'd fall asleep fishin' an' couldn't git back b'fore dat storm hit."

"*What?*" Jonas glanced up from Bell's ankle, his handsome face gone dark as a satyr's.

"Ah give him a gourdful o' de same tea ah gives Miz Sybil," Bell continued, undaunted. "He took it wif him, 'case he got thirsty fishin'. Ah didn't know dat storm wuz comin', but ah knew if he fell asleep, he gonna come t' some kinda harm out dere all by hisself."

"Bell, do you realize what you're saying?" Kate demanded, horrified.

Bell opened her eyes and looked Kate in the face. "Dat weren't all ah done, Miz Kate . . . Ah found dem grouper fingers Mattie was makin' fer de Cap'n,

375

a-fryin' in de cook shed, an' when she wuzn't lookin', ah quick dusted 'em wif poison. If he'da et 'em, he'd be dead, now, too."

"Let's leave her," Jonas snapped, rising. "We'll take Gilbert but leave his scheming, murdering wife behind."

"Ain't nothin' else ya can do," Bell calmly agreed. "Dat's why ah'm tellin' ya dis . . . Dem spirits comin' fer me, an' ah wanna clear mah head b'fore ah has t' meet 'em."

"But Bell, why? Why did you do such terrible things?" Kate wailed.

"'Cause ah'm a slave, Miz Kate, an' a slave gotta obey her mistress."

"My mother *told* you to do those things?"

Bell met her gaze unflinchingly, almost defiantly. "Wuzn't her thought of 'em, but she wanted me t' do sompin', so's you wouldn't lose yer head an' run off wif one o' dem Americans . . . Ah knew it wuz wrong, Miz Kate. But ah also knew dat if ah did 'em, yore Mama—Miz Sybil—would owe me. It give me a kind o' power ovah her, t' have her think mah magic was strong 'nuff t' kill a white man. De onliest power ah got comes from mah magic. But sometimes an Obeah Woman has t' h'ep magic git de job done."

"She didn't mean no harm to *you*, Miz Kate!" Gilbert fearfully blubbered. "It's jus' dat slavery sometimes meks a body do bad things. Bell never could stomach bein' a slave; ever since she ben a young gal, she's always ben lookin' fer a way t' be her own person. She like a bird strugglin' t' break free outa her cage."

"What does it matter now *why* she did it?" Jonas snorted. "Kate, we can't delay any longer. We have to leave them here."

"No! No matter what they've done, they're human beings, Jonas! We can't leave them here to die . . . If you won't help me, I'll get them to the ship by myself."

"Christ Almighty!" Jonas swore—or maybe it was a prayer wrung from the depths of despair. He bent and took Bell's arm. "You and Gilbert take her other side. Between the three of us, maybe we can lift her."

At that moment, Fish trudged by them, carrying one of Cassie's children, while Cassie held the other.

"Fish!" Jonas shouted. "Untie yourself and come help us. Kate will take the child you've got."

So Kate ended up with little Ollie in her arms. But before they had Bell on her feet and moving, all the rest of the group—including her mother and father and even Old Tom—had passed them, and the wind was blowing more strongly, propelling them toward the work site. The whining sound had become a demented shriek. As Jonas and Fish half carried, half dragged Bell between them, the Negress muttered in a language Kate could not decipher. It was some kind of African mumbo jumbo that made no sense to anyone but Gilbert, who wept openly and without restraint as he limped alongside.

"Ah, Bell, honey . . ." he sobbed. "It ain't yer fault. Dem spirits know dat. De yoke of slavery wuz jus' too heavy for y'all t' bear . . ."

Kate felt a sickening chill that had nothing to do with the cutting wind and the rain now lashing her back. Never in her life had she really considered what it meant to be a slave and how unhappy some of the plantation's people must be in that condition. In her foolish ignorance and preoccupation with her own problems, she had thought them all satisfied— well-pleased to belong to a family who treated them halfway decently and kept them fed and clothed, if not too richly.

For the first time, she wondered if Mattie and Cal— her friends—were as happy as they seemed to be in her service. Little Ollie whimpered in her arms, and as Kate studied the boy's light-skinned face in the lightning's glare, she saw Edward's eyes looking back at her. Had Cassie *chosen* to bear Edward's child? Or had the pregnancy been forced upon her?

Bell wasn't the only one with a heavy load of guilt to carry! Kate herself had ignored the clear evidence of Ollie's paternity. And what kind of a life had it been for Bell all these years, spending day after day, hour after hour, in the company of a difficult, imperious, occasionally irrational woman?

By the time they arrived within sight of the beach, the water had reached Kate's waist. Rhythmic waves nearly knocked her down with their brutal force and sucking undertow. The lightning was constant, the rain fierce, the wind fiercest of all. Along with the others who had arrived there before them, Sybil and William clung to the cradle of the ship. Despite the urgings of Big Donald and the other men assigned to help them, they were too weak to climb it.

"Cap'n!" Big Donald called, his voice whipped away on the wind. He waded over to Jonas, cupped his hand around Jonas's ear, and shouted into it. Kate couldn't hear everything he said, but she caught the words "winch" and "hoist."

Donald pointed to the hoist they had used to raise the mast and pantomimed using it to lift William, Sybil, Bell, Gilbert, Old Tom, and the others—such as the children—who would never be able to climb the cradle itself to get into the ship. Jonas and Fish propped Bell next to Daisy, then hurried to help Donald, Nimble, and Musket rig up a canvas swing.

The ship loomed high above Kate, its masts and rigging stark against the churning, greenish-colored sky. A stiletto-slash of lightning stabbed at the mainmast but missed it, and Kate breathed a sigh of relief. At least, they had made it this far, and if they all succeeded in getting into the ship, they wouldn't drown no matter how high the water rose. She gave

Ollie to Daisy, then joined Jonas and his crew members in their efforts to prepare the swing. It had apparently been used before, to haul tools and other items up to the ship's deck; the men seemed to know precisely what they were doing, but the rain and wind hampered the operation.

When the swing was finally readied, Jonas insisted on hauling the slave women and their children up first. Nimble climbed the cradle as handily as a lizard scurrying up a tree trunk, then signaled that the sling—with Mattie, Ruthie, and Baby David aboard—should be raised. The rest of the men hauled on the ropes, and Mattie, clinging in fright to her children, swung upward. The swing twirled madly in the gale for several moments, before Nimble caught Mattie's skirt and pulled her toward the safety of the deck.

The process was repeated with Cassie and her two toddlers, then Daisy and her single child. Cal climbed the cradle with little Ernest clinging to his shirtfront like a monkey. Then it was time for Kate's parents. As Kate settled her mother in the swing, Sybil stared vacantly into space. She had retreated to that place inside herself, where no one could touch her, but Kate was less worried than she was grateful that her mother wasn't succumbing to hysterics.

White-faced, Sybil soared into the air beside the ship. A particularly vicious gust of wind caught the swing and swung it like a pendulum, banging it against the side of the cradle. Kate screamed, but her mother never made a sound—insofar as Kate could hear. Leaning far outward, Nimble caught the swing and pulled it to the deck.

A few minutes later, Papa clung, eyes tightly closed, to the ropes, as the swing danced and careened in the wind. Jonas had tied him in place, and that was the only thing that saved him from falling, as the swing flipped upside down, then right-side up again.

379

Kate feared that her father's head would be slammed against the cradle, but Nimble and Cal didn't let it happen. Old Tom went next, and then Gilbert. The swing spun crazily, slamming against the ship's railing as Nimble and Cal struggled to bring the old man into the ship.

Watching beside Kate, Bell saw it happen, and her fingers clutched at Kate's arms. She said something, but Kate couldn't hear what it was. The woman's eyes were enormous; the whites of them gleamed in the flashes of forked lightning that followed one after another, so closely that it was bright as day. The water had risen to the level of Kate's breasts now, and the waves licked hungrily at the ship's cradle. Time was running out for everyone still on the beach. Fortunately, Bell was the last person left to use the swing; the others were all capable of climbing the cradle on their own.

Jonas, Kate, and Edward helped secure Bell in the swing. Then Jonas and Edward both ran—rather, swam—to haul on the ropes. Kate joined them as soon as she could, but Jonas waved her away. "Climb the cradle!" he mouthed to her, and she started back toward the ship.

Bell's heavy body swung high above Kate's head. Just then, a huge wave swept Kate off her feet, water filled her nose and mouth, and she came up sputtering . . . and that was when it happened. A dazzling shaft of light and sound split the sky overhead, rendering Kate simultaneously blind and deaf. Her heart jumped in her chest, and she feared she was dying. Several moments passed before she realized what had happened; a mighty bolt of lightning had struck, leaving behind an awful, acrid odor that stung her nostrils with the scent of something burning.

When her vision cleared, Kate saw that the upper half of the winch was charred and smoking. Only a frayed and smoldering section of rope hung down; Bell and the swing had completely disappeared. "Bell!" she screamed, desperately searching the turbulent water now dashing against the cradle. She saw no sign of Bell or anyone. The rain poured down in a solid, heavy mass, a wall of water half drowning her where she stood, flailing helplessly. She squinted and wiped her eyes, but still could not see clearly.

Strong arms suddenly closed around her waist, and a voice shouted directly into her ear. She couldn't understand a word, but sensed Jonas's panic as he dragged her toward the cradle. One end of it had collapsed, and the other was shaking from the impact of the clawing waves. The wood felt slick as glass beneath her trembling fingers, defeating her efforts to get a good grip on it. Jonas had to clamp his hands over hers to help her hold on—then he gave her a boost, and she started to climb.

If he hadn't stayed beside her, urging her upward, grabbing her whenever she started to fall or let go, Kate never would have made it. She didn't have the strength to climb over the railing of the ship, but helping hands seized her upper arms and hauled her aboard. No sooner did she feel solid deck beneath her feet, when the ship began to sway and rock. Waves pummeled the hull, and what remained of the ship's cradle began to fall away.

Again, it was Jonas who led Kate to safety. He dragged her across the rain-lashed deck, flung open the door to the cabin, and shoved her inside. Everybody else had already crowded in ahead of them. The small enclosure stank of rain, wet clothing, and fear . . . Kate turned to throw her arms around Jonas and reassure herself that they were both still alive and safely aboard his ship. But Jonas was already signaling for his crew members to join him.

As Jonas and his men departed the cabin—braving the jaws of the storm, once more—the ship tilted far to the left, shuddered, hung there a moment, then tilted far to the right. The occupants of the cabin screamed as they tumbled about, like beans shaken in a gourd. Kate realized then that the battle for survival had just begun. During far less ferocious storms than this one, wrecks occurred with predictable regularity. What was there now to keep them from being dashed to pieces on a shoal or on the cay itself?

What irony! What perfect justice. If all the Montgomerys and their people perished in a shipwreck, it would only serve them right. An absurd desire to laugh came over Kate; only the screams of those around her prevented her from succumbing to it. She groped her way to her parents, huddled in a corner. Her father had his arms around her mother, but in the lightning's glare, Kate could see that Sybil Montgomery had no idea where she was, much less that her husband was holding her. Her mouth gaped in wordless horror. Her eyes stared sightlessly.

She's already dead, Kate thought. She died a long time ago. This is only the shell of the woman that remains.

Oh, Mama, I'm so sorry that I never found a way to make you better, or prevented you from harming others!

The sour taste of failure rose like bile in Kate's throat. She ought to have been able to do something to heal her mother all these years—and to stop her father's drinking. Somehow, she had never met their expectations or fulfilled their needs. She had tried— God, yes, she had tried!—but it hadn't been enough. She wasn't Robin, their precious first-born son, and she wasn't her grandfather, whose legacy of pride and stubbornness had supposedly been left to her. Had he lived, had he not been so old—or so crushed in spirit as a result of being tarred and feathered—Grandpa would have made a success of things here on Conch Cay.

He would never have allowed his slaves to be bullied or mistreated, nor shirked his duties, nor been tempted to stray from long-cherished beliefs and values, nor fallen in love with the wrong person. He would have solved problems instead of creating them or making them worse. Grandpa would have had no need to resort to wrecking. And he would have insisted that Mama and Papa face life with the same courage and determination that he had possessed in such great abundance.

That was what hurt the most—Kate hadn't lived up to her grandfather's reputation and faith in her. She blamed herself for her parents' weaknesses and betrayals. And she knew without any doubt that Augustus Montgomery would never be as miserable, uncertain, and frightened as she was now. I have failed in everything I've tried to do, Kate thought, and failed in *not* doing things I should have.

Overcome with shame at her own inadequacies, Kate hid her face in her hands and wept, her tears falling as hard and fast as the rain hammering on the cabin roof.

Chapter Twenty-Seven

Why all of them didn't die that night, Kate would never be able to explain, either to herself or to anyone else. It was a miracle, pure and simple. By mid-morning of the following day, the storm had spent the worst of its fury and subsided into torrential rainfall and only occasional gusts of wind. Incredibly, the *Phoenix* was still afloat, her basic structure intact, though she had lost every scrap of canvas and rigging, and sustained damage to her spars and bowsprit. Jonas's sailing skills had proven to be superb, for he and his men had managed to keep the vessel in one piece, despite having no idea where she was headed, or what lay in front of her.

His strategy, as he explained it to Kate that morning, had been easy in theory but difficult in practice: don't let the vessel take the brunt of the gale broadside. Keep her headed into the wind. True to her design, the *Phoenix* rode the waves like a gull with its wings folded against its sides. She had bobbed furiously up and down, and rolled side to side, but never once had she wallowed in the troughs between the mountainous waves and risked being swamped. Somehow—probably through divine intervention—she had not struck a reef or a shoal, or been driven onto another cay.

Now, with land, sea, and sky all merged into one great, gray, weeping entity, the vessel endured the heavy rain and fog with equal grace and fortitude. Not so the people who huddled, cold, wet, and hungry in her cramped cabin . . . Instead of thanking God for their deliverance, they complained of their deprivations—and debated what should be done to alleviate their many discomforts.

"I say we should sail fer Nassau right away an' fergit about whoever might be left in the Abacos . . ." Edward argued during the meeting Jonas had initiated to discuss the situation. "We can't do nuthin' t' help survivors anyway. We ourselves ain't got a pot t' piss in, much less food or drinkin' water."

"But people on the other cays could be injured or dying, as well as left without food," Kate pointed out. "We have an obligation to rescue them, if at all possible. I doubt the other islands in the chain were as hard hit as Conch Cay, since we customarily get the brunt of the weather. But I'm sure they've suffered enormous damages. It would be irresponsible to sail to Nassau without first checking to see how they are."

"Beggin' your pardon, Miss Montgomery," Big Donald said. "But how long can them younsters"— he nodded toward the sleeping slave children sprawled together in the corner like puppies in a heap—"go without somethin' t' eat? In Nassau, we could tell folks what happened here, convince 'em t' donate supplies, then come back and help the people in the Abacos who might need it."

"That's right, Kate," Jonas agreed, his blue eyes red-rimmed and weary in his beard-stubbled face. "We won't be much good to anyone if we ourselves don't get some food and rest."

Kate's heart turned over with pity for Jonas. He was obviously suffering from exhaustion, as was nearly everyone else. But try as she might, she could

386

not set aside her feelings of responsibility toward her neighbors. Jonas and his men did not know the other residents of the Abacos—all Loyalists, good people who had stuck together through thick and thin, sharing misfortune as well as the precious few good times. Except when it came to wrecking, they habitually and unselfishly looked out for each other's welfare. Kate didn't think she could live with herself if she sailed off to Nassau, and one or more of the other Abaconians died because they hadn't received immediate assistance.

"I want to go back and at least see how the settlements on Big Abaco survived the storm," she stubbornly insisted. "There may be injured people who need transporation to Nassau. Papa . . . tell everyone. We *can't* leave the area without knowing what happened to the other families. Most of them have friends and relatives in Nassau. They'll be asking us questions we can't answer. We'll never be able to face them. It would be like . . . like we ran out on our neighbors during their time of need. Won't it, Papa?"

Kate's father stirred from his position against the wall, where he had been sitting with his arm still around Kate's mother. "Yes . . . Oh, yes, Kate. Undoubtedly, folks will criticize us for not having checked on their relatives."

"So are you truly worried about your neighbors? Or are you more fearful of what folks will say about the Montgomerys, if you don't do what's expected?" Jonas gruffly inquired. "To me, it sounds like the latter."

"That isn't it at all!" Kate burst out. "It's just that we feel an obligation to people who've been here as long as we have, suffered the same trials we've suffered, and shared our exact, same beliefs. They would never abandon us; so I refuse to abandon them."

387

"Hungry . . ." Sybil Montgomery suddenly said, her lashes fluttering against the parchmentlike skin of her cheeks. "So hungry—and thirsty. Where's Bell with my morning tea? I want Bell."

Jonas's eyes caught Kate's across the crowded cabin, for she stood on one side and he on the other. "We don't have any tea for your mother, Kate . . . For that matter, we don't have any Bell."

At the mention of the familiar name, Gilbert began to moan where he lay curled on his side on the hard plank floor. "Bell! Mah poor ole Bell . . ." he sobbed. "Doan know whut ah'm gonna do wifout dat woman."

Gilbert had spent most of the night alternately weeping and muttering to himself, Old Tom, and anyone else who would listen. One side of his face and body was badly bruised from having been dashed against the ship's railing when he came aboard. Kate thought him slightly feverish and wished she had hot tea and blankets to ease his suffering. But there weren't even dry clothes to put on him, and if they did decide to go to Nassau, there weren't any sails to hoist on the masts. Jonas had earlier told her that in order to fashion makeshift sails, the women would have to give up their wet aprons and whatever else they could spare, the men their shirts, and then everyone, including Gilbert, would be more miserable than they were already.

However, if they stayed, they'd be just as miserable, because hot foot, a reliable source of fresh water, and dry clothes would be many more days away. Kate sighed, not at all certain what was the right thing to do. Could her mother, Gilbert, Old Tom, and the children survive several days without basic necessities? Studying her mother's pale, waxy features and poor Gilbert's ashen-gray skin, Kate didn't think so.

"All right," she conceded. "We'll go to Nassau."

It took them most of the afternoon to fashion a

small sail from their drenched clothing. Fortunately, Nimble had stored several awls, a square of leftover canvas, and other necessary items for repairing sails in an old trunk in the hold, along with some of the tools Jonas had purchased on their previous visit to Nassau. By early evening, no one wore a particle more of clothing than was absolutely necessary for decency. Even the sleeves and the bottom half of the women's gowns or skirts had been appropriated to benefit the cause.

Kate was quite proud of their efforts—and disappointed when Jonas skeptically eyed the results and decided to wait until morning to hoist the patchwork creation.

"I thought you wanted to get to Nassau as quickly as possible," she snapped at him.

"I do," he replied. "But if we lose this sail, we'll really be in trouble. Making another will leave us all naked."

"What makes you think we'll lose this one?" she asked, suddenly worried.

"Haven't you noticed? The wind's picked up, and it's raining harder. I don't anticipate another blow like we had last night, but it's probably safer to stay right here than to set sail for Nassau, tonight."

She touched his arm, wishing she dared embrace him, but afraid to risk it. "Do you even know where we are, Jonas?"

His smile seemed forced. "I've been trying all day to figure it out, but without sun, stars, moon, or the navigational instruments I lost in the fire, it's been a little difficult. Don't worry ... At least, the rain ensures that for now, we've got plenty of fresh water. Maybe when it quits, we can catch fish or a turtle and dine like kings."

"Well, if we can't set sail tonight yet, then you must try and get some sleep," she urged. "Maybe tomorrow when we wake up, we'll discover that we're already halfway there."

Jonas's smile turned into a grimace. "With the force of this wind, I wouldn't be surprised. We outfitted the vessel with as heavy a wooden anchor as we could build, but it won't hold us in one spot. At best, it'll just slow us down."

Kate knew what he was really worried about—piling up on a reef, but there wasn't much that could be done without a larger, stronger sail than sewn-together strips of wet clothing. "We'll get there safely," she assured him. "I can't believe we've survived this long, only to be defeated now."

"My beautiful, little optimist," he said and yawned. "Just don't let me sleep too long."

Jonas appointed Musket Jones to stay awake and keep an eye on things during the first watch, then he lay down on the floor in a corner of the crowded cabin. The ship had yet to be furnished with bunks, cupboards, or much of anything else. They had intended to sail it to Nassau and attract a buyer before the final outfitting, so that the new owner could have a say in how the last details should be done. Thus, the cabin wasn't even divided into captain's quarters and wardroom; it consisted only of a single, rectangular room with a total of six portholes, fitted with wooden covers, and two doors, one leading to the bow, and one to the stern.

Kate settled herself next to her parents and prepared to spend a long, queasy, uncomfortable night in the chilly darkness. Mercifully, all of the children and most of the adults were already asleep, for the rigors of the previous night had sapped everyone's strength and energy. By tomorrow, they'd be ravenously hungry, she guessed. Last night and today, several had been ill with nausea, but by now, most had grown accustomed to the ship's motion, which wasn't all that different from that of a dory on a heavy sea. The slaves and Kate herself had spent lots of time on fishing smacks and dories, and Jonas's men were all used to the sea. However, Kate's mother had not been on the water for a very long time, and neither had her father; both her parents had little use for the ocean.

Kate looked over at them and saw no movement. How long it would be before her mother awoke and began demanding things, Kate had no idea, but she hoped it wouldn't be too soon. Mama was accustomed to instant service; she'd probably be more difficult to handle than the slave children, who usually had to wait to have their needs met. Too tired to worry about it any longer, Kate leaned back against the wall of the cabin and closed her eyes.

It was thunder that woke her—and the increasing motion of the ship as it rolled from side to side, tugging on the anchor. The cabin was silent and black as pitch. Only the cracks under the entry doors admitted any light, all of it the greenish hue of lightning. Bracing herself against the wall, Kate sat up. Despite the rocking motion and the drumming of the rain, everyone still slept the deep, unmoving slumber of utter weariness. The room reeked of overcrowded, unwashed bodies, and Kate found it difficult to breathe without becoming nauseated.

She stood up and carefully groped her way to the nearest porthole. Surely, no one would mind if she opened one to allow fresh air to circulate. As she fumbled in the darkness, trying to open it, a pair of hands joined hers and performed the task with the sure knowledge of one who had designed the ship and helped fashion the porthole covers.

A gust of rain-laden, fresh air poured into the cabin; in the accompanying lightning's glow, Kate saw Jonas smiling down at her. "There," he whispered. "Is that better?"

She nodded, filling her lungs with the pure, clean air. "Much better, thank you."

391

They stood close together, inhaling in unison, acutely conscious of each other's presence. Then Jonas's hand came up to stroke her hair back from her forehead. When he touched her, Kate trembled— and was reminded of the previous night's revelations, which she and Jonas had had no time to discuss.

"Jonas, I'm so sorry about . . . about Bell," she said softly, speaking just loud enough to be heard over the drumming of the rain. "I never dreamed she would do anything like what she admitted. I can't believe Mama knew or approved. Half the time, Mama doesn't know what day it is, much less possess the capacity to plot evil in company with Bell."

"Hush . . ." Jonas admonished. "Justice has been served with regard to Bell. *She* knew what she was doing, even if your mother didn't. It's over now. At least, I know what happened to Jonathan. I did find it hard to believe that he wouldn't have had the good sense to get off the ocean before a storm engulfed him. Now, I know why he didn't . . . I'm also relieved to discover the truth about the grouper fingers; now I can enjoy them again without having to worry that I might die for the sake of that pleasure. However, I still suspect that the burning of my hut wasn't accidental—nor, I'm sure, was the accident involving the mast."

"Mama couldn't have done either of those things, Jonas. Despite what Papa claimed, it *had* to be Edward—only I've never known Papa to lie like that. Why would he bother protecting Edward? What mysterious hold does Edward have over him?"

Kate cast a furtive glance toward the spot across the cabin where she knew Edward had bedded down for the night. Edward lay still as a dead man, his deep snores the only indication of life.

"I can't begin to guess, Kate. What concerns me more is the hold your parents have over *you*."

"Don't, Jonas," she pleaded. "Don't start this now.

392

More than ever, my parents need me . . . We've lost everything. We'll have to start all over. I can't desert them to marry you . . . I can't let them suspect that I'm even thinking of marrying you. It would be the same as killing them."

"One day, they'll die anyway, Kate . . . And when that day comes, you'll be abandoned and deserted. You'll look around and see that your whole life has gone by; you'll have sacrificed it on the altar of filial duty and be left with nothing—no sons or daughters of your own, no one to love and comfort you in the dark of night, and no one to care for you in your own old age."

"I don't ever plan to be as helpless and dependent as my parents," Kate scoffed, though his predictions frightened her, causing a chill to run down her spine.

He placed his hands on her shoulders and gazed intently down at her, his face lit by eerie flickers of lightning. "Kate, we are all going to get old someday. We are all going to *need* someone sometime, to help us when we can't help ourselves."

"But that's what I'm doing, Jonas! Helping my parents when they need me."

"No, you're letting them dictate to you and rule your every thought, deed, and desire. I'm willing to help you take care of them, Kate. In time, if you stand up to them now, they'll get used to me . . ."

"If they don't die first, when I tell them I want to marry you!" Kate said bitterly.

"Then let's not tell them yet. While we're in Nassau, we can get married, but we'll keep it a secret until they're both strong enough to deal with it."

"And what if they never *get* stronger? What if it kills them when they find out I've married you in secret? That would be the blow that could finally do it."

"Kate, you've got to take that chance! I admit there's a risk, but . . ."

A sudden loud shriek cut Jonas off in midsentence. Kate knew where it had come from even before she turned to look. She pulled away from Jonas and immediately started for her mother. "Mama? Mama, it's all right."

Sybil had risen to her feet and was leaning heavily on William's shoulder. Intermittent flickers of lightning revealed her disorientation and rising fear. Blinking in nearly equal confusion, William lurched upright and reached out a hand to steady his wife. "Sybil, dearest, what is it? Have you had another one of your nightmares?"

"Bell!" Sybil muttered fearfully. "I dreamed that Bell is dead! The spirits did it! They turned her into a living torch and burned her before my very eyes!"

"Damn!" Jonas swore behind Kate. "She must have seen the lightning bolt strike Bell. It was a sight *I* will never forget."

Sleeping figures began to awaken all around the cabin. In the corner, Baby David began to wail. Mattie tried to quiet him, but the infant's cries rose to mingle with Sybil's.

"Now, they're coming for *me!*" Sybil shrilled, clutching the front of what remained of her nightgown. "They got Bell, but that wasn't enough for them. Now, they want me."

Jonas elbowed Kate aside as he crossed the cabin—stepping over bodies in his path—to reach Kate's mother.

"Mrs. Montgomery!" His tone rang with authority. "Get hold of yourself. There's no such thing as spirits, vengeful or otherwise. Even if spirits existed, they wouldn't be coming after you. Bell said she did those things on her own. She never once blamed you for drugging my brother or trying to poison me. Do you understand? *She* did it, not you. You have nothing to fear from vengeful spirits."

Sybil's eyes gleamed with madness, but they also

394

held a sly awareness. Kate was stunned to realize that at this moment, her mother knew exactly where she was and what she was saying.

"Oh, no, Captain Irons," Sybil crooned. "Oh, no! It wasn't Bell who killed your brother. It was me. I found him lying face down down on the beach before anyone else—even Kate—got there. He was still alive. I know, because he moved and called my daughter's name . . . The spirits led me there that night. And the spirits led me to the big rock nearby."

Sybil mimicked finding a rock on the beach. Then she stooped as if trying to lift it. "I picked it up," she continued breathlessly. "It was very heavy. I dropped it on your brother's head. It fell with a terrible thud—and *that's* what killed him."

Sybil gazed at Jonas unrepentantly. "After that, Captain, I took his watch . . ."

"No!" William shouted, holding up his hand. "Sybil didn't kill him—*I* did!" He grabbed Jonas's arm. "She doesn't know what she's saying, Captain! You mustn't believe her. She's badly confused . . ."

"Then tell me the truth, damn you!" Jonas's anguished cry drowned out the peal of thunder that rolled over the cabin roof. "Stand right there and tell me the whole, damned, blessed truth, Mister Montgomery."

Kate herself could not have moved if her life depended upon it. She stood riveted to the floor, hearing things she didn't want to hear, dying inside with each word she heard.

"For once, I . . . I was determined to be a man and . . . and . . ." William faltered, glanced at Sybil, and seemed to draw strength from her. "I had always disappointed my wife, you see . . . She married me for love, but all I ever gave her was sorrow. First, I lacked the courage to stand up to my father and tell him I agreed with *her* family, not with mine . . . Then it was too late to convince anyone that my own sympathies lay with the Americans. After my father was tarred and feathered, we had to flee with the Loyalists to save our lives. And because we had to flee, our precious Robin—the apple of his mother's eye—died during the first stage of our exile . . . And then we came here, and still, I failed at everything to which I put my hand . . ."

"So why did you kill my brother, if your sympathies have never been Loyalist?" Jonas gritted.

"Because . . . because we were—*are*—Loyalists. By then, the choice had been made, and we couldn't change it. Everyone we knew and loved had rejected us . . . The agony of it . . . the shame . . . all but destroyed my poor, dear Sybil. She rightly blamed me; I could do nothing—ever—to please her, after that. Not until that night on the beach, when I came upon her trying to kill your brother. She wanted him dead, so he couldn't take Kate away from us . . . and so, I killed him. I picked up the rock and smashed it down on his head, over and over, until I *knew* for certain he was dead . . . Then I led Sybil back to bed, and shortly thereafter, Kate found his body on the beach . . ."

"No, no! You couldn't have done that!" Kate cried, not wanting to believe it. "You couldn't be so cruel . . . Not you—not my own parents . . ."

She stumbled toward them, but her legs didn't want to work. She felt mortally wounded—torn from breast to belly, as if her heart had been cut out.

"I'm sorry, Kate . . ." her father moaned. "If I'd had time to think about it, I'd never have done it . . . I acted on impulse. I just wanted to please your mother. For once in my life, I just wanted to please her . . ."

Kate's mother smiled at Kate—a smile as sweet and gentle as a mother's smile could be. "We did it for you, Kate," she said. "Because we love you and couldn't *bear* to let you go."

"Love!" Kate almost strangled on the word. "What kind of love would lead you to do something so monstrous?"

A loud crack of thunder punctuated the question. But Sybil didn't answer. Instead, she turned toward the porthole, where the lightning's flash illuminated her high cheekbones and disheveled hair.

"They're coming for us, William," she said tremulously. "We've been very bad, and the snakes, the spirits, all of them . . . They're coming for us. Only I'm not afraid. I mustn't be. I, too, can be strong like my daughter. I *am* strong, just like Kate. She gets it from *me*, not from her grandfather . . . I won't be a coward; I'll go to meet them."

"Mama!" Kate snatched at her mother's torn sleeve. "Mama, look at me!"

But Sybil had retreated inside herself; her eyes had that shuttered expression, as if she saw things no one else could see and heard things no one else could hear. "Yes . . ." she whispered. "Yes, I'm coming . . ."

Before anyone could think to stop her, Sybil bolted for the nearest door. Kate belatedly tried to intercept her. Jonas did the same. Both of them forgot about Gilbert lying in the middle of the floor. Kate tripped over the old man; Jonas caught her as she fell. She struggled to break free from Jonas's grip, as rain and wind rushed into the cabin from the door Sybil had opened.

"Let your father handle . . ." Jonas started to say, as William hurried after Sybil.

They could hear him calling her. "Sybil! Sybil, wait!"

"Let me go!" Kate screamed, pummeling Jonas's shoulders. "Jonas, let me go! I have to save them! I have to stop Mama from doing something foolish! Jonas, let go!"

She thought he was deliberately preventing her

397

from leaving, but then he released her so suddenly she almost fell again. Righting herself, she caught sight of his face, rigid and straight-lipped. "All right," he said. "All right, Kate . . . Go . . ."

She fled onto the rain-slick deck just as it tilted beneath her feet. She had to grab hold of the mast and hang on tight to keep herself from being thrown against the railing. Rain drove into her face; wind buffeted her. The flickering light revealed a deck barren of everything. She peered into the darkness, searching the entire ship with her eyes. Her father and mother were gone. Like Bell, they had simply vanished.

Then she saw the broken railing—the gap big enough for a body, or two bodies, to have fallen through. She ran to it, screaming into the wind like a lost child, begging her parents not to leave her. "Mama! Papa!"

They didn't answer, and they didn't come.

Chapter Twenty-Eight

Jonas stood at the broken railing and watched the watery dawn flood the eastern horizon with pale lavender light. The sea was calmer now, and the rain had stopped. Heavy clouds still obscured the sky, but he now knew the location of north, east, south, and west, and today, he would raise the patchwork sail and set a course for Nassau.

He didn't expect to see anything, but his gaze kept straying to the foamy ocean below. Considering the rain, darkness, and heavy seas, the search for Kate's parents had been as thorough as he could make it. But William and Sybil Montgomery had disappeared without a trace. Kate had admitted that neither of her parents had ever bothered to learn to swim; that was probably why they had drowned so quickly. However, she also seemed to think he was somehow responsible, along with herself, of course.

When Sybil first ran out of the cabin, he had held Kate back for several moments. As he recalled it and later tried to explain to her, he had been trying to give her father a chance to deal with the situation, which indeed, William had attempted to do. As usual, as Kate had always done, she had interfered, stepping in and taking over the position that rightfully belonged to William.

Unfortunately, Kate didn't recognize this error in either her past or most recent behavior. Employing the distorted logic of grief and guilt, Kate blamed herself for not reaching her parents in time, and Jonas, for having held her back. She blamed herself—and him, too—for her mother's worsening instability and whatever misbegotten impulse had sent her running out into the stormy night. Undoubtedly, he was more at fault than she, because just by living and breathing, he had disturbed Sybil's safe, secure, little world and threatened her with change.

But if anyone should do the blaming, it really ought to be *him,* Jonas thought with a bitterness that wouldn't be quelled. Sybil and William Montgomery—aided by Bell—had killed his brother. While Jonathan had lain helpless on the beach, the elder Montgomerys had brutally, deliberately killed him. Despite his many sins, not the least of which had been chasing pretty women, Jonathan had been an innocent lamb fallen among wolves. He hadn't stood a chance; his weakness for a pretty face had finally been the death of him, just as Jonas had teasingly warned him it one day would be.

Jonas felt sick at heart, not just for Jonathan, but also for himself and Kate, and yes, even for her weak, miserable parents. Eventually, he hoped, Kate would put the past behind her and begin to think about the future—his and hers—the one he still wanted to build together. No matter what her parents had done, he loved Kate and wanted to marry her. She was sleeping now, worn out from sorrow and self-recrimination, but as soon as she awoke, he intended to tell her how he felt and set things right between them.

He wouldn't give her up without a fight. Part of the guilt Kate felt—and ascribed to him—derived from the fact that the death of her parents freed her to follow her heart's desire and marry him. Mixed with the guilt, there had to be relief; Sybil had not been an easy person to live with or love, and William had been nearly useless. Kate had never openly criticized her mother or father, but she wouldn't be human if she hadn't, at times, resented her parents' manipulation . . . and that resentment must also be a cause for guilt.

Jonas promised himself he wouldn't allow that guilt to fester and become a permanent wound that refused to heal. The Montgomerys had suffered enough from such festering wounds. Over the years, old hurts and slights, both real and imagined, had ruined any chance for happiness they might have had. Jonas didn't understand all of the emotional injuries they had suffered, but he was quite sure that Sybil and William would have been far happier and less prone to murder had they openly discussed their hurts and sorrows, instead of brooding on them and allowing their bitterness to feed on itself and grow.

Alerted by a sudden footfall behind him, Jonas turned to see Big Donald approaching, in company with Nimble, Musket, and John Ferguson. Donald's coppery hair and beard bristled in the morning breeze; more than ever he resembled a big, amiable bear.

"Cap'n, we come ta see if yer ready t' raise that sail," Donald boomed in his typical gruff way.

"Yes, I am, thank you—and thank you also for everything you did last night and during the entire time we were building this ship. You're a fine bunch of men; I'm proud to work with you and call you my friends."

Nimble's Adam's apple worked convulsively for a moment, before he finally got up his courage to speak. "Cap'n . . . Me an' the men was talkin', an' we know this probably ain't a good time t' bring it up, but seein' as how we're goin' t' Nassau . . . well, we

401

need t' know where we stand."

"What do you mean, where you stand? What's bothering you, Nimble?"

"Well, Cap'n, we was wondrin' what yer plans are now, if ya got any. Are we gonna go back t' Conch Cay an' build more ships? Or should we be thinkin' about findin' work in Nassau, maybe even goin' home t' Salem?"

"See, Cap'n, we figure this hurricane has changed things," Donald hastily added. "It ain't that we don't wanna work fer ya no more, but with the plantation wiped out, an' Miss Montgomery's folks dead, ya may wanna change yer plans, and that'll change *our* plans. Don't fergit that me and Musket still got fam'ly back in Salem, an' Nimble's got his sister . . ."

"Your questions aren't out of line, gentlemen," Jonas assured them. "But I'll need more time before I can answer all of them. Right now, the future depends on whether or not we can sell this ship in Nassau; if we do sell it, we'll be left with no transportation back to the cay or anywhere else. I need to talk to Miss Montgomery, since she's my partner. My decision of what to do depends on hers."

Donald glanced at the other men, then cleared his throat. Obviously, he was trying to be diplomatic, but hadn't had much practice. It simply wasn't in him to be subtle. "I guess that's what's got us worried, Cap'n . . . Even b'fore this hurricane, Miss Kate didn't seem too pleased with yer partnership. She stopped comin' down t' the beach to help, and never even showed up to admire the ship when it was all done. At first, we all thought you two was sweet on each other, but then things changed between you, and now . . . Now, she's got that overseer feller in there with her, tryin' t' talk her inta marryin' him when we get t' Nassau!" Donald finished indignantly.

"Edward? Edward's in there *proposing* to her?"

Jonas was simultaneously thunderstruck and furious. "Why that no-good, sneaky, son of a . . . !"

He shoved past the knot of men, heading straight for the cabin. When he got there, he kicked open the door in his agitation. Sleepy faces lifted from the floor. Their owners took one good look at him, and then stumbled to their feet and made a quick departure. Anticipating trouble, parents silently carried or shoved their children ahead of them and out the door.

Finally, only Edward, Kate, and Mattie remained. The tall, black woman knelt protectively at Kate's side. Kate herself sat on the floor, her head leaning back against the wall, and her eyes closed. She looked very pale, tired, and vulnerable. Taking advantage of that vulnerability, Edward knelt on her other side, whispering urgently into her ear.

Jonas struggled to keep a tight grip on his emotions which were clamoring for him to seize Edward by the scruff of his neck and toss him out of the cabin on his behind. "Mattie, would you excuse us, please?" he asked with as much politeness and self-control as he could muster.

"Yessir, Cap'n," Mattie said, rising with great dignity. "I was wonderin' when you was gonna come an' put a stop t' this." She nodded at Edward.

"Shut yer mouth, bitch!" Edward snapped, then, seeing the look on Kate's face as her eyes flew open, and she gazed at him in frowning disapproval, he amended the order. "I mean, hush up. This ain't got nothin' t' do with you. This is between me an' Miz Kate alone."

"Wrong, Edward," Jonas corrected. "It also includes me."

Edward got to his feet, hitching up his pants as he did so. "No, it don't, Cap'n. Kate an' me goes back a long way. I'm the man her mama an' papa wanted her t' marry . . . Yer jus' the latest piece of trash t' wash up on the beach.''

Jonas balled his fists, ready to smash Edward's face, as he'd been longing to do for so long. But Kate suddenly came to life and scrambled to her feet between them, her golden eyes blazing. "Stop it, you two! I'm not a bone for two dogs to quarrel over. I'm a woman with some enormous, troubling responsibilities. I have to decide what to do about them, now . . . what's right for me . . . and what's right for the people who still depend on me . . .''

"Marryin' *me* is the right thing, Kate!" Edward snarled, brutish as an ill-mannered cur. "You know it is. It's what yer mama an' papa both wanted.''

"You don't have to do what your parents want, anymore," Jonas reminded Kate. "I'm sorry they died, but they're gone, now, Kate . . . Now, you can finally do what *you* want.''

"*I don't know what I want!*" she burst out. Her voice was ragged with pain. Her eyes shimmered with tears. "How can I still want a man who prevented me from saving my parents? And how can you still want a woman whose parents killed your brother?''

"Kate, when your mother ran out of that cabin, I didn't know what she intended—if indeed, throwing herself into the sea was what she planned. I'm not holding *you* responsible for what happened to my brother; don't hold *me* responsible for what happened to your parents.''

"But we are responsible! You and me, Jonas. *Us.* Falling in love with each other was a terrible mistake. From the very beginning, I knew it was wrong. You should have known, too. You suspected that Jonathan's death wasn't an accident; but you let your . . . your lust for me overrule your common sense.''

"*Love*, Kate, not lust. From the very beginning, it was more than lust.''

"It was never anything but!" she denied. "Love

404

doesn't destroy people. It isn't selfish and self-serving. Whatever it was that brought us together, it ought not to have happened. You shouldn't love me; you should hate me. And I shouldn't love you; I should—and do—hate you!''

Jonas moved to take her in his arms and shake some sense into her, but Edward barred his way. "Leave her be, Cap'n. She's made up her mind. She don't want you. She's gonna marry me. She's gonna do what she shoulda done all along, an' if she *had* done it, her mama an' papa an' yer brother would still be alive.''

"You bastard!" Jonas hissed. "What kind of a man are you to play on her guilt like that?''

"It's true, Jonas," Kate said, her tone curiously flat and dead. "If I had married Edward when he first asked me a long time ago, none of this would have happened. Your brother would still be alive. So would my parents. They'd be happy and proud. I'd probably have given them their first grandchild by now.''

"You despise this man!" Jonas shouted. "He'll make you miserable—and for what, Kate? What will you gain by marrying him, now?''

She refused to meet his eyes. All the spunk had gone out of her, and she suddenly seemed ten years older. "Peace," she said wearily. "And maybe forgiveness—if my parents, wherever they are, can still forgive me, and I can forgive them.''

Edward draped his arm possessively around Kate's shoulders. "I'll make her happy," he belligerently claimed. "An' I'll make her rich, too. I'll build her a better house than she had before, an' Conch Cay will have the best plantation in all of the Bahamas.''

Jonas searched Kate's vacant expression—her lovely golden eyes now held no emotion—and saw something he had never seen before: a strong resemblance to Sybil Montgomery. "You'll make her a walking replica of her mother," he said. "Is that what you want, Kate—to be like your mother? To spend your life running away from problems, instead of facing them?"

Her face crumpling, she sagged against the wall. "I don't want to *hurt* like this ever again, Jonas . . . I can't bear this pain, this agony . . . this terrible conflict going on inside me. You and my parents are the people I care most about in this world—but now, I've learned to hate all of you! How can I love and hate at the exact same time? How can I . . . ?"

Her voice broke, and she couldn't continue. Edward thrust himself between Jonas and Kate, blocking Jonas's path to her. "Leave her alone!" he demanded. "All yer doin' is makin' her feel worse. She was all calmed down b'fore you come in here . . . Now, you got her cryin' again."

Jonas could see Kate's tears for himself; he didn't need Edward to point them out to him. Still, his own lacerated emotions drove him to try one more time to reach her. "Kate . . . Do you want me to go? Shall I leave here and never speak to you, again?"

"Yes!" she sobbed. "Oh, yes . . . I *never* want to see you again, Jonas. The sooner you're gone, the better. Then I can pick up my life and forget I ever met you *or* your brother."

He stood there a moment longer, hoping—praying—she would change her mind . . . that she would remember what they had felt for each other, what they had shared, the tenderness and passion each had aroused in the other. But Kate wouldn't look at him and wouldn't stop weeping. Edward awkwardly patted her shoulder, and when that had no effect, put both arms around her. Kate clung to him and buried her face against his chest.

It was too much. Jonas turned on his heel and left the cabin.

*   *   *

Kate could not eat. She could not sleep. She couldn't even drink the rainwater Mattie brought to wash down the thin, tasteless gruel made from a single, small fish Cal had managed to catch.

"Give my share to one of your children," she told Mattie, who hovered nearby, ignoring the cries of Baby David. Little Ruthie was holding and rocking the infant, but he still wouldn't be quiet, probably because he was as hungry as the rest of them.

"Ain't David, Ruthie, or Ernest ah'm worried 'bout, Miz Kate—it's you!" Mattie argued. "This broodin' an' grievin' ain't like you at all! An' agreein' t' marry Edward *sure* ain't like you. You gotta come back t' us, Miz Kate. We all need you . . . An' once you start actin' like yer old self, yore gonna realize dat marryin' Edward is a big mistake!"

Kate closed her eyes, the better to shut out Mattie's accusing face. "Leave me alone, Mattie. It's all decided. I can't take care of all of you anymore. Edward will do it. He's not that bad, really. He says he's changed. At least, he loves me, and he'll work hard to get us back on our feet again."

"Miz Kate, dat man ain't capable of love!" Mattie snorted. Glancing furtively around the cabin, deserted now that the sun was out—there was only Gilbert snoring in a corner and Ruthie with the fussing baby—she continued in a quiet but still heated tone. "All he wants is t' be boss of Conch Cay, Miz Kate. Dats all he's ever wanted, an' he doan care whut he hafta t' do t' git it. Soon's he gits whut he wants, he gonna sell me and Cal. You wait 'n see. He ain't nevah liked us . . . an' he gonna keep on makin' poor Cassie's life a pure misery, too. Doan think he won't do it, 'cause he will."

"I won't let him sell you, Mattie, or bother Cassie anymore either . . . I know you don't like Edward,

407

but can't you see how much we all need him? We've lost everything. I'm hoping Lord Dunmore in Nassau will assist us with a loan, so we can rebuild. That, together with my share of the profits from selling this ship, should enable us to start over. We'll do what we've always done—fish, plant crops, and wait for wrecks to happen. For all of those things, I need a strong man to help me. I can't do it alone anymore, Mattie; I just can't do it!"

"But, Miz Kate, what about Cap'n Irons? He's de man who really loves you. Any fool can see dat. The two of you is made fer each other. Why, if you marry him, you won't haveta go back t' wreckin'. Y'all can build ships instead."

"It isn't that simple, Mattie! We've each done unforgivable things . . . or been part of doing them. My parents killed his brother, and because of Jonas, Mama and Papa are dead, now, too. Sometimes I think he held me back because he *wanted* something bad to happen to them, and it did . . . How can we both forgive and forget things like that? I know I can't, and Jonas can't either. In time, we'd come to hate each other, just as Mama always hated Papa for taking her away from America."

"Miz Sybil wasn't right in de head, Miz Kate . . . Doan go comparin' yerself t' her. Mebbe y'all can't marry de Cap'n, but dat doan mean ya gotta marry Edward. Edward's done lots worse things den Cap'n Irons. He wuz de one who made Cal, Benjamin, an' Fish tek out dem lanterns dat caused de ship-wrecks . . . He wuz de one who sent de Cap'n's brother out t' fish when dat storm wuz comin' an' he knew it . . . He wuz also de one who tried so many times t' kill de Cap'n hisself."

Shaken out of her lethargy and depression by these revelations, Kate sat up straighter against the wall. "What do you mean, Mattie? What other times did he try to kill Captain Irons?"

408

"Why, Miz Kate, ah ain't got no proof, but Cal an' me think Edward had somepin' t' do wif dat big log topplin' dat almost killed de Cap'n . . . an' we think he knowed dat musket he give de Cap'n durin' de boar hunt wuz no good . . . an' we're purty sure he done started dat fire in de hut dat night it burnt down. Or if he didn't do it hisself, he made Fish do it."

"Fish!"

"Now, Miz Kate, ah doan wanna git Fish in no trouble, but Massah Edward can be mighty persuasive, when he wanna be. He threatens folks wif sellin' or beatin' 'em, an when dat doan work, he promises 'em things like rum. Everybody knows dat Fish sleeps all de time 'cause he gits drunked up jus' like yore papa an' Edward. An' where'd he git de rum, if Edward ain't been given it to 'im?"

"*I* didn't know Fish was getting drunk or Edward was giving him rum! Why didn't anybody tell me?"

Mattie just looked at Kate, as if the answer should be clearly obvious. But it wasn't. "Why, Mattie?" Kate repeated. "If everybody else was too afraid, why didn't you or Cal tell me?"

"Miz Kate . . . Ummm . . . You is a good person," Mattie hemmed and hawed. "An' you an' me is de closest thing t' frien's dat a slave an' her mistress can be . . . But ah cain't risk tellin' y'all things b'hind Massah Edward's back. Yore papa an' Massah Edward wuz frien's. Dere wuz plenty bad Massah Edward could've done t' me an' Cal an' mah babies—wif yore papa's approval—dat y'all would have never knowed about . . . No, Miz Kate, ah jus' couldn't risk it. Sometimes, y'all fergits ah's still jus' a slave . . . Ah ain't got no rights. Ah probably shouldn't even be talkin' dis way now, only ah hate t' see ya end up married t' a man like Edward. You deserve better den Edward, Miz Kate."

"Thank you, Mattie—for being my friend," Kate

said and meant it with all her heart. She felt a debt of gratitude to Mattie for forcing her to see matters in a different light. Instead of thinking seriously about her future and everyone else's, she had been wallowing in hurt, anger, grief, and self-pity, exactly as Jonas had accused her mother of doing all these years. Sybil had trapped herself in her own misery until she couldn't escape it even when she wanted to do so. If Grandpa Montgomery could see Kate now, he would be ashamed of his sniveling granddaughter.

"Does dat mean yer gonna tell Massah Edward de marriage is nevah gonna happen?" Mattie inquired, her dark eyes brightening.

"No, it doesn't mean that exactly—at least, not yet. But this conversation has given me an idea. I know how I can discover for myself exactly what Edward feels for me, and how much he's really changed . . ."

"Whut you gonna do, Miz Kate?"

"I'm not going to tell you, Mattie. I want you to be surprised. Aren't we due to arrive in Nassau shortly?"

"Cap'n say we gonna be dere by tomorrow mornin'."

"Fine . . . Then you must tell all my workers I'd like to see them gathered together on deck first thing in the morning. Tell Edward, too. I'm sure he'll want to hear what I have to say."

Mattie narrowed her eyes at Kate. "Miz Kate, jus' whut is you plannin'? If y'all tell me, ah won't tell nobody else. Ah swear it."

"Patience, Mattie . . . You'll find out soon enough." To herself, Kate added: *And I'll find out a few things that I really need to know now, too.*

Chapter Twenty-Nine

Early the next morning, under a brilliant blue sky, the *Phoenix* sailed into Nassau's harbor. As Kate came out on deck for the first time since the storm, the rising sun nearly blinded her. She was struck anew by the beauty of the Bahamian waters, colored blue, green, and purple, then sprinkled with diamonds.

Hope and optimism bubbled up in her heart; somehow, everything would turn out all right. She had survived the monstrous blow of Jonathan's death, and she would survive learning the truth about her parents and having them die on her, just as she had withstood Robin's death and that of her grandfather. Death was a natural consequence of living; one must accept it and move on. Her parents' betrayal was a little harder to accept, but somehow she must make her peace with what had happened. To do any less, to grieve too long and too hard, or to permit resentment and bitterness to smolder unchecked, was an insult to one's Creator. Beauty and solace surrounded her; all she had to do was open her eyes and *look* at it.

"Miz Kate?" Mattie hesitantly questioned. "You sure you're feelin' up t' this? Ah got everybody t'gether like y'all wanted."

Only then did Kate notice that all her people stood

411

quietly in the bow, while Edward, broodingly watching her, leaned against the ship's railing. A couple of Jonas's men stood off to one side, also watching, but Jonas himself had his back to her and seemed unaware of her presence. His eyes scanned the harbor ahead, while Musket steered the vessel toward town. But Jonas would be able to hear what she said, Kate realized, absurdly glad of it. Though her actions today had little or nothing to do with him, she *wanted* him to know what she was doing. Surely he would approve.

"Yes, Mattie, I'm up to this," she said, stepping forward. "Please listen closely everyone. What I have to say involves your future and mine . . . As you may or may not know, Edward and I are planning to marry, but there will be other changes at Conch as well—changed directly affecting you . . ."

Every black face watched Kate impassively; every pair of dark, lustrous eyes fastened curiously upon her; every ear strained to listen. Kate drew a deep breath before continuing. Once said, the words could not be unsaid. Once given, the joy could not be withdrawn. To change her mind later would be the ultimate cruelty. Some of her people were ready for this—others not. They had been born into slavery and had never known anything different. For some, her speech might inspire terror, rather than gladness.

"From now on, from this day forward, each and every one of you is a free person . . . I grant you your freedom. You are no longer slaves. I also award each of you an acre of Conch Cay land on which to build your own homes and grow your own gardens . . . I hope you will want to remain on the island and help me build a plantation, plant new crops, and . . . and so forth. I will pay you in supplies and clothing at first, and later, when times improve, I'll pay you wages. If you prefer to remain in Nassau, you're welcome to do so . . . I'll prepare the necessary

412

manumission papers. Freedom is my gift to you on the occasion of my wedding. It's the only way I can think of to celebrate . . . You have all served my family faithfully and well. You deserve to be free . . . I grew up with slavery, but lately, I've come to question the rightness of it. I now believe it is terribly wrong . . . Please wish me well as I marry Edward, as I wish you well in your new life of freedom. I regard you as my friends, no longer as my servants, and I hope and pray we may always be friends . . ."

A moment of stunned silence followed Kate's declaration, then Mattie cried: "Oh, Miz Kate! Oh, mah darlin' chile!" Tears streamed down the black woman's face. Cal grabbed his wife's hand, and the two of them stood together, unashamedly weeping, while their children clung to them in mingled excitement and curiosity. The little ones didn't totally understand what was happening, but they sensed it was something wonderful.

Old Tom shuffled forward, his craggy, lined face alight. "Bless you, Miz Kate! Oh, Gawd bless you!"

Then all the slaves—freedmen and women, now— began talking at once, uttering exclamations of surprise and elation, until a mighty shout froze them all in their tracks.

"What're you thinkin' of, woman!" Edward bellowed, elbowing Negroes out of his path as he strode toward her. "What in thunderation are you thinkin' of?"

Kate remained where she was, and Edward ground to a halt in front of her. "Have you plumb lost yer mind?" he shouted. "You can't free these people! How're we gonna run a plantation without slaves? Who's gonna do all the work?"

"These people are—were—mine, Edward. I can free them or not as I please," Kate calmly responded. "I hope they'll remain and help us, only now it will be their choice to do so, if they desire."

"Ya don't *ask* 'em, Kate, ya *tell* 'em! These people can't think fer themselves; that's why they're slaves. They ain't got no mental capacity. When God passed out brains and morals, black folks wuz hidin' out back of the garden gate, probably stealin' whatever wuzn't nailed down!"

"That's enough, Edward!" Kate snapped. "You're hardly one to talk about brains or morals. The best thing you've come up with for saving the plantation was setting out false lights to lure ships onto the reef for us to plunder. And as for morals, why . . . I have a few questions I'd like to ask you about certain threats you made to Fish and the others, if they didn't do the ugly things you ordered."

"What things I ordered? I ain't done nothin' wrong. All I did was try t' keep you from throwin' yer life away on two no-account Americans yer folks hated. I ain't gonna apologize fer that. Besides, most of whut I done was Bell's idea—or yer ma's."

"But you never tried to talk them out of it, did you? Three times you endangered Captain Irons's life, and if you consider *that* morally defensible, you're a worse man than I ever thought you were!"

"I only did whut I had t' do, Kate! There you was—fallin' fer another Irons fellah, an' there I was—eatin' my heart out over it—an' yer folks was sufferin', too. I couldn't let you marry the man, Kate. I couldn't lose all I been workin' fer all these years."

"That's what *really* motivated you, wasn't it, Edward? The thought that you might not get to be boss of Conch Cay, after all. You don't love me; you love what I represent, what I would have brought to you. Marrying me would have made you the new master of the island, free to do whatever you please . . . Tell me, Edward. Now that we no longer have slaves to do all the work, do you still want to marry me?"

414

Edward glared at her a long moment, his jaw working soundlessly. Then he said: "You ain't signed any papers yet, Kate. They're still slaves until ya sign the papers."

"I'm going to sign them, Edward. But as far as I'm concerned, they're slaves no longer."

A cheer went up as she finished—Mattie, Cal, Benjamin, Daisy, Cassie, Gilbert, Old Tom, Fish, and all the children old enough to join in—cheered at the top of their lungs.

"You did this jus' t' spite me, didn't ya?" Edward shouted. "Ya did it jus' t' git back at me!"

"No, Edward ..." she said softly. "I did it because it's right and just. However, now I can see how much you truly love me—and how little you've really changed ... You haven't changed, have you? You never intended to change ... Oh, you're a bad man, Edward. You've plotted evil, lied, been a bully, and used your authority to accomplish your own wicked ends. Tell me about Jonathan's watch, Edward. You took it to Nassau and sold it to a gem shop there, didn't you? My mother gave it to you to sell, and you sold it in Nassau."

Edward cast a worried glance in Jonas's direction. Jonas still stood with his back turned, but the rigidity of his stance indicated he had heard every word.

"So what if I did?" Edward bristled. "She told me t' sell it. I didn't have nothin' t' do with murderin' Jonathan! All I did was sell his watch in Nassau an' split the money with yer ma."

"But that means you knew how Jonathan died. You knew my parents had killed him, and you never told me."

"That don't mean I *did* it!" Edward cried. "Don't you try an' pin his murder on me, Kate, 'cause you heard yerself how the whole thing happened!"

"Yes, I heard ... and the fact that you knew how Jonathan died gave you a powerful influence over

415

my parents, didn't it, Edward? That's why Papa wouldn't listen when I told him I didn't want to marry you. That's why he let you get away with anything and everything. Weak as he was, my father still loved me, Edward! He would never have defended you so much or listened to me so little, if he hadn't been afraid of what you knew and might tell me!"

Edward shrugged his shoulders and glanced away. "Wasn't me killed Jonathan. *They* did it; they had t' pay. I told 'em I wanted their help t' git you t' marry me, an' they gave it. Yer ma was desperate fer you an' me t' get hitched. I didn't have t' persuade her very much. She was more than willin'."

"Because you played on her fears, didn't you? You kept reminding her of what might happen if I did marry someone else. Oh, Edward. What a fool I was to think—even for a minute—that you truly cared for me. As Mattie says, you're incapable of love. You mistreat everyone—whites and blacks alike. I'll never marry you, Edward—and you'll never find another position as overseer here in the Bahamas. I'll tell everyone what kind of man you are. I'll see to it that you starve before you find work in the islands. When we get to Nassau, you better hop on the first outward-bound ship available, because there's nothing left for you here."

A new round of cheers went up from the slaves— ex-slaves, now—people whom Edward had mistreated and abused. Not one of them offered a word in his defense. As the cheering rose about him, Edward's face grew redder and redder. His angry glance swept the jubilant faces, then returned to Kate.

"Damn you, bitch! You've ruined me forever!" he roared, flinging himself across the deck toward her.

Kate felt his large, heavy hands wrap around her neck, and then he was throttling her, squeezing her throat shut so she couldn't breathe. She brought up

416

her knee, but he anticipated such a move and shoved her backward, knocking her off balance. His hands around her windpipe kept her from falling, but a blackness was creeping up on her, threatening to overwhelm her. She caught sight of Jonas's enraged face as he came up behind Edward, but whatever Jonas did had no immediate effect. Edward's hands continued to choke her. Her lungs felt on fire. Then she couldn't see; red spots danced before her eyes. A roaring began in her ears.

She suddenly realized she was dying; incredible as it seemed, her life was being snatched away, before she had had a chance to live it . . . *Jonas!* Her only regret was Jonas. Now, she would never be able to tell him that she loved him . . . and regretted so many things she had done: holding it against him that he was an American, blaming him for her parents' death, resenting it because he told her truths about herself that she didn't want to hear . . .

Oh, Jonas! she thought. I'm so sorry . . . I love you, Jonas. I'll always love you . . . My darling, my dearest one . . . forgive me, please . . . forgive . . . forgive . . .

For a long time, it seemed to Kate, she drifted on a fog-shrouded, gentle sea, unable to get her bearings, speak, move, or even lift her head. She heard voices, smelled food cooking, felt the brush of stiff, clean-scented sheets against her cheek. Wonderment and curiosity filled her. She knew this place, these voices, those tantalizing smells . . . She had many times experienced the soft comfort of this particular bed, but she couldn't make herself wake up enough to remember precisely where she was . . . and she could not recall how she had gotten there.

Darkness came, and someone lit a candle to hold back the shadows. Several times, she felt herself

417

slipping toward some deep, mysterious abyss, but then a voice would call her name, a warm hand would grip her cold fingers, and she knew that if she let herself slide down into the waiting black hole, someone—someone she loved—would grieve and weep for her.

Amazingly, she didn't fear the yawning abyss. It wasn't half so frightening as she might have expected. Comfort and oblivion awaited her there; she sensed a sweet serenity and peacefulness in those velvety depths. But she couldn't leave just yet—she *couldn't!* A man's familiar, compelling voice kept calling her back.

She wanted to answer him, sooth his fears, and reassure him she had no intention of beginning that irreversible descent . . . But she also knew that she lacked the power of speech. Her throat hurt so much that she avoided even the simple act of swallowing. Pain would accompany full consciousness; as soon as she made the grueling effort to awaken, she would pay for it with agonizing pain.

So she drifted—dimly aware of her surroundings, deftly skirting the abyss, yet refusing to return to the world of the living. For a little while, until her strength returned, she could escape reality, with all its harsh and bitter problems, awaiting her attention. It was a relief not to have to think or plan; more than just her throat felt raw and sore. Lately, there had been pain of a kind that defied medication or physical remedy. She couldn't remember why she had been so anguished, but she knew she bore wounds neither a doctor nor an Obeah Woman could possibly heal.

She contemplated drifting on this peaceful foggy sea forever, but the voice—that relentless, persistent voice!—made such self-indulgence impossible.

"Kate," it kept saying. "Kate, sweetheart, can you hear me? Oh, Kate, please wake up . . . Please don't die . . . I love you, Kate. I want to love and cherish you forever. I want to make it up to you that your parents were so weak, foolish, and selfish. It doesn't matter about my brother, Kate. It doesn't matter about your mother and father. We can't let what's happened destroy our love for each other. I knew you couldn't marry Edward. I knew that as soon as you were yourself again, you'd realize you'd made a mistake in consenting to marry him. Edward's out of our lives, now. He'll never bother us again. All you have to do is wake up, Kate . . . Oh, God, Kate, please wake up! How can I reach you? How can I bring you back?"

Kate found it very pleasant to listen to Jonas—it *was* Jonas, she abruptly realized—begging her to wake up. His love enfolded her like a giant, warm blanket wrapping her from head to toes. She basked in the comfort of being loved so much that this strong, harsh-looking man with a scar over one eye would actually weep when he whispered her name. *I love you, too*, she thought—but still, she couldn't rouse herself to move.

For the first time in her life, she lacked the driving compulsion to be everything to everyone, to meet the needs of so many. For once, she could lie still and let someone else shoulder the terrible burdens . . . except she couldn't ignore Jonas's hands on her body nor his heated mouth pressing against her forehead. With infinite tenderness, he kissed her closed eyes, her cheeks, and then her mouth. His hands skimmed her waist, lingered lovingly upon her breasts, traced the curves of her hips. Oh, his touch made her feel so warm and glowing! . . . so exquisitely alive!

Then she heard a door opening. Jonas's hands and mouth deserted her, and a new voice shattered the stillness. "Captain Irons, has she regained consciousness, yet?"

Kate recognized that voice, too! It belonged to

419

Emily Culpepper—the wife of Bertram Culpepper—friends with whom she always stayed when she came to Nassau. How had she gotten to the Culpepper's house?

"No, she's not awake yet, I'm sorry to say," Jonas answered. "However, her color has improved. Why don't you go to bed, Mrs. Culpepper? I'll sit up with her. As I told you earlier, I won't leave her side until she comes out of this—this coma, or whatever it is."

"Poor girl," Emily clucked sympathetically. "She's been through so much. I don't wonder that being half strangled to death has left her like this. Well, we must hope for the best, mustn't we? Perhaps the doctor is wrong in his assessment. Perhaps your love and devotion to her will prove to be the one medicine that can work a miracle, when all other remedies are counted useless."

"She won't die—or become a hopeless invalid—if I can help it," Jonas growled. "Just keep all your doom-saying doctors away from her. They know nothing whatever about what makes a person want to live or die."

Emily uttered a deep sigh. "I do wish you'd let me send for Mama Rosa . . . She's the best Obeah Woman in the islands, except perhaps for Kate's Bell. Those two have long been rivals; with Bell gone, Mama Rosa is now the greatest. We whites may not be able to understand their powers, but we can't possibly deny them. Mama Rosa may be able to help her."

"No," Jonas responded in a tone of voice that told Kate he was glowering like the devil himself. "No Obeah Woman is going to get near her. I'll see to her care for however long it takes her to recover. If the time comes you no longer want us here, I'll find somewhere else to move her."

"Oh, please, Captain Irons! Don't insult me by

talking like that. I'm deeply relieved and glad that you brought her to my house. Sick, injured, or well, Kate is always welcome. We Loyalists learned long ago to stick together. Perhaps that's why we still call ourselves Loyalists, even though we can hardly remember anymore why we fought or fled the colonies in America.''

"I hope your husband feels the same way," Jonas grunted.

"He does, Captain. Bertie is a gruff sort of man—much like you, if you don't mind me saying so—but his heart is in the right place. He bade me tell you that both you and Kate have a home here for as long as you need it. He will also see to it that there will be no gossip regarding the nature of your relationship to Kate. If the times comes—I mean, *when* it comes—he'll fetch a minister to oversee the exchange of your marriage vows. You can't know how pleased we are that our dear Kate has finally found a man suitable to become her husband. We never did care much for Edward Garvin. He wasn't nearly good enough for our Kate.''

"Mrs. Culpepper . . . marriage is *my* intention—not necessarily Kate's. She did tell Edward she wasn't going to marry him, but she *hasn't* yet consented to marry me. Her refusal was why Edward attacked her.''

"That awful man!" Emily burst out. "I'm so glad you beat the stuffing out of him and frightened him so badly that he forgot about the possibility of sharks and jumped overboard. I hope the sharks *did* get him.''

"Whether they did or not, I think we've seen the last of him. He was stroking hard for Nassau the last I saw him. I just wish I'd gotten to him sooner, before he did so much damage to Kate. It all happened so quickly. How could he have hurt her so badly in the few moments before I got to him?''

"Unfortunately, these things can't be planned, Captain," Emily commiserated. "Please don't hesitate to call me during the night, if you need me. Kate's servant, Mattie, is also available—and a bit upset that you won't let her up here to take care of her mistress. Kate's slaves are certainly devoted to her."

"They aren't slaves any longer, Mrs. Culpepper. Kate freed them only this morning, shortly after we arrived in the harbor."

"Dear me! What was she thinking of to go and do that? I admit that slaves are sometimes as much of a burden as they are a help, but someone must do the heavy labor, especially on a plantation."

"If I can just get Kate to wake up, she'll have plenty of help. As you said, her people are devoted to her. They all want to return to Conch Cay and assist in rebuilding what the hurricane destroyed."

"Well, I'll leave you to carry on, Captain . . . Good night. And may God bless your efforts to revive our dear friend. It's clear she has much for which to live."

The door closed again, and Kate remained completely motionless—willing Jonas to return to her bedside. He did so, and a moment later, the bed creaked as he lay down beside her and gently gathered her into his arms. He nuzzled her hair, and then her cheek, kissing her once more where her shoulder met her neck.

"I won't let you die, Kate . . ." he whispered. "Or like your mother, turn your back on life. If you'll live, if you'll only wake up, I'll spend the rest of both our lives making you glad you did . . ."

Tears squeezed out from beneath Kate's eyelids and dribbled down her cheeks. She wanted so much to reciprocate and love him back, but a terrible weariness prevented her from so much as raising her hand to wipe away the tears. With his face buried in her hair, Jonas never saw them, but as he lay beside her, holding her close, his hand touched her breast and gently closed over her heart.

"I love you," he repeated. "I love you, Kate. As long as your heart keeps beating, we've still got a chance."

Chapter Thirty

Worn out from worry that Kate would never again be normal, Jonas slept. In his dreams, Kate was well again, snuggled against his back, and caressing his body with a knowing, persistent hand. Wherever she touched him, his flesh burned and quivered, yet he dared not move for fear that he would awaken and be disappointed to find it all a magical dream. She stroked his chest muscles, explored his navel, and ventured lower still, finally clasping him intimately, so that he groaned in mingled frustration and pleasure.

It was the groan that woke him. He opened one eye and determined it was almost morning; objects in the room were dimly lit, but discernible. Then he made a another, more shocking discovery: Kate's hand was precisely where he had dreamed it was, and while he lay there, digesting this fact, she gently squeezed him.

"Kate?" he breathed softly, hoping she had regained her wits and knew what she was doing.

She didn't answer, but instead squeezed him again. Breaking contact with her hand, he rolled over to face her. Golden eyes greeted him with a shimmering, love-filled gaze. Her lips parted, as if she meant to say something, then she grimaced and painfully swallowed.

"Don't talk, if it hurts, love," he quickly advised. "Just nod or shake your head in answer. Are you all right?"

She nodded.

"Does any other part of you besides your throat hurt?"

She shook her head.

"Do you want something to eat or drink?"

Another shake.

"Can I do anything at all for you?"

Still another shake, and then a nod—a vigorous nod. She moved closer to him and slid her arms around his waist, pressing her soft, warm body against his.

"Surely, you aren't strong enough to be wanting *this*," he chided, all his senses leaping in hopeful anticipation that she was, indeed, strong enough.

He response was to slip her hand between their bodies and resume fondling him. He couldn't stop the groan of desire that escaped him. Despite his reservations that she hadn't recovered enough to be making love—not yet, not after all she had been through—he found it impossible to push her hand away. He lay unmoving as she kissed him on the lips and entwined her arms and legs around him. The temptation proved irresistible.

With a halfhearted groan of protest, he deepened the kiss and began exploring with his own hands. Kate was all sweetness, honey, and liquid warmth. She was musky, sensual female, demanding and giving, surrendering and conquering. Somehow, their clothing came off, their naked bodies came together, and she enfolded him in the luscious, secret depths of her. He tried to be tender and gentle, to hold back from taking his pleasure, but she clung to him with a need equal to his and squeezed the juices from him as if he were a ripe, bursting fruit.

Taking care not to crush her with his weight, he

pumped his very essence into her, then lay to one side, panting and ashamed of his lack of control. She sighed with repletion, but he wondered if he had satisfied her—so quickly had he found his own release. After a few moments rest, he rekindled their mutual desire with long, slow kisses and caresses calculated to arouse them both. He stroked and petted her, seeking to tell her of his love using the language of touching, rather than words.

This time, upon reentering her, he kept his thrusts slow and gentle, until he felt her shudder with lusty tremors that shook her delicate body from red-gold head to perfect, pink toes. Only then did he abandon himself to his own unquenchable needs. When it was over and he lay spent in her arms, she circled his ear with her tongue, as if she simply relished the taste of him. The simple, artless gesture deeply touched him; he felt humbled by the gift she had given him of her perfect, exquisite surrender.

Kate had loved as she had always loved—without a moment's shyness or hesitation. She loved as only Kate Montgomery *could* love—with all her fiery spirit and tender innocence. A wetness on his shoulder suggested tears, but she wouldn't look at him when he sought to lift her chin and gaze into her eyes. Bluish-purple bruises marred the whiteness of her throat. He touched them with renewed anger and a fervent wish that he had killed Edward Garvin while he'd had the chance.

"Your throat hurts, doesn't it?" he growled.

She nodded.

"The bastard . . . He took a flying leap over the railing when he realized I meant to kill him, Kate. He almost killed you. I was so afraid for you . . . I think I went a little crazy. Big Donald had to hold me back to keep me from jumping over the railing and going after him. Then, when I saw that you were still unconscious and showed no signs of waking up, I no

427

longer cared what happened to Edward; I couldn't get to Nassau fast enough. Do you know where we are?"

A lock of reddish-colored hair dipped over her eyes as she nodded a second time and mouthed: "The Culpeppers."

"That's right. Emily Culpepper fetched a doctor. He examined you and said you had been gravely injured—as if we were too stupid to see that for ourselves. He said it was possible you might die from being deprived of air too long, and there was nothing he could do for you . . . I nearly booted him out the door, the useless, old fool. It may be some time before you can talk again, Kate, but one thing we've got is plenty of time. I don't want you to worry about anything. You must rest and recover; then we'll discuss the future."

She surprised him by placing her hand firmly over his mouth. She tried to speak, but nothing came out, not even a croak, and she dissolved into tears again.

"Kate, what *is* it? Why are you crying? Say it slowly, and maybe I can read your lips."

"I'm sorry," she mouthed.

"Sorry for what?" he demanded. "I'm the one who should be sorry. Maybe if I *hadn't* held you back, your parents wouldn't have gone through that railing. You might have gotten there in time to stop them. Who knows what would have happened? As for what you said to Edward—about his forcing your workers to set out false lights, about the attempts on my life and his selling my brother's watch—I'm not blaming you for all that. Even before Mattie told me she had a little talk with you, to remind you of Edward's basic wickedness and to reveal the full extent of it, I knew you couldn't have known what he was doing. If you had known, you would have tried to stop him."

"Sorry . . ." Kate repeated, forming the words

428

through silent sobs.

"Oh, all right," Jonas said in exasperation. "I accept your apology, especially if you're apologizing for agreeing to marry Edward, instead of me . . . You ought to be sorry for that, Kate. I'm the one who loves you, and you love me. Knowing that, how could you possibly consider marrying Edward?"

She shrugged her shoulders helplessly, the tears sliding soundlessly down her cheeks.

"Don't, Kate . . . Oh, please don't cry." Jonas gathered her against his chest, attempting to comfort her but at the same time reveling in the feel and scent of her. "Kate, let's get married . . . as soon as we can. The Culpeppers will be delighted to arrange it. By the way, all of your people want to go back to Conch Cay with us, and all of my men want to stay and build more ships. We can do it, Kate . . . It will take a lot of hard work, but we can do it. We'll use the *Phoenix* as collateral to get a loan. We don't have to sell her yet— and we'll repay the loan when we sell the next ship. I've got it all figured out; all I have to do is design the vessel we're going to build this time . . ."

She pulled back from him, smiling through her tears, and pantomimed something with her hands. It took him a moment to decipher what she was saying. It had something to do with starting right now to draw the designs for the ship. Typical Kate, he thought, always practical and not afraid to be bossy, either.

"No, not yet," he protested. "Not this very minute. It's still early, Kate. We don't have to get up, yet. Come, lie down with me and rest. For a little while, I just want to hold you."

She nodded, and docilely curled up, kittenlike, beside him in the bed. But they didn't sleep. Kate's hands started to explore again, her soft fingers touching him in ways that made him wide awake, sublimely happy, totally in love, and extremely eager

429

to touch her back. After so long a time being apart from each other, he couldn't get enough of touching Kate Montgomery. He doubted he ever would get enough of it. She belonged to him, now—or soon would, when they married, and he intended to take care of that little matter before the sun set this very day. By tonight, she would truly be his, and he'd never sleep apart from her again.

Kate wore a lacy, white nightdress of Emily Culpepper's for her wedding gown. She married Jonas while sitting up in bed, pillows plumped at her back, and Jonas standing proudly beside the bed. The minister stood at the foot, frowning slightly because he disapproved of such unseemly haste. Before he would agree to perform the ceremony precisely at sunset, it had been necessary to inform him that she was already sleeping with her groom— had, in fact, spent the night in his arms—and intended to sleep there every single night from now on. Finally, he had consented to waive the posting of the banns and perform the ceremony exactly as requested, just as the sun was sliding out of sight behind the trees.

At this moment, a lovely rose-colored light bathed the room and illuminated the faces of all the onlookers crowded inside it. Flower petals lay scattered across the coverlet, and a wreath of flowers encircled Kate's head. Their heady scent had made her slightly drunk, and she smiled and nodded as the Culpeppers, all of her workers, and Jonas's men congratulated her and Jonas and wished them well. Emily Culpepper then shooed everyone out of the room, eliciting their cooperation with the promise of food and drink downstairs.

Before leaving, Mattie kissed Kate's cheek and gave her a quick hug. "Doan worry 'bout nothin', Miz

Kate . . . Yore voice gonna come back, an' so will yer strength. Ah jus' knows it. Y'all gotta a gran' life ahead o' ya . . . Be patient an' rest while you can. When we gits back t' Conch Cay, there'll be more work den you can shake a stick at.''

Her inability to speak, what had happened to Edward, and whether or not her horses and other animals had survived the hurricane were the only worries Kate had tonight. In the wake of her marriage, all her other worries had mysteriously vanished. Someday, she'd have to confront her ambivalence regarding her parents, but she no longer felt the acute anguish about it she'd known before. The future loomed bright and promising, because she was facing it in the company of the man she loved.

She returned Mattie's hug, then lay back on the pillows, anxious to be alone with her new husband. Jonas watched indulgently from the doorway, and after Mattie left, firmly closed the door behind her and came toward Kate with a determined gleam in his eye.

"Feeling sleepy, wife?" he inquired. "Are you worn out from all these festivities?"

She shook her head and held out her arms to him, but instead of joining her on the bed, he took his time about lighting the large candle in the heavy candlestick on the bedside table. When he had lit it, he picked it up and stood for a moment, grinning down at her. "Sorry, my beautiful bride, but despite everything I've promised myself—and despite how fetching you look in that bed—I'm not sleeping in here tonight. You've had enough excitement for one day. Now that you're mine, I intend to cherish and cosset you, beginning by seeing that you get enough rest. Emily agrees with me that all of this activity has probably exhausted you, and she's made up a bed for me in the room next door."

431

Fuming with indignation, Kate gestured that he should put down the candle and join her that very instant. He didn't do either. Wagging his finger at her, he backed toward the door. "Kate, this is for your own good. We . . . ah . . . indulged in more than enough physical activity this morning. Then there was the wedding itself, with people crowding all about you. I'll never forgive myself if you take a turn for the worse. It will be my fault. You see, I can't trust myself to lie down in that bed beside you and do nothing more than sleep. That's all I intended last night and this morning; I was just going to hold you, not make love to you . . . But it seems I can't control myself when I get close to you—so the only answer is *not* to get close."

Never in her life had Kate been so frustrated; her inability to speak made it impossible for her to argue with Jonas. Could he really believe such nonsense? She tried to pantomime that she wasn't sleepy and, in fact, felt better than she ever had in her life—except for the rawness in her throat, which was hardly life-threatening—but Jonas was adamant.

"No, Kate . . . I'm not going to keep you up all night. There will be plenty of time later to indulge ourselves. Perhaps when you regain your voice . . ."

When she regained her voice! That might take weeks—and she might not *ever* regain it. Stubbornly ignoring the pain, she attempted to force his name past the huge, raw lump in her throat. She managed only a slight gust of air; making any sound whatsoever was beyond her, and the agonizing effort brought fresh tears to her eyes.

"You see? What you need is rest—and more rest, not physical exertion," Jonas lectured. "I'm going to make sure you get that rest. You're hardly in a position to argue, Kate, so you might as well give up and go to sleep."

Kate made one last effort to defy the order. She

swung her legs over the side of the bed and tried to stand up—a grave mistake. A wave of dizziness rolled over her, so that she had to grab the bedstead to keep from falling. Jonas was beside her in an instant. Setting down the candle, he clamped an arm around her waist, then made her lie down. After that, he tugged the quilt up to her neck, causing flower petals to fly in all directions. Adding insult to injury, he bent over and bestowed a paternal kiss on her forehead.

"Good night, sweetheart . . . Rest and get better. I'll see you first thing in the morning."

Jonas then departed, taking the candle with him. Seething with anger and frustration, Kate lay rigid in the darkness for more than an hour. This wasn't how she had intended to spend her wedding night. She ought to be trading fiery kisses with Jonas right about now; instead, she was all alone, lonely, and ready to scream from the injustice of it. She was no invalid—and no child, either! But the memory of that wave of dizziness kept her from rising to seek out Jonas and make him understand that she wouldn't be treated like some fragile, porcelain doll.

After a time, as the house grew quiet, she finally dozed—only to awaken abruptly, certain that someone had entered the room. Hoping Jonas had changed his mind, she lifted her head from the pillow and searched the darkness with her eyes. Someone was breathing heavily. The floor creaked as he came nearer.

"Kate?" a voice whispered. "Is that you in here?"
Edward.

Oh, God, he had found her! She ought to have realized he might come looking for her and would know exactly where she was. She always stayed at the Culpeppers when she came to Nassau. Edward had many times been to this house. A scream rose soundlessly in her throat; she scrabbled on the bedside table for something she might use as a weapon, but there was nothing there. Jonas had taken the candlestick with him.

Edward bent over the bed. She knew him by smell, not just by the sound of his voice. He had never been overly fastidious in his personal habits, and his sweaty scent was familiar. When she had agreed to marry him, how could she have forgotten how he smelled? Nausea rose in her throat, as he reached down and grabbed the front of her borrowed, white nightdress. At the same time, his other hand found her mouth and closed off any sound she might have made—had she been capable of sound.

"It's you, ain't it?" he growled. "I knew you'd be here, only I wuzn't sure which room you wuz in. I come fer you, Kate. I didn't mean t' hurt you yesterday—but you made me so mad, freein' all the slaves like that, then rubbin' my nose in it . . . I barely got away in one piece, but ole Edward is hard t' kill. I swam t' shore, lay low then waited 'til after dark t'night t' come an' git you. We're gonna find us a preacher, Kate, an' git married, jus' like we planned. I'm gonna tek care of you. Yore gonna have my babies. Somehow, I'll git us some new slaves. I didn't much like the old ones anyway . . . They was too uppity. Maybe a slave ship'll go down off Conch Cay, an' we can save 'em. We'll use lights all the time, an' make our fortune wreckin', the way I always knew we could."

As he spun out his plans, Kate tried to think of what to do. She knew that if she made a wrong move, she might infuriate him, and weak as she was, could never restrain him if he again became violent. Screaming was out of the question, but maybe she could make some other noise to alert Jonas to what was happening. Until then, she must appear to be docile and accepting—even glad that Edward had found her.

He cautiously removed his hand from her mouth

434

and seemed much heartened when she didn't scream. "Whaddya say, Kate? Let's put the past behind us an' start over. All right, Kate?"

She could sense his rising anger as she failed to answer. It was too dark for him to see the bruises he had left upon her throat—and she couldn't explain why she couldn't respond. He leaned closer and hissed in her ear.

"Listen, bitch—don't think you kin ignore ole Edward. I'll kill ya b'fore I let another man have ya. I've waited too damn long, as it is . . . Now, are you gonna come along peaceable, or do I hafeta tie an' gag ya?"

A light suddenly flared in the hallway. Over Edward's shoulder, Kate saw Jonas's figure silhouetted against the brightness. Behind him stood Emily and Bertie Culpepper in their nightcaps and wrappers, Emily clutching a candle in front of her.

"Well, Edward," Jonas said in a granite-hard voice. "It seems the sharks didn't get you, after all, did they? What a pity, because now I'll have to find another way to get rid of you."

Edward whirled to face Jonas. One hand fumbled at his waist. Candlelight glinted along the wicked-looking blade of the large-handled knife he extracted from his belt. "It don't surprise me, findin' you here," Edward snarled. "This time, I'm ready fer ya, Cap'n. This time, I'll cut ya up like fish bait, an' yer friends can feed whut's left t' the sharks."

Kate forgot that she couldn't speak; she forgot everything but the danger to Jonas. "Jonas . . ." she rasped, her voice sounding like a rusty old saw drawn across a rock. "Jonas, be careful."

She sounded so terrible that Edward jerked around to look at her. His eyes questioned whether or not it was really her lying in the bed. The momentary distraction was all Jonas and Bertie Culpepper needed. They reacted instantly. As Jonas dove for the

435

knife, Bertie drew back a meaty fist and slammed it into Edward's jaw. Regaining his feet, Jonas followed Bertie's blow with a second one that toppled Edward like a maderia tree succumbing to the ax. Edward never made a sound, except for a heavy thud as he hit the wood floor.

"Oh, my!" Emily cried, rushing into the room and holding up the candle. "He's unconscious, isn't he?"

Jonas kicked savagely at the inert figure. "Wake up, damn you, so I can kill you properly!"

"Now, now, Captain . . . Let's not be hasty," Bertie Culpepper intervened. "I've a much better idea for what to do with him."

"What?" Jonas demanded. "I want him out of our lives permanently. As long as he remains in the Bahamas, Kate and I will have no peace."

Bertie rubbed his fist—the one he'd used to punch Edward—and grimaced. "I know of a schooner leaving at first light for Jamaica. If you help me carry the fellow downstairs, I'm sure I can arrange to have him delivered in chains to that ship. The captain is a close friend of mine, and he owes me a favor. He'll see to it that Edward finds . . . er . . . new employment in the Jamaican cane fields, so that you'll never have to be bothered by him again."

"A brilliant solution to a distasteful problem. I'll give you a hand, as soon as I check on my wife."

Jonas hurried to Kate's bedside, but Emily Culpepper had beaten him to it. "I'll take care of Kate, Captain. You help Bertie dispose of that awful man."

"Hurry back," Kate begged, in a voice reminiscent of an ancient hag. Good lord! Would she always sound this bad? she wondered.

Jonas nodded. "Oh, I'll certainly hurry back. Recovered your powers of speech, I see," he remarked, grinning. "Such as they are."

"Yes." She smiled triumphantly. "Which means I no longer have to sleep alone."

His grin widened. "If you say so . . ."

"I do say so," she retorted, then bit down on her lower lip to hide the pain the effort of speaking was costing her.

A scant hour later, Kate was once again being kissed good night and tucked into bed, but this time, Jonas didn't leave the room. Blowing out the candle and lying down beside her in the darkness, he carefully maintained a safe distance, leaving enough room so that another person could have crawled between them. He had also, she noticed, stayed on top of the quilt while she was lying underneath it.

She snorted in disgust. "Jonas . . . Don't make me beg—or talk more than I have to. Please get under the covers with me."

"Kate, it's late, and you must be exhausted. Go to sleep, or I swear I'll leave and spend the rest of the night next door."

"Please, Jonas?" she whispered.

She heard his long, drawn sigh. Then he got up, pulled back the quilt, and grudgingly crawled beneath it. She scooted over to him and was terribly disappointed to discover that he was still fully dressed. But that was something she could change in a hurry. As she struggled with fastenings and tugged at fabric, he groaned and pulled her into his arms.

"What am I going to do with you, Kathleen Elizabeth Irons?"

"Love me," she grated in her awful voice. "Love me forever, Jonas . . . as I love you. And promise me that whenever we argue, disagree, or hurt each other's feelings, we'll always talk it out and forgive each other. We won't make the same mistakes my parents did . . ."

"All that will be easy," he muttered. "The hard part is making sure you get enough rest."

"We'll rest afterward," she promised.

And they did.

Epilogue

"Oh, Jonas! She's beautiful!" Kate crowed, sliding down from Neptune and grabbing his hand. "She's the most beautiful ship in the whole, entire world, isn't she?"

"Well, I don't know if I'd go that far, but she is one hell of a ship," he said, his pride fully evident.

"When will you take me and the babies out on her? We *must* accompany you on her maiden voyage. Perhaps we can go with you to Nassau when you leave to sell her. That would be a wonderful experience for Jonathan and Emmy—their first voyage on one of their daddy's wonderful ships!"

Jonas took Neptune's reins from Kate's hand and turned to walk down the beach with her, away from the newly finished vessel, which was as yet unnamed. "Don't you think the twins are a bit young for an ocean voyage?" he soberly inquired.

"Three months of age isn't too young," Kate objected. "Besides, if *they* don't go, that means *I* can't go, and I refuse to be left behind, Jonas . . . I *deserve* to go. Haven't I been a good, devoted wife and mother all these months—staying home taking care of myself and the babies instead of helping to build this ship, as I was longing to do?''

"I must admit you've been remarkably demure and responsible," Jonas conceded. "Not that I would have permitted you to climb a ship's cradle and haul heavy logs when you were so pregnant you couldn't see your toes anymore."

"Exactly!" Kate exclaimed. "Now that I've recovered from childbirth and the babies are so big, strong, and healthy, it's time for me to get back to work. I can't sit idle while there's work to be done."

Jonas stopped walking and turned to her. "Kate, is that why you're riding Neptune again, because you're rebelling against the quiet, sedate life you've lately been leading? You could get hurt riding Neptune . . . and you could get hurt building ships. Jonathan and Emmy may be all of three months old, but they need you just as much now as they did when they were three weeks."

Kate emitted a husky sigh of impatience. The deep huskiness was the only remnant of her brush with death from strangulation. At first, she had fretted over her unladylike voice, until Jonas convinced her that it added to, instead of detracted from, her feminine appeal. She had always had a husky voice, he reminded her. Now, it was doubly provocative.

"Jonas, I'm not planning to *abandon* the twins! I just want to become more active and involved in *our*—not just *your*—work. I have plenty of help with the babies, you know; everyone begs me to let them take care of the twins. As for riding Neptune, he was so happy to see me after we returned to the cay that he's been gentle as a lamb ever since. I want to teach him to drive as well as ride, Jonas. And I want to break Neptune's foals so that the children will have suitable mounts when the times comes, too. We really do need the horses. It's a miracle they all survived that awful hurricane; now it's time to train

440

and make use of them."

Jonas lifted an eyebrow skeptically. "Let me see if I've got this right. In addition to mothering twins, directing the running of the household, as well as doing half the work yourself, overseeing the planting of an indigo crop, the harvesting of salt, and the feeding of all of us, you want to train horses and help me build my ships."

"*Our* ships, Jonas. Yes, I can do all that. The babies *are* three months old, after all—and as I said, I do have plenty of help."

Jonas shook his head. "I should never have let you come to the work site to see the new ship. I knew you'd get ideas. I just didn't realize how *many* ideas you'd get."

"Oh, Jonas!" Kate flung her arms around her frowning husband. "Don't you realize by now that I'm not happy unless I'm busy? And the more time I can spend with *you*, the happier I am. You have to let me and the babies go with you to Nassau."

She leaned back and gazed up at him through the fringe of her lashes. His frown detracted from his handsomeness and made him look a little like a devil. She wanted to see his sea-blue eyes light up and thought she knew exactly how to accomplish that. "Besides, didn't you build a small, private cabin on this ship?"

"Yes, but what has that got to do with your accompanying me to Nassau or building the next ship or training horses . . . ?"

"I want to try out that cabin, Jonas—to . . . to christen it, so to speak."

As she had hoped, the idea of what they might do in that private cabin distracted her lusty husband from his disapproval of the other things she wanted to do. A smoky look came into his eyes, provoking a tightening in her lower abdomen, accompanied by a queer sort of breathlessness. Kate quickly slipped off the crude bridle she had fashioned for Neptune, and the horse whinnied and set off at a brisk trot for the forest. Slipping the bridle over her arm, she smiled at Jonas expectantly. "I'm ready if you are."

"Wait a minute," he growled. "If we're going to do a proper job of christening our new ship, then we're also going to have to give her a name. Fortunately, I have an excellent name in mind for her."

"You do?" She fluttered her lashes flirtatiously. "What might that name be?"

He gave her a long, searching look. "I'm thinking of calling her the *Sybil*."

The breath exited her lungs in a loud whoosh. She had to swallow hard before she could speak. "Jonas . . . You don't have to do this for me . . . really. I'm not even sure I *want* you to do it."

The sea-blue eyes seemed to probe the depths of her soul. "It's time, Kate . . . We've got to forgive your parents. If you think about it, there's no better time than this—when our own lives are so happy, content, and fulfilled. Your poor parents never had that, or if they did, their happiness was all too brief."

"But they murdered your brother, Jonathan! They knew how I felt about him, and still, they murdered him! If the opportunity had presented itself, they would have murdered you."

"Yes, but they also produced you, Kate . . . I lost my brother, but I gained *you*. I, too, have conflicting feelings about them, and I want to lay those feelings to rest. Isn't our love big enough to spill over into forgiveness for two people who were, after all, touched by madness?"

"Oh, Jonas!" Kate threw her arms around her husband and hugged him tightly. "What did I ever do to deserve a man as loving, kind, and gentle as you? You're the most wonderful man in the world!"

"Let's not overstate my virtues, Kate. All I'm suggesting is that we name this ship after your

442

mother . . . and not go on pretending she never existed. Don't you have a few good memories of your parents tucked away somewhere? Surely, the memories aren't all bad ones."

"No, they aren't all bad," Kate admitted, remembering some of the better times. "Once, when I was little and extremely ill with the croup, both my mother and father stayed at my bedside for two days and two nights. I think it was their love that helped me to get better. And another time, I recall my mother tearing up her best gowns in order to make new dresses for me, because I'd outgrown all my old ones. Yes, Jonas, I do have good memories tucked away in the back of my mind. Only in recent years had my parents become helpless and dependent; before that, before my mother succumbed to madness and my father to drink, they demonstrated their love for me in countless little ways I took for granted or hardly noticed."

She leaned back and gazed up at him through a haze of sudden tears. "Jonas . . . what would you think of . . . that is, how would you feel about . . . ?"

"Spit it out, Kate."

"Well, I was thinking that if someday we have another son, I'd like to name him after your father . . . and mine. I'd like to put the two names together: William Bartholomew or Bartholomew William . . . something like that."

"I think that would be fine, Kate. I have no objections. Whatever the sins and faults of our parents, they gave us life. For that alone, we should remember and honor them. Now that I'm a husband and father myself, I can better understand how a man can make terrible mistakes in his life and still love his wife and children. Your father was a desperate, unhappy man who went too far trying to prove his love for your mother. I pity him, but I can't hate him."

"Dearest Jonas!" Kate again hugged her husband. "And one of our future sons must bear the name of my grandfather—Augustus."

Jonas chuckled. "Or—if we don't have *that* many sons—we can use the name for one of our future ships. Now, about *this* ship, Kate . . ." He held her away from him, rubbing his fingers up and down her arms, and the smoldering look was back in his eyes. "You mentioned something about christening her . . ."

"Oh, yes! Of course! But . . . but what if we should be . . . interrupted, Jonas?"

He flashed his charming, irresistible grin. "Give me credit for a little forethought, wife. The cabin comes complete with an inside lock."

"My goodness!" she cried, wiping away her tears. "I really must see this wonderful hideaway! Surely, people will pay extra to have a ship with a private cabin and a door that locks."

"I intend to charge them extra—not only for the lock and the cabin, but the extra-wide bunk I installed."

"An extra-wide bunk! Do show me these wonderful things, husband."

"I shall be delighted, wife."

He led her over to the ship's cradle, where the newly named *Sybil* gleamed in all the beauty of her fresh, polished wood. Grinning down at Kate, Jonas began to climb, and she eagerly followed, anticipating what awaited her in the cabin above.

With any luck at all, Jonas would forget about the tedious restrictions he had placed on her activities and his ridiculous overprotectiveness. Of course, she wouldn't tell him she might already be pregnant again. Some things he didn't need to know just yet, and besides, she herself wasn't certain. It did seem incredibly soon for such a thing; Mattie had told her a woman couldn't get pregnant while nursing, but

444

maybe Mattie was wrong. Kate hoped she was pregnant. *William Bartholomew Irons*. The name had a lovely ring to it . . . and after that, Augustus Irons . . . and if they had another daughter, they ought to name her after Jonas's mother, too.

Oh, she wanted a whole boatload of babies! How else could she and Jonas build a dynasty of shipbuilders to populate the Abacos?

"Here we are," Jonas said, giving her a hand to help her over the railing.

Kate inhaled appreciatively. "I love the smell of a new ship. The deck and railing are truly beautiful, Jonas—such craftsmanship! Such attention to detail!"

"Wait until you see the cabin," he boasted, tucking her hand beneath his arm.

They strolled the gleaming deck, descended a narrow flight of steps, and entered an enclosed area containing the captain's cabin, wardroom, and two smaller cabins, set aside for passengers. Kate exclaimed over everything she saw, but it wasn't until Jonas opened the door to the captain's cabin, that she let out a squeal of delight and surprise.

"Oh, Jonas! You did this on purpose, didn't you? You knew I couldn't stay away much longer, and you had this all ready and waiting."

She danced ahead of him into the cabin, which was furnished with a table set for two with candles, flowers, fruit, cheese, bread, and a bottle of wine—and the extra-wide bunk made up with clean sheets and scattered with flower petals. As she spun around the chamber in delight, he chuckled and began to strip off his shirt.

"I admit I had a little help from Mattie. As soon as you announced you were going in search of Neptune, so you could take a ride, Mattie sent Fish with a basket of goodies and instructions to get everything prepared for your arrival. She and I planned this a long time ago . . ."

Kate rushed to embrace her romantic husband. "Oh, Jonas, I'm so happy! You *are* such a wonderful man! We *do* have such a marvelous life together!"

"Yes," he said, enfolding her in his arms and crushing her against his naked chest. "For a Loyalist and a son of Liberty, we've managed to achieve great things together, haven't we?"

"And we aren't finished yet. The truth is we've only just begun."

He was smiling as he lowered his mouth to hers. "Do you want to eat first, or to . . ."

"Do you have to ask?" she whispered against his lips. "Of course, I'd rather . . ."

She never got a chance to finish the sentence. As usual, when she and Jonas finally managed to be alone together, they found better things to do than talking . . . so they did them. They stayed in the cabin a long, long time, hardly realizing that they were starting a new tradition, a new way of christening ships . . . But that's what it turned out to be—The Irons Christening Ceremony. And every new vessel they built, they christened in the exact same way.

Afterward From the Author

Conch Cay is a fictional island based on the many real cays that make up the Abaco chain in the Bahamas. Shipwrecks were common in that part of the world, and wrecking was a means of survival for many uprooted Loyalists during the post-Revolutionary War period.

Gradually, wrecking gave way to more reputable pursuits, such as shipbuilding, and it is that era of change I wanted to capture in this tale. The displaced Loyalists were a courageous, tenacious lot, who grappled with tremendous challenges and overcame huge obstacles to build new lives in an alien environment. Their story has rarely been told—hence, my interest in telling it. I hope you enjoyed meeting Kate and Jonas, as much as I enjoyed researching and writing this book. Watch for the next Katharine Kincaid adventure, coming soon from Zebra Books.

FEEL THE FIRE IN CAROL FINCH'S ROMANCES!

BELOVED BETRAYAL (2346, $3.95)

Sabrina Spencer donned a gray wig and veiled hat before blackmailing rugged Ridge Tanner into guiding her to Fort Canby. But the costume soon became her prison—the beauty had fallen head over heels in love!

LOVE'S HIDDEN TREASURE (2980, $4.50)

Shandra d'Evereux felt her heart throb beneath the stolen map she'd hidden in her bodice when Nolan Elliot swept her out onto the veranda. It was hard to concentrate on her mission with that wily rogue around!

MONTANA MOONFIRE (3263, $4.95)

Just as debutante Victoria Flemming-Cassidy was about to marry an oh-so-suitable mate, the towering preacher, Dru Sullivan flung her over his shoulder and headed West! Suddenly, Tori realized she had been given the best present for a bride: a night of passion with a real man!

THUNDER'S TENDER TOUCH (2809, $4.50)

Refined Piper Malone needed bounty-hunter, Vince Logan to recover her swindled inheritance. She thought she could coolly dismiss him after he did the job, but she never counted on the hot flood of desire she felt whenever he was near!